THE DISTANCE

THE DISTANCE

HELEN GILTROW

First published in Great Britain in 2014 by Orion Books,
an imprint of The Orion Publishing Group Ltd
Orion House, 5 Upper Saint Martin's Lane
London WC2H 9EA

An Hachette UK Company

1 3 5 7 9 10 8 6 4 2

A CIP catalogue record for this book
is available from the British Library.

ISBN (Hardback) 978 1 4091 2662 1
ISBN (Export Trade Paperback) 978 1 4091 2711 6
ISBN (Ebook) 978 1 4091 2712 3

Typeset by Deltatype Ltd, Birkenhead, Merseyside

Printed and bound by CPI Group (UK) Ltd,
Croydon CR0 4YY

The Orion Publishing Group's policy is to use papers
that are natural, renewable and recyclable products and
made from wood grown in sustainable forests. The logging
and manufacturing processes are expected to conform to
the environmental regulations of the country of origin.

www.orionbooks.co.uk

THE DISTANCE

Prologue

Day 25: Saturday

Karla

There's blood in my hair. Twelve hours and I've still got blood in my hair.

'Are you all right?'

The uniformed officer standing guard by the door is staring at my face in the washroom mirror. Breaking rules: she's been ordered not to talk to me. Maybe she thinks I'll faint.

They took my coat away from me last night, at the scene: the blood had soaked through to the lining. There was blood on my face too, and blood on my hands, working its way into the cracks around my nails – the doctor who examined me cleaned most of it off before declaring me fit to be interviewed. I dealt with the rest as soon as I could, ignoring the pain, scrubbing my skin red-raw to get it out.

Nobody told me about my hair.

I pick at it with my good hand. A brownish clot glues the strands together. I wish I had scissors. I'd cut it out.

Don't think about it. Don't.

It's ten o'clock on Saturday morning. That's what my watch says; without it I couldn't even guess. I last slept, for a few broken hours, on Thursday night. Thursday … We had a plan in place then. I'd ceased to kid myself that I had the situation under control, but at least we had a plan. We could see a way through all this.

Now there's just me, in a police station toilet, pulling at my hair, trying to ignore the knot in my chest, holding myself together, sticking to my story. How many times have I rehearsed this situation in my head? But it's nothing like I imagined.

My whole adult life I've devoted to the pursuit of information, the analysis of patterns; to data and cold fact. This is just another fact, isn't it? And that's how I'll get through this, how I'll remain professional, detached.

But it hurts. I never guessed how much it would hurt.

3

The officer's still watching my reflection.

'I'm fine,' I say. 'Really. Thank you.' I try to smile at her, diagonally, through the mirror, but my face is gaunt and slack.

Her gaze skates away. 'We'd better go back,' she says.

On the interview room table the plastic cup of cold coffee by my seat has developed a greenish-white scum. My stomach flips and I push the cup away. Immediately the officer says, 'I could get you another?'

'No—' Too abrupt: she's only being kind. Try again. 'Thank you, but no.'

She takes the cup and goes out, shutting the door. There are voices in the corridor outside, then silence. I'm alone.

More than anything I want to put my head down on the table and weep.

But any minute they'll be back, with their questions. *Just one more time, Charlotte, from the beginning.* What did I see? What did I hear? They're checking the details from different angles, listening for a piece that doesn't fit. Because they have to be absolutely certain how much I know; or how little.

So I'll start again, from their beginning, the one that makes the story neat and containable, and my part in it entirely innocent. But there are other beginnings.

Eight years ago: a stranger sitting in a warehouse with a bright light shining into his face, a stranger who should have been afraid, and wasn't.

Or the eighth of December, just over a year ago: a woman in a dark coat crossing a hallway, her face unreadable.

Or a Wednesday in January less than four weeks ago, when Simon Johanssen found me, and I learned about the impossible job.

4

Part I

Karla

I've always known the past might hunt me down, despite all my precautions, the false trails and the forged histories and everything else I've done to distance myself from it.

But not like this.

It happens while I'm standing in the interval crush of a Royal Opera House bar, listening politely as a portly banker expounds on the proper staging of *Götterdämmerung*'s final act: I glance up, and in that second my two lives – lives which I have taken so much care to keep apart – grind against each other like tectonic plates, and set the room rocking.

He's loitering at the edge of a nearby group but angled fractionally away from them: he isn't with them, though you might be forgiven for thinking that he is. The beautiful suit, the tie, the glass of champagne held loosely in the fingers of his right hand, even his haircut and his stance, mark him as someone who belongs here. Only I know that he doesn't.

Two years. Two years, and only one reason he'd be here. He's come for me.

A beat – I swallow my shock – then I turn back to my companion and smile and provide the right response. But my peripheral vision strains for a fix on him. I need to watch him, as if he's some unpredictable animal, potentially dangerous. I want to turn and stare. But right here, right now I'm Charlotte Alton – polite, wealthy, idle Charlotte Alton – and she emphatically doesn't know the man I've just seen. Instead I must manoeuvre myself so I can survey the crowd over the banker's shoulder. By the time I've done so, he's vanished.

Carefully, discreetly, I sweep the room.

It's a sold-out performance and the bar – the biggest in the opera house, like a giant Victorian glasshouse under a high curved roof – is

7

packed, the north and south balcony tables full, people crowding around the circular copper counter of the central servery. Too many men in dark suits who could be him, but aren't. A wall of rippling mirrors doubles the size of the place, reflecting the elaborate ironwork of the huge arched window and turning the crowd into a throng. He and his reflection have melted into it. At the top of the mirrored wall the glass oblong of the upper bar's balcony seems to float suspended above us: the people lounging against its rail look like boxed exhibits. I glance up there too. He isn't among them.

But he's here, somewhere, and he's found me. Of course he has. *And whose fault is that?*

The five-minute bell goes. Around me glasses are drained. 'Here, let me.' The banker takes mine but as he turns away another of our party, a senior City lawyer, lays a hand on my arm. 'Charlotte, I was hoping for a word – shall we?' So I fall into step beside him as we join the patient shuffle towards the auditorium, and I smile, and focus, while the blood beats harder behind my eyes.

Even though I'm searching for him I don't see him until he's right beside me. He doesn't look at me, but his hand finds mine. Then he's gone, blending into the crush around me.

The lawyer and I move along the corridor towards the Grand Tier. The lawyer is on the board of a charity, there's an auction coming up, might I possibly ...? The object nestles in my closed hand. It's sticky and warm with perspiration when, bending to take my seat, I slip it into my clutch bag.

It is a tiny Christmas-tree decoration, a little red-and-purple bauble that has embedded glitter into the skin of my palm.

The lights dim. The final act begins. Wagner's tale of assumed identities, broken promises, betrayal and murder storms towards its end. I barely register it.

The bauble is a message, a prearranged signal in a code devised on the fly years ago. Simon Johanssen wants a meeting. But not with discreet, well-bred Charlotte Alton. Johanssen wants a meeting with Karla.

The easy excuses come unbidden. *You haven't been near a client in months. You're out of the game. Send Craigie. He'll deal with it. It's what you pay him for.*

It's a pointless debate. I'm going anyway.

*

The early hours of the next morning. The cold is like grit, stinging the eyes.

Up on the main road in this part of east London there are glass-fronted office blocks and new-build light-industrial units, and in the distance the towers of Docklands – my apartment building among them – glitter like something out of a fairy tale, but from down here they're invisible, and a world away: a burned-out van slumps on its axles beside the approach road, and the gutters are choked with rubbish.

An amusements company uses the site for storage: decrepit fair-ground rides, tatty street decorations. Broken machinery litters the yard like the fossilised remains of prehistoric beasts: a giant petrified octopus with its tentacles drawn up around it, a stretch of track like the curved spine of a tyrannosaur. Inside the warehouse underpowered fluorescent tubes send a grimy wash of light across the aisles, illuminating a sheared-off dodgem car still with its pole, a painted board with the words THE ULTIMATE THRILL.

It's January, I've been here for twenty minutes and I'm cold. Perhaps that's why I miss it.

Not movement. I would have spotted movement. He is simply there, in the gloom, watching me.

'I'm sorry,' he says, but still I find myself sucking in air.

It's as if he's been here all along, among the grinning plastic Santas, the concertina'd Chinese-New-Year dragons, and only a change of focus has brought him into view. Or as if he's developed fractionally, like the grass growing or the accumulation of dust: the shadows thickening into human form.

He's thirty-eight years old. Six foot tall and spare, with the lean muscle mass of a distance athlete. The beautiful suit's gone; now his clothes are understated, anonymous, his wristwatch mass-produced. The bones of his knuckles are prominent, and scarred.

As always I'm struck by his stillness.

'I wanted to be sure we were alone,' he says. His voice is quiet, polite. The flat northern vowels betray his roots; nothing else does.

Two years since we last met. Fielding couldn't tell me where he'd gone. The trail he left petered out in Amsterdam. A scatter of rumours after that came to nothing. I'd almost come to believe that he was dead. But here he is.

So why now, after all this time? Why come to find me now?

Instead I ask, 'You didn't try the number?' and I sound calm.

He says, 'I didn't know the man who answered.'

'He works for me. He's safe.'

He nods, but his gaze goes sideways, away from me.

'Two years,' I say. 'I thought we'd lost you.'

'I was keeping my head down.'

'Any particular reason?'

He just shrugs.

What does he want? Up until two years ago a meeting like this meant he simply needed an ID, or information for a job. That's what people came to Karla for: the unauthorised obtaining of data, whether by bribery or blackmail or hacking or straightforward physical theft; the deliberate destruction of other data that would, if left intact, be of benefit to law enforcement agencies; the forging of identities, or their deletion.

It can't simply be that, not after two years of silence. But perhaps he's out of the game too, perhaps he's ceased to be the man who—

'Tell me about the Program,' he says.

One extra second of silence, that's all. But I've schooled myself too long and too hard, and nothing else shows.

You could call it a prison, but it's like no other prison standing, apart from the wall, and the wire.

When Johanssen left two years ago it didn't exist. It came only after the prison riots. Which came after the recession, and the crime wave, and the prison overcrowding, and the budget cuts … Five thousand inmates dumped out of overflowing jails and into the care of a private security firm, to be housed – temporarily – in a collection of run-down suburban streets that had been emptied for redevelopment just as the economy crashed. A stopgap, certainly – but a stopgap that might run for years, so they pasted on a snappy Americanised name and set up a website extolling the theory behind the move.

And they came up with the experiment.

'And this experiment?' Johanssen asks, though he must know the answer already. It's on the Internet, after all.

'Teaching criminals to function within a self-regulating society.'

'A self-regulating society made up of other criminals.'

'That's right.'

'And in return for taking part they get …?'

'"Enhanced individual liberty and responsibility within a secure environment."'

Keys to their accommodation. Access to TV and newspapers. The opportunity to sit on self-governing councils, make rules. Educational support, vocational training, small-business initiatives. Healthcare, sports facilities, even a restaurant. According to the website.

'Sounds too good to be true,' he says.

'Then it probably is.'

'Is it safe?'

'"Regular patrols by armed officers ensure the safety and well-being of all residents."' Then, 'Charlie Ross went in there when it opened. One of the first batch. He was dead in three months. Came out in bits.'

He doesn't blink. Of course: he knew that too.

'So who's in there?'

'Mainly career criminals. Thieves, racketeers, pimps, dealers, people traffickers, murderers ... but no paedophiles or terrorists.'

'Psychopaths?'

'Officially, no: can't be trusted to take their medicine. Unofficially? Dozens at least, maybe hundreds. All learning to be good citizens.'

'You know people in there?'

'Knew.' I smile. It feels glacial. 'We're no longer in touch.'

'Internal surveillance?' he asks.

'Cameras.'

'Communications?'

'A landline system for inmates, all calls recorded. No mobiles.'

'Security?'

I've been asked that question so many times that I can reel it off in the blink of an eye; in a heartbeat.

'Double perimeter wall: forty foot high above the surface, thirty foot below. Electric fence, razor wire, heat and motion sensors. Twenty-four-hour guard on the walls. Air exclusion zone above. All underground connections are sealed apart from the main sewer; the contents of that are – *processed* – as they pass under the perimeter. A rat couldn't get out.'

'What about in?'

'No one wants to get in.'

'What if I did? Could you get me in?'

I say, 'There's limited visitor access.'

'More than that.'

More than that? 'A staff ID? Something that will get you in as a warder – a guard?'

'More than that,' he says, and he looks at me—

'As an inmate?'

—and then away again.

So it's a job. An anticlimax with a whiplash sting of irony: a job, it's just a job, for which he needs an ID. Warders – guards – work in teams, to strict rotas; civilian staff are heavily protected. Only inmates can move freely in that place. He has to pass for an inmate, for what he's planning to do—

A sudden sense of dread.

'It can't be done,' I say.

He glances at me. 'You sure?'

End this now, just end it. 'We don't have an in with the operating company, and we can't hack prison system records. Too well defended. Believe me, it's been tried.'

He says, 'By people who wanted to get out. Not in.'

I just shake my head.

A silence between us, as if there's something else to say. At last I break it. 'Is that everything?' A fractional nod. 'Well, then: if you need me again, use this.'

I hand him a card with no name, just a phone number. He reads it once, twice, and passes it back. We're done. Two years, and this is all we have to say to each other.

I push the card back into my coat pocket. 'I'd better be going.'

He doesn't say goodbye.

The car – not the Merc Charlotte Alton's used for the last year but a saloon with shell-company plates – is parked a street away. Robbie's on watch beside it, arms folded across his barrel chest, breath smoking in the cold air, heavy grizzled head cocked, alert to every sound.

A year since I last called him, since I last asked him to do anything like this, but he's worked for the network right from the beginning and he knows the rules. He opens the door for me without a word or a look.

I slide into the passenger seat and there it is, that brief smothered pang, *You should have stayed, you should have said something, you should have asked*—

I close it down. Close down, too, the image of Johanssen standing there in the shadows, listening as the car pulls away. For all I know, he's gone already.

*

We take the usual precautions. It's gone 4 a.m. when I get back to Docklands.

The building I live in overlooks an arm of the West India Dock, on the north side of Canary Wharf. Once they unloaded cargoes of sugar here, but all that's left of the industrial past is a pair of monumental cranes on the wharf, the dock itself – a shivering oblong of water that has to be skimmed periodically for cigarette butts and takeaway paper cups – and a run of low brick warehouses converted into bars for the tourists and the office workers. Everything else is new, and my building is among the newest. It caters for the nervous rich: over-scaled rooms, heavy on security, cross-webbed with CCTV. It's possible to hermetically seal the place from the outside world; I don't get surprise visitors. Even at this hour there's a uniformed guard on patrol out front, and inside a night porter on duty behind a bank of switches and monitors. We nod to each other as I cross the lobby to the lift.

From the forty-first floor the views are glittering – the offices of Docklands, the riverside warehouse conversions of Limehouse Reach, the curve of the Thames and the skyline of the City of London – but tonight when I look out, I barely notice them.

Did Fielding track him down in some obscure corner of the world? *Something's turned up, son. Right up your street.* Or did he just decide to come back, and discovered this waiting for him? A job inside a prison. Looks impossible.

That sense of dread again: of course he'll try to do it.

I walk into the small room I use as an office. Switch on the computer, plug in a hard drive. Enter passwords, run decryption, and open a file I haven't touched in a year.

The first click brings up a set of five coloured rings, one inside the other – outer security, inner security, the first wall, a narrow no-man's-land, and then the second wall – all formed around a dark, blank heart. I click on the central blank and a numbered grid appears. Place a cursor on one of the squares and click again, and the square expands to fill the screen with detail: roads and buildings, a canteen, a vocational training block, a football pitch. Click again and a delicate tracery of sewage pipes and electricity cables runs beneath the streets like veins under skin. Again, and icons scatter themselves across the plan: a random punctuation of little blue diamonds, green dots, yellow squares. Some are command centres or observation

13

posts; some represent cameras and listening devices. Others we simply can't decipher.

We started gathering data on the Program, assembling this map, when the place was still in the planning stage. And ever since it opened its gates people have come for the map. Except they don't come to me any more, they come to Craigie, and it's not really the map they want, it's an answer to the question, *Is there a way out of there?*

The answer, as it has been since the Program opened, is no.

But that's not what Simon Johanssen's asking for. He wants something else.

And still I don't phone Craigie, although I know I should. I phone Fielding.

I phone using a line that no one will be able to trace. The person who picks up the phone just grunts, but it's him.

'Hello, Fielding.'

A pause that stretches out to ten long seconds. Then, '*Karla*.'

One word, but Tony Fielding manages to load it with a heavy freight of superiority and contempt. He's never liked me – he prefers his women younger, and grateful. I'm a cold bitch, aren't I? In a way that's liberating.

Fielding says, 'Well, here we are again,' and his voice is like rust. Still smoking then. 'I take it you had a visit.' He sounds smug.

'Why are you letting him do this?'

He snorts. 'Why not? You worried he's out of practice? I think he'll pick it up again soon enough.'

'A job in the Program.'

Fielding says, 'Look, he wants to work. I've already told him it's impossible. But that's what he does, isn't it? The fucking impossible. Put money on it, Karla, he's going to do it. Question is, are you?'

End this. End it now. The same argument trotted out again, deadpan. 'You know the system in there. We can't hack it.'

'Sure about that, Karla? Well, your choice. There's other people who can set this up. They'll get him in there. Course, they're not as *careful* as you, but beggars can't be choosers.'

The words are out before I've time to think. 'You can't put him in there.'

'Watch me.'

'John Quillan runs the Program.'

But Fielding says, 'Does he, Karla? Good old John Quillan. I'll make sure Johanssen knows.'

When he's gone, I walk back into the main room of my apartment, go to the window and look down: the black water of the dock ripples back at me.

Walk away. Just walk away. You don't live the old life now. You're not Karla any more, and you owe Simon Johanssen nothing.

But I can't walk away.

You like to think you make your own decisions. You like to think that it's all conscious, planned. But sometimes the decisions are made for you, and you only find out when it's much too late. Sometimes the borders are invisible; you cross them in the dark.

Before Johanssen told me about the job. Before I even walked into that warehouse—

That moment in the opera house when I looked up and saw him: the future was set then.

Somewhere in the Program's security there is a loophole, and I will find it, and use it to put him in there. Because if I don't someone else will, and they won't watch his back.

John Quillan – professional criminal, gangster, murderer – runs the Program.

John Quillan wants him dead.

Day 2: Thursday

Johanssen

3.13 a.m., Thursday. A north London street in what they call an 'up-and-coming area', bars and estate agents slowly replacing the old pound shops and cheap clothing stores. A taxi took him part of the way here, and a night bus, but now he's on foot: the usual drills. A sniper's habit reduces the world to distances.

Three metres to his left, a teenage couple huddle at a bus stop, their breath clouding the air around them. Eight metres right, a drunk zigzags down the opposite pavement, immune to the cold, then pauses with one hand against a wall and doubles. Johanssen keeps moving. Six paces take the man out of his field of vision. There's the sound of vomiting, and above his head a CCTV camera swivels impassively to catch the action.

No one is watching him.

He's seen her again. He's spoken to her. Now he's carrying that memory through the yellowish dark almost as if it's an object in his hands, with weight and shape. Sometimes it's fragile, precious – the light in her hair, the turn of her head – but never for long. He crosses a street, passes a row of houses, and it changes into something sharp, or corrosive, like the look in her eye the second after she saw him.

He got it wrong, didn't he? He thought it would be different, but he got it wrong.

He cuts down a side road, turns right and walks until he comes to the first of the tall Victorian terraces. Less than five minutes from here the streets are crowded with builders' skips, but the tide of gentrification hasn't reached this one yet: there are too many buzzers on the entryphone panels, too many bins and broken bicycles and old sofas in front gardens, and the basement flat's front door opens to a familiar smell of damp.

Inside, the living room curtains are open and the outside security light is on. Beyond the glass doors the shadows of a plastic garden chair and a dead rose bush are knife-sharp. He closes the curtains and opens the doors to the bathroom and bedroom, switching lights on, checking windows, looking for any sign of disturbance. There's nothing.

He sits down in the only comfortable chair, the one that faces the TV, and thinks again of Karla in the opera house bar: Karla, in her green dress, her head tilted to one side, listening to the fat man, pretending not to be bored, the moment before she looked up and saw him.

And there it is, the same fist-clench in his guts, as raw and immediate as ever.

And nothing's changed.

Eight years ago. First meeting, if you can call it that: him in a chair with a bright light in his face, and her just a voice behind the light saying, 'I can make you safe.' Is that all it took, those words? Delivered at the point when he'd screwed up everything – proved the army right, lost his nerve, watched a man die screaming – when he was sleeping rough, shaving in public toilets, eating out of supermarket bins, avoiding daylight, scared to walk down a street in case John Quillan's people spotted him and did to him what they'd done to the others. When carrying on living was no more than a reflex and a product of his training—

I can make you safe.

And she did: took every reference point in his past existence and wiped it off the map – wiped him clean – then pasted on a new ID, gave him an airline ticket, told him to run and not come back.

Except he came back, though only when the men who knew what he did the night Terry Cunliffe died were all behind bars, or dead. Came back because it was the only way to put that night behind him: working for Fielding, all the difficult jobs, and every one of them clean and tight and tidy, no raw edges or loose ends or mess. No hesitation either – every job proof that he could hack it after all, that Spec Ops were wrong, that Cunliffe was a one-off, a bad night that caught him off guard, nothing to get worked up about. That the man who went to pieces wasn't him.

For every job he went to her for information.

One day she stepped out from behind that light.

And one day she gave him one of those rare swift almost-smiles of hers, and for a moment anything seemed possible; but then she turned away.

You couldn't hack it. You couldn't hack it, Spec Ops knew, then Cunliffe proved them right. And one look at you eight years ago and she saw all of it. And she won't forget.

Until one day the only thing left to do was walk away. He had no idea then that it would take so long to come back. But he couldn't return while she was still in his bloodstream, like a drug – while he still thought of her the way he did; still dreamed of her. So six months passed, then twelve, then eighteen. And slowly she ebbed out of his system, until his dreams were of all the old things: a man at a desk, a rooftop at night, that farmhouse. That was when he knew he should come back.

The first thing he did, once he was sure it was safe, was try to reach her.

The old phone number was answered by a man, a Scot whose voice he didn't recognise. He hung up without speaking. She wasn't at the old address either. But he still had an old code for a meeting, a place and a time. All he had to do was find her.

And now he's seen her. And it was all right, wasn't it? He kept it professional.

That's right, you keep telling yourself that. Asking her all those questions when you already knew the answers, as if she wouldn't notice. Talking just to keep her there. Stalling on that last big question, scared the answer would be no and the moment she said it there'd be nothing else to say.

What did he think? That he'd come back and things would somehow be different? That he'd feel nothing?

Or that she'd be *pleased*?

She never even asked him where he'd been.

So what does that leave him with now? The job? A hit in the Program?

Even she can't get him in there.

Night has tipped over into morning before he sleeps, and tonight he dreams one of the old dreams again. Though it is less of a dream, more of a memory.

He's in an office, standing to attention in front of a desk. Behind the desk a man in uniform sits, his hands clasped on top of a paper file.

'This is no reflection on your abilities,' the man says, and at that point he wakes with the familiar deadweight in his stomach, the taste of failure in his mouth.

His mobile's ringing. He picks up – 'Hello?' – and Karla says, 'I think I can find a way,' and something inside him twists just at the sound of her voice.

'One thing,' she says, and he can guess what's coming. 'John Quillan runs the Program.'

'He doesn't know who I am.'

There's a short silence from Karla, then she says, 'I'll get back to you.'

'Well?' Fielding says. He's angry – tight-shouldered in his ex-pensive cashmere coat, his fists clenched beneath the cuffs, his seventy-year-old face all crags and lines. It's as if he's come here for answers, except there aren't any. 'Well?' he says again, then, 'Fuck you.'

Johanssen digs his hands into his jacket pockets. It's a cold pale day. They're on a scrap of riverbank east of Woolwich. In front of them the Thames slides by, fast and grey: the tide's turned. At their backs there's a hoarding with a picture of neon-lit glass towers and behind that, a building site. Cranes pivot against the sky. It's an exposed place: nothing to stop the wind slicing upriver, and too much sky.

'This is a joke,' Fielding says. The old routine. 'This is a fucking joke.'

Johanssen says, 'It's just a recce. I go in, I look around, I come out. Forty-eight hours. That's all.'

'I don't believe this,' Fielding says. 'John Quillan runs the Program.' As if he didn't know right from the start, from the moment he first outlined the job, smoking his cigar in the dark of a Soho backroom, his smile oozing smugness: *You'll love this one, this one's fucking Mission Impossible, the client's out of their tiny mind.*

Johanssen looks away.

But Fielding's stare is still locked on to him. 'And what? You think there's some statute of limitations operating in there? Or Quillan's got amnesia, has he? After what happened to Terry Cunliffe, you think he'll have *forgotten*?'

'He doesn't know who I am,' Johanssen says, then, 'It's just a recce. If it's not safe I pull out.'

Fielding says, 'Safe? Course it's not fucking safe. And how d'you think you're going to *pull out*? It's a prison, a fucking *prison*. You can't just walk away.'

A pair of gulls comes screaming overhead and on the building site something mechanical judders into life behind the hoarding, belching diesel fumes.

Fielding mutters, 'We should be using inside talent. Place is full of murderers, let one of them do it. Find a guy who's just been sentenced, get to him before he goes in – someone with kids on the outside – we lift one, we make it clear how far we're prepared to go—'

The thought sickens him, but it's irrelevant anyway. It isn't going to happen. 'I'm doing it,' Johanssen says.

Of course he is. He's never failed a job. And still Fielding comes up with this stuff, reminding him how difficult it is, pretending to try to talk him out of it, because that's what makes him want it, isn't it? One day he'll say, *You can stop now. I'm already committed.* He hasn't, yet.

'And Karla? Can she get you in there?'

'She's looking into it.'

If Fielding's pleased he doesn't want to show it. He turns his head away.

On the other side of the site a piledriver rams supports into the mud. Through a gap in the hoarding they watch.

At last Johanssen says, 'Have you got it?'

But Fielding hasn't finished yet. He says, 'Why should I give it to you? You should be sitting this one out. This is the one you can't deliver, and you know it. Everyone's got a limit, son. Even you. But you don't want to hear that, do you?'

The piledriver cuts out.

'Have you got it?' Johanssen says again.

Fielding reaches into his coat, pulls out an envelope, pushes it into Johanssen's hand. 'What is it with you?' he asks bitterly. 'What the fuck is it?' Then he says, as if it disgusts him, as if it goes against everything that's right and proper, 'It's not even like you want the money.'

The envelope is plain, brown, unmarked. Johanssen doesn't open it. 'What did they do?' he asks.

Fielding just says, 'Something bad.'

He waits until he's got the front door locked, the curtains tightly drawn, before he opens the envelope.

It contains a single sheet: a photograph run out from a cheap domestic colour printer, on office paper. For a long time he just stares at it. Then he puts it back into the envelope. Within twenty minutes it will be out of his hands.

The image sits in his mind, whole and perfect.

For some reason he wasn't expecting a woman.

Day 2: Thursday – Day 5: Sunday

Karla

I have a dinner party to go to on Thursday night – or Charlotte Alton does, though tonight she's less than sparkling company. The envelope's waiting for me when I get back to my apartment just gone eleven: the night porter catches my eye as I cross the lobby, and holds it out to me.

Two glasses of wine evaporate from my bloodstream in the time it takes to ride the lift up to my floor. As soon as I'm through the front door I rip the seal and pull out the sheet of paper.

She's maybe thirty, slim, with hair the colour of pale butter, and in the photo she's wearing a high-buttoned grey suit. It has an expensive look, and so does her hair: she could be a corporate lawyer, well bred, locked down. Her smile is like armour.

I swear I know that face.

There's no accompanying name, no background details, just the picture.

What did she do, this closed-down rich girl? Why does someone want her dead?

But it's simple: she's a convicted criminal, like everyone else in the Program, and at some point her face has been splashed across tabloids and TV screens. Less than a second and my imagination has assembled a front page: alongside the photo the word MONSTER! stands out in eighty-point capitals.

Revenge hit, it has to be. Payback for some gangland betrayal? Or victim's family. One or the other. Odd that Fielding hasn't given a name, though. We should have more than this.

Hands on the keyboard. Our dialogue, stripped of its origins, bounces through proxy servers on three continents. My lack of jargon marks me as an outsider but I don't let it bother me these days, and if it bothers Finn, Finn never says.

The answer comes back almost instantly.

<K?>

I read surprise into that. Over the last year Finn, like many in my network, has become used to dealing with Craigie.

<exploit 4 U Private job Usual $ Inmates Program secure facility Get details Names FACES Hists RSVP me only>

We can't hack the system, but we don't need to. All we need is a copy of the data.

A pause. Finn is thinking about this, or the servers are running slow.

<ddline?>

<asap>

<let u no> Finn's standard response. It used to annoy me. But it's not like it is in the movies; this could take days, weeks. Finn has no idea. *I'll let you know* is as much as I'm ever going to get.

I sever the connection and sit back in my chair.

I spoke to Fielding again this afternoon, pushed for details about the client, but they're nameless too: Fielding has rules about anonymity. 'They've come with references' is all he'd say this time. Someone else, someone he's done business with and trusts, has vouched for them; again he wouldn't say who. Then he asked me if I knew how I was going to get Johanssen into the Program, and I stonewalled right back at him: said I was working on it. Trust is a two-way street and we're not on it. In fact I've spent my day locating the man who'll be my key to this, though he'll never know. The prime candidate's image is staring from my screen right now. Later I will go back through his life, hunting for any reason to rule him out, but for now I'm content to leave him there, though he committed crimes I don't want to contemplate ... I think back to the woman in Johanssen's picture. MONSTER. They'd make a lovely couple.

Just then the digital clock in the office blinks from 23:59 to 00:00. Today is Friday.

It's time I talked to Craigie.

I never meant to get into this life. Some things just happen.

I got involved with Thomas Drew before I knew what he was, or what he did; you can do that when you're twenty-three and innocent. He had a clever mind, smooth hands, the liquid gaze of a charlatan, and a self-belief I've never seen in anyone else, before or since. We met at a party in Kensington; two hours later we were in bed.

A week passed before I asked him what he did. The sign outside his office just read DREW. 'Investigations,' he said, and smiled.

A month after I came to work for him – routine surveillance, basic IT, answering the phone – I realised what he was really doing: the network he was building, and its clientele.

A year later and I knew it better than he did.

He had an accountant: Alex Craigie. Thirty going on fifty, dark-suited, tight-lipped. I always assumed he didn't like me much. My ally was Robbie: a Staffordshire bull terrier of a man, solidly built, genetically loyal, dangerous in a scrap. He'd been a foot soldier with one of the old East End crime families but gave that life up when his wife died, leaving him with a seven-year-old son to raise. He was Drew's man for driving and surveillance, occasionally muscle. He and I once kissed in a car during a surveillance op, in those very early days; it was for entirely professional reasons, but when I want to embarrass him, I still remind him of that.

Then one day we couldn't find Drew anywhere. Information he'd supplied for a bank job had turned out bad, two men were dead – shot by police – and a notable London gangster was on his way to discuss the consequences.

Drew had fled.

Robbie told me to get out of there. I sent him home, to his son. I expected Craigie to vanish too – slide a bundle of financials into his briefcase and walk away – but to his credit, when I decided to hold my ground, he stayed.

We have not always agreed, then or since, but a year ago, when I decided it was time to trust someone else with the day-to-day running of the network – minimise risk, get myself a life – there was only Craigie. He knows my sources, he pays my suppliers, he insulates me from my clients. He ensures my invisibility, keeps my hands clean, keeps me safe. Keeps me away from people like Simon Johanssen. That's the theory, anyway.

It's dark at the back of the warehouse when I arrive on Friday, but I know my way. I know every one of our locations; I scouted them all myself. So I enter almost soundlessly, past the man on watch – just a faint creak from the door, the softest shuffle of a footstep. Still Craigie turns and frowns. When he sees me his narrow face angles a little to one side – curiosity, calculation? – but he says nothing. Right now it's someone else's turn for questions.

In front of us, and separated from us by a bank of bright lights pointing straight at him, a tall man in his early sixties sits head down, elbows on knees, hands hanging limp. He's slim, his grey hair well cut, his clothes casually expensive. Handsome in a hawkish kind of way; in a TV drama he'd play the upright patriarch, the ageing general leading his men into one last battle. But this place and everything it took to get here – the hood, the van, the searches – has eroded his dignity: his face is pouchy and lined, and he's sweating. Through the pricey aftershave I can smell his despair.

'I resigned,' he says. 'I simply felt that it was time to move on.' But his voice quavers.

'You resigned, Mr Hamilton? You weren't asked to step aside while something nasty was brushed under the carpet?' Craigie's kept his son-of-the-manse demeanour along with his East Kilbride accent. At times like these I can believe there's not one chip of pity buried in his flinty soul. 'You'll have to do better than that.'

The man says nothing. He must realise this is part of the price to be paid. But Craigie isn't doing it out of cruelty. Disclosure: we always insist on disclosure. We have to be sure what we're dealing with.

Craigie says, 'Let's run over the story, shall we? You stepped down from your position with no wrongdoing, no blame attached, not a stain on your record and a nice pension to boot. You have no dirty secrets and no one's blackmailing you. Yet you've come here offering a lot of money in return for a new life. People only do that when they're running, Mr Hamilton. The question is, what are you running from?' He pauses. 'Well?'

I don't even hear the answer.

Eight years ago I was in another warehouse just like this one, but the man in the chair with the light in his face was Simon Johanssen.

Clean shaven, brown hair. Dressed casually, in greys and blacks. Tidy, too: you wouldn't have guessed that he'd been living rough. Trace evidence that he'd been in a fight – scabbed knuckles, fading bruises to his face – but none of the bulky bravado of the self-proclaimed hard man. Nothing flashy or distinctive either. Mister Nobody. You wouldn't look twice.

He'd been hooded, searched, thrown into the back of an unmarked van with untraceable plates and driven across London. He had a price on his head. He should have been sweating, and he wasn't.

'You have to tell us everything,' I said. 'Complete disclosure is vital.'

Except that I didn't need him to tell me what he was running from. I already knew. Everyone knew.

Of course I'd read his file.

Born in Salford, onto a working-class street. Father a Swedish ex-sailor who liked to drink and use his fists – there were drunk-and-disorderly arrests, 'domestic incidents' at the damp little house he grew up in, before his mother decided she'd had enough. (He was six when she left, but she didn't take him with her.) Then the patchy school attendance, the poor grades. There should have been a record of juvenile crime too – minor theft, that sort of thing – but even back then he was smart enough never to get caught.

And after that, the army records. Squaddie, then sniper. Service in the Middle East. Commendations for courage under fire. The army saved him, didn't it? Gave him family, structure, discipline, self-respect. Showed him what he could become, if he wanted it badly enough. And he wanted it.

It ended with selection for 'additional training'. The euphemism for some branch of Special Ops, tucked into a dark corner between British intelligence and the MoD: people disappear into it and they don't always come out. But Johanssen did. Five months away from his unit – a scatter of codes in his file – and then he returned to standard combat duties. No mention of why; he said he didn't know.

Soon after he returned to his unit, he quit.

The records ended there. Nothing on the months he spent adrift. Nothing on the drink with a friend of a friend in a London pub. Nothing on his recruitment into the gangster Charlie Ross's private army. And nothing on the first job Johanssen was sent on, in the company of three others: to abduct a man called Terry Cunliffe, and send a message to his boss.

When I asked Johanssen what happened, all he said was, 'It went wrong.' But for the first time since they'd taken the hood off him I saw a flicker of emotion, something in his eyes and mouth, something that might have been shame.

It wasn't enough, not to make up for what happened to Terry Cunliffe. I looked at him and thought, *You're going to die.*

'Fraud,' Craigie says, and he shakes his head. He doesn't believe a word of it.

We've moved into a small room with the windows boarded: it holds two uncomfortable chairs and a desk. Hamilton's gone, hooded and hustled out of sight. I can make out faint clinks and scrapes and rattles as someone takes down the lights.

'So who is he?' I ask.

'William Arthur Hamilton. Worked for Hopeland, the medical giant. He was the contracts man. "Director of Collaborative Ventures". Four million flu jabs? Government quarantine facility for biowarfare casualties? You went to him. Lots of offshore work and private contracts, but Whitehall jobs too.' Craigie's mouth is tight and humourless.

'Plenty of room for fraud there.'

Craigie gives another neat decisive shake of the head. 'There's more to it than that. He's not just been lining his own pockets, taking aid money for vaccines that never existed. He's too scared.' He smiles, a brief sardonic smile. 'Maybe he's been accepting bribes from some nasty little regime to ship something he wasn't supposed to. Maybe he didn't deliver. Whatever he's done, he thinks they're coming after him. Or why demand the safe house?'

'He's not keen to share.'

'He'll change his mind. Give me a week and we'll have it out of him.' Craigie has a ruthless streak: in his dark suit and coat he looks like a small-town undertaker, but he's a predator. But then his hard black eyes latch on to me. 'You know I'd have preferred it if you hadn't come.'

We meet once a week, every Friday without fail, to run through the latest developments in the business. Usually the meeting takes place at my apartment, Craigie with a briefcase of bogus financial paperwork to back up the story that he's some sort of financial adviser to me. But once in a while I ask to sit in on an interview. Just to keep my hand in? Or out of boredom? I don't know. Charlotte Alton is my real name, the name I was born with. But for a long time she was just a cover, and even now, for all my efforts, I'm still not convinced she's real. She lives only just enough to maintain her own fiction. She moves among people who accept her at face value and wouldn't dream of asking personal questions. She is a pleasant companion, an easy conversationalist; she can be relied upon to support charitable causes, and can be seated next to awkward dinner guests. But if she were to disappear from the face of the earth tomorrow, how many people would notice?

I stepped back from the running of the network to build myself a normal life. A year on, and I don't have one yet. So sometimes I come to stand at the back of the room – hidden behind the lights, saying nothing. Still Craigie doesn't like it.

'You're doing a fine job,' I say.

'But you wanted to make sure.'

'Nothing like that.'

'And you don't know Hamilton.'

It's true, Hamilton could easily be one of Charlotte Alton's tribe. We might have rubbed shoulders in a theatre or a concert hall. He's the type: affluent, well connected … but he's a stranger. I shake my head. 'It's just a site visit.'

Craigie purses his lips. 'Your coming here exposes you to—'

'If it's safe enough for you, it's safe enough for me.'

Craigie's look tells me that's not how he sees it. That look's like a little jab at me. But isn't this what I pay him for? To be cautious, and conservative, and risk-averse. To pay as much attention to the details as I would myself. It still irritates.

I swallow it. We have business to discuss.

'So what have you got for me?' I ask, and we begin.

An approach from a Russian group: well capitalised, but their internal security seems based largely on excessive and bloody violence; we'll turn them away. A new Japanese intelligence source that looks secure: Craigie will check him out. An upgraded firewall at a European bank but we have a contact in the software developers. And on, and on … Craigie's narrow face creases with concentration as he pulls the facts out of his memory: potential clients, potential sources, potential threats. He's trained himself never to make notes.

It's only when we're done – when Craigie stands and dusts down his coat – that I say, 'You remember Simon Johanssen.'

His expression says it all. Of course he does.

'He's been in touch,' I say.

Instantly his gaze sharpens. 'With you? How did he contact you?'

Calmly, as if it's nothing that need trouble us: 'The opera. Last night.'

'He approached you? In public?'

'We were careful. No one saw.'

'But he knew to find you there.' And then, more quietly, almost to himself: 'This was always going to happen—'

He breaks off. He's said enough. Already the old argument's filling

28

the air between us. On everyone who's seen my face, everyone who can identify me, we hold incriminating information, and we make sure they know it. All except Johanssen.

Finally he asks, 'So what did he want?'

'The usual. An ID for a job.' I pause. 'It's in the Program.'

Craigie gapes.

'He asked if I could get him in there. As an inmate, temporarily.'

'You said no.'

'I said I'd look into it.'

'He'd need an inmate ID. It can't be done.'

I let the moment play out. 'It can't,' he says again. So I tell him.

Ryan Jackson is thirty-five, though he looks older in the photo I've got. He was born in Britain but moved to the US at the age of twenty-seven – drawn to LA for all the wrong reasons. He shacked up with a local girl, a waitress, and for a while succeeded in evading the attention of US Immigration. Succeeded, that is, until the girl got sick of him and dumped him for another guy; at which point he went to her home, shot the guy, sawed off his head, placed the corpse in a chair with its back to the door and then waited for the girl to turn up. She let herself in and crossed to the chair, with no idea of what was waiting for her.

Afterwards he shot her too. It took her six hours to die; he sat watching throughout. He later told police she'd had it coming.

When they asked about the boyfriend he just shrugged.

He must have had a good lawyer: California has the death penalty, but he's serving a life sentence in Victorville Penitentiary.

Ryan Jackson is scum of the lowest order. But he's in the right age range, he's the right height, and his physical resemblance to Johanssen is close enough.

Craigie's shaking his head. 'And he comes to the Program why?' he demands. 'Visiting friends?'

'Our story will be that he's got links to US organised crime. He's got information. Which he's offered to share on condition he gets a transfer out of the US and into the Program. The US authorities will ask for UK co-operation on this: their man in the Program for three weeks, to see if he'll crack. But officially in that time he remains a US prisoner, a US responsibility, who's entered the Program of his own free will. Effectively he's a volunteer. So he never shows up on the Program inmate system. Ryan Jackson gives us the complete story: why Johanssen has to go in there, why he has to keep in touch with us while he's in there, why he walks out at the end.'

'When Ryan Jackson goes back to California.' For a moment Craigie sounds bitterly impressed.

'It'll be like he never left.'

'And Jackson has no UK criminal associates?'

I shake my head. 'Not as far as I can see. Though I'll keep looking.'

'He'll need a chaperone.' Then something clicks behind his eyes. 'Whitman. You phoned him before you came here. That's why you were late.'

Mike Whitman's an intelligence contractor, a tall dyspeptic American with a faint Alabama twang to his accent and thirty years' experience of working the US system – fifteen of them behind a CIA desk. He knows me as Laura Pressinger, has done for years; he's not entirely sure who Laura's people are – she doesn't go in for business cards – but they're definitely intelligence community. She's legit. But occasionally she needs help from someone with a US passport, an inside knowledge of US intelligence and a willingness to look the other way.

Whitman inhabits a grey world where anything can be fixed with the right contacts and plausible paperwork, and where some form of double-dealing is standard business practice. Add to that a late first marriage eight months ago to a beautiful French girl and a move to Paris – at her insistence – and Whitman's cut off from the contractor honeypots of Washington and Langley. He has money worries. He wants the work. When I told him what I wanted he said drily, 'You're still doing that James Bond shit, Laura,' and I replied, 'You'd be disappointed if I wasn't,' and he laughed, but not like he meant it.

He's catching the Eurostar from Gare du Nord today.

'If anyone can make this look good, it's Whitman,' I say.

'And Washington?' Craigie asks. 'US Department of Justice playing along with this? One phone call is all it will take.'

'We can give Johanssen enough paperwork in the UK system to go through on the nod. It'll be on all the right desks by Monday. This sort of thing, everyone just wants to make sure their arses are covered. And they will be. Johanssen turns up with an escort and they'll be expecting him.'

'Three weeks, you said. Where did that come from?' The smart question, as ever.

'It's all we need.'

He says, 'Or that's how long you reckon you've got before some-one calls Washington. And does Johanssen know the risks? If anyone looks hard at this – or if anyone does make that call to Washington while he's in there—'

'Of course I'll tell him.'

'But he'll do it anyway, won't he?' He shakes his head. Then, more quietly, he says, 'It's a hit in a prison, Karla,' and I know exactly what he means. It could be a trap.

'Fielding's checked out the client. And Fielding's a shit, but I trust him not to risk his best asset. I checked the Met too: if someone in Organised Crime's running a sting operation to catch a hit man, no one's heard a whisper. In any case, does this look like a sting to you? You don't make traps this difficult to walk into.'

'And you? What about the risks to you?'

'There is no risk to me.'

'Karla, a year ago we agreed—'

I know what we agreed. 'It's one job,' I say firmly, 'nothing else. Just one.'

For a moment Craigie's silent, looking down at the floor. He says quietly, 'You can't be part of this.'

'I already am. He came to me. He's my responsibility.'

'Why, Karla? What makes him so special?'

But I don't have an answer.

I think he's done, but at the door – briefcase in one gloved hand, the other on the door handle – he pauses and looks back, and his pale narrow face is tight with disapproval.

'Think carefully about Simon Johanssen,' he says. 'Isn't he un-reliable?'

I know why he says it. But every job Johanssen's ever done has been clean. Except for the first. Except for Terry Cunliffe.

Terry Cunliffe: forties, a little overweight, round-faced, permanently cheerful. A decent guy. He worked for John Quillan, small time, and maybe four or five times a year he came to me, his master's emissary for minor trades – a request for information, or something to sell. He wasn't tough and he wasn't brave but he suffered the indignities of our security procedures with gentle good humour. I liked him. I liked him a lot, though I never let him see my face.

Terry was a nobody until John Quillan went to war with Charlie Ross, and Terry became a target.

And Simon Johanssen was a nobody too, an ex-squaddie on the streets, until Charlie Ross recruited him and sent him after Terry; though he was only there to make up the numbers, in case there was trouble.

The trouble didn't materialise. Terry was alone.

They put him in a car and drove him to a remote farmhouse. After that things ran out of control. Before the night was over Terry was dead. Not the clean way, though; not the bullet-to-the-head way.

By the time Johanssen got to me, events had taken a predictable course. The three other men who'd escorted Terry to the farmhouse were dead too – two in a quarry, one in a burned-out car on a country lane – killed on the orders of Terry's boss John Quillan. All three had been tortured before they died.

Johanssen would be next.

He didn't know that I knew Terry. He'd simply come to me to disappear. He had no reason to lie, no reason to know that when I said, 'Complete disclosure is vital,' I was bracing myself to hear about the last, horrific hours of a man I knew and liked. But I had to know. Knowing what happened would justify what was to come. The moment when I told him, *I'm sorry, we can't help you.* The moment when we put him back out there, unprotected, and turned away while Quillan's people closed in.

Complete disclosure is vital. Of course I thought I knew it all already. It turned out I was wrong.

We made him disappear. We went through his life, piece by piece: his National Insurance number, National Health number, tax reference code; every place he'd ever lived, every school he'd ever attended, every job he'd ever done. We took his passport, his bank details, his credit cards, his driving licence. And we wiped him from the record.

Craigie didn't understand what we were doing. Ironic, since he found the clue when we were stripping out the last of the physical evidence, deleting every little scrap of Simon Johanssen's past: an MoD memo referring to a set of psychological test results from the very end of that Special Ops training. The memo itself was in opaque military jargon but in the margin someone had scribbled, 'Unreliable.'

Craigie saw that word and thought, *This man's a psycho, ticking like a bomb*. But Craigie wasn't in the room that night. He didn't hear the story. He doesn't know that there are other kinds of *unreliable*, and Johanssen's one of them.

It doesn't make him less dangerous; some would argue it makes him more so. I understood that at that time. Still, I had to let him live.

I deleted Simon Johanssen's past, then sent a message to the squat where he was holed up. In less than fifteen minutes he'd gone, as if he'd never been there. Within twenty-four hours he was out of the country, on a fake ID that he would abandon shortly afterwards in Tunis. And that was the end of it; that's what I thought.

I didn't know that he'd be coming back; and coming back a different man.

At 9.54 on Saturday night my safe phone rings.

Robbie's East End accent: 'He's on his way. With you in six.' He sounds peeved: it beats him how anyone manages to get so close without being spotted.

At ten on the dot Johanssen arrives at my apartment. I hesitated before giving him the address, but he had it already. Of course he did.

Tonight he has the scrubbed carbolic cleanness of a man who doesn't spend time on how he looks, but that's an illusion. He's studied hard to make himself a blank canvas, edit out any element of his appearance that might snag on the memory, and now his anonymity is perfect. He could be anyone.

And before twenty-four hours is up he'll be someone else again: wearing different clothes, shackled to a different past, answering to a different name.

So few people can do what he's about to do. Most can't cope with the discipline of it all, the loss of contact with their own lives. They become restless, and then they start to break the rules, out of carelessness or frustration. But not men like him: for them, the shift from one life to the next is nothing more than taking off one jacket and putting on another.

Some of this is the result of sheer willpower. But some of it is down to isolation. He cut all ties with his family years ago. He has few associates and no close friends. He sleeps alone.

Perhaps that's what makes it so easy for him: because he has so little life to miss.

33

'You're going in as a man called Ryan Jackson, British born but US resident, and down for life in Victorville Penitentiary, California: murder, two counts. We're going to borrow his ID.' I push a paper file across the coffee table to where Johanssen sits. Immediately he starts to flick through it. It contains everything I've managed to glean about Jackson's life. There are even photos of the girlfriend, as she was when she first met Jackson, and then afterwards, as the police found her. The wounds are shocking, but he just blinks three times, rapidly, then turns the page without a word. He's seen it all before.

'Your escort is an American contractor called Whitman. He knows you're not Jackson. That's all he does know. He doesn't know why you're going in, and he won't ask. How long do you need for a recce?'

Johanssen doesn't glance up from the file. 'Forty-eight hours.'

'All right. When forty-eight hours is up, Whitman will get you pulled out for a little chat. At that point you get to choose: stay out or go back in.'

'How long have we got, all told?'

'From first entry to final exit? I reckon three weeks, after which he pulls you out of there permanently. Is three weeks enough?'

He gives the ghost of a shrug: it'll have to do.

'And in that time we need to keep you as low profile as possible. If anyone gets restless, starts asking questions, we'll get you out, but there's always a danger with these—'

'I know,' he says.

'Whitman will also give you a number you can reach him on, any time, day or night. If you have a problem, call him saying you're ready to talk and he'll get you lifted.'

'There won't be a problem,' he says.

I push a second file towards him – 'The Program,' I say. 'Run by a private security concern and ruled by John Quillan.' I lean forward in my seat, willing him to meet my gaze. 'He'll wonder who you are.'

He doesn't look up. 'I'm Ryan Jackson,' he says. As if that's an end to it.

Of course. Only Charlie Ross could ID him, and Charlie Ross is dead.

He begins to read, and while he reads I watch him.

He doesn't seem to resent my scrutiny, though he must be aware of it. But he's a sniper, with a sniper's overdeveloped ability to focus, and right now he's directing it towards the man he's about to become and the place he's about to go. Once in a while he leans back and closes his eyes, reviewing the information, replaying it to himself. Sometimes his hands move fractionally as he does so, and the scars on his knuckles shine in the light.

Another empty room, same set of lights. Simon Johanssen again, but two years later. Terry Cunliffe's horrific death reduced to the scar tissue of memory. John Quillan and Charlie Ross both behind bars, unlikely to get out.

Johanssen had a different name this time. He worked for Fielding, and he wanted information. We'd brought him in with all the usual precautions: black plates on the van, a hood over his head. This time we kept the hood on.

I stood before his chair and said, 'Remember me?'

For ten seconds he didn't move. Then he said, 'I never got your name last time.'

'Karla,' I said. 'You can call me Karla.'

'A spy's name,' he said.

'George Smiley's nemesis.' I hadn't pictured him reading Le Carré.

'Who?' he said.

'Nothing. So,' I said, 'you want information.'

It was for a hit.

That was where we began again, though for another two years after that we only ever met in empty rooms, with the light between us: me in shadow and invisible, him in the glare and blind – but always quiet, patient, reticent, polite, sitting very still under those lights, only ever asking the necessary questions; never pushing at the boundaries of our relationship, never presuming anything.

Four years ago I let him see my face.

He specialises in the difficult jobs, the technical ones, the ones requiring care and patience, with a high degree of risk; his record is unbroken. And he has rules, though it took me time to work them out. He doesn't talk about them.

Some like to watch the aftermath. They sit through the customary four-second frozen silence in order to see the horror unfolding on the onlookers' faces, the mouths stretching into screams; see them clutching at each other as they flail for cover. He isn't one of them.

35

Some accept that collateral damage – a bystander down, a little extra blood on the pavement – is an occupational hazard. He isn't one of them either.

And some will loose off a second bullet into the chaos, even though the job's over. Just for fun. Their treat. To him they are sick. He is careful with the lives of others.

His targets never know and never suffer, even the ones who might deserve to: the gangster with a taste for torture, the woman who traffics children into the sex trade, the paedophile who's walked free on a technicality. That's the narrow focus of Johanssen's morality: not whether they die – someone else has decided that – but how.

Does this make him a good man, or a hypocrite? I'm not sure. I live in a world where there are few good people. Perhaps I have no frame of reference.

Craigie's baffled by him still. He's said it more than once: 'Any sane person would have had screaming nightmares after what happened to Cunliffe. Simon Johanssen just got better at what he did.'

He's right: in six years Johanssen's only ever been efficient, methodical, professional, each hit clean and perfect.

But still I can't help wondering if the man who fled that farmhouse after Terry Cunliffe died – the man the army branded *unreliable* – is sitting before me now.

He just won't let me see it.

He has a version of the Program map in front of him – there are landmarks he must memorise, refuges he may need if this goes wrong – and he's scanning it for details when I say, 'If you have a problem, get to a phone. Call Whitman. He'll get you lifted as soon as possible. But there are restrictions. The patrols?'

Without taking his eyes off the map he says, 'Snatch Land Rovers, three-man crews, armed.'

'Officially they circulate day and night. But at night the Program goes into a sort of lockdown. Gates are closed. Patrols go back to their secure bases and on the whole they stay there.' I lean forward. 'You have a problem, get out by six. Because after that you're in there until morning.'

Johanssen nods, still doesn't look up from his map.

'As for the target, we're still awaiting access to inmate records. We may get in within the next few days, we may not, so there's a chance you'll go in without knowing—'

'It doesn't matter. All I'm doing is a recce.'

'Fielding say what she did?'

'Just something bad.'

'That's all?'

He shrugs.

Not murder, though. We would have found her; she would have made the news, would have left a dirty smear across the media and the Internet. The women always do. But I've searched through trial reports and wanted lists and even the specialist true-crime websites, and there's no sign of her.

'I can't find her,' I say. He doesn't reply.

'Johanssen, checking her out is due diligence.'

For the first time he looks up at me. His eyes – a bleak North Sea grey in this light, though I know they are blue – are very clear.

'It's only a recce,' he says.

It's after three on Sunday morning when he leaves. As soon as he's gone I walk into my office and begin to destroy the files. I've discreetly tapped into my building's security camera network, and so the live CCTV feed on the office screen picks Johanssen up as he crosses the ground-floor lobby, nodding to the night porter. He walks out through the front doors and into the night, an anonymous figure in a dark coat. Mister Nobody. You wouldn't look twice.

I go back to the main window expecting to see his dark shape crossing the walkways, but he's already vanished.

The phone rings. Robbie. 'Tail him?' he asks.

I say, 'Don't bother.'

Someone wants a woman dead; wants it badly enough to pay through the nose for it. They've read the reports on the Internet – read about the Program's sports facilities and training opportunities, its small-business initiatives and its restaurant – and believed every word. Now they want the punishment to fit the crime, whatever it was … I've put away her picture, but still it seems to float in the air before me: the young woman with a smile you can't get past. Yet again I'm back at that imaginary front page, that screaming headline. What's she done? And why can't I find her?

The phone rings a second time. Craigie this time, on a secure landline. He doesn't talk on mobiles: risk, again. For half a second I wonder if Robbie's not the only one who's been watching – if

Craigie's had my building under surveillance too, has seen Johanssen leaving, and now he's going to have one last try at wrenching control of this from me.

Then he says, 'Karla?' and the tension in his voice tells me it's something else entirely.

Most of my clients may be criminals, but by and large we make our bargains and we stick to them: I get them what they want, and they pay me. Few get to see my face, and on those that do I try to make sure I've enough information to wreck their lives comprehensively and for ever. Still, there is between us something like trust.

But for five years and eight months I've worked for another client: a client I can't afford to trust, a client I've never met, never spoken to, never communicated with except untraceably. A client who doesn't even know me as Karla, and who has never paid me.

His name is Peter Laidlaw, he works for British intelligence, and through the fog of my own shock Craigie is telling me that the night before last, with a terminal diagnosis in his pocket, he threw himself under a train.

Day 5: Sunday

Powell

Home, but with no sense of homecoming.

The call on Saturday morning. 'Something's come up. You're booked on a flight.' Thea, dressed as a fairy, had a lunchtime party to go to; was engaged in complex negotiations with her mother over the wearing of wings with her coat. He hugged her before she left, inhaled her strawberry smell, wondered tightly how long he might be away. Promised himself, *Not long*, though he knew it was a promise he was in no position to make.

The 18.15 flight out of Dulles, the short transatlantic night – a little over seven hours in the air – and then the touchdown at Heathrow: 06.20 GMT but winter dark, the runway lights winking across the tarmac, the airport corridors lit a washed-out low-voltage grey, the smell of the flight clinging to him like the aftermath of an illness. His body clock was still on Eastern Standard Time, and he hadn't slept a wink.

There was a driver waiting for him with a sign. 'Hotel?' he asked – he'd have liked a shower before they got started – but the man said, 'Straight to the office, if that's all right, sir,' and he nodded, because he expected as much.

Now they're in the Long Room, the room overlooking the inner courtyard, its windows with their one-way glass baffled to guard against listening devices, the door reinforced so as soon as it's closed no sound leaks in from the rest of the building – or out. Just him and the Section Chief, and between them a Sunday-morning pot of coffee and a plate of synthetic-looking pastries that ought to make things better but don't.

'Laidlaw,' the Section Chief says. 'Peter Laidlaw.' He adds sharply, 'You know the name?'

Powell shakes his head. The name means nothing.

39

The Section Chief pushes a file across the table, two inches of paperwork; either Laidlaw is old, or he's been busy. Powell flicks it open. *Old*, says the photograph in front of him. Early seventies, at a guess. He scans the page. SIS, a Moscow Man, an agent handler; one of the old Sov Bloc master race, retired. *Compromised* – the assumption's automatic – and then, *How badly?* Very badly, if they've brought him back from Washington. He looks back at the file.

Peter Laidlaw has been retired for years. Any secrets he could give up would be old secrets.

You wouldn't have brought me back for that.

The Section Chief sits back in his chair and folds his arms, turning his head sideways towards the courtyard. He looks uncomfortable.

Powell asks, 'What's he done?'

The Section Chief says, 'Where were you five years ago?'

'Here.'

Here in an office down the corridor with no name on the door. *Here* among the clean-up agents of the intelligence and security worlds: the janitors. Three years into the job. One year into his marriage. Thea a bright promise in the future. Everything possible.

'Five years and eight months ago Peter Laidlaw turned up on the doorstep of Thames House with a plastic bag and refused to go away.'

Thames House: home of MI5, by Lambeth Bridge. *Wrong building.* Peter Laidlaw was SIS. But he didn't go to his own, to the place where someone would have vouched for him. 'Why not Vauxhall Cross? Why—'

The Section Chief says crisply, 'Those were his instructions.'

'Instructions from …?'

The Section Chief gives him a look. 'You sure you don't know about this?' And Powell wonders, not for the first time, if that's why they sent him to Washington after all. Because he'd handled one too many cases? Because he knew too much?

'Positive.'

The Section Chief says, 'He sat in an office for two hours demanding to speak to an officer out of G Branch. He wouldn't go away. In the end they sent someone down just to get rid of him.' The Section Chief pauses.

There's only one question to ask. 'What was in the plastic bag?'

'*This.*'

He flicks open another file, spins a photograph across the tabletop.

A familiar face looks out: a woman in her forties with an unrelenting stare.

Eileen Granger, the Maternity Unit Bomber.

'Laidlaw produced the tip-off on Granger?'

'The time, the place, her identity, everything. Granger was under everyone's radar – ours, the Americans', everyone's. Nobody knew what she had planned. Except Peter Laidlaw.'

'So how did he know?'

The Section Chief blinks, blandly. 'Received it from an anonymous source.'

There's a hare to be chased down, but it can wait. Powell sits back. 'And then what?'

'Nothing for four months. By which time MI5 had scaled back surveillance on him: tired of following an old man at his errands. They'd decided it was a one-off when he turned up again.'

'Another plastic bag?'

'Envelope this time. Tip-off about a money trail: someone funding an extremist cell in the States. Two months further on, he's got news that a source is about to be compromised. Another month … And so on. Of course by this time MI5's watching him round the clock, because they'd like to know where all this is coming from.'

'And?'

'Whoever it is plays by Moscow Rules. Tradecraft. Chalk marks on trees. Dead drops. We're talking old school, minimal technology.' The Section Chief pulls a sour face.

'And Laidlaw? What did he say?'

'He claimed he'd no idea.'

'Is that likely?'

The Section Chief doesn't answer that one. He says, 'It has to be intelligence community and it has to be Russia.'

'Ident?'

'Laidlaw called them Knox.' He shakes his head. 'MI5 took to diverting his mail.'

'And?'

'A note arrived, from Knox. "Stop the diverts."'

'Knox knew?'

'Or guessed.'

'What did MI5 do?'

The Section Chief snorts humourlessly. 'Backed off. Next thing they know, Laidlaw's phoning them in the middle of the night.

From a call box, of all places. There's going to be a shooting in an Aiya Napa nightclub.'

'That was Knox?'

'That, and the Birmingham network they rolled up two years ago, and the ricin plotters.'

'*All* of those came from Knox?'

The Section Chief nods. 'Though MI5 repackaged the product, made it look like it came from several sources, as you would. Tech stuff went out under the name Albatross. Al-Qaeda spin-offs were Alchemy. Money laundering was Green Man. Knox accounts for at least seven different brands. Last big spectacular was a year back. One of Five's own tech ops guys obviously felt he wasn't being paid enough. Put a list of all their live surveillance operations up for auction. Who was being watched, and how. Bidders were queuing up to get a look.' The Section Chief pauses. 'Knox secured it for us.'

'And we still don't know who Knox is?'

The Section Chief shakes his head.

'So how many people are up on this?'

'Apart from the MI5 high-ups? Very few. Laidlaw had his own handler – you can imagine, it wasn't the easiest job in the world, handling a Moscow Man. A couple of analysts, a reports officer ...'

'The Americans?'

'Saw the product. Didn't know it all came from the one source.'

'Did *we* know about Knox?'

The Section Chief hesitates. This is an awkward point. 'No,' he says at last. '*We* weren't informed. MI5 felt they could handle it themselves.' *Or they didn't want to admit they were running a source they couldn't validate.* 'Leeson – do you remember Leeson? – was assigned to the MI5 ops list auction; she identified the culprit. But no one told her the original tip had come from Knox. We didn't even know Knox existed.'

'So what changed?'

The Section Chief says, 'On Friday night Laidlaw threw himself in front of a train. Suicide.' He adds, 'He had cancer. Brain tumour. Brutal ... The news has been embargoed but of course these things get out.' He sighs. 'As soon as they realised what they were up against, MI5 came to us.'

He looks at Powell again, expectantly. Powell looks again at the photograph. Peter Laidlaw is jowly, humourless ... a keeper of secrets, a details man. One of the old guard.

The Section Chief says, 'They haven't the first idea who Knox is. Their best source, and they've lost it.' He says again, 'It has to be Russia, doesn't it? Someone within the SVR, skimming off their own product – someone who knew Laidlaw, or knew *of* him. Anglophile, maybe.'

And doing it out of the goodness of their heart? Powell says, 'Knox never asked for anything in return? Money? Promise of safe harbour?'

The Section Chief shakes his head.

They just haven't got round to asking yet.

'You want me to find Knox.'

'Establish a means of contact. But don't have any direct communication, is that clear? Anything you get, you send up to me immediately.'

Powell nods. Doesn't ask why. The Section Chief wants this one for himself.

'Oh, and I want interim reports.'

Powell says without thinking, 'That's not how we normally—'

The Section Chief says, 'I know how we *normally* do things here, I do still run this place. I know you wouldn't *normally* expect to file a report until your investigation's complete. But nothing about Knox is *normal*. Nothing.' He shifts in his seat, uncomfortable again, then settles. 'As for resources, just tell us what you need.' The Section Chief nods, as if that's everything.

'Do the others know I'm back?' Powell asks.

'Of course not.'

'Who's still here?'

'Morris, though she's seven months off retirement. Carter. Leeson. Kingman – he's after your time I think. Ex Special Branch.'

'What will they be told?'

'The usual,' the Section Chief says. He means, *Nothing.*

'And unofficially?'

'You've come to clean the Augean stables,' the Section Chief says. He allows himself a little smirk.

Powell says, 'And what are they supposed to make of that?'

'Whatever they want,' the Section Chief says. 'Whatever they want.'

Another office with no name on the door. A security pass on the desk. Beside it, a letter with the address of a serviced apartment which will be his for the duration, however long that is.

He drops Peter Laidlaw's file on to the desk. It lands heavily.
To the apartment; a few hours' sleep; a shower; then back to work.
09.35 GMT. 04.35 Eastern Standard Time.
Thea has been in bed for hours. He never said goodnight.

Part II

Day 7: Tuesday

Johanssen

Johanssen dreams of a man in an office. The man sits behind a desk, with his hands clasped on top of a file; the file has Johanssen's name on it.

The man's lips form words but no sound comes out.

Johanssen wakes. The light filtering through the thin curtains is sodium yellow. The digital clock beside the bed reads 6:02. On the streets, traffic's already stirring.

They brought him here yesterday, to a three-bedroom flat in a privatised south London housing block. Three men are with him, on rotating shifts, two on duty at any one time. The American, Whitman, is tall, bony, weary-looking, seen-it-all; he pops antacids constantly, could have an ulcer on the way. The other two are younger, late twenties, British, experienced: Johanssen can smell army on both of them. They watch him warily. Given who he's supposed to be, it's little wonder.

Mostly he's done nothing. But he's used to waiting before a job: wearing the same clothes for days on end, living off tinned food, listening to others going about their lives – voices and TV and the thump of bass from a speaker … On one side they have a harassed single mum for a neighbour: he hasn't set eyes on her, but her voice and the kid's sound through the thin wall. The kid – boy or girl? – must be only three or four. Sometimes the mum sings along to the radio. She chain-smokes; the smell seeps through from next door. The kid has a smoker's cough already.

No sound comes from the flat on the other side.

So he waits. Twenty-four hours is nothing. A lot of the time he simply clears his mind, blanks himself. Better not to think about what might happen. On a job like this you don't want expectations, don't want a picture in your head of how things will be. Nine times

47

out of ten that picture will be wrong. He has focused instead on the facts, the map, Karla's data—

There is no gas supply in the Program.

Chemicals are not supplied to residents if, in combination, they become combustible.

—he's tried to ground himself in that and not imagine what anything might be like. Imagination, like expectation, is a flaw.

So some of the time he thinks of Karla's data. But some of the time he thinks of Karla.

When she called to fix the briefing she asked him straight out, and sharply, 'Do you have my address? Do you know where I live?' And he said yes because it was the truth, even though it was information he shouldn't have had. He didn't expect her to say, 'Then come here.'

Two hours of anti-surveillance drills is his standard; that night he did three, for her.

She opened the door herself, and when she showed him into the apartment's main room – cool, pale, vast, he could have fitted his current flat in that one room with space to spare – there was nobody else waiting; nobody he could see anyway. Perhaps they were tucked away in a side room: a bodyguard, or the Scot who answered the old number. He couldn't say. At least she'd wanted the illusion they were alone.

But there were no pleasantries, no small talk, nothing to suggest he was anything but another client ... except once or twice, while he was reading the files, he thought he sensed her measuring the distance between them. As if she might cross it? But as soon as he finished with the last file she began to talk about the patrols, and they might as well have been in a warehouse again, with her behind the lights, invisible.

So many years he thought about the place where she might live. Thought about being there with her – waking up beside her in a clean quiet room and finding her still asleep, her face relaxed, her hair cloudy against the pillow, her breathing slow ...

But you don't belong there. You never will.

At 6.30 a.m. Whitman comes in, escorts him to the bathroom, where he pisses, then back into the bedroom to dress.

In the kitchen he's given cereal with milk, and some lukewarm tea. He finishes it and that's it. They're leaving.

48

They'd cuff him but they don't want to attract attention. Instead Whitman explains, again, what will happen if he tries to run.

Outside the early light's grey. The radio's on in the next-door flat, the mum singing, then the kid starts playing up and she shouts. Still no sound from the other side: it's empty, or the occupants keep different hours.

Ryan Jackson has a dad alive in a small Lancashire town, but they're not in touch. No old friends in contact either. Unlikely anyone would go to the trouble of springing him. Still, the younger guys mark him all the way down to the car, eyes everywhere. One of them opens a rear door. Johanssen gets in, and the man gets in beside him.

Where civilian contractors are required, they work under the protection of armed security.

Armoured vehicles patrol the streets, operating from secure command posts.

Whitman and the other man get in the front, the engine starts, and they're away.

You can tell it's coming before you see it. You know, because everything starts to die.

It shows in the ex-council housing on the other side of the dual carriageway: alongside the outbreaks of stone cladding and the tacked-on porches there are weeds in the drives, peeling paintwork, grey steel anti-vandal boards at the windows. The stain of neglect. A few businesses cling to life in the little shopping parade – a discount furniture dealer, a hairdresser's, a pound shop slewing bright plastic goods across the pavement – but most of the shops are boarded up. There's a curry house and an ugly barn-like pub offering cheap lager and big-screen sporting events, but the only place doing any real business is the drive-through restaurant up on the main road, shovelling out fast food to people who have to eat but don't want to stop.

From the flyover a small newish light-industrial park looks like a reminder of a forlorn hope. The sign boards are mostly blank and only two cars sit in the car park.

Then the carriageway turns and there it is: Karla's map made real.

First there's the waste ground, the areas of land they cleared around the main site but never built on: weeds sprout among the concrete footprints of demolished buildings. Inside that: parking areas, storage hangars, warehouses. Everything's still new and clean. Signs point to Visitor Reception, Administrative Services, the Staff Restaurant. A big green modern block has the word INDUCTION on a board by the entrance. A smaller blue unit calls itself the Emergency Medical Centre. There's a helipad beside it. The whole thing might be a modern commercial estate, one that houses particularly nervy businesses: the roads are dotted with checkpoints, yellow sentry boxes, red and white barriers, and cameras on stalks monitor all the approaches.

Beyond the buildings the wall looms.

The exit comes up. The car pulls off at the ramp, the road sinks, and the Program disappears from view.

They stop at the first security barrier. Guards ask Whitman to state his business, peer at Johanssen in the back, consult a clipboard and then wave them through. They park next to the big green block and get out.

On the other side of the building's glass doors, two warders man a metal detector. As the doors slide open they turn and stare.

Whitman says to the others, 'I'll take him from here.'

Johanssen breathes in, filling his lungs. Adrenaline kicks in his bloodstream: suddenly everything's brighter and harder and clearer. This is it.

'Can you tell me the purpose of your visit, Mr *Jackson*?' asks the clerk behind the armoured-glass screen, without irony. He's middle-aged and overweight, with a bland soft face like uncooked dough. The plastic badge on his lapel says RESIDENTS' RECEPTION. He talks with an exaggerated slowness as if he's used to dealing with idiots or people whose English is weak, and he has a habit of overstressing the last word in his sentences.

On the desk in front of him sits Johanssen's application to enter the Program.

Johanssen says, 'I want to see what it's like,' and Whitman snorts.

The man pauses, perplexed. The form obviously doesn't have a category for people like Ryan Jackson. Eventually he murmurs to himself, 'Checking inmate conditions.'

He makes a tiny mark on the form, in biro. The room they're in is windowless and smells of nylon carpets.

It's taken an hour to get to this point. An hour of sitting or standing – in rooms like this one, or in corridors – while memos are consulted and calls made. Throughout it all Whitman has maintained a weary ironic patience: he's come here to do his job and sooner or later they'll let him. If he has worries about Karla's paperwork, they don't show. He's given Johanssen the occasional order – 'In here,' 'Sit down' – but rarely looks at him. Johanssen is now Jackson, and Jackson is scum.

At last the clerk is finished. He pushes the form back under the screen for Johanssen to sign: three signatures, all in the name of Ryan Jackson. When Johanssen passes it back the dough-faced man says, 'You are advised to deposit all valuables before you enter the Program.' He smirks to himself. 'Things have a tendency to go *astray*.' Then he says to Whitman, 'What about induction? There's usually a video presentation—'

Whitman says, 'I think we can skip that. He'll pick it up as he goes along.'

Another room. Hand- and fingerprints and a retinal scan. Photographs, face-on and profile, against a height marker. A blood sample and a scrape of DNA from the inside of his cheek.

Whitman and the dough-faced man have followed Johanssen in. Whitman says softly, 'You load this to your system?' and the dough-faced man says, 'Not unless he's confirmed as a permanent resident.' Whitman just nods gravely.

Then Johanssen's handed a lidless metal box and told to turn out his pockets; except there's nothing in them.

A third room: tiled, with a sink and an examination table. Inside three men in warders' uniforms with batons on their belts are waiting, one of them snapping surgical gloves over his hands.

Gloves steps up to him. 'So you're off to the zoo,' he says conversationally. 'Open your mouth.' The man peers inside, probes with a finger: the glove squeaks against enamel. Johanssen stares at the man's right ear. The man grunts. 'Close.'

After that he's told to strip. The warders observe while Johanssen undresses and places his clothes in a plastic crate, which one of them takes outside.

Gloves says, 'So where you in from, then?'

'Victorville.' Johanssen keeps his head down, avoiding eye contact. 'It's in America,' he says.

'Huh,' the man says as if he's heard that one before. Then, 'Strip-search. Turn around, you know the drill.'

Once the strip-search is finished the two warders go out, leaving

Johanssen shivering under the blank gaze of a security camera.

At last they bring the crate back, order him to dress and escort him to a kiosk, where Whitman is already waiting. A bored girl with flat brown hair sits behind another screen. Above her head is a sign: NO UNAUTHORISED WEAPONS OR DRUGS BEYOND THIS POINT.

On his side of the screen there's a handprint reader and a retinal scanner.

Without looking at him the girl says, 'Place your hand on the panel and look into the screen.'

When she's satisfied she issues him with ID: a credit-card-size oblong of green plastic with an embedded chip and a copy of his digital photo.

'Currency?' she asks.

Johanssen glances sideways at Whitman. Whitman asks, 'How much can he take?'

'One hundred,' she says.

'Then give him a hundred.'

The girl stares at her monitor, punches a couple of keys, and a flood of little plastic discs, red and blue and yellow, rattle down a chute into a metal tray in front of him. He scoops them out: they're like counters from a kids' game.

Last of all she takes a printed map which shows the perimeter wall and the tracery of streets, and with a fat blue marker puts a cross against a building. Next to it she writes 'Grisham 24' in rounded childish writing. She pushes it through to him, along with a pair of keys on a ring.

He's still staring at the map when Whitman says, 'You got what you wanted. You go in there, you think about it, then we'll talk. Two days.' He nods, turns, and walks away without another look.

Johanssen's taken outside.

Across a stretch of tarmac the Program's perimeter wall rears up: forty foot high, topped with wire. Dead ahead is a metal gate; above the gate, in sheeny black lettering against a white board, are the words RESIDENTS' ENTRY POINT WEST.

To one side of the gate is a sentry booth: a guard is watching electronic screens. As Johanssen draws close he glimpses images: the wall, the exterior of the sentry booth, an empty corridor.

Johanssen's escort halts him in front of the gate. 'Name?'

'Ryan Jackson.'

The man in the booth consults a clipboard.

The same bored instruction: 'Place your hand on the panel and look into the screen.'

He does as he's told.

Outside the sentry booth a green light comes on and the guard says, 'Clear.'

The metal gate slides open. Johanssen steps through it.

He is in a whitewashed corridor of breeze-block walls and concrete floor, lit high up by caged wall lights. Above his head two cameras peer down at him. Gas nozzles stud the ceiling. Only two metres ahead of him the corridor turns at a right angle.

Behind him the gate slides shut and bolts clunk home.

He follows the corridor. Turns left, right, left again. No sounds but the sounds of his own footsteps, his own breath.

He turns another corner, and a second metal door comes into sight. Same cameras above. Same gas jets. He waits.

Nothing.

Ten seconds pass. Fifteen, and he's counting now. Still nothing.

Then a metallic click, and the door slides open.

A big empty room. A couple of CCTV cameras, no furniture. He's alone. A sign in six languages says, WAIT HERE. On the other side of the room is a door marked EXIT.

When he tries the handle it opens.

He steps outside, blinking.

A forty-metre no-man's-land of cleared ground. Then the buildings start, and beside them, a command post with a tower bristling with aerials, like something out of Troubles-era South Armagh. Left and right, the inner perimeter wall curves away, the wire on its upper edge winking in the pale winter light.

No guards that he can see.

He checks his watch: 10:39.

Then he crosses the no-man's-land and walks towards the command post and the buildings. He's barely halfway across when he knows he's been marked.

A glance and it could be a street in any run-down London suburb. It could be, if you can forget what you've just come from: the strip-search, the wall, the razed ground, the command post.

Houses line the road – kicked-about houses with junk and refuse in the front gardens, but inhabited. Then he walks on and the houses morph into a row of shops ending in a small 70s shopping centre. Some of the shops are boarded up, but some look like they're doing business, though what they're selling he's not sure. There are things he'll need to get, but they can wait. On the other side of the road there's a pub, only it can't be a pub now. The sound of hammering comes from inside. Outside three men stand in a tight group, talking without looking at each other, eyes on the street. In charge. Johanssen switches his gaze away. Already he's read the rule book for this place. *Don't attract attention. Don't look weak. Don't get in anyone's space. Don't meet their eyes.*

He keeps walking.

A middle-aged black guy shuffles past in slippers like an eighty-year-old. A younger woman with a pale face and dark Slavic eyes pauses to light a cigarette. A tired-looking white man clutches a plastic bag ... Ordinary faces from an ordinary town on a tough day; you wouldn't mark them as special—

Another man standing in a doorway, watching the passers-by with a predatory alertness. His gaze settles on Johanssen, and it's like a current moving through him; instinctively he tenses until the man's attention moves on.

There are no cars, no buses, no kids.

And still he's being followed. No surprise there. Walk into a place like this, alone, out of the blue, and someone will want to know why.

At a corner he comes across a sign of hopeful private enterprise, two stalls set up under plastic sheeting. One sells old clothing, the other small electricals. A radio crackles out tinny music. A young Asian walks past carrying an electric lead and a bag of potatoes – head up, moving quickly, with business to attend to. A patrol in a snatch Land Rover trundles by.

He reaches a crossroads. Another command post at the junction, bigger this time, with a high razor-wired wall around a yard. Another snatch is pulled up outside. Up ahead are ageing council-built residential blocks, three-storey, with mean tight windows, their facades punctured by stairwells behind wired glass, but he turns right and south, homing in on that blue cross on the map.

A block beyond the junction he reaches it. The sign outside calls it the Grisham Hotel. A few trees have been planted in front but most of them are dead, broken trunks spiking out of the earth at intervals. The main structure has been built on so many times that

54

it's lost in a jumble of add-on boxes. A first-floor window is patched with tape, another has torn sheets for blinds.

The front door's open. Inside a middle-aged woman's chain-smoking listlessly on the other side of a small barred hatch knocked through the wall. Johanssen shows her the map and the keys but when he starts to explain she cuts across him – 'Stairs' – and points.

The staircase walls are utility green darkened by patches of damp. Signs on the second floor direct him along a corridor greyly lit by low-voltage lights. Room 24 has a single bed and a chair. There are stains on the pillow, greasy smells rising from the bedding. He crosses to the window, tries the catch – it opens. That's something. Two and a half metres below, the roof of a ground-floor annexe juts out from the side of the building. An exit, if he needs it. Though the chances are, whoever's watching will have thought of that.

Through another door there's a tiny squalid bathroom: shower, dirty toilet, cracked sink. The bolt on the door is cheap and pathetic: one swift kick is all you'd need.

He sits on the bed. Somewhere close by: music, and a low moaning from another room.

He waits fifteen minutes, but nothing happens. At last he goes back down the stairs, past the woman and out into the street again. And there's the tail, slotting into place.

He walks north, back to the central command post, then right and east, past the council blocks, checking off the landmarks against the map in his head. A light-industrial unit with a sign outside that says SKILLS DEVELOPMENT CENTRE, a handful of men loitering by its doors and three more kicking a ball idly around an empty car park.

Program residents are offered a choice between participation in employment schemes, vocational training, and study.

More shops, and a side road with a pair of snatches parked at the junction; on Karla's map the housing beyond it was marked WOMEN'S AREA. He doesn't try that way, instead turning north to skirt the edge of the council flats again, then leaving them behind. A mosque is doing brisk business, but up the road a small chapel has been boarded up. Beyond the chapel queues stretch down the street, dozens of people shuffling forward in a line that ends at the door to a square white building: the central admin block. A command post overlooks the street, and another snatch is parked nearby. When a scuffle breaks out its crew watch, but don't intervene. Other men

– residents, civilians, prisoners, take your pick – step forward and separate the fighters.

Beyond that the buildings end: he's back to the waste ground and the wall again. This time he turns left, following its curve. There are more high-level cameras on posts along its length, and one of them swivels to track his progress. He keeps his head down.

He's still being followed.

After ten minutes he reaches a railed area of muddy grass with two benches bolted onto concrete rafts. Beyond the grass a big modern windowless building juts out from the wall. He goes in.

Inside it's one enormous room like a warehouse, with seating for a few hundred and a barracks smell: cabbage and sweat and disinfectant. The canteen. Above the heads of the diners, on a big screen, a girl singer in a scrap of dress mouths words at the camera. Her lips are soft and glossy, her skin's coffee coloured, taut, perfect. At the tables and in the queues men watch, heads up, jaws slack, the food cooling in their mouths. There are only a handful of women in the room.

Johanssen joins the back of a queue. Following the next man's lead he picks up a plastic bowl and a plastic spoon and shuffles forward in the line until he comes to a bank of nozzles. He slides the bowl under a nozzle: a grey-brown stew with the consistency of vomit discharges automatically into the bowl.

He finds an empty table. Both the chairs and the table are bolted to the floor. The food is lukewarm and tastes mainly of salt.

In Johanssen's head the woman in the grey suit smiles her armoured smile.

She's out there somewhere. But she's a different woman – the fitted suit, the closed-off look, all that's history. Since that picture was taken things will have happened to her that have changed her for ever … He thinks of her: thinner, ragged, older – hardened by this place, or broken by it.

Then for the first time since he entered the Program, he thinks about the job.

There is a process to these things. You locate your target. You follow them or you have them followed. You learn their habits. You survey their environment and you find the one place where you can do the job cleanly, then you do it and you leave.

There is a process and it assumes you aren't yourself constantly watched, constantly followed. It assumes you can find a way to disappear – among shoppers or commuters or casual workers loitering on a corner waiting for the gangmasters to drive by. It assumes you can pass for a street drinker or an addict or a workman or a man in a fluoro vest emptying bins. But someone invisible.

How long before he becomes invisible in this place? A month? Two? Six?

He has three weeks.

Someone says, 'All right, mate?' in a high breathless voice, and he looks up into a narrow face framed by stringy hair. A man is standing by his table, holding a tray. He gives a scared placatory smile – 'All right if I sit here?' His eyes are darting everywhere. Inside his shirt his pulse must be racing like a snared rabbit's.

Johanssen doesn't move.

'All right then,' the man says brightly, and he sits, and straight away bows his head over his food and starts to eat. His fingernails are bitten down to the quick.

After a minute the man glances up. Another nervous smile. 'So where you from then?'

This is not the man who followed him. A good tail needs nerve and he hasn't got it. But he knows Johanssen's just arrived. Whoever sent him in here told him so.

Refuse to answer? No point.

'Victorville,' Johanssen says. 'Penitentiary. California.'

The man's face twitches into a desperate grin. 'California, eh? You don't sound—'

'No, I don't, do I.'

'So why you here?' the man asks.

Who wants to know? But he'll find out soon enough.

'Transferring,' Johanssen says. 'Maybe.'

'Nicer here, eh?' the man says.

'Yeah.'

'So what you doing today?' the man asks.

Johanssen says, 'Taking a look around,' and the man brightens.

'Yeah,' he says, 'like sightseeing.'

It takes him all of two minutes to gulp down the rest of his food and then he rises with another fleeting, frightened smile and leaves, sliding his tray on to a rack and heading for the door. Going to make his report.

*

The next man is waiting outside, on one of the benches, watching the canteen door: a man with fair hair and the delicate face of a damaged angel. When he sees Johanssen he smiles, dazzlingly – deep and warm and genuine – and gets to his feet, angling his head. Then he turns towards a gap between two buildings. He glances back once over his shoulder, to check Johanssen's following, and he smiles again, encouragingly.

Johanssen hesitates.

He has a choice now: follow, or wait. Or even run, though running only does you any good if you have somewhere to run to.

Johanssen follows, because whatever comes next is probably going to happen anyway.

Two in the afternoon now, and already the January light's beginning to fade. The gap between the buildings is in shadow.

The man's picked up his pace. He's five metres ahead of Johanssen now. 'Slow down,' Johanssen calls out, but the man doesn't stop, or turn, or look back. He walks through the gap between the buildings.

Johanssen's just level with the gap when a door bursts open to his left and a stranger comes rushing out towards him, head down, fists swinging.

The guy telegraphs the first blow long before it connects: Johanssen feints, drops back away from it and gets in a couple of punches of his own but now there's someone behind him and another coming head-on between the buildings – early twenties, pockmarked face, yellow wolfish teeth. A fourth one, scrawny and dark, barrels out of the doorway. Do some damage, try to get out of there? But the first one's back on his feet now and the scrawny one – it might be a girl – has a knife.

He half-turns, kicking out at the knife, and a blow from behind drops him.

They are on him in seconds, dragging him through the doorway, pinning him face down. Hands empty his pockets. They've got his ID card. A voice – the voice of the fair-haired man? – says pleasantly, 'Mr Ryan Jackson ... welcome to the Program.'

After that they force a hood over his head.

But he's already seen their faces. This is for something else.

They tie his wrists behind his back and hobble him, then haul him to his feet. He sucks in air through the hood and tastes someone else's saliva, someone else's blood.

The man who spoke before says, 'Watch him.' A door opens and closes.

He sways in the dark, straining into the silence, trying to gauge the size of the room, how many are left, if they're moving towards him.

The first blow's not a hard one, more of a slap. Then another, and this one's harder. They're close, circling him: when they laugh he can smell their breath through the hood. Someone kicks him and he falls – that's funny too, so they kick him some more and then someone says, 'Hey, get him up,' and they pull him to his feet again and throw him against the wall – 'Fucking stand up, fucking cretin, what are you? Fucking cretin' – and they laugh again.

He presses himself into the wall. The strap bites into his wrists.

More kicks and slaps and then they turn him and punch him so that he doubles, and again so he's on his knees. A hand grabs the hood and wrenches his head sideways. A whisper in his ear – 'Know what we're going to do to you?' The speaker's mouth is inches away: Johanssen can smell his excitement, raw and chemical. 'We're going to piss on you and stamp on you, and then we're going to get a big stick and fuck you with it—'

'Fuck him with it,' says a breathy echo, it might be the girl.

'Yeah and then we're going to pour petrol on you and set you alight—'

'You're going to fucking burn, know that?'

'Fuck him with it,' says the echo again.

He closes himself down then. He's no longer in the room. They're talking to someone else. Someone else will take the blows, stand up when they tell him to, fall when they knock him down.

More slaps. More kicks. More threats. But there's a point beyond which they don't go, however much they want to.

Because this isn't the main event. This is just the start.

Day 7: Tuesday

Karla

2.05 p.m., Tuesday. Johanssen's in the Program now. Whitman phoned this morning to tell me so. 'They had to make some calls.'

'Of course.' And we had it covered: memos on desks in the Home Office, the Ministry of Justice, the Prison Service, and a call from someone in the States, senior, busy, making time – *the information he holds could be crucial … your co-operation much appreciated …approval at the highest level … you appreciate the seriousness … absolute discretion required.* The trick is to know who will ring whom, and what questions will be asked, and then ensure those questions can be answered easily, simply, to everyone's satisfaction. And that every person in that chain of checks and balances feels they cannot be held to account: that however much shit flies later, none of it can possibly hit them. That they can say, *I did my job, I followed procedure, it's someone else's fault.*

'They know it's just temporary?' I ask.

'And that he's out again in forty-eight hours.'

'And in the meantime if he needs to be lifted …?'

Whitman sighs. 'I'll be by the phone. He likely to have a problem in there, Laura?'

I bat it back at him. 'The place is pretty stable.'

'But you still want me on standby.'

'Naturally. Oh, and phone calls are monitored.'

He sighs again. I wait.

He says, 'Every contact I have with this guy raises his profile. I take him in and out of that place, people are going to talk. You know they are. People are going to ask questions – of me, which is fine, but not just me. Yeah, yeah, you're keeping Washington out of the loop, you don't want to make it official until you have to—'

Washington again. And Whitman knows how Washington works, he knows where the risks lie, where the screw-ups will come.

'We've got three weeks,' I remind him.

'You estimate. Could be sooner. And even if it isn't—'

But Johanssen will be out of there by then, we'll see to that. 'I told you, we've got it covered.'

'And you'll square it with them if you have to?'

'You know I will.' Another beat of silence, his scepticism humming down the line. 'It's a promise, Mike.' I wonder if he hears the lie.

But he hasn't asked why I've put a man inside the Program. He doesn't want to know.

So Whitman isn't happy; and I'm not either, though for different reasons.

I wanted a delay. There's no sign of the target through all the regular searches, and Finn still hasn't got me that copy of inmate records yet, and that gap in my knowledge nags at me. We should have traced her days ago. But *it doesn't matter*, Johanssen said, and it's true, it doesn't, not to him. *It's just a recce.* And he's the client; the choice is his, not mine. So I've let him go, and now all I can do is wait.

That's what I'm doing when Craigie arrives at my apartment. The CCTV feed on the screen in my office catches him crossing the lobby in his familiar dark-grey overcoat, briefcase in hand, his narrow face angled away from the camera.

I show him in. 'Let me get you a drink.'

'Tea would be fine.'

I keep three single malts in my cabinet; Craigie's never touched one of them. But I suspect his whisky is a private pleasure, in the same way that pornography is for other lonely men.

When I come back from the kitchen he's over by the window. The winter sun's already dipping. To the south the office blocks are dazzling bronze mirrors; west, over the shoulders of the smaller buildings, the Thames is a curve of polished pewter. But he isn't admiring the view; he's gazing down towards the dock below my window. Forty-one storeys down, matchstick figures people the walkways. The wind is gusting hard, tugging at their clothes, shattering the surface of the water in the dock. Craigie's upper body angles towards them. He's removed his overcoat. In his dark suit he looks like a question mark.

When I hand him his cup he says, 'The man they've brought in to go through Laidlaw's files? We have a name.'

*

Laidlaw is dead. Laidlaw is dead, and I shouldn't be shocked. He was an old man, he'd lived his life, he'd made his decision, perhaps his time had come. But the fifty-nine hours that have elapsed since I first heard the news haven't taken the edge off it.

Our alliance was triggered by a story, told to me by a troubled criminal contact and involving hospital plans and a woman called Eileen. I looked into it, and the more I looked, the more troubled I was too. We've all seen the images: a London bus with its roof peeled back by the force of the blast, a burning skyscraper folding into dust. It's the thing you don't want to contemplate: that you knew, you knew all along, you could have stopped it and you didn't.

Peter Laidlaw was the man I chose to give my information to.

He'd been an agent handler at the fag end of the Cold War. Quiet, intent, good with secrets, cautious to a fault, he'd been in the inner circle that handled the Soviet mole Gordievsky, had contacts in MI5's old K3 subdivision, and kept his job when the Wall came down and for a while the Russians were our new best friends. But by the time my package arrived on his doormat, he'd retired to read his books, sip warm beer in dark pubs, ignore his garden and be bored out of his mind.

I picked him because I knew he'd be careful, and tenacious, and diligent – because I knew he wouldn't rest until he found someone to take that package seriously.

And I picked him because I knew that everyone who wondered who I was would look east, to Laidlaw's old contacts in the former Soviet Union, and not towards me.

At the time it was to be a one-off; I had no intention of becoming a source. Nine months and four contacts later, we had something like a relationship, or a habit. Perhaps it eased my conscience. Or perhaps I'd realised that if the security services ever knocked on my door, I wanted to be in a position to call in favours.

Peter Laidlaw wasn't on my side. I never believed he was. He served his country all his life; that wasn't about to change. But he was a Moscow Man, with suspicion rooted in his soul, and when MI5 bugged his house and began to follow him he knew and liked it about as much as I did. I like to think we raised our games accordingly – that ours became an alliance of the wary, an unspoken contract between two people who didn't trust each other but still found they shared a common adversary: the very people they were trying to help.

But in the end he had me fooled. I hadn't even known that he was ill.

'Powell,' Craigie says. 'His name is Lucas Powell.'

The name means nothing to me. He must pick that up. 'He was in Washington, on secondment. They've brought him back specially. You got the shots?'

Tall, black, good cheekbones, good suit. Officer class. I nod. 'What do we know?'

Craigie says drily, 'He's not Laidlaw.'

'There's a surprise.'

There will be no more Laidlaws. Laidlaw was the last of the old guard.

'So tell me about this Powell.'

'Straight as a die. Graduate intake, fast-tracked through the ranks. Careerist. Ambitious.' Craigie's face is grim.

'Janitor?'

'Of course,' he says.

One of the tight crew of investigators – ex-MI5, ex-SIS, ex-Special Branch, belonging to none of them – who are brought in whenever their masters turn over a stone and find something they don't like the look of. They operate in isolation and almost complete secrecy, can access files denied to most other security and intelligence personnel, and are incorruptible. No wonder it's taken this long for Craigie to come up with a name.

'Are you picking up chatter?'

'He says he's come to clean the Augean stables.'

'He actually said that?'

'So I hear.' Craigie adds, 'Too clever to use the word "shit", evidently.' Craigie's a grammar-school boy: he knows his classical allusions. Clearly, so does Powell.

'Thinks he's Hercules, does he? Oxford or Cambridge?'

'Cambridge. A first. Then straight into the service.' A pause, then Craigie says, 'He's looking for Knox.'

'Of course he's looking for Knox. Powell said it himself: he's here to clean up any mess. Find out what was going on, tidy up, write a report. These people don't like being in the dark about their own operations.'

Craigie's shaking his head. 'Twenty-two tip-offs in five years—'

'Not all of them led anywhere.'

63

He says darkly, 'Some of them did. You've made yourself a prize, Karla. A prize, and Lucas Powell's out to win it. He's after you. He's going to dig through Laidlaw's past until he finds you.'

'Then good luck to him. I'm not in Laidlaw's past. That's the whole point.'

Craigie's still stony-faced. 'We don't know what records Laidlaw kept.'

'Laidlaw was old school. His sort didn't make notes.'

Craigie says, 'You sure about that? He was an old man. His memory was failing.' Then, 'What about the flat in Ealing?' Owned by Laidlaw, under a different name, and kept for his occasional private use.

'Has Powell found it yet?' I ask.

'Not yet.'

'Then let's have it watched.' But I say it too dismissively for Craigie.

'You're not worried about this?'

'If Laidlaw knew who I was, he'd have found me himself. Craigie, we sanitised *everything*.'

Twenty-two drop points in over five years, never the same one twice. Calls from clean phones, single-use, untraceable numbers. Goods and services paid for by credit cards registered to shell companies. A briefcase in a bar, no prints. Once we even sent him information in a box of mail-order shoes. That was how Laidlaw and I did business, *because* he was old school: the set-up precisely calculated to appeal to him – and to reinforce the message that I was old school too. Craigie hated it. But the traffic was all one-way. Laidlaw couldn't contact me. We made sure of that.

Now Craigie's look tells me he doesn't believe it.

For a moment we fall silent. Above the City's profile fat grey clouds are piling up, pregnant with rain, and the Thames has changed from pewter to lead.

'And Simon Johanssen?' he asks.

'Went into the Program this morning.'

His mouth tightens, but he says nothing. Shortly afterwards he leaves.

At 3.15 p.m. an icon winks on my computer screen. At last: Finn.

Finn, and a read-only copy of the Program's inmate records, cloned from a government server. Names and reference numbers, criminal records, psychological profiles, DNA data. And photos.

We're in business.

I've already reduced the target's image to biometrics: to the computer she's a series of measurements. All I have to do is match that data to the corresponding inmate record. Any minute now I'll know exactly who she is.

While the timer counts down I leave my desk and walk into the main room. In doorways forty-one storeys below my window, office workers snatch at cigarettes, huddled against the January wind. Muffled tourists idle across the lime-green metal bridge that spans the dock; a toddler chases pigeons. In the office blocks, behind the reinforced glass, people make money out of money. West towards the City, everything is sky.

When I walk back into the office, the search program has run its course. The answer sits squarely on the screen. No match.

My data must have corrupted. I pull up the scan of the original image, click on 'Biometric breakdown' and 'Export'. On the screen a new timer counts down. Done. I reopen the inmate file, click 'Compare'. This time I don't leave my desk.

No match.

Something cold settles in my stomach.

But there's a further list: deceased inmates. I pull it up, run the data once more.

No match. The woman in the picture is not on the Program's inmate list.

But there are other explanations. Maybe she's being held elsewhere, on the point of being transferred, or maybe she's already in transit, her data in a virtual pipeline, migrating from one system to another—

Or maybe she's a nobody, a face plucked at random for a job that doesn't exist.

<URGENT locate female within prison sys Not in Program list Try other prisons Also check data migrating Prioritise this Use all trusted help>

I attach the biometrics I've generated.

A pause, and then the usual response: <let u no>

For once it isn't good enough.

I call Fielding. The phone rings seven, eight times before he answers. When he hears my voice he grunts. I don't wait for the put-down.

'She's not listed in there. You said your client was sound. So are you lying? Or are they?'

65

Three seconds of silence, which I don't like, before Fielding says, 'She's in there.'

'She's not on the inmate list.'

'She's in there,' he says again.

'Wrong, Fielding. Who's the client? Not someone fronting up for John Quillan, by any chance?'

Fielding doesn't answer. Instead the line goes dead.

It is now 3.46 p.m. Just over two hours to go before the gates close and the Program goes into its unofficial lockdown. I call Whitman.

'We may have a problem. I need you to get our man out of there.'

There's a short silence from Whitman. Then he says, 'Laura, he's only been in—'

'*Now*, Mike. *Now*.'

4 p.m. comes and goes. 4.15. 4.30. Time. It all takes time. I pace out the three-million-pound views of my apartment. I sit on my sofa. I make coffee, fail to drink it, throw it away. The light fades. The street lamps come on. Whitman doesn't call.

But perhaps she isn't an inmate at all, perhaps she's a volunteer or a social worker, perhaps she's security.

<Finn Check other Program lists Check volunteers security staff>

How long before I get a result?

5 p.m. On the walkways forty-one storeys down, the office work-ers have started their homeward stream, little dark-coloured specks of humanity drawn in swathes across the pavements like iron filings following the pull of a magnet.

Still Whitman doesn't call back.

I stand by the window and I try to focus on the lights of Docklands, but the clock face across the room seems to pulse like a clot on the edge of my vision, and the tiny sliver of wristwatch is heavy on my arm.

5:30. 5:45. Nothing from Whitman. He's cutting it fine, that's all.

5:58, 5:59, 6:00. The gates close. But maybe Johanssen's being processed now: sitting in an empty room while they recheck his ID. Any minute now, and Whitman will phone to say he's out – any minute now—

The phone rings and I snatch it up.

'Laura,' Whitman says.

I know just from his voice: we've lost him.

'They checked out his accommodation,' Whitman says. 'No sign.'

Then, wounded, as if he thinks I might somehow – unjustly – hold him responsible: 'They can't keep tabs on everyone, the place is self-regulating, right? They're watching the surveillance feeds for him. And they'll search again tomorrow morning.'

Tomorrow is too late.

'Laura?' Whitman says tentatively.

But he's only going to ask what the problem is, and I can't tell him.

'Tomorrow morning,' I say, and ring off.

My stomach's sour with anxiety. *Keep a lid on it. The army trained Johanssen as a sniper. He knows how to survive, undetected, within enemy territory for days. One night in the Program is nothing. Whatever has happened, wherever he is, of all the people you know he's the best equipped to deal with it—*

And the woman? The target who isn't even in the records? What is that? *Coincidence?*

With anyone else – anyone else at all – my fears would have a different script, different images. Johanssen snatched off the street in a Land Rover. Or asked to step aside – 'This way, Mr Jackson' – as he went through the gates. I'd be putting out feelers – among the specialist departments of the Met, the intelligence services, even offshore agencies – for the first hint of a high-value prisoner undergoing interrogation. And wondering how far those five months of Spec Ops training would take him: standard police questioning won't be an issue for him, but the same people who taught him to withstand interrogation could be involved in the process of breaking him now. How well did they do their job all those years ago? How far have they refined their techniques since then? How good is he, how long will it take to break him, and how soon before they get to me?

But this isn't anyone else; it's Simon Johanssen, and he's gone into the Program.

Four men in that farmhouse when Terry Cunliffe died. Quillan went after all of them. He caught only three. Johanssen he never found. Until now.

Day 7: Tuesday

Johanssen

He's on the floor, on his side, when the door opens. Hours could have passed, he's not sure. A grunted instruction, and he's yanked back onto his feet, still bound and hobbled, still with the hood over his head.

There's a thick ache in the back of his skull, the copperish taste of blood in his mouth. His guts are raw.

They make him walk.

Out through the door. Darkness, and the pinprick glimmer of electric lights through the hood. It's night. No point in trying to memorise the route, too many turns. Halts and starts, murmured conversation. They're in no hurry. Sometimes he stumbles, but they keep him upright.

At last they stop. Somewhere close the damp air fizzes with an electrical charge. A metal gate unlatches and creaks open. They march him on and the gate rattles shut.

Now they have him by the elbows and they're steering him forward fast. Another halt. Footsteps moving away. Up ahead a door swinging softly on its hinges, open and closed. A wait of how long? Four, five minutes? He sways on his feet. Distant voices, a conversation just outside his range: he strains but he can't pick up any words. Then through a door, and the quality of air and sound changes: they're inside now.

His boots rasp on concrete. He trips and falls forward: his shins crack on stair treads. Hands grab him, haul him up. A turn at the top. Another corridor, another door. They push him through.

Carpet muffles his footsteps. Different smells too, clean homely smells, food and polish. The air's warm. Faintly, in the background, a TV mumbles.

He's pushed down into a seat, and they pull the hood off.

He blinks in the light.

68

He's in a neat, old-fashioned sitting room. Holy pictures on the wall: the Madonna in blue, one hand raised in blessing or appeal, and a teenage saint shot through with arrows, casting tragic eyes to heaven while his wounds open like tiny mouths, and bleed. Below the pictures, a houseplant on a stand. A veneered mahogany cabinet: a concealed fluorescent strip lights up someone's best china, dishes and soup-tureens and gravy boats. Through an arch to one side is a kitchen: a brief glimpse of gleaming worktop, coffee mugs on a little wooden tree.

Across the sitting room a TV is playing with the volume turned low: a sitcom is showing, the dialogue a low blur of sound, punctuated by canned laughter.

A small elderly man with skin like a corpse's sits in an armchair, watching the TV.

But it was always going to be this, wasn't it? Always.

A minute passes and then John Quillan speaks.

'Welcome to the Program, Mr *Jackson*.' His voice is quiet. He sounds bored. He hasn't taken his eyes off the TV. 'How do you like our little social experiment?'

The blond smiling man from outside the canteen has taken up a position behind Quillan's chair. He watches Johanssen, head tilted to one side. He's still smiling. Johanssen says nothing.

'Do you know who we are?' Quillan asks.

Something has closed his throat. He has to force the words out, one by one. 'You're – in – charge – here.'

For the first time Quillan turns his head to look at Johanssen. His eyes are pale blue and watery, the whites bloodshot as if he has trouble with them. 'My name is John Quillan,' he says. 'Does that mean anything to you?'

Three men dead, one in a quarry, two in a car, all tortured before they died. He can still remember their faces. 'Yes.' His voice cracks.

Quillan's mouth gives a little twitch of satisfaction.

'We are the law,' he says, as if Johanssen hasn't spoken, 'and you are on our territory. Under our *jur-is-dic-tion*. My *job*—' he leans forward '—is to keep order here.' He sits back again, as if he's made a point. 'Do you think that's easy, Mr Jackson?'

Johanssen says nothing. His guts squirm. Quillan turns his gaze to the TV again.

'Governing the violent, the addicted, the sick … You'll under-stand the need to be firm. To make an example, where necessary.'

From the set the canned laughter crackles again, a rasping mech-anical sound.

'So you're from America,' he says, and he smiles at the TV, though his skin seems too tight for it and the expression fades instantly.

'Victorville Pen,' Johanssen says. A hard knot of something has formed below his lungs.

'Don't know it.' *Don't want to.* Quillan's gaze swivels, locks back on to him. 'What brings you here?'

'I asked for a transfer.'

'Ah, like *football*.' Quillan nods. 'Thought your prospects would be *better* here?'

'I heard – I heard about this place – I thought—'

'You thought you'd have an easy life here, Mr Jackson? What were you down for in *Victorville Pen*?' The name spat out, like a bad taste.

He doesn't know who I am.

'Life. Double murder.'

'But life means life in the States, doesn't it? What would persuade them to agree to your request? The kindness of their hearts?' Quillan asks, reasonably, 'What have you offered them, Mr Jackson?'

He hasn't lured you here, this isn't revenge. He doesn't know. The relief almost swamps him.

'They think I've got some information.'

'And have you?'

'They think I have.'

'Shop your friends for an easy life in the Program? It wouldn't be the first time.' Then he says, 'Or maybe it's something else.'

Johanssen says, 'All I want is—'

'To come here. To come here and keep your head down and your nose clean, just like everyone else. You know what my problem is? I don't trust you, because *I don't know who you are.*'

'My name is—'

'Ryan Jackson, so you say, serving life for double murder at *Victorville Penitentiary* but no one here's ever been to Victorville Penitentiary and no one can vouch for you.' He sits back in his seat. 'Are you a clever man, Mr Jackson? I think you might be. But what's a clever man doing, walking into a place like this with a story that he's about to shop his friends? Why would he own up to that?

Unless it's just a cover ... Oh, did you expect to be taken *on trust*? That's not how things work around here.'

'Talk to the screws, I came through Reception this morning, they've got my file—'

'The screws?' For a second Quillan looks almost pleased. 'Oh no,' he murmurs, 'no, Mr Jackson. We have a different way of checking our facts here.' His gaze switches back to the TV. 'Mr Brice.'

The interview is over. The smiling man steps forward.

The knot of hope in Johanssen's guts turns to water.

Quillan says, 'Mr Brice will take care of things from here.'

They bundle Johanssen back along the corridor at a stumbling run, punching their way through fire doors.

Back to the stairs, and down. Right, along a bare corridor, and then they open a door and throw him in.

It's the room he's been expecting all along. No furniture. Breeze-block walls. One window small and high. The floor is sticky with dark stains.

The blond man, Brice, strolls in behind them. He looks down at Johanssen. Now his smile's a smile of regret. 'You realise what we have to do, don't you?' he says gently.

Johanssen says nothing.

They force him to his knees and turn him towards the wall.

Someone kicks him in the kidneys. He goes down. The second blow, to his guts, doubles him, gasping.

Brice bends over him. His gaze is focused, intent. 'Are you a fast learner, Mr Jackson?' As if he genuinely wants to know. 'I hope so, for your sake.'

Johanssen says nothing.

Brice steps back, signals to the others. 'If you would.'

They get on with it, fists and feet, picking up where they left off, but harder this time. Twenty seconds' worth and they step back. He's on the floor now, on his side, unable to rise. When Brice steps forward the toes of his boots are inches from Johanssen's eyes.

Brice crouches and reaches out a hand: delicately his fingertips brush Johanssen's face. 'You don't understand,' he says, 'none of this is necessary. Now, you can tell me: who are you really?'

Johanssen swallows, puts the words in order. You stick to your story or you say nothing. 'I told you—'

Brice straightens. 'I'm sorry,' he says.

71

Johanssen blocks it all out then, shuts it down. He has to get to the other side of this, that's all. He concentrates on that. There's nothing else he can do.

After a while they go out, and he lies on his side, in the dirt, and practises breathing.

Somehow he sleeps, in fitful, broken snatches – it must be sleep because noises keep bringing him round, voices, doors banging.

Somewhere between sleep and waking the face from the photo comes back to him: the woman in the grey suit with a smile like a shutter coming down. He tries to blank it out but up it floats again, like a drowned face rising through water.

Footsteps in the corridor outside jolt him awake in a sweat, his senses raw, guts lurching, every muscle screaming.

A lock rattles. A wedge of light: the door, opening.

Something clatters at floor level. Something metallic.

He tries to gather himself. Any minute it will begin again. He has to be ready for it.

The light goes on, a single bulb, painfully bright. Brice is standing over him. He crouches down, tilts his head to one side.

'Thinking this was all a bit of a mistake, eh?' he says. The others are behind him.

Johanssen doesn't move. Moving will only provoke them. He forces himself to go limp, swallowing the pain as they haul him upright again.

Another beating? But the one with the yellow teeth has a length of tubing and a funnel in his hands, and the metal thing on the floor is a bucket with something stinking in it.

He mustn't fight it, he must stay relaxed. It'll hurt less that way. But when they force his head back and his mouth open and jam the gag in place, raw instinct kicks in and he fights against them, ignoring the screaming pains in his back, his shoulders, his ribs.

The tube goes down his throat.

When they've finished they take the bucket and the tube and the funnel, and they turn the light out. The door closes, and the darkness surges in again.

He lies there in his own vomit. The night stretches ahead of him like an endurance test.

Day 7: Tuesday

Karla

I have phoned Fielding again. I had to. 'Your man's missing in the Program.'

A pause. A silence I can't read. I forge ahead. 'Give me a name for the client.'

'Fuck off, Karla.'

'Johanssen's disappeared and the target isn't in there—'

'I spoke to the client. She's in there.'

'She's not.'

'She is.'

'Who are they?'

Another pause. He's weighing up how much to tell me.

'Fielding, you said the client came with references.'

Stonily: 'No one who connects to John Quillan.'

'Which side of the line?'

'Civilian.' An ordinary citizen, then, a member of the public. Or claiming to be. 'Karla, they've got grounds—'

I snatch at that. 'What grounds? What did she do? Because it never made the news. A name, Fielding.'

'Dream on.' And then he says, 'She's in there. He'll be fine. He's always fine.'

Because of me, he's always fine because of me, because I've made sure we always had the data. Except now I haven't.

And still I'm recounting to myself everything I've done to keep him safe, trying to draw some reassurance from that. *We wiped his ID, we deleted everything. No one can say he isn't Ryan Jackson, and Charlie Ross is dead. There is no way John Quillan knows who he is, no way that he can tie him to that farmhouse.*

Pointless, telling myself that. If Quillan knows, then how is irrelevant. What matters is what happens next. What's happening now.

*

73

At 8 p.m. the last of Finn's inmate search results come in. There was, and is, no trace of the woman within the prison system.

And then, just gone 10 p.m., Finn gets into the list of volunteers working in the Program. There aren't many. The woman isn't among them.

Which only leaves clutching at straws.

<Try Staff Try Security>

Finn replies, <Already have>

In my apartment the blinds are up. Electric lights illuminate the empty shells of the offices opposite. To the west, the sky above the City is a yellowish black.

Not in the Program list. Not in the prison system. Not a volunteer, not security, not staff. Where does that leave us?

I phone Craigie and tell him what's happened. Immediately he says, 'I'm coming over,' and I know he isn't thinking of John Quillan. He's thinking of that other scenario: the prepared security services trap, Johanssen being sweated in an interrogation suite, the slow collation of names ... how much Johanssen knows about me, how he was able to contact me, how traceable I am.

He's thinking we still have time to wipe the files, destroy the hard drives, erase every last trace of Karla and of Charlotte Alton. If we have to.

And I can't argue against it. The woman in the picture is not in the Program. Johanssen knows who I am, and he's walked into a trap.

Suddenly, in a breath, in a heartbeat, less, in my head the scenario flips.

The woman in the picture—

When Craigie arrives, the first words he uses are 'damage limitation'.

I know what he's about to say: that I must leave, tonight, within the hour, and I must leave assuming that I'm never coming back. But I'm not leaving, for one reason and one reason alone.

If I were baiting a trap for Johanssen I'd assume he would check it out, and he'd be thorough.

I'd use a real prisoner.

Day 8: Wednesday

Johanssen

He has no idea what time it is when the door opens. Someone flicks a switch: the light is a sickly fluid stain on his retina.

'Get up,' says a voice he doesn't know.

But he's weak with vomiting and in the end they have to haul him to his feet.

It's daylight outside. The sky is yellowish-white, streaked with grey, like marble. They half-walk, half-drag him around the building and into a narrow yard hemmed in with blank walls, no cameras. A blind spot. Off the record.

The first thing he sees is Quillan. He's sitting in a lightweight folding chair, wrapped in a big coat, like an invalid at a picnic. His eyes slide over Johanssen, dispassionately.

Brice is standing at Quillan's shoulder, out of the older man's line of sight. There's a baseball bat propped up against the wall beside him. His smile is the smile of something higher up the food chain, too many teeth.

In Johanssen's memory the tube goes down his throat, and he gags.

There are maybe a dozen others in the yard, Brice's crew among them, and they're all looking at him.

'Mr ... *Jackson*,' Quillan says.

Quillan has a red scarf tucked inside the collar of his overcoat. The colour beats like a pulse in the winter light.

He has to focus. Stay in the present, pull it together.

'So it's true,' Quillan says, 'you'd shop your friends for a place in the Program,' and he gives one of his stretched smiles, as if the skin might split. 'I like that. I like to know what a man's priorities are. You'd do anything to stay, wouldn't you?'

Anything. It's not even a word when it comes out of his mouth, just a dry croak of sound. He swallows.

75

'Again, we need to put that to the test.' Quillan turns his head, speaks over his shoulder. 'Brice?'

Brice steps forward and his smile broadens. 'Mr Jackson,' he says. 'I'd like you to meet a friend of mine. Jimmy?'

At the sound of his name he comes forward: a bright-eyed, bird-like man in his forties. He has a nervous, eager smile, and there's a weird neatness about him, as if he's dressed for an interview: his thin dark hair carefully slicked down, his shirt buttoned up to the collar under a cheap jacket.

Focus.

'Time for some proper introductions,' Brice says. 'Mr Ryan Jackson, meet Jimmy. Jimmy's offered us his assistance. That's right, isn't it, Jimmy?'

Jimmy nods – there's something pathetic about his enthusiasm – and reaches into his jacket. He pulls out a handful of photos, family snaps. 'Photos,' he says.

Brice says to the little man, 'Not the photos, Jimmy, not this time,' then confidingly, to Johanssen, 'Not all there, is Jimmy.' Louder, he adds, 'Jimmy's first task is to help us with a little demonstration.'

Jimmy's still smiling. He doesn't see it coming, but Johanssen does.

Brice steps forward, jabs Jimmy hard in the guts, and as he doubles, grabs his arm, twisting it savagely, wrenching it against the socket. The photos scatter. Jimmy yelps and goes down, face in the dirt. His legs are working, trying to pivot him away from the pain, but Brice's knee has settled between his shoulder blades, pinning him down. His snapshots have fanned out around him: a man and a woman in party hats raising glasses to the camera, a kid chasing a dog across a lawn …

'You see, Mr Jackson,' Brice continues conversationally, 'we need to know how committed you are.'

The words run through Johanssen's head like water. Sweat's trickling cold down his back. All the colours merge. *Focus focus focus.*

'You did say you'd do anything, didn't you?' Brice glances over at Johanssen and his face creases with concern. 'You don't look very well. Ryan – I can call you Ryan, can't I? I hope this isn't making you uncomfortable.'

Johanssen's stomach squeezes in on itself.

In the dirt Jimmy whimpers. Brice gazes down at him. He's still got the little man's arm wrenched behind his back. He murmurs,

'Or maybe you don't realise how serious we are. Maybe we have to demonstrate our seriousness to you.'

Wrench and twist. The angle's impossible. Something snaps and Jimmy screams like an animal.

Brice glances up at Johanssen. 'Would you say we're serious?'

Johanssen's stomach twists, his eyes sting. He opens his mouth, closes it again.

'Sorry, didn't catch that,' Brice says.

'Yes,' Johanssen says. The word cracks.

'Good,' says Brice. He releases Jimmy's arm and rises, dusting his hands. 'Your turn. Mr Quillan wants to see how serious you are.'

The words have to fight their way through the mess in his head. Brice wants him to—

'Well?' Brice asks. His eyes are very bright, and blue. He's still smiling.

Three metres away Quillan leans forward in his seat, his gaze darting between their faces.

'I hope you're not wasting our time,' Brice says pleasantly. Then, when Johanssen still doesn't move: 'Sorry, don't you get it? Need another clue?'

'No—' Johanssen says but Brice is already moving. Jimmy tries to lever himself away from the other man, dragging his useless arm but Brice grabs him by the shoulder, slamming him down and he screams again and then he gives a little strangled sob.

Brice glances questioningly at Johanssen.

'All right,' Johanssen says.

'Sorry?'

'I'll do it.'

'Sure?'

Johanssen gulps down bile, nods. He can't speak.

'That's good,' Brice says. 'Good.' He steps back. His hands sign an open invitation: *Be my guest*. 'Over to you then. Impress Mr Quillan.' Then: 'Oh – it doesn't matter how much noise he makes. No one will come.'

Johanssen looks at Quillan. The bright red scarf's bleeding its colour across the air between them. *Jesus Christ focus*. For a second their eyes meet. Quillan's face gives nothing away.

Down on the ground Jimmy starts to cry, incoherent pleading bubbling out in a mess of snot and saliva. Johanssen blocks it out.

He takes a step towards the little man. Everything hurts. His back, his throat, his guts, shoulders, limbs. The light surges and fades. He sways on his feet. Behind him someone sniggers.

Do it. Just do it.

Can he make it quick, clean? Does he have anything left for this?

Pull it all together. You know how it goes.

He maps them. The little man snivelling in the dirt. Brice off to one side, his breathing shallow, his lips drawn back in anticipation, keen for the fun to start. Quillan sitting forward in his chair, eyes hawkish, watchful: waiting to be impressed. Johanssen himself at the centre of the freak show, vomit down his shirt, swaying on his feet—

Three deep breaths. Go on the third.

—raising one knee, lifting his left foot and letting it rest lightly on Jimmy's buckled shoulder (no weight, no pressure but Jimmy still screams), ready to stamp down and twist until he feels the bones grinding through the sole of his boot—

—and Brice leaning forward, all his concentration focused on that one point of impact—

Go.

Two moves in the same instant. Sidestep and jab. His hands connect: fingers into Brice's eyes, fist into his throat. Pivot. The boot into the kidneys. Brice doubles against the nearest wall. Johanssen follows through, grabs his head, smashes it back against the blockwork. Snatches up the baseball bat left-handed and spins away from the wall—

He is surrounded. Five of them: two blocking the path to Quillan, the other three moving in on him. Quillan has one hand raised. The gesture telegraphs, *Wait, wait* … Johanssen tries to read his face. Impossible.

He has nothing left now. He's spent. The shakes hit him and this time he can't stop them.

Quillan nods at Johanssen's left hand. 'Drop that.'

The baseball bat slides easily from his fingers and clatters to the ground.

'You interest me, Mr Jackson,' Quillan says. His eyes are small and cold and hard, like marbles, like glass. 'One blow from that could shatter a man's skull like eggshell … Tell me, would you have used it on me?'

Up against the wall Brice's head sways. There's blood on his face. His eyes flicker open and he coughs, shifts, tries to get up.

'Why did you do that, Mr Jackson?' Quillan asks.

He should have an answer. What is it?

Brice makes it to his knees. His head comes up and his stare locks on to Johanssen. The rage coming off him is pure and hot.

'Be honest with me, Mr Jackson,' Quillan says quickly, 'while you can still talk.'

Brice is on his feet now, balling his fists, sucking in air.

Johanssen says, 'He told me to impress you.'

'Ah,' Quillan says. 'Well, if it's any consolation ...' he smiles, sadly: 'I was impressed.'

One blow and Johanssen's down. A boot into his stomach and he gags but there's nothing left to bring up. Another blow and all the injuries of the last twenty-four hours connect, a hot grid of pain.

Brice grabs him by the hair, presses his face into the dirt. The man's breath is on his cheek.

'We start with your fingers,' he says, and then, to someone else: 'Bolt cutters.'

Oh Jesus.

He's face down. They wrench his arms out on either side, kneel on his elbows to keep him spreadeagled. He clenches his fists but they're so much stronger: they force his hands open and splay the fingers.

There's going to be pain, a lot of pain. He needs to take himself out of this but he can't, there's nowhere in his head he can go.

Brice crouches down beside him again, selects a finger, prises it straight. Right hand, trigger finger. The metal of the bolt cutters is cold against his skin.

Across the dirt, beyond the scatter of photos – weddings and barbecues and party hats and the smiling face of a man who could almost be Charlie Ross – Jimmy's eyes are open. His stare meets Johanssen's but nothing passes between them, no understanding, nothing.

'The first one goes like this,' Brice says.

A movement, fast – a flash, bright and hard, on the edge of his vision.

And a woman's voice, very close. 'Do not *fucking* make me, Brice, because I will.'

Everything stops.

All he can see are the photos, and Jimmy. All he can feel is the metal against his finger, hard and cold, and squeezing, squeezing.

'Quillan?' The woman again, as if it's a threat.

Above Johanssen, Brice shifts his weight. Seconds pass. The pressure on his finger eases. He breathes, once.

The pain swamps him.

After that, nothing.

His fingers. They are going to cut off his fingers.

He balls his fists, turns them in towards his chest but they're prising his hands open, and there's the cold touch of metal.

Jesus Oh Jesus Oh Jesus

He opens his eyes. The light blinds him. He squirms away from it as if he's been burned. Flails, thrashes, but they pin him down. Someone's shouting, he can't make out the words.

Fight it fight it fight it

A male voice: '—the fuck's that sedative?'

Above him a blank-eyed boy readies a needle.

Minutes later, or hours. He has no idea. He cannot feel his own body.

Voices float past him. A man and a woman.

The man: '—Outside.'

And the woman: 'So?'

'He says you've got to hand over—'

'*I know.*'

How long has he been staring at the wall, and what do the scratches mean? Are they keeping score?

The light changes. He drifts.

He wakes on the edge of pain.

He's down on the floor, on a mattress. On the far side of the room in a nest of bedding by the door, a woman sits. Her face is gaunt and there are dark shadows under her eyes, like bruises. Her exposed wrist is brittle, skeletal. In her hand there's a blade.

Somehow he must get it off her but he cannot move.

He sleeps.

Behind a door in a farmhouse, a man is screaming.

Day 8: Wednesday

Karla

I sweat my way through Wednesday.

The gates open again at 8 a.m. but I'm at my desk long before that. Over twenty-two hours since Johanssen entered the Program, fourteen since the gates closed for the night; I've had maybe three hours of broken sleep and I'm nauseous with tiredness.

But any moment this could be over. Any moment, and he could be out.

Whitman's already in Program Administration, talking to the staff, impressing on them the urgency of finding Ryan Jackson. I wait as the digital clock on the computer clicks round to 8:00, then 9:00, then 10:00 – wait by my phone for the call that says he's out, he's safe. It doesn't come.

Craigie wants me out and safe too: out of here, and untraceable. I've refused. *To bait a trap they would have used a real prisoner.* Craigie doesn't believe it. Even over the phone he twitches with stress. He's gone hunting for Johanssen in the darker corners of the security services' domain, the interrogation rooms and high-security suites. But he won't find him there, he won't. Johanssen's in the Program still. I'd swear it.

I send to Finn, <internal surveillance ntwrk Program access? URGENT>

Although the Program is a privately run enterprise, various interested government parties require access to surveillance footage. The Prison Service and the Ministry of Justice have round-the-clock feeds; the Met and the security services also have on-demand access, as do a select few high rankers in other areas of public policy. Each point of access may have a security loophole; Finn must find one.

Finn doesn't respond. Doesn't answer chases either. But then, at 4 p.m., as the light's fading, I receive a link, with the comment, <fk of a lot easier thn inmate rcrds>

Finn has got me access to the Program's surveillance feeds.

I'm passive: I can only watch what they watch. The cameras pan across, zoom in and out, at someone else's whim. An empty interior that might be a classroom, a convoy trundling down a darkening street, a man loitering in the doorway of a small shop.

I search all the faces. I don't see Johanssen.

Should I take it further? Attempt to eavesdrop on comms traffic in the Program? Check for news of a corpse, white, male, six foot, blue eyes? Check for body parts coming out with the refuse collections? I won't be squeamish. These things have to be faced. I know what happened to Charlie Ross. They couldn't even return complete remains to his widow; had to identify by DNA. He'd been dismembered.

At 5 p.m. Whitman rings.

'They got a sighting,' he says. 'In the canteen: Jackson seen talking to some guy, but he left alone.'

I snatch at that. 'Today?'

'Yesterday.'

'And the guy?'

Already my hand's on the mouse, reaching to click into the inmate records, but Whitman says, 'They wouldn't give a name.'

'Persuade them.'

'I can't just—'

'*Find a way.*' Snapped back at him, too hard, but there's still an hour to go before the gates close again and the place locks down for the night. Still time.

Whitman's silent. At last he says, 'I don't like this, Laura. You want it both ways. We're keeping it unofficial, you said, we're just borrowing this guy's ID, Washington doesn't need to know. Fine: then we keep it low key. I act concerned but I don't go in there telling these guys how to do their job. I tell them they're doing great. Or I go in there and I kick these guys around, but in that case you'd better find someone in Washington who'll back you because you're going to need it. I can't make a big noise and keep your guy off the radar. Every time I open my mouth, his profile goes up a notch.' There's another little silence; a weary shrug on the other end of the line. 'You choose, Laura.'

He leaves just enough space to be sure I'm not going to reply, then he says, 'I'll try again tomorrow,' and he hangs up.

On the screen in front of me the Program goes about its business. The light diminishes, the patrols pull back, the gates close.

It is now over thirty-two hours since Johanssen entered the Program.

At 7 p.m. Craigie calls on me again. He sits with his tea cooling on the table beside him, his narrow face pinched with anxiety. But he's found nothing to suggest that Simon Johanssen is in the hands of the authorities.

'He's still in there,' I say, and this time he doesn't argue.

'Could someone have ID'd him?' he asks.

'Ross is dead.'

'Someone he served with in the army, then?'

But I've been through inmate records for any ex-squaddie who could identify him as Simon Johanssen. There's no one. No one who's likely to have known the real Ryan Jackson either. Everything's a blank.

When Craigie's gone I eat in my office, watching the surveillance feeds. The official patrols have stopped circulating now, but others have taken their place: men on foot, in twos and threes, moving with quiet purpose. Quillan's men.

So far there have been no reports of a wounded civilian. No reports of a corpse. I try to cling to that.

But you know what Johanssen is. And you thought he'd retire to some beach in Thailand? Wear cut-offs, grow a beard, smoke pot, take up fishing? Grow old?

No.

They all go, sooner or later. All of them.

There is a pattern to these things: a phone call first, a tip-off, and then a few hours later a news bulletin, police tape across an alleyway, the TV camera zooming in on the remaining traces of blood. That's what happens to people like him.

Only this time maybe there's no contact calling in. Certainly no TV coverage. Maybe he's just gone.

That night Charlotte Alton goes down with the flu, and phones her friends, rearranging her diary; and I stay at my desk.

I've returned to the woman in the photo. I've stopped thinking of her as an inmate – in my mind the newspaper front page, the

83

screaming headline, has vaporised. But her guarded smile remains, and so does the conviction that I've seen her before.

Johanssen said that who she was didn't matter. He was wrong.

So I sit up late into the night, searching the databases for the woman in that photo. And I keep chasing the memory of her face, but always it drifts ahead of me, just beyond my reach.

Day 9: Thursday – Day 10: Friday

Johanssen

Another voice, in another life.

'Ryan Jackson.'

Pain tells him he's alive: his head pounds and his guts ache as if someone has taken them out and stamped on them.

'Ryan Jackson,' the voice says again.

The name is familiar.

He opens his eyes. A sharp-featured man with a receding hairline is gazing down at him. 'So,' he says, 'you still know your own name.'

Johanssen blinks at him, bewildered.

'One lucky bastard, aren't you?' the man says sarcastically.

The man helps him sit up. The pain in his head doubles, roaring, and when he breathes too deeply something sharp lances into his ribs.

'Here.' The man holds a beaker to his lips. He swallows and pain rips into his throat, and everything rushes back: the bucket and the funnel and the tube, the narrow yard, the old man Quillan in his picnic chair, Jimmy on the ground screaming, the bolt cutters—

His fingers. He stares at them. A red ring circles the index finger of his right hand. A cannula's pinned into the back of his left; an IV line runs to a drip stand next to the mattress.

'Brice—' he says.

'Fuck Brice,' the man says. 'Drink.' He pushes the beaker against Johanssen's mouth, tips it. He's in his mid-forties, hardbitten, wiry. There's strength in his hands, and his forearms are lean and knotted, the veins standing out over muscle, tattoos for 'Mum' and 'Baghdad'.

Five gulps and Johanssen pushes the beaker away, gasping. 'Jimmy?' he asks.

The sharp-featured man grunts. 'Medevacked.' He pushes the beaker into Johanssen's hands – 'Take it, you're not a fucking kid' – then he gets up and goes out, shutting the door. His footsteps clump down a flight of stairs.

There's a dull light in the room. The only window has a piece of blanket nailed across the frame to block out the day but strands of light creep round the edges. Bits of scavenged furniture are pushed against three of the walls: a chair, a rickety picnic table with a plastic bowl on it, a chest of drawers in cheap fake-pine laminate. On the fourth wall someone's been keeping count: there are marks on the plaster, vertical lines in clusters of five, dozens of them. Some are neat, some crude and wonky. Some look like they've been gouged into the wall with a blunt nail. Clothes and junk and bedding are scattered across the floor.

The window is two metres away.

He pulls the cannula out of the vein on the back of his hand and rises slowly, testing the pain at each stage. Another sharp jab when he breathes in too deeply. Could be a cracked rib. His chest, arms, thighs are bruised – marks from fists and boots – and one knuckle has been grated into a mess of dirty shredded skin and raw flesh. Crossing the room, everything hurts.

At the window he peels back the edge of the blanket.

Daylight outside. A drop to the ground, two storeys. An expanse of tarmac marked with the scuffed white outlines of parking spaces. Ahead and to his right, an L-shaped block of low-rise housing in red-black brick. To his left, on the far side of the car park, an eight-foot wire fence, a cluster of people loitering around a gate. Beyond the fence there's a road and then the three-storey council blocks begin.

He is inside a compound. Quillan's compound. Already, automatically he's measuring the angles between the buildings, looking for the blind spots, the dead ground, but it's a prison within a prison. He won't be leaving yet.

He finds a stained bucket in a corner and pisses into it, then he lies down again.

After a while a different man – balding, with weak harmless features – brings him a bowl of food and a spoon. He says his name is Vinnie. 'I'm leaving soon,' he adds confidingly.

'That right?'

The man nods, pleased with himself, and goes out.

Swallowing still hurts but he keeps the food down. He crawls back under the bedding and sleeps again.

*

86

Later – it must be early afternoon now, from the light – the sharp-featured man brings him clothes, but no boots. 'Here,' he says, 'get dressed.' He gives Johanssen a slow look, then he adds, 'Name's Riley.'

'Jackson.'

'I know.'

'What day is it?'

'Thursday.'

'Jimmy,' Johanssen says suddenly. 'Brice broke his arm.'

'I know what Brice did.'

'Why Jimmy?'

'Nicked stuff,' Riley says. 'Photos.' He goes again.

Johanssen dresses slowly, pushing the pain away. The clothes fit him but they have someone else's smell.

On the far side of the tarmac yard the compound gate rattles. Running footsteps approach – four men, no, three – carrying something. There's shouting. He hobbles to the window but they're inside already. Downstairs a door bangs. More shouting, several voices this time. Instructions? He goes to the door of the room, opens it. Outside a narrow staircase goes down to a landing.

Are they coming for him? How much does he have left? Where are his limits now?

But the noise has formed a knot somewhere below. After a moment he begins to make his way down, wincing at each step. The shouting intensifies.

He pauses on the first-floor landing. Below him, at the foot of the stairs, a door's open a crack, and the shouting comes from beyond it. He waits. No one comes through the door.

He goes to the foot of the stairs and peers through the crack.

On a treatment bed a man's body is leaking blood. Hands reach across it, cutting clothing away, exposing wounds, applying pressure. Out of sight Riley says, 'What the fuck's he doing here? Gates are open, aren't they?' No one answers him.

'They should have taken him out,' Riley says a moment later, but more quietly, as if the argument's dying within him.

He's not the one in charge here.

Johanssen shifts his position and she comes into view: the gaunt woman with the blade. She's working on the body, fast, efficient. Someone asks her a question and she raps out a reply without look-ing up. He doesn't take in what she says.

Once she was polished, controlled, aloof. The photo Fielding gave him proves it. Without it you'd never guess.

Before three weeks are out, she will be dead.

He drags himself back up the stairs to the muffled room. Her room. Her clothes, her junk, her nest of bedding by the door. Her mirror screwed to the wall above the washing-up bowl – in it his face is bruised and swollen and split, one eye still half-closed. And the marks on the wall, they're hers too.

He crouches, ignoring the pain, and goes through her possessions. In a corner under a dirty jacket he finds a handmade wooden box with the name 'Cate' carved carefully into the lid.

Cate. Her name is Cate.

Quillan is the authority here. Quillan runs the Program. And Brice works for him, Brice punches with Quillan's weight behind him. But this woman Cate has another sort of power.

In the yard – yesterday, was it yesterday? – Brice or any one of his crew could have forced her down, stamped on her hand, used the knife on her. But she held a blade against Brice's throat and said, 'Do not fucking make me,' and no one touched her. She said Quillan's name like a threat, and Quillan backed her against his own man.

Downstairs the noise has faded. They've evacuated the man, or he's dead. Johanssen's staring at the marks on the wall, the little clusters of five, when Riley walks back in carrying his boots. 'Put them on,' he says.

Johanssen does. Riley watches as he rises to his feet – Johanssen tries to keep a lid on the twitching pain, tries not to let the hesitation show – then looks him up and down. 'Tough bastard, aren't you? Smart money said you were a stretcher case.'

He leads Johanssen down both flights of stairs and through the door at the bottom. Just inside it there's a slick patch that smells of bleach. The room beyond is an improvised clinic. Chairs, a couple of trolleys, a curtained recess, a sink, cupboards, a cluster of drip stands. Shelves stacked with medical supplies, cartons of gloves and dressings, odd-sized plastic bottles. A newish defibrillator in a rack on the wall.

Riley sees Johanssen looking. He says, 'How do you like our *overnight treatment facility*?' His voice sketches bitter quotation marks around the words. 'Oh, during the day you're fine, walk-in clinics, armoured ambulances, the lot. But at night? Six o'clock they close the gates, no one in or out – except for *emergencies*, only you can be lying in the street under their noses with your guts hanging out, they don't give a stuff. Too risky, isn't it? Could be a set-up, could be an ambush. Safer to just look the other way, safer for them anyway. So—' he surveys the room, the tatty furniture, the improvised kit '—it's this or a body bag. And it ticks a box in the rehabilitation brief, doesn't it? Shows we're learning *social responsibility*.' His glance switches to Johanssen again. 'Happy memories, eh?' he says. Maybe he sees uncertainty in Johanssen's face. 'No?'

Johanssen shakes his head.

'You fought,' Riley says, half-resentment, half-admiration. 'You fought all the fucking way.'

On a work surface a small sterilisation unit hums and winks to itself. A flip-top bin has SURGICAL WASTE scrawled on the lid in uneven black marker. A smaller one is labelled SHARPS.

'And this place is Quillan's?'

'Yeah, he's big on altruism, didn't you notice? Or maybe it's because then he gets to say who comes in here, and if it's four in the morning and you're bleeding out and he won't let you in, you're dead meat. It's hearts and minds, isn't it? Hearts and minds.'

'You work here?'

'Like a fucking slave. We're a man down.' Riley pulls a face. 'Natural wastage.'

'Jimmy got medevacked,' Johanssen says.

'You're quick, aren't you.'

'But not me.'

Riley shows his teeth. 'Oh no, my friend, not you. Brice thinks he's earned his fun with you.'

'But Cate won't let him.'

When he uses her name Riley's eyes go still, but all he says is, 'So who's going to win, eh?' He jerks his head towards a door. 'Out.'

The next room is full of mismatched chairs, with a muddy vinyl floor and a payphone on the wall. Through another door, and they're outside. It's late afternoon fading into winter dusk: the buildings around them are in shadow, but the sky's a bright remote blue. A group's still huddled by the gate in the wire-mesh fence, their cigarette smoke rising through the cold air. One of them, a woman, laughs, and the sound rings out clear across the tarmac.

Riley leads him across the yard. Johanssen walks like an old man. He won't be able to run.

He glances back once, to the building they've just left. It must have been built as a row of shops. The big plate-glass windows are blanked out with cardboard.

There's a guard on the main door to the housing block. He steps aside and in they go, up the flight of stairs and along a corridor to a door where another man waits, a big man with the damaged face of a boxer. He opens the door as they reach it. Riley stops. 'In.'

Through a tiny hallway and into the same room. The teenage saint and the Madonna on the wall, china gleaming quietly in the cabinet, the kitchen mugs on their wooden tree through the arch. Quillan's in the same chair as before but he's alone, his TV switched off. This time Johanssen has earned his complete attention.

Quillan nods briefly towards a chair. His bloodshot gaze doesn't leave Johanssen's face. Johanssen sits. The door closes.

For a moment they stay like that, both of them waiting. A clock ticks sedately among the tureens. Outside, in the yard, someone shouts. Neither of them reacts.

Then Quillan says, 'So, Mr Jackson: what are we going to do with you?'

Johanssen says, 'I don't want trouble.'

'Bit late for that, though, isn't it? You humiliated Brice, publicly. Good move?'

'Brice told me to impress you.'

Quillan sits back in his chair. 'Brice isn't happy about what you did to him.' He pauses, as if he's expecting a reply. Johanssen says nothing.

'Now, giving you back to him would cheer him up. A little present, a toy for him to play with. You've seen what he can do ... And that's just the start. Brice doesn't kill, you know – doesn't get the same entertainment value from a corpse. But he'll make you wish he did. So where do we go from here? Back to the little room downstairs? Brice's gang with their boots and their buckets?' He narrows his eyes. 'Look at you now, Mr Jackson. Look at you. Barely walking. You're good with the pain, aren't you? But this time he won't be starting from scratch. You're *primed*. Every bruise, every cut ... He'll have you begging in seconds. But he won't stop this time, not after the first finger, or the second. Thorough, is our Mr Brice. Very thorough.'

Quillan looks at him for a long moment, speculatively: that scenario's playing out in his head.

Suddenly he asks, 'Where'd you learn to fight? America?'

'Here and there.'

'You've been trained.'

'Picked it up as I went along.'

Then Quillan asks, 'So what is it you want? Don't tell me. You want Mr Brice to conveniently forget what you did to him. You want a nice quiet life—'

'I want to work for you.'

'Oh yes?' He snorts softly to himself. 'And what could you do for me? Use your fists? There's not what you'd call a *shortage* of violent men here.'

'Clinic's a man down.'

'Is that my problem?'

'Clinic's part of your plan for this place.'

'So now you know all about my *plan*, do you?'

'Clinic helps keep you in charge here. Hearts and minds.'

'And you can help with that? What, you're a doctor now?'

'No. But I can pack a wound. I can splint a break. I can put a line in. I can use a defibrillator, I can do CPR. I can recognise a bleed on the brain. I can drain a lung. I don't need much sleep and I don't want anything in return.'

'Except Brice off your back.'

'Yes. Except that.'

Quillan leans back in his chair, still staring at Johanssen. 'First-aid skills also something you just *picked up as you went along*?' Then he turns to the man waiting by the door. 'Get her in here.'

She walks in fifteen minutes later. She glances at Johanssen once, a flat look that slides off him, then she turns to stare at Quillan.

Quillan raises his hands. 'What can I say? He came back.'

She's lost all trace of the gloss she had in the photograph. Her skin's greyish, and she has that look of war-zone exhaustion he's seen before in cities under bombardment, sleep-deprived and strung-out on adrenaline. Her clothes are too big for her, and her hair's raggedly cut as if she did it herself, in a hurry and in poor light. She looks like she's already heard the question and the answer is no.

Quillan says mildly, 'Mr Jackson wants to work at the clinic. He says he can *help*.' Quillan turns to Johanssen. 'Tell her.'

He begins again. 'I can put a line in, I can splint a break, I can do CPR, I can use a defibrillator—'

She snorts. 'And Brice?' she says to Quillan.

'I'll put in a word.' Quillan smiles reassuringly, then spikes the smile: 'Provided he passes the entrance exam.' He turns to Johanssen. 'All this talk, but talk's the easy part, isn't it? You can't make these claims about your abilities and expect us to take them on trust.' His gaze snaps back to the woman. 'The next one bleeding out is his. No interventions.'

They lock him in a room with a wired-glass panel on the door. There's a chair, and sometimes he sits, and sometimes he gets up and stretches in an effort to stop his injuries stiffening, stop the bruises from clogging his movements. His throat's dry and sore but they haven't given him water. From time to time people peer in at him through the glass, but no one enters.

Outside the daylight shrinks and fades. Four o'clock, five. Somewhere close by, the woman who calls herself Cate is arguing with Quillan, but it's an argument she loses: the look on her face tells him that as soon as she opens the door.

'You coming?' But she's gone before he can reply.

He limps behind her, back across the compound to the row of boarded shops. It's dark now, the sky black hazed yellow by street lights, the floodlights white at the compound gate; strips of light show at the tops of the blanked-out shop windows, where the sheets of cardboard don't quite reach. She walks through the central door into the room full of chairs. There's a man by the payphone, about to push a prepaid card into the slot, but one look at Cate and he puts the phone down and goes.

She swings round to face him. 'Is this a joke?' she demands. 'Is it?'

He pulls himself upright, and all his injuries sing out.

'Don't make me laugh,' she says, 'you can hardly walk. So what's the plan, huh? There is a *plan*, isn't there?'

'I meant what I said. I can do all those things.'

'Oh, I hope so,' she says, 'because if you're lying and you fuck up, Brice can have you.'

'I won't fuck up,' he says, but she's already turned on her heel and is heading for the door into the clinic.

'Wait,' he says. 'How often do you get people bleeding out?'

Her hand's on the door. She turns and there's that flat look again, the mouth a compressed line, the eyes cold. She says, 'Tonight I'd put money on it.'

Three people are in the clinic: Riley, the middle-aged man Vinnie, and a boy who can't be more than seventeen. The boy turns his head first: he has the dark, depthless gaze of the psychologically damaged. Vinnie's mopping the floor. Riley's over by the counter, laying out instruments on a blue paper sheet. He glances up. His eyes meet Cate's.

'We got us a new recruit,' she says.

Riley looks at Johanssen and then at Cate again. 'He should be on a fucking trolley, not—'

'Make sure he can cope with a bleeder.'

Riley gapes at her. Then he says, 'How soon?'

'How should I know?' she says.

Just then the door bangs open behind her and one of Brice's lot, the one with bad skin and yellow teeth – the one with the funnel and the tube – saunters in smoking a cigarette. He grins and nods at Cate – her stare jabs back at him – then he turns lazily to Johanssen. 'Don't mind me,' he says. He takes up a position against a wall. He looks pleased with himself.

Soon, Johanssen thinks, and the tension in his chest rises a notch.

'I'm fine,' Johanssen says, to anyone who'll listen. Yellow Teeth sniggers.

Riley says, 'You done this before?'

'Yes.' Part of his Spec Ops training. And once in the field, for real.

'They live?' Riley reads his expression. 'Christ. All right. You know what you need?'

He's still grabbing dressings and kit from the shelves when Brice walks in.

Johanssen's got his back to the door, but on Cate's indrawn breath he turns.

She must have snatched up a syringe – the needle wavers in the air – but Brice doesn't even glance at her. His gaze finds Johanssen. He smiles.

He says, 'Mr Jackson ... I hear we're getting another demonstration of your skills.'

Riley looks like he's just put down whatever he was holding in case he has to step in, throw his weight around. Vinnie has backed up against the wall, his knuckles whitening around the mop handle – he doesn't like confrontation, wants it all to go away. The blank-eyed

93

boy simply stands there, neutral, unfathomable, his head tilted to one side: things just got interesting. Over by the door two new arrivals – Quillan's? – shift on the balls of their feet. Yellow Teeth prises himself away from the wall, grinning.

Cate's mouth is thin and tight. 'Get out now.'

Brice's smile doesn't fracture but his eyes go blank. 'I'm here to see fair play. Check with Quillan.'

'*Get out.*' She takes a step forward. The needle in her hand lances the air.

Yellow Teeth says, 'Fuck off, bitch.'

Quillan's men shift again but Brice raises his hand. 'No need for that,' he says, and behind him the door bangs open.

A man's body lolls lifelessly between three handlers. His clothes are heavy with blood, almost black with it; as they drag him he leaves a tarry smear on the floor.

Brice's brow furrows briefly. 'That looks bad,' he says, and he turns his smile on Johanssen again. 'Your turn.'

He grabs pressure dressings, a drip-set, a squidgy pack of plasma substitute. They've dumped the man on a trolley. His head rolls. Johanssen pulls the man's tongue clear, checks pulse. It barely whispers.

Behind him Cate's voice, low and fast: 'He's not doing this alone.'

'Mr Quillan's terms,' Brice says placidly.

Expose the wound. He cuts the man's clothes away. The abdomen's been slashed open, showing the yellow lip of fat, the blue glisten of organs drowning in red.

Yellow Teeth giggles, high and sick. 'Look at that.'

Johanssen snatches a plastic bottle of disinfectant, hoses out the cavity, once, twice. Hunts the source of the bleeding. *There.* The wound surges. He pushes gloved fingers against it. *Now clamp it.*

With his free hand he gropes for a clamp, misses – it clatters to the floor.

Brice murmurs, 'It's only his fingers, Cate.'

He blinks the sweat out of his eyes, reaches for another clamp. Blood's pulsing out under his fingertips. Behind him Yellow Teeth sniggers. 'Gonna die,' he sings softly, and then, 'Chop chop.'

No.

Forget them all. There's no one else in the room – no Cate, no Brice – and nothing beyond it, no yard, no bolt cutters, just him and

94

the man on the trolley with his guts open. *Come on, you bastard, don't die on me.*

Again. This time the clamp holds. Immediately the flood of red eases. He backs it up with a pressure dressing, taped hastily in place.

Now get a line in. He grabs the needle, exposes the man's forearm. The flesh is pale and slack. He digs with the needle, probing. Once, and then again, and then again. Nothing. The veins have collapsed. *Come on.* And there – flashback, the telltale glimpse of blood in the tube. He slides a cannula over the needle into the vein, pulls the needle out, plugs the drip set into the outer end of the cannula, attaches the first litre of plasma substitute to the drip line.

Ventilate him.

Cate says sharply, 'You've done enough, step aside,' but Johanssen doesn't look up.

Mask. Bag.

Someone moves behind him. Yellow Teeth says, 'Oh yeah?' and Riley hisses, 'You fucking touch her—'

Johanssen places the mask over the man's nose and mouth. Cate's hand slides over his, holding it in place. 'Enough,' she says, 'you've done enough.' A glance at the blank-eyed boy. 'Drill? Ventilate him.'

Johanssen steps back.

Yellow Teeth mutters, 'Fucking bitch,' but Quillan's men are moving in and there's a scalpel in Riley's knotted fist. 'Fancy some of that, do you?' he hisses. 'Do you?'

Brice hasn't moved.

He is still smiling: smiling like a man at a cocktail party. Only a tiny twitch in the corner of one eye betrays him.

Then he turns and strolls out of there, as if he paused to watch events unfold and now he's lost interest.

Yellow Teeth backs away behind him: he can't take his eyes off Riley and the scalpel. 'Cunt,' he bawls at Cate before he plunges for the doors. She's working on the man on the trolley. She doesn't even blink.

Riley drops the scalpel onto a bench and shouts, 'Vinnie!' and Vinnie scuttles forward with his mop and makes a wet red smear across the tiles.

Johanssen's eyes are stinging with sweat. When he goes to wipe his forearm across his face, his own skin is slick with blood.

*

As soon as the man is stable Cate stalks out through a side door. After a moment Johanssen follows.

Beyond the door a small room houses two decrepit metal cots, an old ventilator and a thicket of drip stands. Cate's sitting on one of the cots, eating a biscuit.

She looks up at him as he comes in, then reaches into the breast pocket of her overall and pulls out a little packet of biscuits, just three in a sealed cellophane wrapper, the kind they leave next to the coffee at business presentations. She holds it out to him. There's an identical one open in her lap. 'Fucking take it,' she says.

He takes the packet from her without touching her fingers, opens it and begins to eat.

'So how do you know this stuff?' she asks after a minute.

There's nothing in Ryan Jackson's personal history that would have given him medical training so he shrugs.

Her head comes up. Her stare is like a punch. 'Brice set that up. That man was cut to order. You were supposed to fail.'

'But I didn't.'

'And now you want to stay,' she says. 'Why? Don't tell me you just want to help, don't tell me you want to say thank you—'

'I know what I'm doing,' he says. 'I'm not here for the buzz and I'm not here to prove myself. I can be useful.'

'*Useful.*' It comes out sick with disbelief.

'I won't let you down,' he says.

She's finished her biscuits. She screws up the cellophane wrapper, watches it uncurl in the palm of her hand, pushes it into her hip pocket. Her face is a small cold mask. Her eyes are brutal.

'All right,' she says, 'this is how it works. Anyone who turns up at the compound gates between the hours of 6 p.m. and 8 a.m. we assess. Walking wounded we patch up, critical cases we resuscitate and stabilise. If we can. Nothing fancy, just keep them alive until the gates open. Then get them out, eat, sleep, start all over again. There's no Aids here; they're screened for it on entry. But not hepatitis, so you have to watch out when they spit. Oh, and sometimes they hide weapons in their clothes. But you knew that, didn't you?'

'They're not searched at the gate?'

'Of course they are. You don't rely on that. You don't leave anything sharp where someone can grab it. You don't turn your back on anyone who isn't restrained. You never assume they're out cold, and you never assume they're going to stay that way.'

'So I can work here?'

'I think you'll find it isn't up to me.'

'You stopped him,' he says. 'Brice. In the yard, with Jimmy. What did you do?'

'Appealed to Quillan's sense of fair play.'

'You had a blade.' The dirt of the yard against his cheek, Jimmy wide-eyed, watching him, the cold of the bolt cutters on his skin and that sudden bright hard flash at the corner of his vision. *Do not fucking make me, Brice.*

She says, 'I'm five foot four. I don't weigh much. I have only two advantages in a fight. Surprise. And knowing exactly where to cut.' She leans into his face. 'So what's your advantage?'

He shrugs, and in the next room a door bangs and Riley starts shouting.

'Do better than that,' she says. 'Because Brice isn't finished with you. This won't go away until you do.' She rises to her feet.

'Don't you want to know what I'm in for?'

'Double murder, in the States. Quillan told me.'

'It was a shooting.'

'The easy way. Feel good about it afterwards?'

Ryan Jackson told police the girl had had it coming. He says nothing.

'I think we're done here.' She's heading for the door.

He says, 'And you? What are you in for?'

She looks back at him, a look that's all hard edges, razor wire and spikes.

She says, 'I killed someone.'

When he follows her out into the clinic Riley has just finished strapping a man down on a trolley. The man's eyes are wide with terror. His face is a mess of blood. Just then the boy bends over him with surgical tweezers, and begins to pick shards of glass out of the cuts.

Close by, Vinnie is mopping up: the air holds the ammonial tang of piss.

I killed someone. He's not surprised at all.

Quillan blinks, a slow reptilian blink. He says, 'So you passed.'

It's 8.15 in the morning, a kids' show on the TV: happy, brightly coloured figures, bouncy music. The night shift's over, but its smell seems to cling to Johanssen's clothes: the smell of blood and piss and shit and disinfectant, vomit, cigarettes, sweat, raw alcohol, decay, and once, when the door opened, the smell of cooking, wafting in from somewhere else. He's very tired and he aches as if he's been kicked, and kicked again.

Quillan says, 'You can stay.'

The TV shows a field of singing daisies, yellow and white against grass that's a chemical green.

'And Brice?' Johanssen asks.

'I'll do what I can.' But his voice is bland and his eyes have switched back to the TV. After a second he angles his head towards the door: *Now go.* Johanssen rises but as he reaches the door Quillan says, 'The business with Jimmy. Brice made a mistake. Tell me what it was.'

Brice in the little yard, teeth bared, eyes fixed on Jimmy, waiting for the fun to start ... 'Brice enjoys his work too much,' Johanssen says.

'So he does. And your mistake? What mistake did you make, Mr Jackson?'

Johanssen's still groping for an answer when Quillan smiles. 'You let him live.'

At the clinic the armoured ambulances have come and gone, taking the night's consignment to the Emergency Medical Centre beyond the wall. The others are clearing up. Riley catches his eye, jerks his head towards the stairs. 'Come on,' he says.

Johanssen follows him up to the first floor. Through a door and into a kitchen – a couple of electric rings, a sink unit, a table and chairs, a grubby white fridge. On the other side of the kitchen another doorway leads into a darkened room.

Riley reaches into his shirt pocket for a cigarette that's been smoked almost down to the filter, lights it and draws on it sharply, greedy for nicotine. He leans back against the counter, blows out a stream of smoke. Takes his time. His eyes don't leave Johanssen.

'So,' he says, 'America.'

'California.'

'Lifer?' He nods. 'But you done a deal to come here.'

'They want me to talk.'

'So what is this? A try-out? See if you like it? See if it's worth snitching for?' Riley says. 'Meantime we're stuck with a complete fucking stranger. We got to count the scalpels morning and night, in case you decide to take one to bed? Am I going to wake up with my throat cut?'

'It was a shooting,' Johanssen says.

Riley takes a last drag on the cigarette and grinds it out on a dirty plate. 'Well thank fuck for that,' he says.

Riley walks through the open doorway and clicks on a light.

It's a narrow bunkroom: four metal-framed beds sit end on, two on either side of a central gangway, each bed boxed in, head and foot, with plywood screens for the minimum of privacy. At the foot of the first bed on the left someone's covered the screen with photos of a dog, an overweight Rottweiler cross whose eyes are glazed blue or red by the flash. Dog in a garden. Dog on a beach. Dog with a kid's party hat sliding off its head, its pink tongue dripping slobber … The bed on the right is surrounded by clippings from wank mags: girls with pneumatic breasts and collagened lips pout at Johanssen and touch themselves.

On to the next pair of beds. The one on the right has only three objects taped to its screen: a piece of bright turquoise plastic, the feathered wing of a small bird, and something metallic that glints in the light.

The opposite bed is unmade, the bedding in a roll at its foot, nothing on the plywood screen but a few scraps of tape.

Johanssen unrolls the bedding. Behind him Riley says casually, 'Watch your stuff. Place is full of thieves.'

He eats with Riley and Vinnie. Vinnie asks Johanssen a few questions, personal stuff: is he married, does he have kids? Vinnie talks a lot about his dog. He says he'll be out soon.

Riley asks about Victorville, and California.

The boy – they call him Drill – eats alone, sitting on his bunk, the one opposite Johanssen's, and talks to no one. He's already under his blanket when Johanssen lies down to sleep later that morning, but his eyes are open, and he watches Johanssen, unblinking.

Johanssen must have dozed, because he dreams.

We will make you run.

Another dream that's also a memory. Three months into Spec Ops training; when failure was still unthinkable, and only other people got kicked off the course.

He is on a rooftop. It's night.

He's lost count of the times he's been scared beyond belief, but now the fear is beginning to slick off him as if he's developed some sort of protective layer, or maybe he's just learned to accommodate it: it's become something to be tolerated, respected, befriended even. It's part of his life.

Tonight the exploit's a pursuit. He has to get from A to B. They – and he doesn't know who they are, or how many – have to catch him.

Street lights below, skeins of traffic, the sweet kick of adrenaline.

He is on a rooftop, and he is running.

The sound wakes him. Not in the bunkroom, but overhead.

Someone's scratching at the wall. After less than a minute it stops.

There are scratches in the plasterwork of Cate's room: clusters of five, some neat, some wild and jagged.

Cate is keeping score.

He wakes again when the clinic's outer door bangs open. Shouts, footsteps – this time they hit the stairs. Already he's on his feet, adrenaline slicing through the pain. Something in his head is screaming at him to run, but there's nowhere to run to.

Through the bunkroom door they come. Three men – he knows their faces from the yard. Riley's on his feet too now – 'What the fuck?' They just push past and grab him, and this time he can't fight it.

Down the stairs, barefoot, half-naked, grunting with the pain as they haul him along. Through the door at the bottom, into the clinic – Brice, are they taking him to Brice? His hands clench, fingers curling tight on a reflex, uncontrollably. Straight through the next door into the room full of chairs—

Quillan's waiting, huddled in his coat.

The men stop, and Johanssen stops too, sagging between them, gasping for breath.

'Seems you're needed elsewhere, Mr *Jackson*,' Quillan says.

He inclines his head, and the men haul Johanssen through the next pair of doors and out into the compound yard and daylight, the cold tarmac biting into the soles of his feet, towards the fence and the gate. Behind him Riley's still shouting, and a woman's voice: Cate, it must be Cate.

In the road beyond the fence an armoured van is waiting, engine idling in a cloud of diesel, rear doors open. The two armed guards beside it watch, impassive, as he's dragged towards them.

The compound gate swings open. They pass through. The men holding him push him into the back of the van – he slams into the floor, the breath knocked out of him, the pain searing across his ribs again – the door bangs shut, the engine surges and they're away.

He stays on the floor of the van. The vibrations of the engine and the road rattle his skull.

Finally it stops. The doors open. They help him out. And there's Whitman, gaunt in the pale daylight, the outer wall with its glint of wire looming behind him. When he sees Johanssen's face he says, 'Looks like we broke up the party just in time.' It takes Johanssen seconds to realise he's talking about the bruises.

Then Whitman turns to the guards who surround them; the dough-faced administrator's there too, shivering in his shirtsleeves. 'Thanks, guys. He got lucky.'

But he doesn't feel lucky. He feels like he's just been through a test from Spec Ops training, something tough and brutal, and has seen the end in sight, and then been told he's not allowed to reach it.

Day 10: Friday

Karla

I'm standing in my office, hugging myself. *He's out. He's safe.*

I was in the main room with Craigie, in the middle of our routine Friday meeting, when the call came, and I excused myself, walked into the office and picked up the phone with no sense of hope whatsoever. Three days – more than three – since Johanssen vanished. Perhaps I'd finally given up.

In my ear Whitman said, 'They've found him. They're bringing him out now,' and for a moment everything stopped.

'Alive?'

'Yeah, he's alive,' he said.

'Injuries?'

'He was in some sort of compound in there, in the hands of a guy called Quillan … He's been beaten.'

Something spasmed in my chest, but I kept my voice even. 'Fine. Thanks for letting me know. I need to speak to him.'

Whitman hesitated, then he said, 'I'll see what I can do.'

Quillan. I was right. It brings no satisfaction. But we got to him. We got to him in time.

Craigie's still in the main room, with his cup of tea. We are in the middle of our agenda. The Russians have gone but they'll be back. The Japanese contact is being developed, the banking software people have agreed a fee, the ex-pharma boss Hamilton is tucked away in a safe house somewhere, still insistent that his life is in danger, still reluctant to disclose the details of the fraud he claims to have committed. We are watching the flat in Ealing that belonged to my old intelligence contact Laidlaw; if this new man Powell knows about it, he hasn't bothered to visit. A client isn't paying their bill: at what point do we apply pressure?

In a minute I'll go back in there, and Craigie will look up, and say,

'Any news?' And when he does I want to be clear, and focused, and professional. But right now all I can think is:

He's out. He's safe.

Forty-five minutes pass before the next phone call. Whitman's voice again, softly – 'Here he is' – and then a rustle as the phone is handed over, the clunk of a car door closing.

'Hello?' Johanssen says.

I cannot say, *Thank God you're all right.*

'It was Quillan, wasn't it?'

He doesn't reply. But Whitman's around – maybe he can't talk freely.

I say, 'We got into the records – we've been through all the lists. She's not in there. This has all been set up but we can handle it—'

'She's in there,' he says. 'I've seen her. I'm going back.'

I think I sound calm when I phone Fielding ten minutes later, though of course I'm not.

The line connects. A muttered aside – 'Hey, I'll be right with you' – and in the background a cocktail-party murmur. Fielding drumming up business?

'Yeah? Who is this?' Fielding's voice again but louder now, and guarded, wary. The background noise has dropped away. He must have stepped into another room, closed a door.

'He's out. He says he's seen her.'

One of Fielding's three-second silences. There's gloating triumph in this one. 'What did I tell you?'

'They scooped him out of a compound. He's been beaten. By Quillan.' And into the silence that follows that: 'He wants to go back.'

Another pause. Then Fielding says, 'Client's been in touch. Small change of plan … The maintenance crews in the Program, who tells 'em what to do?'

What is this? 'Supervisors. Responding to work tickets. Fielding—'

'What if we needed a crew to do a job for us? Could you fake up a work ticket?'

'Fielding—'

'There's a tank, been capped off. We need the bolts on the cap loosened.' As if it's all still going to happen, even now.

'Fielding, what's this about?'

'Check it out, get a price, get back to me. Oh, and he and I need to meet.'

'He's undercover.'

'A meeting,' Fielding says. 'And don't tell me you can't fix it, you *fucking* well got him in there, you can *fucking* well get me a meeting.'

And all the time: *She cannot be in there. She cannot.*

I want Johanssen somehow to be wrong.

Already I know he's not.

Day 10: Friday – Day 11: Saturday

Johanssen

They hustle him through the Induction block. This time there are no formalities. They find him some clothes to wear, and boots; the dough-faced administrator hisses anxiously, 'Do you wish to make a *complaint*?' and Johanssen shakes his head, and everyone looks relieved.

To the building's exit – the metal detectors, the guards, the glass doors opening with a faint soft squeak on their runners ... Whitman takes hold of his arm, but as if he might fall, not run. With his eyes still on the doorway he says softly, 'You're a mess. You need a doctor?'

'No.'

The car's parked in the same place as before, Whitman's men beside it.

Whitman puts him in it, hands him the phone, closes the car door and walks away, motioning the other two to follow.

Karla's voice: 'It was Quillan, wasn't it?' A sort of fierce compression in her tone. Anger? She's telling him Cate isn't in the records, but all he can think of is going back.

They drive across London. He wakes outside the privatised flats to the tick of the cooling engine and the fleeting conviction that the last three days have been a dream. When he tries to get out of the car his injuries have stiffened again.

Inside, he manages half a frozen ready-meal, microwaved to scalding point in the flat's little kitchen with the TV blaring in the main room. Through the doorway its images dance meaninglessly in front of his eyes.

He goes to bed in daylight, like a child. He doesn't dream at all.

He wakes when Whitman walks into the room. The clock reads 07:13 a.m. He has slept for seventeen hours.

'Get up,' Whitman says, then so the others will hear: 'That

meeting you wanted? You got it. But after this we want to see some co-operation.'

Johanssen hauls himself upright, snapping down on the pain. He doesn't ask where. Karla. It has to be Karla.

He showers, dresses, eats – swallowing with only a little difficulty – and then they pile back into the car, all four of them. The two ex-army guys are watchful, nervy, but they seem to have bought Whitman's story, that this is all part of getting Ryan Jackson to talk.

The route they take could be going anywhere.

At last, just gone 10.30, they pull up outside a run-down parade of shops in Lavender Hill.

Whitman says to him, 'It's just you and me from here.' He adds wearily, for form's sake, 'Don't try anything.'

The door is wedged anonymously between a barber's and a book-maker's, with 7A in stick-on brass-effect letters and the tiny bulging eye of a spyhole. Whitman knocks.

Karla, it has to be Karla—

But the bullet-headed man who opens up is one of Fielding's regulars.

He's a professional, and anyway he's probably seen worse, much worse, in his time: he regards Johanssen's damaged face with blank indifference. Then he nods, and Johanssen and Whitman edge past him, over a pile of free newspapers and takeaway menus. Already Johanssen can smell Fielding's cigar.

He climbs the stairs alone.

Fielding's in an uncarpeted room on the second floor, sitting on a folding chair in a band of rancid yellow sunlight. For a long moment he stares at Johanssen.

Then he says, 'Fuck you' – anger and relief and resentment all in two words – and he laughs, a corrosive laugh. 'Three days,' he says. 'Three fucking days. Christ. Look at you.' He draws on the cigar and exhales: smoke twists and billows upwards in the light.

Johanssen says, 'I found her. I can do it.'

Fielding shakes his head. 'Not this time, son,' he says. 'It's over.'

Fielding has walked to the window and stands close to its edge, peering down into the street. He says, 'The bloke you came in with, the thin guy.'

'He knows not to ask.'

'And the pair across the road?'

Johanssen says, 'They don't know anything,' and Fielding grunts, satisfied. He turns away from the window. 'Client's made a new request. They want the body delivered. To a location within the Program, chosen by them. You like the sound of that?'

He pauses – for effect? For Johanssen to respond? When Johanssen doesn't, Fielding goes on anyway.

'There's a place in there, a workshop, a garage, something like that, bunch of immigrants used it for stripping the lead out of batteries – they dumped the acid in a tank in the floor. When the place went over to the Program no one bothered to drain the tank, just sealed it up. According to the client. So this is what they want: when you're ready to go, we get the tank unsealed, you take the target there, you do the job, put her in the tank, get away. Forty-eight hours after it's opened up, we get it sealed again.'

'This is the client's idea?'

Fielding nods. 'Yeah. And I told them, battery acid won't dissolve a body, not completely, not unless it's in there a very long time. They won't have it: say it's the only way to keep it quiet, stop her turning up. Which they don't want. But it's all a bit too thorough, isn't it? A bit too precise, and I don't like it. So: time to think about alternatives. Like subcontracting: use someone else. Someone inside, someone a bit more ... disposable. This guy I got in mind, uses a knife – he does women, that's his speciality.'

That again. Fielding knows the button's there; he can't resist the urge to push it. 'Who's the client?'

Fielding shakes his head. 'You know I can't tell you that.'

'But you said they're sound?'

'I know what I said.'

'Our side?'

'Civilian. Now, you'll get something for your trouble, I'll make sure of that. Call it a research fee. You found her and we can use that, right? So don't look at it as a failure.'

'Where's this tank?'

'In a garage – how the fuck should I know? All I got is a grid reference. Now, you've seen the set-up in there. You tell me where to find her, I pass it on to my guy, he does the business. You had a plan? Right, now that's his plan.'

'It won't work.'

'What are you, fucking indispensable? It'll work for you, it'll work for him.'

107

Johanssen says, 'She's Quillan's tame doctor and no one in that place'll risk touching her because they know what'll happen if they do.'

Fielding says, 'Quillan's *doctor*?'

'She works in a clinic. Run by Quillan from a compound. Give me the location.'

'Quillan,' Fielding says. He eyes Johanssen's bruises. 'It was Quillan who did that?'

'Guy called Brice. He works for Quillan.'

Fielding mutters, 'Christ—'

'He wanted to check who I was.'

Fielding narrows his eyes. 'But he doesn't know, or you'd have come out of there in a bag.'

'Quillan gave me a job.'

'What?'

'In that clinic. I work for him now.' Johanssen holds out a hand. 'Give me the location,' he says again. 'I go back in, I check it out, I say yes or no. If it's not safe it's a no. If it's a yes, that's it. I do it. There won't be a problem.'

Fielding says nothing.

The sunlight hazes the dust on the windows. Sound filters up from the bookie's below and in from the road outside: another bus grumbles past, and someone shouts.

Then, 'Fuck you,' Fielding mutters. He dips into his pocket, pulls out a folded slip of paper and holds it vertically between two fingers, but when Johanssen reaches for it he flicks it back.

Fielding says, 'You check it out, you call me.'

'They monitor the landlines.'

'Who knew?' Fielding says. 'You call me. And remember: six years we've worked together. Six years, and you know what that means? It means every time you open your mouth I can read every fucking thought in your head. So if you say it's safe you'd better be sure of it. One tiny little doubt—' he raises his free hand; index finger and thumb measure a sliver of space '—and I'll know. We'll go with my guy, and you'll get out of his way and you'll stay out. Have I got your agreement on that?'

Johanssen nods.

'Say it.'

'Yes.'

Still he pauses, holding the paper, and his eyes stay on Johanssen one, two, three seconds too long. Then suddenly he flicks it forward again. Johanssen takes it, glances once at it – a row of scribbled figures – pockets it without a word, and as he does so the sun blinks out, and the room's cold.

'She killed someone,' Johanssen says.

'She tell you that?'

He nods. 'Why isn't it in the records?'

Fielding grunts. 'Client said it got covered up. Maybe someone's got friends in high places. Who knows with this stuff?' Then he says, 'So she was a doctor, was she? That figures.'

'What?'

'You trust someone when they're a doctor. Hippocratic oath and all that. You think a doctor kills someone, it's going to be quick, it's going to be clean. Not …' He shakes his head. 'Client talked about it. You should have seen the state they were in.'

He pauses, reflective. 'Our line of work, we can't afford to stress about the rights and wrongs of it. But this one?' And his eyes have a flat look in them. 'This one deserves it.'

Day 11: Saturday – Day 12: Sunday

Karla

2 p.m. on Saturday, and I'm in an alleyway in the borough of Wandsworth, with a key in my hand. As I slip it into the padlock and turn it a voice behind me says doubtfully, 'You don't want to go in there.'

An elderly man with a woven plastic shopping bag is shuffling towards me through the dusk. 'There's bad people use that place,' he says. 'You want to be careful.' The alleyway's narrow, and his shopping bag scrapes harshly against the brick wall. Up on the main road a market's selling pirated DVDs, cheap cleaning materials, giant bags of sweets. Maybe that's where he's heading, maybe this is his short cut.

He says, 'They block up the windows, see, but that don't stop 'em, they just break in again. It's drugs.' He nods sagely. 'Drugs.'

He's right beside me now. I step into the doorway to let him pass, but he doesn't. Instead he stares expectantly at the door. 'I remember this place before they closed it down.' He sounds suddenly hopeful. 'Years since I've been inside.'

The last thing I need is nostalgia. I slip the last key into the door's Yale, then turn to the old man. 'Not safe in there, mate. You'd need one of these.' I tap the hard hat I'm wearing: its harsh yellow plastic is jagged in the overcast alleyway. I'm conspicuous, but sometimes this is the best way to hide: in plain sight.

'What you doing then?' the old man asks as the door swings open. He squints past me, into the gloom. The stench of urine and decay belches out at us.

I step inside. 'Health and safety, mate,' I say cheerily. 'Health and safety.'

When I pull the door shut the old man's still peering in after me: his watery grey eye in the diminishing slit is the last thing I see before the dark closes in on me.

The building is a big Edwardian-era pub, boarded up for the last three years, sliding into patient disrepair as it awaits the attention of the developers. I've come in via a side door, a staff entrance opening onto a dingy, windowless corridor. The darkness magnifies the rich clammy damp.

My torch flares, the beam nosing through the rubbish on the floor. Used needles glint among the refuse. To my left a narrow staircase rises to the first floor. Upstairs there'll be peeling bedrooms, rust-spotted baths, frayed death-trap electrics ... or maybe it's all gone, torn out, and the floorboards are failing. I don't go up. We agreed: the ground floor.

Beyond the staircase there's a fire door. I open it and immediately I'm dazzled.

On instinct I put a hand up and the beam glances away. Behind its bright afterglow Whitman, invisible, says, 'Laura, where do you find these places?'

I didn't see his men outside. 'You alone?' I think he nods. 'What have you told them?'

He sighs. 'He wants to meet some old contacts and we need to keep him sweet.'

'They OK with that?'

'They're paid to be OK.' But there's something non-committal about the way he says it. He thought it was going to be simpler than this.

I've finally blinked the dazzle out of my eyes. Whitman angles his head towards the bar. By torchlight his face is more cadaverous than ever. 'In there,' he says. 'He's not pretty.' And he steps past me, closing the fire door behind him. Whatever comes next, he doesn't want to hear it.

The bar's boarded windows face the main street. Through the boards filter noises – traffic, voices, the thump of bhangra music from a passing car – and a little light. In the corner the outer double doors that once opened on to the street are nailed shut. The glazed inner doors are empty frames, the glass glittering in tiny fragments on the dirty tiles. I play my torch beam around: there's rubbish everywhere, empty bottles, more drug paraphernalia, graffiti on the walls.

Johanssen's down on his haunches with his back to the far wall, so still he might be petrified.

The gloom has smoothed his features into a mask, but as I

approach he rises and nods a greeting – 'Karla' – and a strand of light crosses his face, and something thumps in my chest.

The swelling's gone down but the bruising's still bad, purple-black and red fading out to yellow and brown.

I've seen enough. I switch off the torch, pocket it and fold my arms, and for a moment we both stand there in silence.

At last I say, 'It's definitely her?'

'It's her.'

'She's not listed anywhere. Not as an inmate, a volunteer, a member of staff.' A hidden inmate in the Program and someone wants her dead. I don't like this. I don't like it at all.

He just repeats, 'It's her.'

I bite back my anxiety. For now.

'So what happened in there?' I ask. 'We looked for you. The surveillance feeds.'

'You can access them?'

'We can now. It took a while – we only got in on Wednesday. Whitman said they found you in Quillan's compound.'

'Quillan doesn't know who I am,' he says. His face shifts in the light. There are cuts too, to his lip, his ears, around his eyes.

He tells me the story then – but quietly, and as if he wasn't part of it, and not all of it either. The interview with Quillan and the night in the cell, but not the beating. The little man Jimmy but not exactly what was done to him, or what Johanssen was expected to do. Or what punishment his refusal had earned him, before the woman called Cate stepped in to save him, with a knife.

I wonder if this intervention will bother him, but all he says is, 'Turf war. Cate and Quillan's deputy, a guy called Brice. A day later she was threatening to hand me back.'

'And she's an inmate? You're sure? Not a volunteer medic?'

'Killed someone. She told me herself.'

'She killed someone?' All those hours scouring the reports ... 'Then it's been covered up.'

He nods. 'Fielding said.'

But doctors who kill get put on trial, locked up. Not hidden away. What makes this one special? I'm watching Johanssen, but his gaze comes straight back at me. He has nothing to add.

At last I ask, 'So what did Fielding want?' though I've a suspicion I already know.

He digs in his pocket, hands me a scrap of paper. A string of numbers has been scrawled across it.

Co-ordinates: same as the ones Fielding gave me a few hours ago. I hand them back. 'Medium-sized structure, in the south-west sector of the Program. Houghton Street. One camera, inside. I checked the feed: not a lot to see. Brick-built, semi-derelict.' A wall smeared with graffiti, and one enormous window with every pane broken.

'He told you about the tank.'

'He told me. It's possible to get it opened up. Fake work ticket, and a story about a safety inspection: we say there's toxic fumes inside, hopefully no one will lift the lid to take a look before they seal it up again.' I pause. 'But if she's in with John Quillan and she disappears, he'll start looking. Someone'll remember opening up that tank.'

'I'll be gone by then,' he says. And he's right. It won't be his problem.

'Client came up with this, didn't they?' He nods. Of course. It's not Fielding's style, this much detail; had to be the client. 'Fielding told me they're civilian, but for a civilian they know a lot about the Program. Contacts inside? But they're using you.'

'She's Quillan's tame doctor,' he says. 'No one inside will touch her.'

'Even so …' I don't need to outline the risks, if the client's got eyes inside. They could have people watching the location. They could have people waiting when Johanssen arrives. A paid killer isn't always considered a valued employee once the job's done. 'What does Fielding say about all this?'

He looks down. 'Fielding says I should pull out.'

Doesn't he always? Playing up the risks, raising the stakes, knowing that with every move he's reeling Johanssen in – that the harder he makes the job appear, the harder it is for Johanssen to walk away.

'And if you don't do it, who does?'

'Guy with a knife.'

A nice image to plant in Johanssen's head; set the ghost of Terry Cunliffe walking again. *You bastard, Fielding.*

'But a guy with a knife couldn't get near her?' He shakes his head. 'Could you?'

'I've got a job in the clinic where she works.' He looks away. 'There was a guy they brought in, hurt.' He shrugs, leaves me to fill in the details. He's got the training: Spec Ops saw to that.

So he's got close to her. 'And you think you can get her to go with you to this place? With Ryan Jackson's record? She going to take a walk with a man like him?'

'I told them I went down for double murder. A shooting. That's all they know.'

And they looked at him and thought: gangland hits. He won't tell them the truth, not if he can help it. Because he needs her trust.

So what do we have? An inmate without a record in the Program. A murder covered up. A civilian client who wants her not just dead, but obliterated, so she never comes to light; someone who knows more than any civilian should about the Program—

Someone who's dictating how the hit should go. Who could be watching the moment it happens ...

'You want me to check out the client? See if they're safe?'

'Fielding won't give me a name,' he says.

Bloody Fielding and his policy of anonymity. And stalking him won't get us anywhere. He's been in this business too long. We could have him followed every day for a year, we could hack every email and tape every call; still there'd be a meeting we didn't see, a phone call we never heard. In any case, the whole thing's already set up: from now on, his contact with the client will be minimal.

'All right then, what about the victim?'

'Fielding said the death was messy. Client was in a state talking about it.'

'And they're going to all these lengths to get her killed ... It's personal for them. Victim's family, then, or someone close.' They've seen justice give them the slip once and they won't let it happen again. That would explain the demand to hide the body, too: they know if she's found, the trail could come back to them.

And that gives us our break.

'What if I can get the client's name? If we can ID her and find her victim, we'll know who they are. If they look anything less than solid, you pull out.'

There's a stillness in Johanssen's features that says *I don't pull out.*

But he's thinking of all the other jobs. This one's different.

'In any case,' I say, 'you've got less than three weeks. That's all we can give you.'

He says, 'That will be enough,' and I know I'm dismissed.

But as I turn to leave he says softly, 'Karla?' and I stop, and look back. The gloom has softened his injuries: in the dim light he seems unchanged, undamaged.

'There's been a clean-up. What if there's nothing left for you to find?'

'There's always something,' I tell him.

For a moment he's silent, thinking; then he says, '*She* knows what this is all about.'

'Will she tell you?'

He doesn't answer, and after a few seconds I know he isn't going to, and I turn and leave.

Whitman's still waiting on the other side of the fire door, playing his torch beam through the rubbish.

He says, 'We're putting him back in there, aren't we.' He's not stupid. 'I thought there was a problem?'

'Apparently not.'

I'm back at my apartment in time to see Johanssen on the surveillance feeds, picking his way across the strip of rubble that separates the perimeter from the buildings. It's dark now, and the floodlights seem to strip the flesh from his face, giving his features the intensity of a skull's.

Four minutes later, flipping between cameras, I lose him.

In the end I give up, and switch to another camera. Brick wall, graffiti, broken panes. The workshop.

Say he can get her out of that compound. Say he can take her across the Program, unhindered, undetected. He's going to bring her here.

Cate, her name is Cate, she was a doctor once …

Hours later I'm still at my desk, and staring at my computer screen.

In front of me are the faces of women. I'm scrolling through identities, searching for her – for a closed-off half-smiling blonde, for a fragment of memory. I haven't found her yet.

Was her hair different when I saw her before? Longer? Darker? Tied back, pinned up? I don't know. Forget the suit too, forget its connotations of wealth and taste, it's just a costume – but no, somehow the suit is right, it goes with the guarded smile, it's part of her armour.

The faces keep coming: faces from passports, from security records, from employment files. Most of the subjects have taken to heart the instruction not to smile. Harsh lighting has bleached out skin tone and warmth: even with make-up their faces look scrubbed, plain, exposed.

She isn't among them.

I've been sitting in the wrong position for too long. My feet are cold and there's a pain in my right shoulder, and the finger resting on the mouse button has frozen. When I try to move, my joints respond sluggishly; everything needs to be coaxed or bullied into action. I push my chair back, stretch my fingers and my spine, walk out of the side office to the big south window. Lights reflect off the oily ripple of the dock but beneath the surface there's something dark, indistinct, vaguely menacing ... I count taxis on the approach roads in an effort to empty my head, but all the time back it comes again, the memory of that hard-edged smile. I know her.

I turn away from the window, go back to my desk. Another database, another batch of photos. These are all victims, women with bruises and black eyes and broken teeth, whose emptiness is more than a trick of the lighting. No one had to tell them not to smile ... But she isn't one of them, either. I've seen this woman before and she was never a victim.

I close down that database. Go onto the Internet. Adjust my search parameters. And—

Match.

I'm so fugged with caffeine and sleeplessness that for a moment I'm convinced this is my own confusion at work here, my tired brain playing a trick on me.

Her face stares back at me: clever, guarded, smiling that closed smile beneath a year-old headline pasted into a blog. I have found her.

I read the coverage once, twice, and again.

Whatever I was expecting, it wasn't this.

Day 11: Saturday – Day 12: Sunday

Johanssen

He re-enters the Program.

A check on his ID against the record from last week. The strip-search. Dressing again. The nod from Whitman, and the walk under escort to the sentry booth – 'Place your hand on the panel and look into the screen.' The metal gate sliding open; through it and into the big room beyond (still empty) and then on through the next door. A pause on the edge of the rubble, five seconds only, enough to take one breath and let it out – white floodlights and hard black shadows and cold air – then, *Go. Go now*.

Across the waste ground to the command-post tower, and into the first street. Thirty metres, and he's picked up a tail. His pulse quickens. Quillan's? Brice's? No way of knowing.

On past the houses, the half-abandoned shopping centre, the pub with the sound of hammering. Threading through the dark streets, from one puddle of street light to the next. The tail's still there, the voice in his head whispering, *Behind you*. Left just before the central guard base – six o'clock, the shutter rattling down as it seals itself in for the night. At the wall the entry gates are closing, the authorities turning the Program over to itself.

Shadows shift behind glass. Somewhere close a door bangs, someone calls out, and up ahead running feet recede into distance. He keeps moving. Skirting the council blocks on their west side – steering clear of doorways, taking corners wide, straining for the first premonition of ambush, the line of men strung out across the street with Brice at their exact centre, brandishing his bolt cutters.

When the council estate ends he takes the first right, and there it is, up ahead: the electrified wire, the knot of men at the gate. They've spotted him: one head turns, then another. Someone splits from the group and sprints towards one of the buildings. Who's he gone to warn? Quillan or Brice? Closer and he tries to make out the faces, looking for Brice's crew – the one with the yellow teeth, the skinny dark one—

He reaches the gate. Four strangers stare at him.

Ask for Cate? But it was Quillan who stood and watched him leave. Only Quillan can let him come back.

Quillan's in his usual armchair. On the table beside him is a tray with the remains of a meal, cauliflower cheese and a glass of orange squash. Invalid food. The TV's showing a wildlife documentary: iridescent butterflies flood the screen. Quillan isn't watching it. Instead he's staring at Johanssen.

'Well,' he says at last. 'I think you owe us an explanation, Mr *Jackson*.'

'The Americans,' he says. 'They wanted to talk to me.'

'Oh yes, keen for you to shop your former associates. And did you?'

'No.'

Quillan corrects him: '*Not yet*. And now you're back.'

'I still want to work for you.'

A ticking silence. Quillan's look is cold, assessing.

And then he smiles as if the calculation he's been doing in his own head has solved itself to his satisfaction; but the smile fades quickly, and all he says is, 'What are you waiting for?'

Johanssen crosses the compound yard to the clinic building. In through the main doors, through the room full of chairs – a man already seated there, a bloodied bandage around one hand – and into the clinic itself. Four faces turn: Cate, Riley, Vinnie, Drill.

Riley says, 'You're just in time.' Cate looks away.

And here they come. Broken fingers, chest pains, burns. A young Asian with slash wounds to his chest and arms, refusing anaesthetic, taking his pain seriously. A man who's been stabbed in the shoulder: it takes two of them, Johanssen and the blank-faced boy Drill, to pin him down while Cate fastens the straps. He screams a lot – high-pitched screams that are nothing to do with pain – until the sedative takes effect.

Johanssen does what he's told when he's told, finds stuff to do when he's not. He fetches things, holds things, straps patients down. Administers painkillers, splints a limb, cleans and dresses a wound.

Helps Vinnie wash down the room they use as a mortuary, blocks a punch aimed at Riley's head. Ignores the buzz of tiredness, and the aches. He knows he's being tested.

From time to time he catches Cate or Riley or Vinnie watching him, and always the look is the same. They're wondering about him.

Drill watches too, but what he's thinking is anyone's guess.

The armoured ambulances arrive, under escort, shortly after 8 a.m.

After they've loaded and left he queues for a shower, then eats with Riley and Vinnie. There's no sign of Cate, just a dirty plate in the kitchen sink. Drill eats on his bed. Vinnie tells them about his dog again; he'll be out soon. Johanssen washes his plate, then Riley walks him across the yard to meet a man who sells him a phonecard for probably twice the going rate.

Johanssen uses the payphone in the waiting room. He calls on one of the safe lines: the number will be untraceable.

He dials, bracing himself for the impact of Karla's voice, but the line connects to an automated message on an answering machine.

He keeps it brief. He's fine, he'll be all right, this is the number he can be reached on. 'Tell Dad,' he says. He hangs up.

Ryan Jackson has a father. They haven't spoken in years, but it'll wash.

He walks back into the clinic.

She's on a stool at a counter, with surgical hardware – clamps and forceps, scissors, saws, scalpels and retractors and something hooked that he doesn't know the name of – spread out in front of her on a long blue paper strip. When he comes in she doesn't look up. Her hand strays across the sheet; she reaches for a scalpel, holds it up. The blade winks in the light.

'So,' she says flatly, 'you came back.'

'I want to be useful,' he says.

'You said.' She puts the scalpel down again, very precisely, on the blue paper sheet. 'Not worried what Brice has got planned for you? He's not known for his patience.'

'He'll want an audience.'

'Yes, he will, won't he.'

She picks up a clamp and puts it down again. The conversation's over.

He goes upstairs to the bunkroom. His own bed is as he left it. He undresses quickly and crawls under the blankets.

Fielding said, *This one deserves it.*

Somehow he must get her to trust him, talk to him, make him safe.

He doesn't know where to begin.

He's still lying awake when Cate's footsteps pad up the stairs, past the door and on up to the floor above. Her door opens, then closes. A few minutes later the sound of scratching starts: slow, careful. This time it lasts only a few seconds.

He's dozing when the cry comes from above: a ripped, ragged sound, there and gone again.

He's on his feet, out of the bunkroom and across the kitchen when a low voice behind him says, 'Leave it.'

Riley's standing by the partition.

'She gets nightmares,' he says. 'Just leave it.'

Johanssen goes back to his bed and lies awake, watching the dust motes turning in the light that seeps around the makeshift blackouts.

She doesn't cry out again.

Part III

Day 12: Sunday – Day 13: Monday

Karla

I called him at 4.30 a.m. on Sunday. Anyone else might fumble the phone, blurred with sleep at that time of night. Not him.

'*Karla*,' he said. Pin sharp as ever, and with that dangerous confidence in his voice that always puts me on edge. As if the call wasn't a surprise to him at all. As if with one word Detective Inspector Joseph Ellis had already got me just where he wanted me.

'Don't tell me,' he said, '4.30 in the morning and you want a favour. Funny, could have sworn it was my turn to ask. And don't you leave this sort of thing to your boyfriend now?' He meant Craigie.

'This one's personal. Just for me. And it's urgent. It's a file.'

'Sorry, our business hours are—'

I said, 'It's Missing Persons.'

A pause on the line. That wasn't what he was expecting.

At last he said, 'So what's in it for me?'

The place is a tyre workshop in Harringay, north London.

The owner, a Turkish Cypriot in his fifties, arrives at 7.30 on Sunday morning to open up, and finds a Ford Mondeo parked on his forecourt and me in the driver's seat. He looks at the Mondeo's tyres seriously – they're borderline legal – and says yes, he can help me, but he's only here early to catch up on paperwork; for tyres I'll have to wait until his men arrive. There are chairs in the workshop's front office, and a coffee machine, but instead he suggests that I wait in the back room: it will be warmer there. He shows me through the garage – the biting cold deadening the smell of rubber and oil – to a small room with a few tatty armchairs, a TV, a week's worth of discarded tabloids, an elderly electric heater which he switches on, and a collection of calendars in a style I thought had gone out decades ago.

And that's where I stay, for more than two hours, until Joe Ellis arrives, clutching a tan-coloured plastic cup from the coffee machine and with a leather document case tucked under his arm.

He's young for a DI, only twenty-nine years old. Not tall, but with a whiplash sharpness about him, a lean aggression, that his meticulous appearance (smart-casual, designer stuff) does nothing to diminish. He looks like a man who'll fight dirty if it means he wins, though to my knowledge his collars have always been the real thing: he's never fitted anyone up. Where and how he gets his tip-offs is another matter, though.

He was already a DS when we first met three years ago, already on the way up: 'looking to progress further', as he put it. And progress he has, thanks to his wealth of useful contacts, his high conviction rate. I am one of those contacts. But he operates on a two-way street, and the tip-offs I give him are part of a much bigger trade. He's bought his meteoric rise with inside information on Met operations.

I have records of that: careful proof of every little deal. Move against me, and he not only loses his best source, his best chance of fast-tracking it all the way to the top; he ends up in prison. That's one reason I'm prepared to meet him face to face, even though it means he can ID me as Charlotte Alton. He knows what I can do to him, and he knows I won't hesitate.

But there's another reason why I'm here.

Some people you're better off dealing with at arm's length. Not Joe Ellis: he's one enemy best kept close. I feel safest when I'm in the room with him. Safest when I can see the whites of his eyes.

'Mind if I take a seat?' he says. When he sits he tosses the document case into the chair next to him, the one furthest away from me. It's heavy, lands with a soft thud. He's brought me the file. But the scent of a deal has charged him up, and the way he smiles and sips his coffee and takes his time tells me this isn't going to be as straight-forward as I'd like.

'So,' he says after a moment. ''S been a while. I was beginning to think you'd retired. South of France, maybe.' He narrows his eyes. 'Not Spain. Not your style.'

'I've taken a step back,' I say, as non-committally as I can.

'Yeah, leave it all to someone else, why not? I would if I could. So: personal favour eh?' His hand rests lightly on the document case.

'That's right.'

I want him to open the case, hand over the file, but he doesn't move. He's watching me. He knows I don't do 'personal', so he skim-read every page in that file as he pulled it off the Met's Missing Persons database this morning. Now he's wondering what this is all about.

'Christmas, eh?' he says. 'What is it about Christmas?' And he smiles, showing white, even teeth. 'I blame the ads. All those happy families, kids all smiling, peace-on-earth-good-will-to-all-men … Like a knife in the guts to all the fucked-up lonely people.' He looks at me as if it's me he has in mind. 'No wonder you're more likely to top yourself at Christmas.'

'But she didn't,' I say. 'She was gone weeks before Christmas. Walked out on the eighth.'

The date was in the news coverage. On the eighth of December, just over a year ago, Dr Catherine Gallagher applied to the London hospital where she worked for a couple of weeks' compassionate leave to visit her mother, who had – she said – been taken gravely ill. Dr Gallagher was due back on the wards on Christmas Eve, and when she walked out of the hospital on the eighth everyone assumed she was coming back.

'Yeah,' he says, as if I've just proved his point. 'Maybe she wanted to avoid the Christmas rush.' He pauses again to look me over.

'So tell me about her.'

'What d'you want to know?' It's nowhere near as helpful as it sounds. He's looking for my angle on this.

Keep it neutral; safe. 'For a start, she wasn't expected back at work until the twenty-fourth, but she was reported missing on the twenty-first.'

He shrugs. Bastard.

I try again. 'She missed an appointment.'

Still Ellis doesn't respond. He's finding this entertaining.

'Ellis, busy people miss appointments all the time. It doesn't usually trigger a Missing Persons enquiry.'

This time he can't resist. 'It does when it's your shrink and he's got you down as suicidal.'

That wasn't in the news article. 'A shrink? She was seeing a psychiatrist?'

Ellis's eyes flick over me, assessing me. He's a copper: always waiting for the lie. But he seems satisfied my surprise is real.

'Guy called Ian Graves. Appointment was for the twentieth. And she's a good patient, regular as clockwork, never misses, so when she doesn't show and doesn't contact him to reschedule, he worries. He tries her mobile and her home number but she's not answering. Goes round to her flat, no one home. Would have tried her work except it turns out she'd lied about that: told him she worked for some ad agency. Didn't want her bosses to find out she was a potential wrist-slasher.' Ellis snorts softly to himself. 'Anyway, he reports it to us. "Concerned for the safety of a patient." He says she's a suicide risk. Wants it taken seriously. You know what these people are like: always worried about liability, scared someone's about to slap a lawsuit on them. He comes to us, it's our problem.' He pauses and drains the sludge from the bottom of his cup.

'Course,' he says, 'quick check tells us she's a doctor. Call to the hospital: they say she's on compassionate leave. Dying mother. Stood to reason at the time: your nearest and dearest's at death's door, you don't always think to check your diary, do you? Mum's in a nursing home in Kent. Alzheimer's. We call the nursing home.' Ellis smiles, though this one's joyless. 'And Mummy's fine. Doolally, but fine. They haven't laid eyes on Dr Gallagher in over a month.'

'And you've got a Missing Persons enquiry.'

'Oh no, we're looking for a body.' He hunts round for a bin, spots one, pings the cup into it.

'Graves was that sure?'

He nods. 'Everyone reckoned overdose. Well, it fits the MO, doesn't it? With farmers it's guns, with commuters it's trains, with doctors it's drugs. Overdoses, they're most often at home or in their car. A crew went round. She lived alone. Wapping, one of the new blocks. Nice place, apparently, if a bit—' he fishes for the word '—soulless. Two weeks' post and no body. No note but no clothes taken either, as far as they can make out, just her coat and her bag. Passport's in a drawer, car's in the street outside.'

'Bank account? Cards?'

'Last credit card use the weekend before. Last cash withdrawal on the seventh. A hundred quid, so she wouldn't have lasted long on that. Last calls on her mobile and her landline on the evening of the seventh. Last known sighting on the eighth, 8.15 at night. There's a security camera on the door of her building. She came home from the hospital, changed, went out again.'

'Neighbours see anything?'

'Nothing. Our lot knocked on doors, half the folk didn't even recognise the photo. Pretty enough girl but kept herself to herself.

Same story at the hospital – she worked all the hours, didn't social-
ise. Colleagues rather than friends. "Acquaintances."'

'Lovers?'

'Not a trace.'

'Family?'

'Only child, Dad's dead, Mum doesn't even know her any more.
She walks out of her flat, she's got nowhere to go, not that we could
find.'

'Missing Persons circulated her details.'

'Hospitals, shelters, women's refuges …' He shrugs again. It's one
of his settings, indifference; he uses it sometimes to lull interviewees.
'She could have had a breakdown, ended up on the streets. It happens.'

'A bit organised, booking leave first.'

'Some people are funny like that. Or she might have been the
type who fits her life into little boxes. Work in this box. Social life in
another. Maybe she's got a reason for that, maybe she's into kinky
sex with strangers, you wouldn't want that getting out at work. Oh,
we did check: Internet use, contact sites … Nothing.' He sits back.
'Missing Persons got a press release out, media ran with it for a few
days. Not much going on between Christmas and New Year, nice
blonde female doctor disappears … They like that sort of thing, it's
a story.'

I must have glimpsed her photo then, on TV or on a news site.
Police are concerned for the safety …

'Any good leads?'

'A few sightings. Most of them ruled out. The helpful but mistaken. And of course the usual nutters and attention-seekers crawled
out the woodwork.'

'Confessions?'

'As you'd expect.'

'And then?'

'And then nothing. She's on the database. Every time an unknown
white female pops up, alive or dead, the system looks at her.' Ellis
sniffs. Still in indifferent mode. 'Richardson thinks she's dead.'

'Richardson?'

'Guy who ran the original investigation, after she disappeared. I
had a word.'

Already? On a Sunday morning? I didn't ask him to do that, and
he doesn't usually do things he isn't asked to, or isn't going to be
paid for. He's latched on to this one, hasn't he?

'Did he add anything?'

He grunts. 'Screwed-up high achiever, suicide risk, tidy flat, CCTV shows her leaving alone, no sign of foul play, no note, no leads.' Another shrug. 'He thinks she topped herself. Holed up somewhere she wouldn't be found, big needle full of morphine and it's Goodnight Irene.'

'Why would she hide?'

'Shame. That's the thing with doctors: always supposed to cope.' He nods at one of the calendars on the wall. 'Nice tits,' he says and then, although his voice is as casual as ever, suddenly he switches his copper's gaze to me. 'So what's your interest?'

'Natural curiosity.'

He snorts. 'Yeah, right. What's Catherine Gallagher got to do with you? Did you know her?'

'If I had, I'd have been asking questions a year ago. Not now.'

'So: what? Where do you fit into all this?'

'I don't fit.'

'You want the file. You're asking questions.'

'It's what I do.'

'Makes two of us.' He's still watching me. 'This *is* personal, isn't it?' Then he leans forward, fixes on me. 'You think she's been murdered, don't you?' And he's lost that casual tone completely. 'Cut me in on this, Karla. You know you want to.'

I shake my head. 'It's nothing like that.'

'Oh no?' he says, then, almost to himself, 'You didn't know her but you're asking questions. She's dead and there's something we missed.'

I leave first. Park the Mondeo on a meter in Fulham – it will be collected from there within the hour – walk half a mile and then take a taxi to South Kensington, then a bus and finally the Jubilee Line to Canary Wharf. By the time the escalators deliver me out into the weak sunshine again it's almost 1 p.m., and the file's burning a hole in my bag.

I get back home to a winking message light: Johanssen, with a number for a payphone. 'Tell Dad,' he says. His voice is low and tired.

Fielding can wait. I pull out the file and go straight for the images, and there it is, the photo from the Internet, the same one Fielding gave to Johanssen. Catherine Gallagher.

By rights I should never have identified her. The blog piece I found was a freak survival; in every other Internet article on her disappearance, above captions reading MISSING DOCTOR CATHERINE: NO LEADS and HAVE YOU SEEN THIS WOMAN?, the space left for her picture is now blank.

Catherine Gallagher was thirty-one when she vanished. The file itemises her appearance – the slim build, the blonde hair. The photos are the sort you find on membership cards and in employment files. No informal snaps, nothing taken in a pub or at a party or on holiday. In all of them – even the ones in which she's smiling – there's something shuttered about her face.

There is only one unposed shot, and that's the record of the last firm sighting of her: a blurry CCTV image of a pale-haired young woman in a long coat, frozen in movement, passing through a lobby towards a door. The time code in the bottom corner reads 20.15-08-12. The eighth of December, 8.15 p.m.: Dr Catherine Gallagher walking out of her life.

She worked in the intensive care unit of a major London hospital, on her way to her first consultancy among drugged, passive patients. She worked hard, kept herself to herself. She came over as a little cold maybe, a little distant, but highly efficient and trustworthy. *Professional.* None of her colleagues knew about her depression. To them she was self-contained, a loner, a high achiever. Good at her job, hard on herself. Driven.

The only person she allowed anywhere near the inside of her head was the psychiatrist, Graves.

They interviewed him at some length. I skim the notes. *Fifteen months, regular appointments.* (Ellis was right: she was always punctual, never missed a session.) *History of depression. Low self-worth. Self-harm an evident risk.* But no indication of why.

Because she'd killed, and it had begun to crack her open? But she wasn't going to tell anyone that, not this one.

So what happened on the eighth December?

She realised someone knew.

I go back to the CCTV grab: the woman in the long coat, heading for the door. Where's she going? Not to the Program, not in her mind, not then. She's told everyone her mother's sick and now she's making her escape. I can't make out her expression clearly, but her body language is relaxed; for someone in full flight she's very calm.

Still, running; just not fast enough.

They caught her and they put her in the Program – dropped her into that dark pool like a weighted corpse, the waters closing over her without a ripple. That's the thing: even when the alert went out for her – although someone must have supervised the fingerprinting, the retinal scan, the strip-search – no one ever said. She remains a missing person, her case file still open, the police convinced she killed herself and it's only a matter of time before they find a body.

Who did you kill? And why is it a secret?

And then: *Who wants you dead?*

Some people fit their lives in little boxes ... There's a box somewhere that holds the truth behind all of this. And I must find it.

Where to start? Her friends? She had none. Her colleagues? The psychiatrist? But I can't risk flagging my interest; it has to look routine, coincidental. A police investigation? A last quick trot through the facts before the file's quietly shelved?

Ask Ellis?

But Ellis wants this too badly. Cutting him in would be a mistake.

'So what is it this time?' Ellis asks. It's gone 2 p.m. when I get hold of him. He's in an upmarket pub somewhere, I can tell from the background noises, the voices and the rattle of glasses and cutlery, the low throb of jazz: 'So What' from Miles Davis's *Kind of Blue*.

'Catherine Gallagher,' I say.

'Just a moment.' He's with someone – aside he adds, 'Sorry, I've got to take this.' The background noise surges, then clears. 'What about her?' he asks.

'It wasn't suicide.'

'You got remains?' There's that sharpness in his voice again.

'No.'

'But she's dead.'

I brush past that. 'Something happened. Could be something to do with her job. Something she did, something she knew. And I think someone may have come after her for it. If we can find out—'

'We?' he says.

'We.'

Ellis falls silent again. The offer's on the table. He's trying to work out what's behind it.

'You know more than you're telling,' he says at last.

130

'I'm telling you as much as I can right now. The fact is I don't have a lot.'

'So what makes you think it's to do with her job?'

'You read that file. Her work was all she had.'

'You think she did something bad? What? She offed a patient? You think she could have been another Shipman?' he says. 'Or who was that other one, the nurse?'

He's thinking of the god-complexed control freaks easing their charges prematurely from this world; or the adrenaline junkies inducing heart failure for the thrill of resuscitation, the chance to play the hero. But it wasn't like that – it was messy, it was horrific – the client told Fielding so …

Ellis says, 'Cos it's not clinical error, or if it was, there's nothing on record,' and that startles me. So he's checked her HR file too, has he? That was quick.

'Maybe it never came to light. Maybe it was hushed up. No one knew about her depression. Maybe she was good at keeping stuff hidden.'

'And you want someone to go back to the hospital, dig around.'

If he wants to believe she was murdered, let him. 'When your friend Richardson interviewed her colleagues, everyone assumed she was a suicide. Even Richardson thought so. Someone needs to introduce the idea of foul play. Find out if anyone might have had a motive. See what comes out.'

'And what do I get?'

'The usual.'

'Cash for questions, eh?'

'You wanted in. Your choice. If you're not interested, say so now.'

He grunts, but he's going to do it. He's a copper. He can't help himself. Any more than I can.

Maybe that's why, as soon as he's off the line, I pull out Catherine Gallagher's address in Wapping and I make another call.

She lived in a cobbled street of warehouse conversions and newbuilds one block back from the river. When I arrive at 10 a.m. on Monday a young property rental agent is waiting for me, in a suit, statement dark-framed glasses and too much aftershave. He beams at me and shakes my hand. 'Mrs Christie? Shall we go in?'

The CCTV camera in the lobby isn't working today – we've seen to that – but even so, as I cross its path I can't help seeing my own blurred form with the time code superimposed below. Like Catherine Gallagher on the eighth of December, except Catherine Gallagher was going the other way. Catherine Gallagher was walking out of her life.

The police searched her flat back then, and they still hold a bare handful of her personal possessions – a diary, bank statements, a laptop. But the police were looking for a suicide, not a motive for murder. I'm counting on the chance there's something they missed.

Up the stairs to the first floor. The agent has the key and opens the door – 'I think you'll like the decor' – and I step in.

A tiny hallway. A mirror, a bland watercolour landscape; a year's quiet dust furs the frames. The air is still, unused and stuffy. The place smells like something kept in a drawer for too long.

The agent closes the front door carefully behind us while I pull on latex gloves. 'I'll wait here,' he says and gives me an empty, professional smile as if what I'm doing is perfectly normal. His glasses wink at me. 'Take as long as you like.'

His name is Sean, and he's Robbie's son, though he looks nothing like his dad – doesn't have the stubborn bulldog head, the barrel chest. He's slim, light on his feet, and there's a delicacy in his features that he gets from his mother, a woman I've seen only in photographs; a woman already cold in the ground by the time Robbie began to work for Thomas Drew. Sean was seven then, a small boy in a West Ham strip. Robbie dreamed of a career as a professional footballer for his son – would have settled for an electrician, or a plumber, but maybe some things are in your blood; now Sean's twenty-one and working surveillance beside his dad. And as soon as I outlined the scenario to Robbie yesterday he said, 'Use Sean.'

Before I arrived Sean had already established his credentials as a property rental agent with the caretaker. I did the groundwork myself on this one: a rush job, and the paperwork's a little flaky. But no one seems particularly interested in Catherine Gallagher after a year. Sean looks, sounds and smells right, and no awkward questions have been asked.

I open a door: the light from the hall spills into a small sitting room. The blinds are closed. I won't open them. Instead I grope for the light switch, flick it on.

A sofa, a table and chairs, TV, iPod dock. A bookcase of medical textbooks and neatly filed journals. But no family photos, scribbled shopping lists, dirty mugs, dead houseplants – none of the usual poignant reminders of a life abandoned. It's like a room setting in a furniture store, with space left for the customer's imagination to dress-in their own possessions: *See, you too could live in a place like this.* But she didn't really live here, did she? She lived at the hospital, in the ICU. No wonder this place is like an empty shell.

I spent last night reviewing Catherine Gallagher's professional history. There's a sheeny gloss on it all: the pristine exam results, the extra year in med school to acquire a further degree in medical sciences, the house jobs in top teaching hospitals, the list of published papers dating back to her student years – dense studies into the management of neurological problems within intensive care that descend into jargon within a paragraph. What lies behind that history? The emotional immaturity of the hothoused over-bright, the brittle calculation of the very ambitious, the steady loneliness of the workaholic? The HR files don't give a clue, but they back up colleagues' accounts: she lived for her work, chose a life that revolved around it.

Somewhere in that life there's the reason she has to die.

I've looked at the figures. There's no statistical irregularity, no mortality spike in any of the ICUs where she worked. But one kill would be invisible in the stats amid all those routine deaths, the broken bodies simply giving up on life, too damaged to be saved ... So I'm going through those fatalities, one by one, searching for the ugly death, the one that demanded secrecy. I haven't found it yet.

The kitchen is off the sitting room. I open drawers, cupboards: the tins and jars are regimented in rows. The wine glasses all match. The plates and bowls are stacked tidily: probably Dr Gallagher only ever used one of each.

Then the bedroom. The bed's made. I go to the wardrobe, open it; open the drawers too. Suits, trousers, skirts, shirts, sweaters, a few pairs of jeans, underwear. All good-quality labels and all in colours that must have suited her. There's nothing for evenings out. Nothing silkily indulgent, nothing sparkly. No mistakes either – nothing extravagant or frivolous or ill judged, nothing bought on a whim.

The SOCOs were here a year ago, their quiet latexed hands moving over the shelves, through the drawers, checking the pockets. They found nothing. Now it's my turn.

I go through every garment in the wardrobe. I go right through the drawers. I shift furniture, peer under the bed with a torch. In the en suite bathroom the toiletries are neatly ranged in the cabinet.

There is a little make-up – good brands, natural colours – but no perfume. Sticking plasters and a few over-the-counter remedies, paracetamol, antiseptic; nothing stronger.

Back to the living room. The door into the hallway's still open: Sean stands motionless by the front door, awaiting his cue like an actor in the wings.

I empty the bookcase, item by item. I all but strip the sofa and the armchairs. I lift the iPod dock and the TV, exposing their blank shiny footprints in the dust.

I retrieve a flyer for a domestic cleaning outfit and a twenty-euro note, both pressed into service as bookmarks; a dark blue button; a pen that looks like a drug-company handout; a few coins; a paper-clip; and wedged between a shelf and the wall, a creased business card. It's not much.

Around me the dust I've stirred is already settling. What have I learned? That she was tidy and focused and isolated? But I knew that from the file.

Every moment of your life, from when you were a little girl, all you ever wanted to do, all you'd ever prepared for, was to practise medicine. You'd been working sixteen-hour days for years. You had no personal life. When you went to the gym you were never one of those chatting over a cappuccino with girlfriends in the café afterwards. You went alone, you worked the machines, you ploughed your lengths up and down the pool, you showered, you left. You came back to your flat, you heated up supper, you read the medical journals and worked on your papers, you slept and you worked again.

Who did you kill, and why?

In my head the woman in the picture stares back at me. She's saying nothing.

I've been here too long. It's time to go. One last look around: everything is as I found it. In the hallway I strip off the gloves and push them into my bag, and promise to call Sean with my decision tomorrow. I smile, and he smiles back. Fake smiles. Heaven knows why, no one's watching. But I've been careful for so long that it's become much more than a routine; now it's a biological necessity, like breathing.

Back at my apartment I take out my meagre haul from Catherine Gallagher's flat. The business card first: MARK DEVLIN, RECRUIT-MENT CONSULTANT, it says, and the company name: MDR. The pen has what I guess is the brand name of a drug stamped on its plastic casing.

A brief Internet search reveals that the drug is a sedative, and that Mark Devlin is a headhunter specialising in the medical sector. He's in his mid-thirties with a lean smooth face: he half-smiles from his page on his company's website, above a ghosted paragraph that boasts of his track record in 'connecting high-calibre medical professionals with projects at the cutting edge of treatment and research'. It's an intelligent smile with a hint of self-mockery, as if he doesn't take his own profile entirely seriously. His name isn't in Dr Catherine Gallagher's Missing Persons file.

Did she keep the card deliberately, or by chance? Was he a friend? But if he was, he'd have been questioned by police. Maybe he was just a useful contact. Maybe they once shook hands at a conference. I phone Ellis and give him Mark Devlin's name.

'His card was in Catherine Gallagher's flat.'

Immediately he bridles. 'You saying we didn't do our job?'

'I'm saying it was in her flat. Find out what the relationship was. Especially if she was a client. If he was looking to place her in a position, he'll have checked her out. Maybe he heard something.'

'So why didn't he say so when she vanished?'

'The guy's a Big Pharma headhunter, he lives and dies by his own discretion. No one asked, so he didn't say. Start by finding out if she was on his books.'

I put the phone down. Seconds later it rings again. Robbie's gravelly voice, pure old East End, says, 'Karla? Check your inbox.'

While his son was escorting me to Catherine Gallagher's flat, Robbie was monitoring Program surveillance feeds.

The link he's sent me takes me to a view of a wire-fenced compound and a knot of figures at a gate. Three seconds in, Simon Johanssen walks into shot. The gate opens and out he goes. A jump-cut, and there he is a street further on; and again, a little further still. He's making a recce.

The cameras track him towards Houghton Street. But he's being careful or maybe he's being followed; two streets from the workshop he turns away and loops back towards the compound. The gate is opened for him, and he disappears from view.

The screen goes blank.

But tomorrow he'll go out again, and the day after, and the day after that. Let them get used to him coming and going, let them believe there's nothing to worry about. One day he'll have to walk out of there with Catherine Gallagher beside him, and no one must think anything of it.

Day 13: Monday

Powell

Eight days on the case.

If you're going to throw your weight around, the first week of an investigation is the time to do it: before the shine's worn off you, before they've got your measure. But everything's been done before he's even had the chance to ask. Peter Laidlaw's house in Shepherd's Bush secured. The body – what was left of it – ready for viewing. (He declined.) Pathologists on hand to explain their findings. (Laidlaw had been drinking – blood alcohol at 190 milligrams; nothing in his stomach. No needle marks, a clean tox report, no signs of foul play.) Laidlaw's personnel files retrieved and laid out for inspection: the details of every operation behind the old Iron Curtain. (His ID came under Soviet scrutiny in the 70s but he returned twice after that, at some personal risk, under assumed names, to handle meetings with frightened men who wouldn't talk to anyone else.) His Moscow contacts, and *their* contacts, listed – the list given to him in person by Laidlaw's own handler, with a look that said, *Do you think we didn't check?*

He's gone through that list, searching for links to active Russian intelligence personnel – the men and women within the SVR who might be able to get their hands on the sort of information that Knox passed on to Laidlaw. Somewhere there's a point of intersection, a space where the lines all cross, a centre to the web ... He draws a blank.

He's viewed the footage of Laidlaw's own debrief: Laidlaw saying patiently, for the record, time and time again, '*I have no idea who Knox might be.*' A lie, it has to be, but one they never caught him out on.

Resources: ask for whatever you need, the Section Chief had said, so he hand-picked a young woman called Bethany to act as his assistant – he finds her tidy, unreadable, disconcerting – and a tech guy,

Mitch, who is friendly but not quite genuine. They've been given the office beside his in the janitors' blank narrow-fronted building in Victoria, and they're trying to impress him: whenever he walks into their room they have lists for him, of things they've done or things they're about to do, and they look up into his face – it might be guilelessly – for approval.

Beyond them, the other janitors circle, watching. Carter, himself ex-MI5, bluff, affable, eaten up with curiosity. 'Busy, eh? But let's have a drink some time.' A quiet young woman he can just remember as a junior when he left, now a janitor in her own right: must be Leeson, the one who tracked down the tech ops guy after Knox's tip-off. Morris in her end office overlooking the street, seven months from retirement herself, peering over her reading glasses at him, wrinkling her nose. Kingman, the one he didn't know, imported from Special Branch after his own departure for Washington – Kingman came in to shake his hand. 'I've heard a lot about you' – but he didn't say what. All of them eyeing him. The janitors are people readers to a man and woman, and now they're trying to read him. To bring him back from the States means something serious, something bad … Maybe they've heard the Section Chief's rumour, maybe they really do believe something's begun to stink and he's been called in to track the stench to its source. He doesn't confide in them; that's not how it works. Janitors operate in isolation, not only from the rest of the intelligence community but even from each other. After all, anyone could be guilty.

Except he doesn't work in isolation, does he? He's the exception to the rule. Three reports so far sent up to the Section Chief, detailing each careful step he's taken, keeping conclusions to a minimum – refusing to grasp at empty supposition, create theories just to fill the void – but after each report the Chief's come down, 'to talk it through'. The man's looking over his shoulder constantly. He's trying not to twitch.

He works late most days, returning to the serviced flat gone ten – long hours in the office are inevitable when you can't take paperwork home – eating supper alone, Skyping to catch Thea before bed. She has drawn him pictures, which she holds up for inspection: herself in her pink fairy outfit, at the party; him in a suit, with Tori's clear, no-nonsense handwriting below: *Daddy helping people.* So that's what he does, is it?

He tries not to let himself think about the progress he's not making. Falls back on handy clichés: *It's early days . . .* Sooner or later the breakthrough will come.

Today he went back to Laidlaw's house in Shepherd's Bush.

Last Monday, when he visited for the first time, the dead man's presence was still all over it: the washing-up on the drainer, the socks drying on the rack above the bath, a tattered scrap of shopping list in the kitchen (tea bags, bleach). A letter from the hospital pinned to the fridge, a Post-it on the front door: *Bins Tuesday*. Upstairs, a recent and very beautiful edition of the *Iliad* by the bed, and a smell of books and damp that took him back to his tutors' rooms in Cambridge.

It's all changed now. Holes knocked in the walls to admit cameras. Insulation ripped out of the loft. The chimney, drains and sewers examined. The carpets and floorboards lifted.

'And you've found?'

Mitch – in a T-shirt and overalls, dust caking his hair – said, 'Only what MI5 put there.'

Powell nodded. *We bugged it. But Knox knew that, or guessed, and steered clear. Just as Knox knew, or guessed, about the intercept on the post. No meetings here, no phone calls, and no secondary bugging either: Knox never succumbed to the temptation to watch those who were watching him. Perhaps he didn't find it necessary.*

'What about paperwork? Records?'

Mitch gestured at the wrecked walls. 'If Laidlaw kept anything he didn't keep it here.'

Bethany was standing to one side, hands folded in front of her, quiet, fastidious, keeping the dust off her coat. 'Thoughts?' Powell asked her.

Her pale unreadable gaze went around the room. She shrugged. 'He wanted to keep Knox to himself.'

'Because?'

'Because he didn't trust anyone. He expected betrayal.' She paused. Her eyes are a yellowish green; her pale brown hair, in its ponytail, has the sheen of satin. 'And because Knox gave him status. Without Knox he's just another old man.' She turned her head towards him. Her look seemed to say, *Are we done here?*

Now, at his desk, he goes through the surveillance reports on Laidlaw again. Twenty-two tip-offs in five years and eight months. Peter Laidlaw, out of retirement and following the chalk marks on the trees … Bethany is right. *You kept Knox to yourself. You clung on tight to him, and when you stepped in front of that train you took him down with you.*

Bethany works on until seven, then puts her head round the door. A small, surveying pause before she says goodnight. She'll be good in interrogations; you can't tell what she's thinking.

In the logs: Laidlaw doing his shopping. Laidlaw going to the post office, the library. Laidlaw stopping for a quiet pint somewhere. Old man's errands. Did Laidlaw know about the watchers? The MI5 surveillance came in waves, intensifying when a tip-off was expected or had just taken place, falling into abeyance as the months passed and Knox remained silent, until another tip-off fired up the machine again.

Knox had been quiet lately. So there was no surveillance on the last day, when Laidlaw carried out his plan.

Finally he puts the surveillance logs back in the strongbox in the corner of the room and locks it.

Tori has taken Thea swimming today, with friends. He thinks of Thea in her swimsuit, doggy-paddling, her small sturdy brown body slick with water … The thought of her tightens into a fist and wedges itself beneath his breastbone.

He assumed he was the only one in the building, but as he leaves, via the basement car park, Leeson is walking out ahead of him. At the sound of his footsteps she turns. She nods to him but her look is wary. Perhaps she can smell the loneliness on him.

She gets into her car, a small red Citroën, starts the engine and drives out through the barriers.

The tech guy who tried to sell those ops files on the open market got away from her, didn't he? That must have counted against her. Does she still think of that? In her mind is it still pinned to her, a badge of her own failure?

And what if you don't find Knox?

But Knox won't simply vanish, not after five years and eight months. Knox wants something. Knox just hasn't got round to asking yet.

So Knox will resurface somewhere, at a time and place of his own choosing, when he has something to communicate.

It's not supposed to work like that.

Run the source. Win trust. Reward compliance. Control the relationship.

Don't just wait for them to come to you. That's what the rule book says, but Knox doesn't care.

They've hired him a car. He pats his pockets for his keys and then remembers his mac, hanging on the back of his office door—

Sees another door, in a damp house, with a Post-it on it: *Bins Tuesday.*

Laidlaw's memory was failing.

He made notes for his own reference, because he needed to remember, and without the notes he was helpless.

He made notes.

Mitch said, *If Laidlaw kept anything he didn't keep it here.*

Somewhere else, though?

Somewhere he could visit, later, once it was all quiet again, the surveillance wound down, everyone gone home?

There's no other property in his name.

What about the other names?

There are no other names—

And then he stops.

The meetings with frightened men, in the 70s, in Moscow. Laidlaw had other passports then.

Day 13: Monday – Day 14: Tuesday

Johanssen

All residents have access to medical treatment, including 24-hour emergency care and evacuation facilities.

Midnight on Monday: his third night in the clinic. What might pass for a quiet night, for all Johanssen knows.

An old man's complaining of chest pains: he says he's going to die, except the ones who tell you that mostly don't. Two members of rival gangs – one white, one black, minor wounds, not life-threatening – are strapped down on trolleys a few feet apart; occasionally they scream abuse at each other. An asthmatic's breathing comes out in tight panicky gasps. Riley's pumping oxygen into her. And a skinny guy has slashed his own arms. The bright curl of Cate's needle flashes in the light from the overhead bulb but the man doesn't flinch; his gaze, softened and blurred by sedative, is drifting somewhere over her head. For the first time since Johanssen arrived her face is intent and peaceful.

Then the doors bang open and they bring the man in.

His skull is smashed, the grey-white of brain tissue visible through the blood and fractured bone. It's like a battlefield injury, the product of high-cal bullets or explosive. He shouldn't be alive. But then his mouth moves and he says, quite clearly, 'Help me' – as if he's asking for a little thing, a hand with a heavy box or someone to hold a door open for him. Then his face goes slack and his body heaves, once, a basic animal response. He vomits, chokes – one of the gang boys says, '*Fucking Christ*,' and Cate snaps, 'Clear it.'

Johanssen slides gloved fingers into the man's mouth, pulls the tongue to one side – it's slack, inert – and scoops the vomit away.

'Ventilate him,' Cate says. She's at his elbow, trying to get a line in, working in a trance of concentration as if by willpower alone she can keep the man alive while Riley prepares the fluids. But the man

142

fits again, back arching, limbs in spasm, once and then again, and then for the last time, the last rattle of breath, and it's over.

Beside him Cate reaches out as if there's something more she can do – start CPR, try again – but Riley says, 'Cate?'

Straight away her gaze punches out at him, but he says her name again, softly, and she looks away, and her hands drop.

For a couple of seconds after that no one moves. Then Cate says, 'Tidy him up, will you?' and her face has that closed look again. She strips the latex gloves from her hands, bins them and walks out. A second later her feet hit the stairs.

Riley swears wearily under his breath. He crosses the room and bangs out through another door to the storeroom where they keep the body bags.

The gang boys are watching wild-eyed from their trolleys, but the old man craning from his bed seems satisfied, as if all this has just confirmed his view of the world, when Drill leans forward, slides his fingers into the cavity in the dead man's skull, and begins to probe the cooling brain.

One of the gang members gags. The other whimpers. But Drill's face is suddenly very young, and full of wonder, like a child seeing snow for the first time.

Riley says, 'He killed some kids. Three that they know of. Different MO every time. Liked to *experiment*. That fucked the profilers. They got him on forensics in the end – Drill's not the confessional type.' *Flick* goes the ash from Riley's cigarette. He takes another drag and blows out a stream of smoke. 'He's twenty-four, y'know?'

'Looks seventeen.'

'Yeah.'

They're standing outside the clinic doors, in the shelter of the awning. By the compound entrance men huddle in waterproofs, and the floodlights are haloed in rain.

'They reckon he started as young as twelve. Funny kid. Curious. 'Bout life. 'Bout pain. That's why he likes this stuff. Every night he gets to stand outside the human race and look in.'

For a moment Riley goes back to his cigarette. The wind gusts and the rain blows in at them a little, and then away again. Beyond the fence, lights are on in the council blocks, figures moving within. Out of sight, a street or two away, someone's calling a name, over and over.

Riley says, 'He heard about this place. Came to the compound, hung around the gate, kept asking to be let in. Said he wanted to watch. Everyone told him to fuck off but he always came back. Cate got to hear about it. Went out, talked to him, then talked to Quillan. Persuaded him to let the kid in. A week he was in here, every night, still as a fucking stone, watching. You'd be treating some bloke with his guts hanging out and there'd be this weird kid at your elbow.' He shakes his head at the memory. 'Then she started getting him to do stuff. He's good. Doesn't blink, doesn't freak out. You just don't leave him alone with anyone. And his bedside manner's never going to be much. But, fuck—' his sharp features twitch into irony '—we'll make a valued member of society out of him yet.' Riley gives a soft whuffling laugh. 'Spooks you, doesn't he? I thought nothing got to your sort.' Another drag on his cigarette, another stream of smoke. 'The thing you were in for, in the States,' he says.

'It was just something that had to be done,' Johanssen says. It's all he's going to say. Killing the girl could have been a crime of passion, but what happened to the boyfriend makes Ryan Jackson slippery, treacherous, sick, and he needs them to trust him.

For a minute after that they stand watching the slow drift of rain across the floodlights.

'So where d'you learn this stuff?' Riley asks at last.

Johanssen shrugs. 'Around. Just picked it up.' Riley's look says, *Oh yeah?* but he meets it and Riley glances away. Then, 'You?'

Riley grunts. 'Army. Combat medic. Basra, Helmand – oh yeah, I'm a proper fucking war hero.' He draws on his cigarette again. 'Got out after Helmand. A bit of this and that. Ended up with a habit – you know? Needed some money for it, asked this guy, he wasn't playing. I had to get serious about it.'

Get serious. Brice in the yard: *Would you say we're serious?*

Riley says, 'Once I started on him, well, it got hard to stop.' Another draw, another flick of ash. 'You know how it is. It gets hold of you,' Riley says, and he's talking into the darkness. 'It gets hold of you. Life's so fucking cheap, isn't it?'

'Yeah,' Johanssen says.

Another minute passes.

Riley says, 'I was here in the beginning. They were going to knock all of this down—' his arm sweeps out briefly, into the rain '—and then someone decides it's a good idea to put us in here. Took the boards off the windows, hooked up the services and bang, we were in. Fuck knows how they thought it would work. Half the folk wandering around like zombies, the other half ...' He shakes his head.

Johanssen says, 'Quillan sorted it.'

'Oh yeah, he sorted it.' He pauses. 'There's a trick to it, y'know. Doing just enough to keep everyone in order, but not so much the bosses can't ignore it ... That's what he's good at, Quillan. Walking the line. And making any trouble work for him. The gangs in this place? He plays 'em off against each other, keeps 'em at each other's throats, keeps 'em busy.' He takes another drag. 'Same thing with Brice. Brice is a sick fuck and Quillan knows it, he knows you don't leave a guy like that with time on his hands. You give him something to focus on. And that's what Quillan does. Finds someone to dangle in front of Brice, keep him occupied. Absorb his energies a bit.' Another drag, gaze dead ahead.

'Someone like me, you mean.'

Riley turns towards him and his eyes are hard, the light in them very flat. 'Why d'you think Quillan let you stay? Cos you're an asset to the team? And Brice is learning to live with his disappointment, is he?' Riley snorts. 'He wants you and he's going to have you, and it won't be something simple like a knife in the guts when no one's looking, not after the public beating you gave him, no: he'll want to put on a show. And while he's planning that little show, he's under control.' Then he turns away, squints across the tarmac through the veil of smoke and rain. 'Me, I'm just a spectator.'

He takes another drag on his cigarette but it's almost down to the filter: one last draw and he throws it down – 'Fuck this, I'm getting some sleep' – and goes back in through the door.

A handful of casualties trickles through the gates towards the end of the shift. There are no more crises. The old man with chest pains dozes smugly on his trolley, sure of a day trip to the Emergency Medical Centre beyond the wall: a clean modern clinic, a cup of tea while he waits for examination, maybe even a day or two in a ward ... The gang boys have fallen silent, their stocks of obscenity exhausted for now. The self-harmer floats in his narcotic trance. Cate's bandaged his slack fingers so that if he wakes he can't mess with his wounds. His mittened hands give him the look of a bantam-weight boxer out for the count. She scribbles a crude medical history – background, intervention, medication – for the benefit of the staff beyond the gates, pins it to the man's clothing with a safety pin and scrubs her hand across her tired face. Her handwriting's spiky and thin, as if she's struggling to focus.

At the end of the shift she takes her plate up to her room, and later there's that scratching sound again.

He's lying on his bunk when he hears the soft creak of the stairs as she goes down. He waits, straining for the sound of the outer door closing. It doesn't come. She's still in the clinic. After five minutes he rises, pulls on his clothes and follows.

She's at the counter just like before, the blades spread out in front of her. What's she doing? Cleaning them? Counting them? When she sees him she says, 'You're going out again.' She must have watched him leave on that first recce yesterday. He aborted when the tail got nervous but it's given him their measure; he'll try again today.

'That's right.' He goes to the sink, runs the cold tap, scoops water into his mouth. Her gaze has followed him.

'Where to?' she asks suddenly.

'Just out.'

'Why?'

He shakes the water off his hands, meets her look. 'See if Brice will try to kill me.'

'He doesn't kill,' she says, but neutrally: just an observation. She reaches one hand towards the hardware in front of her. Her face is like the surface of flat water: tiny movements like ripples show the currents underneath.

'Quillan's having me watched. I'm safe enough.'

She just picks up another blade.

He thinks she's done, and he's turning away when she says, 'The head injury. You OK with that?' Her eyes are cool. No sign of the woman from the clinic earlier, the one who couldn't stand to lose a patient, who had to keep on trying.

'I'm OK,' he says.

'Seen it all before.' It's not a question.

'Some of it.'

She sits back in her seat, folds her arms. Regards him.

'There's a scar two inches long on your right forearm,' she says. 'From a cut, probably a blade. On your left shoulder, a burn. Old, I'd say childhood. Something flat. An iron? On your left thigh, a puncture wound; quite deep at the time. Ragged. Sharpened screwdriver?

Multiple small cuts to both shins. A scar below your right ear and another above the hairline. A scar by the left hinge of your jaw. And your knuckles.' She pauses. 'It's always been part of your life, hasn't it? And seeing a man with his head blown open, that's just part of your life too.' She shrugs and reaches for another blade.

'There are worse ways to go,' he says.

A man screaming behind a door in a remote farmhouse.

'Yes,' she says, 'there are,' but her face has tightened.

He goes out, across the yard. The crowd on the gate eyes him, but no one says a word. The gate swings open and he steps through it, then turns right to skirt the council estate. Twenty metres on, a tail slots into place behind him. He keeps his head down, keeps walking.

He loops across the Program at random. North-east first, past the boarded-up chapel and the mosque, as far as the admin block with its listless queues. Then due south, along the eastern fringe of the council estate. Music blares from balconies and people watch him pass. At a small shop, dark and musty-smelling, the goods still in their boxes in a roped-off area, he asks for chocolate and cigarettes, pays with counters and comes out again. Dead ahead is the Women's Area, two snatches still parked across the junction. He turns away and angles south-west, back into the heart of the Program, heading for the workshop on Houghton Street.

A week since he first crossed the place. A week, and most of it spent inside the compound, but already he's begun to wire himself into the environment, read its codes. The pecking order and the power struggles and the personalities. The fixers and the operators, the entrepreneurs with their projects, their sidelines, their clever little dodges. The dogsbodies and the victims and the broken people, and the ordinary ones who're just trying to make the best of it. The patrols. And among the loiterers, but apart from them: Quillan's men, keeping an eye on everything, enforcing the rules, taking their cut.

Whatever he does from now on, they'll be watching.

And there it is, just like Karla said: an abandoned brick-built workshop, standing apart on an island of cleared ground as if some-one was about to demolish it when they decided they might have a use for it after all, another training centre or a light-engineering plant. He makes one slow circuit from the cover of the surrounding streets, pretending not to look, then turns away. It's enough for one day.

Four minutes later he begins to notice.

Just small things. The flash of a face turning towards him in the street ahead and then immediately away again. A flurry of movement in an alley as he passes; no one there when he doubles back. They're not Quillan's. Quillan's tail is plodding on behind him. He sharpens his awareness, tries to get a fix on them, fails.

Then he turns left to come up behind the Grisham Hotel again and it happens.

There must have been a signal. Suddenly Yellow Teeth's coming towards him from the left, another man moving to cut him off on the right, and when he spins, a third – the skinny dark one, could be a girl – is closing fast with a knife.

He whips round again, and there's Brice.

Yellow Teeth and the one on the right grab for his wrists, pinning him between them, Yellow Teeth trying to force Johanssen's arm behind his back. The blade presses into his jacket, notching itself against his spine. Johanssen twists again. The tip of the blade bites. He freezes.

Yellow Teeth reaches into Johanssen's jacket, pulls out the green ID card, passes it to Brice. Brice looks at it, smiles at the photo, pockets it. Then takes a step closer, and another.

His mouth dips to Johanssen's ear. He whispers.

The one with the knife takes a sudden breath. It's like a trigger. Brice steps back, turns away. The two others release Johanssen so fast he might be toxic. The knife pulls out. They're gone.

Two of Quillan's men have come up behind him. One of them's craning around. The other says to Johanssen, 'You all right?' He looks rattled. Johanssen doesn't answer.

In the clinic he pulls off his jacket. The back of his shirt is sodden with blood, but when he peels it off and peers at his reflection in the door of a steel cabinet the cut's just a centimetre across and clotting already. Awkwardly he cleans and dresses it, then sponges the jacket where the blood has stained the lining around the tear, and bins the bloody shirt.

Losing the ID means nothing, makes no difference. People must lose their cards all the time. The handprint, the retinal scan, are all the ID he really needs.

But somewhere along the line he's stumbled, slipped up. Brice thinks he's someone else. Brice wants to know who.

Brice wants the card because it has his photo on it.

Brice plans to ask some questions.

But no one knows Ryan Jackson in here, do they? And Charlie Ross is dead.

In the bunkroom he makes his way past the sleeping figures, undresses, lies down on his side.

Soft snores. Someone mutters. From the room upstairs, a single word, a small thin cry, a whimper. Above his head, dust motes spin in a sliver of light. He breathes them in, and counts.

But there's still Brice's breath against his cheek and Brice's voice, all crooning intimacy—

How did it feel when the tube went down your throat?

More than an hour passes before he sleeps.

Day 14: Tuesday – Day 15: Wednesday

Karla

The first of Ellis's recordings arrives on Tuesday.

Just gone noon a man with a heavy Turkish Cypriot accent phones, demanding to speak to 'lady with Mondeo'. 'You leave package behind!' he announces. 'I keep it for you! I keep it safe!' He sounds both proud and indignant. I'll never know why he uses that accent for our phone calls; his English is as good as mine.

For once I'm glad of the distraction, though it means the usual weaving journey by taxi and bus and Underground and bus again, a weird schizophrenic zigzag across the city and back, this morning's surveillance footage playing in my head all the way.

A view of a street, and Johanssen. One second, two at most, to register the tension in his body, the way his head turns and turns again, before three figures come at him from different angles. The struggle's brief. Johanssen freezes. Someone's got a knife.

A fourth person saunters into the frame. One of the others takes something from Johanssen's jacket and passes it to the newcomer. He glances at the item, pockets it, then steps in close—

Is this it? Is this how it ends?

The man turns away. The others release Johanssen and scatter.

Two more figures run on. One just stares at Johanssen. The other looks around wildly: jerky, edge-of-panic movements.

The clip ends.

The first time I watched it, I unclenched my hands to find my fingernails had made half-moons in my palms.

Don't be a fool. You knew what it was like in there, and so did he.

I replayed the clip. Again Johanssen was seized, again he froze, again the man took the item, then stepped closer and delivered – what? Not a blow. A message? A threat? A kiss?

And once more, but this time when the stranger turned away

from Johanssen, towards the camera, I locked the image and opened the copy of the Program inmate list.

It didn't take me long to find him: the angelic features were unmistakable. His name is Brice, his speciality torture. In his mugshot he's smiling.

Johanssen gave me that name in the derelict pub in Wandsworth. Brice is the man who had him beaten. Brice is Quillan's deputy.

The package waiting for me at the tyre fitters' in Harringay is a small padded envelope with no name on it. I break its seal sitting on the top deck of a bus at a red light on the Charing Cross Road: it contains a data stick, nothing more.

Back at the apartment I check the stick for bugs and trackers before I open its contents. One sound file, titled 'Devlin'.

Mark Devlin, whose card was in Catherine Gallagher's flat.

I've done a sketchy background check. I know about the idyllic moneyed childhood (sailing, riding; the family had a country house in Wales), the public school education (Harrow), the brief flirtation with a medical career (Edinburgh; he lasted only two years), the move into recruitment. Four years now at the helm of his own company, with some success. An image search pulls up a handful of PR shots from first nights, fundraisers, and private viewings in the smaller, more fashionable galleries; three times at Royal Opera House events. In every shot a different beautiful girl is on his arm; not Catherine, though.

Now Ellis has interviewed him.

Ellis's voice first. Surly, with an edge of impatience to it. *'It's late so I'll keep it brief. Catherine Gallagher: how did you know her?'*

I wish I could see Mark Devlin's face. Is he frowning? Racking his brains? Blank? Shocked?

'Well, sir?' The 'sir' for form's sake only; insincere.

'We met at a conference.' Devlin's voice is quiet, slightly husky. *'Prague, two years ago.'* In control too: he hasn't risen to Ellis's baiting. *'I run a medical recruitment business; she was a doctor.'* And then: *'We began a relationship.'*

That wasn't in the file.

But Ellis doesn't even miss a beat. *'And how long did this relationship last?'*

'We met occasionally over a month or so – five or six times.'

'You mind telling me how it ended?'

151

'We were both very busy with work … It just tailed off. I wasn't aware it was public knowledge.' Implicit question: How did you find out?

Ellis blanks it. 'Did you argue?'

'No.'

'You knew she was depressed?'

'No.'

'She was seeing a psychiatrist at the time.'

A brief pause. 'I didn't know that.' It sounds genuine.

'And when she disappeared? You didn't think to go to the police?'

'I hadn't seen her in months.'

'Sure about that? Not even in passing? Another conference?'

'Quite sure.'

'So what was she like?'

'Intelligent – ambitious – committed to her job—'

'Were you representing her professionally, Mr Devlin? As well as—'

'No.'

'She ever discuss becoming a client of yours?'

'No.'

'Ever express any worries, concerns? Any problems at work?'

'No. The last time I saw her she was fine. You said she was depressed? You think she—'

'Any fears for her safety?'

For the first time Devlin sounds genuinely shocked. 'No, absolutely not. What's this about?'

I can almost see Ellis's placid, treacherous blink. Indifferent, as ever. 'Just routine, sir. Just routine.'

'So, Prague. Some doctors' jolly. He's glad-handing the talent, she's all shiny and ambitious. They shag. Then they come back to London and shag some more.' He snorts over the phone. 'Intelligent, ambitious, committed. Christ. Sounds more like a reference, doesn't it? But maybe there was more shagging than chat.' Then he says, 'He didn't do it. Yeah, yeah, I know the statistics, always look at the boyfriend.' Again: 'He didn't do it.'

'Why not?'

'What's the story? They shag, she gives him the push, eleven months later he offs her in a jealous rage?'

'We've only got his word for the timescale. Or the relationship, come to that.'

'Oh yeah? So why would he lie? The girl's gone AWOL; he fesses up to a relationship, he'll know he's putting himself in the frame for murder. That's probably why he kept quiet at the time: 's not good for business, is it? Plus there's the phone records – I did check. Bunch of calls two years ago between his mobile and hers. Starts immediately after the Prague conference, tails off after a few weeks. Not a dicky bird after that: home, mobile or office. Yeah, I know: fact they're not talking doesn't mean he's not obsessing over her. But what's with the lie she told about her sick mother?'

'Maybe she was running away from him.'

'So he's what? Threatening her? Stalkers leave a trail, that's the whole point. Texts on her phone, weird stuff through her letter box. Whatever you might think of that first enquiry, they looked. They'd have found him. No. No. He's all wrong for it.' He pauses. 'The way he talked about her. Like she was someone he hardly knew.'

That's the phrase that echoes in my head long after Ellis is off the line.

Ellis isn't a good cop, but he's a smart one. I trust his instincts on this, even though he doesn't know the truth.

I get up, make coffee, stare out of the window, come back to my desk.

Replay the recording of Mark Devlin's interview.

'Intelligent – ambitious – committed to her job—'

Ellis is right: it's much more like a reference. An odd thing to say about someone you once slept with, but maybe it was one of those brief relationships fuelled by raw chemical attraction and nothing more – burning hot and fast, then burning up: from spark to ashes in a matter of weeks. It happens; I know that from experience.

Or maybe he just likes to play the field: insists he likes women, but doesn't get involved. The lovely girls on his arm in all those photos parade before me: never the same one twice. I know that type too.

I scroll back. Replay again.

'Intelligent – ambitious—'

But no, something's wrong. This man rates intelligence, ambition – they've got him where he is today – but his tone is cool, stepped back, as if he's holding the memory of her at arm's length, as if he doesn't want to remember her at all.

Ellis: *'You knew she was depressed?'* And Devlin: *'No.'* Ellis again: *'She was seeing a psychiatrist at the time,'* and Devlin pauses before he says, *'I didn't know that.'* And in that pause I swear I can hear it:

in Mark Devlin's mind a loose piece has just dropped into place. Something he didn't understand before makes sense now. Something about Catherine Gallagher.

He won't tell Ellis, though. Ellis is a nosy copper. Devlin's type don't talk to them.

So will he talk to me?

But he haunts the same places Charlotte Alton does. He could know me by sight already, we could have mutual friends.

And having Charlotte ask him about Catherine Gallagher, the day after the police have paid a visit? Charlotte Alton is my cover story. She can't risk getting involved in any of this.

Even so, by the time the office workers start to pile into the bars beneath my windows, Charlotte Alton is spending rather longer than usual deciding what dress to wear. She's going out.

The exhibition – in a fashionable East End gallery – is called 'Pleasures of the Flesh'. But anyone hoping for a cheap thrill would be disappointed. The sealed display cabinets are full of meat – animal carcases intricately carved into the shape of luxury consumer items, gadgets and handbags, wristwatches, shoes. Some of the cabinets are refrigerated, but not all; sometimes flies buzz around the rotting flesh, or the exhibits squirm with maggots. The artist, a pale, pudgy young man, stands in a corner silently clutching a beer; an arts journalist and a collector converse across him. Waiters drift blank-faced between the exhibits bearing canapés at shoulder height but only a hardy few are eating. I take a glass of wine which I don't plan to drink: it's just a prop, something for my hands to do. Some of Charlotte's opera companions are here – among them the senior City lawyer, this time accompanied by his lipsticked politician wife – and we make polite conversation, but I'm not really listening. I'm watching the door. So I see the couple as soon as they walk in.

Every straight man in the room, and most of the women, would notice the girl first: the long dark hair, the endless legs, the effortless beauty. But I notice the man, because the man is Mark Devlin.

Grey eyes, pale Celtic skin. The sort of ranginess that looks good in two thousand pounds' worth of Italian tailoring. His hair isn't dark, as it appeared from the online photo, but a deep reddish brown. Already he's snared a waiter. He secures the girl a drink, then leads her across to the corner where the artist skulks. Devlin seems to know both the journalist and the collector. Introductions are made. I turn my head away.

A call to this evening's organisers confirmed he was on the guest list. They thought I was his secretary, just checking.

Another call, and Charlotte Alton was on the guest list too.

Now I immerse myself in conversation again, but my eyes keep hunting out Devlin and his companion. They leave the artist's corner and start to move round the room. I'm circulating too, and on three separate occasions I'm close enough to touch Devlin's arm. Fragments of their conversation drift towards me. He's trying to entertain the girl but she's increasingly fractious. First date, or second? He doesn't know her well. He thought she'd enjoy this, or be impressed by it, but for once he's called it wrong: she thinks it's unpleasant and bizarre, and she's making it obvious. He's mortified. They'll move on soon. I don't have long.

I step into the gallery's lobby and make a call. 'Hello, darling.'

Robbie recovers fast. 'Silver Audi, parked thirty metres from yours, left as you come out of the entrance.'

'That's lovely. Thank you.'

Robbie says, 'You sure about this?'

'We've done it before.'

'Years ago,' he says.

As I return to the party, the girl is heading for the ladies', sullen-faced. For a moment Devlin's alone, staring at a decomposing Louis Vuitton trunk overflowing with entrails. I saunter over to stand beside the same exhibit – glance at him, my standard ice-breaking line ready – when he flashes me a quick ironic grimace and says, 'Yes, I know, bad choice of date.'

As if we've known each other for years, as if we're old friends.

'She's very beautiful,' I say.

'Apparently she's vegetarian.' He looks at me again, curiously. He says, 'Somehow I suspect you're not.'

I laugh. It doesn't feel forced and he takes it as encouragement. He says, 'I know you from somewhere,' and just then the door to the ladies' opens, and the girl emerges, her face set. He sees her, and pulls back. 'I'd better—'

'Of course.' I glance at my watch. 'Enjoy the rest of your evening.' I turn away.

A brief flirtatious exchange between two semi-strangers, over in seconds, but it's all I need for now.

I find Charlotte's friends, make my excuses and deposit my barely touched glass of wine on a tray. I pass Mark Devlin and the girl on the way to the gallery exit. They're by the door, about to leave too: he opens it for me. Our eyes meet briefly and I smile my thanks. The girl ignores me. She's frowning; there's an obvious tension between them. As the door closes behind me a scrap of her speech – just the word 'sick' – escapes into the lobby.

I collect my coat from the attendant, pull out my phone, dial Robbie's mobile. The line connects as I step out into the cold night air.

'OK?'

'OK,' he says. He doesn't sound OK. I end the call.

Further along the street there's a cluster of fashionable bars and clubs – a bass line pumps out from a doorway, and lights spill from a restaurant window – but here I'm in a patch of silence. The pavement's bleak and cold, a bitter wind blasting down between the late-nineteenth-century commercial buildings, the darkened design-group shops, the shuttered advertising agencies. My Merc is parked a little way from the gallery. As I turn towards it the door opens again behind me, and I glance back. Devlin and the girl have followed me out. Her face is still sullen. He takes her arm and begins to walk her up the road, away from me. He's trying to tease her out of her bad mood, though she's resisting, making him work. What's her plan for this evening? An expensive restaurant where she'll sulk over dinner, and then – if she's forgiven him sufficiently – back to his, where he'll have to exert himself again to make up for the evening's bad start.

I've reached the Merc. My palms are sweating, my heart starting to race. *You sure about this?*

Devlin and the girl have stopped under a street light, beside a silver Audi saloon. Devlin has a key fob in his hand. He's smiling; the girl isn't.

Any second—

From nearby a squeal of tyres.

Now.

I step out from the pavement just as the van corners wildly into the street.

Thirty metres away Mark Devlin and the girl turn their heads.

I don't know what happens next. The tyres squeal again and someone shouts but by now I'm on the tarmac, the breath knocked out of me.

By the time I've struggled into a sitting position he's reached me.

He's talking. Asking if I'm all right. My ears are still ringing. 'I'm fine,' I say, but my voice is shaky. I'm out of practice. That was too close.

'Did he hit you?'

'No. Let me get up.'

'You sure? You're very pale.'

I hold out a hand. Dirt from the road is crusted into my palms. 'Please—'

He takes it and helps me up. He doesn't let go.

'He almost ran you over,' he says.

This is what I planned, isn't it? But suddenly he's too close, and the world is moving too fast; I'm hanging on to it by my fingernails. Adrenaline has kicked in, redundantly: my pulse is racing and the street lights seem brighter than they should be, the shadows darker too, squirming and alive. Perhaps he sees it. 'Do you need to sit down? Or some water, maybe? Shall I—'

'Really, I'm OK.'

It's the girl who rescues me, arriving at his side. She doesn't even glance at me. The attention-grabbing, electric beauty she had when she walked into the gallery has lost its charge completely; now she looks cold, and furious.

'You could have been killed,' she says, but not to me. To him.

That's when I notice the Merc. The wing mirror hangs limp from a wire, like a broken hand. I pull myself away from Devlin and shuffle round the car, leaving him and the girl to their muttered conversation – 'stupid' is the only word that reaches me. I touch the damage, gingerly. Close. Very close.

'Your car?' he asks. He's beside me again.

'It's nothing.'

'I'm not sure you should drive.'

'I'm fine,' I say, but now I've started shivering. What's this? Shock?

'Let me drive you home,' he says.

'I can get a cab.'

But he says, 'You know I can't just leave you like this,' as if there's an intimacy between us. As if he'd stay all night.

Heels on the pavement make us both turn. The girl is stalking towards the Audi. He must have given her the key: the indicators wink as the locks disengage. 'I told her to go and get warm,' he says.

But she gets in on the driver's side. A second later the headlights come on and the engine fires; the gears grind sickeningly, then the car lurches away from the kerb and accelerates past us. Behind the wheel, the girl's face is tight and closed. She doesn't look at us.

Mark Devlin watches the tail lights disappear. He breathes out, and shakes his head, and smiles to himself: a complex, layered smile full of irony and self-mockery. Then he turns to me and the smile becomes conspiratorial, as if we've just shared a joke. No, as if we're kids, doing it for a dare, and we just got away with it.

'I need a drink,' I say.

'I don't even know your name,' he says.

'Charlotte.' I offer my hand across the table. 'It's Charlotte Alton.'

His grip's firm and warm but the fingertips are cold from the ice in his glass. 'Mark Devlin.' Then he says, 'That wasn't just a line, you know? I recognise you from somewhere.'

The opera house, probably. Will he work it out? Charlotte Alton's undemanding on the eye, elegant but never glamorous, shunning attention, largely unmemorable. No reason why he'd notice. I shrug. 'I go to a few of these things.' A beat. 'I've wrecked your evening.'

He smiles: that lopsided, ironic smile that lifts only one side of his face. 'And it was going so well.'

'Surely she'll have just gone home?'

'I don't think I ever got her address.'

'Her phone number?'

'I was working up to that.'

'At least the car's fitted with a tracker,' I say.

He glances at me; a tweak of his mouth concedes the point. 'As long as she doesn't wrap it round a lamp post first.'

'What happened?' I ask. 'Back there in the street.'

'You nearly got run over by a van.'

'She said you could have been killed.'

'Really? I thought she was talking to you,' he says. For a second his smile's disingenuous, and then it morphs into something almost serious. 'I'd like to take you out to dinner. Would that be all right?'

I hold up my scraped palms. 'Maybe not tonight.'

'Another night.' That other smile now, the smile that makes us co-conspirators. He has a whole repertoire of smiles, each with a different meaning. I'm starting to collect them. Then he leans forward in his seat. 'Can I have your number?'

I write Charlotte's number on a paper napkin – the digits come out ill formed and blotchy – and present him with it, and he smiles as if I've just made his day.

But I won't wait for him to phone. The next move is mine.

Outside the bar the breeze tugs at my coat. A taxi's passing and I've flagged it down, when he says suddenly, 'The Royal Opera House. We weren't introduced – you wouldn't remember.' Then, softly, almost wistfully, 'At *Götterdämmerung* you wore green. Goodnight, Ms Alton.'

He goes to the opera. I knew that already. And he has some clever trick of recall, a memory for faces, and he only said that in the hope I'd feel singled out, noticed, special—

But he was there the night Johanssen came back. Just coincidence, but it doesn't feel like that. It feels like an omen, and it's left me cold.

As soon as I'm in the cab, I dial Robbie's mobile.

'Everything OK?' I ask.

'Fuck it, there was diesel on the road—'

'I'm fine.'

'And him – fucking idiot.' He won't say more. I have to wait until I'm back at my apartment and logged into the CCTV record for the street outside the gallery to find out what happened.

Mark Devlin and the girl turn their heads. The white van that's just swerved past me rights its course, heading towards them. It's accelerating when Mark Devlin steps off the pavement into its path and raises his hand.

The van swerves again, late. Rocks left and right, but doesn't stop. At the next junction it brakes sharply, dipping on its rear suspension, and turns out of sight.

Devlin stands in the road, his expression locked, neutral, frozen: shocked by what he's just done on instinct. *You could have been killed.* Out of bravado? A belief he's indestructible? I can't tell. Then he blinks as if he's just come out of a trance, turns his head to where I must be lying—

My phone rings: one of the safe lines used for business. I pick up on the second ring.

'Karla?' It's Craigie. Of course: only Craigie would ring at this hour. Has something tipped him off to what happened this evening? But he doesn't sound stern; he sounds disconcerted.

'Laidlaw's bolt-hole – the flat in Ealing? They've found it.'

*

The building's a squared-off modern block in pinkish 70s brick on the corner of a quiet tree-lined street. There are two dozen buttons beside the entryphone. At 7.21 on Wednesday morning, as I park up, a girl in dark trousers and a good coat is holding the front door while a young man in jeans and work boots places a large black holdall in the back of an unmarked van. The man has strong hands: he could be a carpenter. The girl might pass for grieving family but she isn't, and anyway she's too composed, too focused. They're both here to work. The bag they've just put in the car will be a basic SOCO kit: they've dusted the place for prints. They want to know who came here. Though I suspect that only Laidlaw did – that this was a private refuge, shared with no one. In any case there won't be traces. Laidlaw may have looked like he dressed in the dark but he served his apprenticeship in the Cold War, when a casual lapse could get someone killed. I'll bet the place is clean.

My bag is on the passenger seat. I rummage in it, pull out a phone, hit a key, start talking. The girl has registered me. She looks long enough at the car's number plate to memorise it. The young man slams the back doors of the van and they both go back inside. Still I keep my head down, look preoccupied. Chances are I'm being watched.

Craigie didn't want me to come. 'We have the place under observation,' he said. 'You don't need to be there. What would you gain?'

But Craigie doesn't have my track record with these people. With criminals, yes, and with sources, but not with the intelligence community. This is one job I can't delegate, one operation I must see for myself. Are they casual, or serious? Are they tidying up, ticking the boxes, or is there more to it than that? I have to know.

And I'm more than prepared for this. Once I did it all the time. Now, sitting behind the wheel of my anonymous car, talking to no one on the phone, I still get that tick of excitement. *You miss the old life, don't you?*

In any case, Lucas Powell won't be here in person. I've read his file. He's not an ops man, he doesn't do fieldwork: he's sent foot soldiers. For hours they'll have been lifting carpets, emptying cupboards, shaking out food packets, delving into the cistern. Any minute now the floorboards will be coming up.

They're looking for Knox. Looking for me.

They won't find me, though.

Unless they've guessed I'd come?

I turn my head away; my one-sided phone call becomes heated.

Some criminals are drawn to the investigations of their crimes, aren't they? They loiter among the crowds by the police tape; they chat to officers. They may be friendly and helpful – may offer useful local knowledge – or they may simply watch. But some compulsion drives them: they have to be there.

So has Lucas Powell put me into that category? Sitting here, do I fit some profiler's pattern? Has he predicted I'd come?

I press a key, drop the phone onto the passenger seat. Time to go. I'm reaching for the car's ignition when the front door opens and out they come again—

No. The young woman's there, but this time someone else is with her, a man who must have been inside the building all along.

Tall – comfortably over six foot – and slim. Black skin, high cheekbones, good posture, good suit, good shoes. Powell.

He's carrying a sealed cardboard crate.

My breath catches. I force my gaze away and grab the phone from the passenger seat.

Talk. Talk and don't look up.

What's he doing here?

Lucas Powell, the security services' Hercules, fresh out of DC and cleaning up the shit. Doing it himself too: not just sitting behind a desk and waiting for them to bring it to him, but coming out here, watching as they dust the flat—

Removing something.

But there should be nothing here to find. The place should be clean, we counted on it being clean. *Laidlaw was old school. His sort didn't make notes.*

They've gone to a different vehicle, an estate car. Powell rests the crate he carries on the car's roof, reaches for his keys, and as he does so his stare sweeps towards me.

Start the engine. Don't look up. Just drive.

As I pull away from the kerb I force my eyes dead ahead. Even so I'm conscious of how Powell's head turns towards my vehicle. And all the way down the road – long after he's lost to sight between the ranks of parked cars – I daren't look in the mirrors, as if just one glance might betray me.

Craigie was right. *You've made yourself a prize and Powell's out to win it.*

And if he wants to do business?

I controlled every aspect of my relationship with Laidlaw. He never knew who I was or where my information came from. He couldn't even contact me. And he settled for that. Ultimately all that mattered was that the intel was good.

Powell will be different. He isn't a man to take things on trust. He'll want to verify his source. He'll want to know who I am, and however good the intel is, he won't stop searching until he's found me.

Day 15: Wednesday

Johanssen

Wednesday morning. It's the end of his fourth night in the clinic. He's on his bed. Broad daylight outside, but only the faintest chinks of light escape around the blackouts, and the noises in the bunkroom are night noises: soft snores and Vinnie muttering in his sleep. Johanssen doesn't know whether Drill's awake and he doesn't look.

He sits up, reaches for his clothes. Pads the length of the room, past the others, into the kitchen where he dresses.

On the stairs he pauses, listening for movement in Cate's room, but there's nothing.

He puts on his boots in the clinic – the cut on his back itchy under the dressing – and goes out through the waiting room into the daylight.

Crossing the yard he gets the prickling sense of being watched from Quillan's building, but he doesn't turn to look.

Through the gate. He heads right, past the council blocks, aware of the exact moment when the tail slots into place.

He leads them through the Program streets, opening doors and wandering into buildings and out again, pausing at a corner so the tail must stop too and then moving on, heading down alleys and doubling back so their paths almost cross – stopping to look up at a window, a roofline, into a tight little yard tucked between buildings, so that there is no pattern to anything he does.

And once or twice he'd swear there's a second tail, someone moving parallel to the first but not with them; but he never sees them.

Brice's crew again? But Brice will be doing the rounds with his ID card, thrusting his picture under people's noses, *Who is he then?*

He won't find anything. Charlie Ross is dead.

The news of the attack broke last night. Riley had sent him out to the storeroom to get more gloves and when he came back he knew, just from their faces: frightened curiosity from Vinnie, knowingness

163

from Riley, speculation from Drill – Drill must have heard about the wound; he'd have liked to watch the knife go in. Only Cate's face was blank.

At last he works his way round to the workshop on Houghton Street. As he crosses the margin of rubble that separates the building from the surrounding streets, two men stop at the edge of the cleared ground, observing him. He looks beyond them for another face: the second tail. He doesn't see it.

The door he opens leads into a poky warren of small damp rooms. Through them, and he's in what must have been the main machine hall. There's a camera here somewhere. Perhaps he's being watched. By Karla? And who else? A large metal-framed window has had every pane smashed out of it: broken glass crunches underfoot. Above his head, a beam spans the width of the structure. A pulley hangs from it, strung with chains. In a circular cut-out in the brickwork, a fan creaks and sighs. Caged safety lights have been fixed up on the walls, linked by rubber-sheathed all-weather cabling. The bulbs glow faintly in the grey daylight. The surveillance camera's high up in a corner. He steps back out of its line of sight. It doesn't move to follow him.

He'll have to deal with that.

In the middle of the floor there's a metal plate, three foot by five; he kicks it idly but it doesn't shift, crouches briefly – five seconds only, any more would be too much – then straightens and moves on. The bolts are dirty and beginning to rust; no one's touched them for months.

To one side there's a smaller second workshop. A few sick-looking pigeons are roosting in there: as he walks in they rise with a clatter of wings and wheel away overhead, out through ragged gaps in the roof. A pair of prefab offices are stacked one on top of the other. They're beginning to collapse in on themselves, the angles out of true, the walls folding like the walls in a house of cards.

He goes back to the main hall, and there she is.

She's muffled up in a big coat, by the door. She's watching him.

The second tail: not Brice's crew, but her. She's good; better than he'd have expected.

She tilts her head. Her gaze travels up, across the scarred walls, following the chains to the crossbeam and the creaking fan, then down again.

'What are you doing here?' she asks.

'Just … looking.'

She doesn't say anything to that. She wraps her arms around herself – she must be cold, despite the coat – and walks out into the next chamber, where the prefab offices sit. He doesn't follow. There are faint sounds, a scrape, something shifting, then she comes back.

'Quillan's men still outside?' he asks.

She nods, chin up, appraising him. 'Having a fag.'

'I made two,' he says.

'It's usually two. They were wondering if they should come in. I told them not to.'

'No one follows you?'

'Why should they? I'm Quillan's doctor. Who's going to touch me?'

She looks up again, at the walls, the chain, the creaking fan. She's still standing like that, head tilted back, when she says, 'Why did Brice want your ID card?' And when he doesn't answer: 'Don't you know? Brice thinks you're lying. Doesn't believe your story.' She drops her gaze, stares straight at him. 'Want to know why?'

He shrugs.

'Yes you do. Quillan enjoys *excellent co-operation* with the authorities. He asked them about you. Who you were. What kind of man you are.' A pause. 'They told him what you did.'

Is he blown? How much do they know now? He blanks his expression, says nothing.

'She was your girlfriend, wasn't she? The woman.' Her face is still, mask-like. Her eyes glitter. Then, savagely: 'Did you love her? Because Quillan said she took a long time to die. Well? Are you going to tell me it's not true?'

He shakes his head. 'No.'

'And the man?'

'I know what I did.'

She stands there, staring at him, moving her head a little to one side, then back again, as if she's trying to sense him across ten feet of distance.

Then she says, 'But you're not like that now,' and she says it as if she doesn't understand.

He says nothing.

'What changed you? You repented? Got God? Or you're not

Ryan Jackson at all; though if you're not it's one fuck of a cover story to pick.'

She gives him one more look, then turns away and walks the length of the workshop, the soles of her shoes crunching on the broken glass. When she reaches the cover on top of the tank she stops and touches the edge of it, lightly, with her toe; then steps over it.

At the far wall she turns back, arms still locked around her, but something has shifted in her face.

'You still think about them,' she says. 'Is that why you can't sleep? Is that why you walk around like this?'

'No.'

'So what's keeping you awake then?' Her voice hardens. 'That burn on your shoulder, the electric iron, that's a childhood scar. Who did that? Mum's boyfriend? Dad?'

She's still digging, still trying to make him snap, but that particular pain's been out of its box so many times he can look at it now without flinching. 'Dad,' he says. 'He drank.'

Ryan Jackson's father drank too, according to Karla's file. Though Jackson has different scars.

'You drink?' she demands.

'No.'

'But you did then. When you—' She stops; and for a handful of seconds after that she looks at him, just looks, and he lets her.

At last she says, 'It isn't in you, is it? You don't carry it around. You've forgiven yourself, then.'

'No. I just – I just do the best I can. Try to do it right.'

'Do what?'

'Everything.'

'And it works for you, does it? Doing it right. That makes it ... *better*?'

Another of those long slow cold looks, but then her mouth curls – irony, contempt? 'Is that what I'm doing?' she says. There's a biting edge to her voice. 'Is that what you think the clinic's about? Doing it right, doing good? It's what I do, it *passes the time.*'

'You were a doctor,' he says.

She makes a small soft *hah* noise. 'Oh yes. And you know what? Every life I saved was proof of how clever I was, how I could beat the system. And I was *good*, all right. Better than good. I was on another level – up there, making decisions ... It was hard and it was technical and I loved it. And my patients *might as well have been another species.*'

She stops. Up above, the fan groans and rattles. Somewhere outside an engine drones, a snatch on patrol.

She says, 'I'm going now.'

But she turns back at the doorway. 'About Brice.'

Johanssen says, 'He's just looking for an excuse.'

'And if he looks hard enough he'll find one, won't he?' Suddenly she says, 'Do you hate him?'

'Should I?'

'After what he tried to do to you? And what he'll still do, the first chance he gets—'

'Brice doesn't kill,' he says.

'What he does will be worse.'

For a moment she holds his gaze. Then she's gone, the sound of her footsteps across the rubble fading out to nothing.

He stands very still in the workshop, listening to the creak of the fan.

Quillan's spoken to the authorities. And Quillan knows the man before him isn't acting like Ryan Jackson should act. But he can live with the discrepancy for now, because he has other plans.

Brice is a sick fuck. You give him something to focus on. He's just the latest in a long line. How far does it stretch back? As far as Charlie Ross?

But Brice doesn't kill, and Charlie Ross is dead.

Sully, the man's name was. If he had a first name, Johanssen never heard it. An army mate, a Scouser Johanssen had served with in Iraq and who was to die at a checkpoint in Helmand, put them in touch. They met in a pub in Elephant and Castle. Sully worked in security, was looking for a bit of extra muscle for a job. A few questions, then he said, 'All right if we go for a drive? Someone you need to meet.'

The M4 out of London, then the A404. Dark by then, and raining softly, the windscreen wipers squeaking against the glass, Sully snatching glances at him all the way.

Through Marlow, all middle-class middle-England quaintness, red brick and tiled roofs, a spindly church spire. Across a suspension bridge, and out the other end. The buildings ran out and the ground rose. A turn into a private road – narrow, edged with big houses overlooking the river on the left: a white place like a miniaturised castle, and a vast black-and-white timbered house.

They stopped in front of a pale house with gables. Ten o'clock on a late summer evening: traffic noise from the main road, and a train passing somewhere nearby, and a bird still singing.

A woman opened the door to them. She looked at Sully – 'He said you were coming.' Not at Johanssen. He might have been invisible.

Sully led him across the hall to a long room, and there they waited, in silence, staring out at the damp summer night beyond French windows, the steps going down to the lawn and the river running by, Johanssen listening to muffled creaks, voices elsewhere, and then footsteps, several men coming closer – a murmur of conversation, 'Yes, very good' – but when the door opened only one of them came in: sixties, and tall, six six or six seven, in slacks and a business shirt, a gold watch on his wrist, the faint smile of a man who knows that whatever joke he tells, everyone around him will laugh.

The man said to Sully, 'So who's this?' and Sully said, 'He's the one I told you about.'

The man looked at Johanssen keenly. He asked, with only the smallest hint of threat, 'And what do you want, eh?'

Johanssen said, 'I want to work,' and killed the urge to add the word *sir*.

'What can you do?'

'Whatever I have to,' Johanssen said. Because this was going to be his life from now on, wasn't it? This was all that was left.

The man nodded and went out. As he passed Sully, Johanssen heard him say, 'Use him.'

That was Charlie Ross, though he didn't know it then.

They wouldn't meet again.

Within months Ross would be under arrest because of what happened to Cunliffe in that farmhouse. A year and he'd be in prison. Another four years, give or take: the Program. Another three months, and he'd be dead.

When he gets back to the clinic Riley's sitting in a chair in the main room. He looks Johanssen over, doesn't smile.

'I heard,' he says. 'What you're down for?' Nods to himself. 'Well. You get a clean slate here, like everyone else. But you touch *her*—' He stops, choked on his anger.

Then he shakes his head, gets up and walks out.

Day 15: Wednesday

Karla

Wednesday morning. The surveillance feeds again.

A brick wall and a broken window: the workshop. At first nothing happens. Then a man walks into shot. He's looking up at something I and the camera can't see, looking with an intent, practical kind of focus. Then he stops, and turns, and glances up into the lens just once, and the image of Simon Johanssen freezes onto my retina.

He moves around the workshop. Crouches briefly in the middle of the floor, straightens. Walks out of sight. Comes back—

It's in his face: someone else is there now, below the camera, out of shot.

His mouth moves, soundlessly. A shadow clips the very edge of the frame, then vanishes – they've gone. He doesn't follow. He waits, his face closed and still, and a moment later they come back.

This time I see her.

How many times have I looked at her photo? And still I might not have recognised her in the poor light: the gaunt pale woman with dirty-blonde hair, bundled up in a jacket several sizes too big for her, her arms wrapped around herself protectively. When she lifts her head there's something dead about her expression.

Has he arranged to meet her here so she knows the place? So next time – and it could be any day now – she won't be afraid?

They're talking again. What are they saying? I lean in towards the screen. Impossible to read. But they're talking. That has to be good, that has to be progress: making her talk, making her tell him what she did and why.

The talking stops. She turns and walks away. Johanssen's face tells me he's alone again.

What did she say to him?

Since then I've stayed by the phone, waiting for a call. It's never come.

Wednesday, late afternoon. Craigie arrives, briefcase in hand, as I'm getting ready to go out.

'What was in that crate, Karla?' The one Powell removed from Laidlaw's Ealing flat this morning.

'I don't know yet.'

'Papers. Has to be. Which means Laidlaw kept records.'

'Records of what? We sanitised everything, Craigie. You know we did. There was nothing to find.' Because that's what I have to tell myself, and him, until we know otherwise. Panicking will get us nowhere.

He glances at my clothes. Discreet dress, minimal jewellery, heels; Charlotte Alton's wardrobe. 'Out tonight?'

'Supper.'

He nods. *At least that's something.* I'm reinforcing my cover. And he likes me to be Charlotte; finds it safer. Supper can't be bad.

He doesn't know who with.

I didn't know if Mark Devlin would be free. I phoned at short notice, on the off chance, even though it's probably too soon. 'Busy tonight?'

When I reach his office in Moorgate it's gone six, and dark. The building's massive atrium spills a wash of golden light across the pavement and the office workers hurrying home. Inside it's a cavern, the triple-height space broken only by glinting perspex sculptures suspended on wires from the ceiling and rotating serenely, like giant Christmas-tree decorations. By the window, ugly modern seats surround coffee tables made from single blocks of limestone, artfully strewn with newspapers in half a dozen languages. Security guards in Armani flank the floor. CCTV cameras track me all the way to the reception desk.

The building houses half a dozen high-end businesses, and their names are displayed behind the desk: a firm of tax specialists, another of corporate lawyers, a stockbroker, a computer security company, a risk management outfit, and Mark Devlin Recruitment.

When I tell the polished girl on duty that Mr Devlin is expecting me, she presents me kindly but firmly with a plastic visitor tag on a ribbon, as if it's a gift I shouldn't dare refuse, and directs me towards the waiting area by the window. The chairs are as uncomfortable as they look.

Two minutes later Mark Devlin walks out of the lift, coat on and briefcase in hand. When he spots the visitor tag he takes it off me gently – 'We won't be needing that' – steps over to the desk, smiles blindingly at the girl on duty, hands her the tag and walks me out of the door.

'She thought I was here for a meeting. Do I look like a doctor?'

'Consultant neurosurgeon,' he says. 'Definitely. Are you hungry?'

And right on cue a voice behind us says, 'Mr Devlin.'

I know the voice; Devlin doesn't, not immediately. He turns towards it. Ellis is closing in fast. 'Mr Devlin … I was hoping I'd catch you.'

Devlin shoots a look at me. Am I going to witness something he'd rather I didn't? He says to Ellis, 'Excuse me, this is hardly—'

Ellis ignores him. 'Just a small thing: the eighth of December, a year ago – you couldn't tell me where you were that evening? We're trying to account for the movements of everyone who knew Dr Gallagher, on the night she disappeared.' He glances at me – a glance you'd give a stranger – then back at Devlin: patient, stony-faced. You'd never guess he doesn't give a damn.

Devlin says tightly, 'Offhand I can't remember but …' But he'll co-operate with the police. He has to. Ellis is virtually daring him not to.

Devlin's fished out his smartphone and he's thumbing keys when Ellis says, 'It's all right, Mr Devlin, it doesn't have to be now. But if you'd call me with it? You've still got my card?'

'Of course,' Devlin says. His voice is still taut, but he's confused too. Why has Ellis so suddenly backed down?

'Well.' Ellis nods at Devlin, then at me; blank again. 'Have a lovely evening.'

We make to move past him. But he's not quite done: he holds his place on the pavement and when I step round him he shifts suddenly, forcing me to brush against him. But Devlin's half a pace ahead, and I don't think he sees.

The place Mark Devlin takes me to has a dining room on the second floor. He knows the maître d', and we get a table by the window. Beyond the triple glazing, the rush-hour street below is a homeward crawl of brake lights and exhaust, but up here the only sounds are the tinkle of a piano, the murmur of voices. The lights are a low honey-yellow.

We talk. At first about last night: my bruises, the state of his car, the girl, the exhibition, why he stepped out in front of a speeding vehicle ('He could have killed you,' he says, as if that's a reason, ignoring the fact he could have died too), the ridiculousness of it all ... Between us we turn it into a funny story, a shared adventure we can look back on and laugh at. The waiter arrives to take our orders, and after that Devlin asks me about myself, though the questions are all quick-fire, offbeat, elliptical: when I last went abroad, where did I go? What can't I live without? What do I like most about the place where I live? When I dream, what do I dream of? I answer fast, dodge the supplementaries and throw the whole lot back at him. But all the time my head's full of different questions – *What do you know about Catherine Gallagher? Why was everything you said about her cold? And what suddenly made sense to you, the moment Ellis mentioned the psychiatrist?* – except that I don't get the chance to ask.

My steak arrives bloody, with a knife sharp enough for surgery. He's ordered grilled fish on the bone, which he dissects efficiently, prising the flesh from the skeleton with tiny delicate cuts, talking all the while, drawing out my opinions, making me laugh.

When we've finished he sits back in his chair. One finger idly rubs the stem of his wine glass. His hands are strong and masculine, the nails square-cut and very clean. In the low light his hair has bright strands of amber in it, like fine hot wire.

'And now the other question,' he says, and he's serious.

'What question's that?'

'The one you haven't asked. A police officer stops me in the street ...'

'You might not want me to.'

Because you always give them the chance to back out, always. They have to remember afterwards that talking was their choice, not yours.

For a moment he's silent: staring at his glass, rubbing its stem, picking up the hum of its vibration. Then he says, 'Two years ago I had a brief relationship – I met her at a conference, she was a doctor. It lasted a month ... ran out of steam – you know.' He pauses. 'Eleven months later she disappeared. Walked out of her job, vanished. Never seen again. No one knows what happened.'

'But that would have been over a year ago.' He nods. 'So why are they asking you now?'

He shrugs. 'I suppose they're re-interviewing everyone she knew.

172

We're all potential suspects.' He grimaces – no humour in his expression. 'The inspector told me she was seeing a psychiatrist. He said she was depressed.'

'Then surely they must think—'

'She killed herself. I know.'

'Is that what you think happened?'

Another hesitation before he answers. 'I'm not sure. She was very steely, very ... *impressive*.' He shakes his head. 'I never saw it coming.' And he says it in a way that lifts the hairs on my neck, though I don't know why.

'Not at all?'

'No. But what do I know?' Another of those complicated expressions. 'Half a dozen evenings, spread over a month – how much can you learn about someone in that time?'

I don't know why, but I think of Johanssen. 'Sometimes a lot.'

'With some people, maybe. Not Catherine.'

But he's holding back, I know he is. 'You don't think she killed herself.'

He glances at me, then back to his glass. Another pause. He's weighing up his answer. 'Sometimes people do just want to vanish. People who no longer want the lives they have. Just walk away, and leave it all behind.'

'So she no longer wanted her life? Or there was something in it she couldn't live with any more.'

His gaze comes back to me. I've said too much.

Then he says, 'I think that she was capable of things other people aren't. I don't mean clever things, though she was clever. I mean her boundaries weren't set up like other people's. So when she disappeared—' He stops.

'You thought she'd done something? What?'

He shakes his head. 'It's just a feeling.' And I know we've hit the limit.

Another glance at me. 'You find all this intriguing, don't you?' But he says it sadly.

He takes his women as he finds them, doesn't he? An opportunist who acts like a gentleman throughout, provides good company and uncomplicated sex and something that might pass for intimacy; who doesn't ask tricky questions, doesn't want to own the women he sleeps with, won't make promises he doesn't intend to keep ... Suddenly I'm back outside the gallery under the too-bright street lights, and he's saying, *I can't just leave you like this …* Did he look at Catherine Gallagher like that? And did she think, why not? Something quick and meaningless, to satisfy an appetite? To help her forget what she'd done?

And now a police officer's stopping him in the street, questioning him about her, making him feel like he's a suspect; making him remember, too, that sense of something dark in her that he didn't want to understand.

I never saw it coming. But he did, didn't he?

We order coffee and loiter over it. He tells stories of his own, funny stories in which he portrays himself as a hapless idiot. We make each other laugh. At last we ask for the bill and then argue over who'll pay; in the end we split it. When he walks me outside it's raining, a light misty rain like a memory of childhood seaside holidays, and we huddle under his umbrella to wait for a cab; his shoulder is warm against my cheek and I can smell his aftershave, a discreet whisper of ozone laced with something darker.

Mark Devlin: corporate headhunter, womaniser, man about town. And Catherine Gallagher's ex. But also: a man who doesn't believe his own publicity, whose smiles have their own complex vocabulary, who steps in front of speeding vehicles. I like him more than I thought I would. More than I thought I'd allow myself to … Just then he turns his head towards me and murmurs, 'Or we can go on somewhere else?' When I glance up he's smiling, and this smile's like a shared secret, it whispers, *Come on, this will be fun …*

I think of all those girls pictured on his arm, and I understand.

He isn't a beautiful man, with his imperfect features and his irregular smile. But there's something bracing about him: being with him is like standing on the edge of a sea cliff on a windy day – breathe in too deeply and you feel dizzy—

A voice close by says, 'Mark?'

A woman has hesitated a few feet away: early thirties, discreetly well dressed, delicately lovely. 'How funny,' she says, 'seeing you here.' Her voice has a silvery quality to it, an artificial brightness that doesn't fit with the searching look she gives him. Then she glances at me and smiles, though in the second between the glance and the smile there's a sliver of cold assessment, less than the thickness of a knife blade, and I know I'm standing where she wants to be.

Devlin says to her smoothly, 'Anna, this is Charlotte. Charlotte Alton. A friend from the opera.'

'Hello,' I say, and we all smile; but the smiles ring false, and when she excuses herself and leaves, he visibly relaxes.

He glances down at me and says, 'Anna and I go way back.' As if that explains it all. But she's thrown him off his stride, the moment's gone, and he knows it.

I'm in the taxi when Ellis phones. 'Got what you wanted?'

'Not really.' It's a half-lie. Now I know what piece dropped into place the moment Ellis said the word 'psychiatrist' to Devlin: not that she was depressed, not that, but broken, broken in ways that had made her dangerous—

'Told you so,' he says.

'And that brush pass was poor.'

'Really? You seemed to enjoy it.' He hangs up.

Back at the apartment I take out the stick that Ellis passed to me in the street. The sound file on this one is titled 'Roberts'.

This time the background noises are pub noises. Not a raucous evening shout but a soft blur of voices, piped music, the clink of glasses and cutlery. It sounds like lunchtime in a gastropub in one of London's middle-class enclaves, all scrubbed tables and leather sofas.

'So how would you describe Catherine Gallagher?' Ellis.

And then another voice – cultured, careful, educated: 'Oh, highly intelligent. Reliable. Hard-working. Good with technically difficult cases. She had an interest in research – she might have done something special, if . . .' His voice trails off. If she'd lived.

A flick through the files has given me the speaker's name: Aylwyn Roberts, consultant anaesthetist, fifty-three years old, father of two, and Catherine Gallagher's last boss.

Ellis says, 'She a good doctor?'

'Very knowledgeable. Very focused. Very committed. In her own way.'

'And what way was that?'

'Precise. Careful. Determined.'

'Patients liked her?'

'Most of our patients are heavily sedated. You save your bedside manner for the families. And the families liked her. She had confidence. Authority. They felt secure with her. They had every reason to. I can't fault her professionally.'

Ellis jumps in on that. *'What about personally?'*

A hesitation from Roberts. I wait for an echo of Mark Devlin's comments – the sense of darkness, something broken in her ...

'She was a pleasant colleague. A little distant, sometimes.' The strain's creeping into his voice. *'A private person.'*

But he doesn't say more than that.

Roberts hadn't known she was seeing a psychiatrist; had only found out when the police arrived. *'I know, I know, we should have spotted it. Heaven knows, depression isn't uncommon among doctors. Even when nothing's said, you can usually sense it: the lack of engagement, the feeling of being ... unsupported. But not with her. That was how she was. Private. Closed. Anything could have been going on.'* A pause. *'Even when she sought treatment she made sure it stayed out of her medical records. She didn't want anyone to know. The effort that must have taken, to seem normal, to keep pretending ...'*

'Why would she do that?'

'There's no stigma attached to mental illness in the police force? I congratulate you. The medical profession's different. We all like to think we can cope. We don't want to admit it when we can't.'

'And it would have affected her career, wouldn't it? If people had known about the depression.'

A sigh. *'Officially it should make no difference.'*

'But it does.'

'But people think it does.'

'And she was ambitious?'

'Her career was important to her, very important. Add to that, the fact that she was a perfectionist: of course she covered it up. Anything else would have been an admission of failure.'

'When you say perfectionist ...'

'She set high standards for herself. Prided herself on never making mistakes.'

'Good for her patients.'

'Yes. But hard for her.' He seems to think about that for a moment. *'Maybe that was part of the problem. It's an ICU. People die. Despite your best efforts, they die.'*

'She had problems with patients dying?' Ellis asks sharply. *'Any particular patient?'*

'No one patient in particular.' A pause, as if he's struggling to explain. *'As doctors we like to feel we're in control, but we're not, even with the best will in the world. Losing a patient reminds you of that.'*

'So she needed to be in control.'

'Yes. Maybe suicide's the ultimate expression of that? The only way she could stay in control.' Then he says, 'I saw the picture from the CCTV, you know. I still think of her leaving home that evening. As if she was just going on shift. But she wasn't.' Another pause. Is he shaking his head? 'I hope you find her, I really do. I don't like the idea of her lying out there somewhere. But it's like her: not wanting to be found. It's like her.'

A long pause, then Ellis says, 'She asked for time off work. She told you her mother was sick. Anything unusual about that?'

'I knew her mother had health problems.'

'She seemed worried?'

'She seemed ... a little agitated. But she was very diligent; she took her responsibilities seriously. That was what I put it down to: the fact that she was asking people to cover for her, at extremely short notice. Of course I realised afterwards, she was – well.' Aylwyn Roberts' voice fades slightly; perhaps he's turned his head away. 'She must have been planning it then.'

But he saw no change in Catherine's behaviour in the weeks before. Because she didn't know what was coming? Or because she did, but kept it hidden?

And then at last, the big question from Ellis: 'Can you think of anyone who might have wanted to harm her?'

Roberts sounds appalled. 'You're suggesting that someone—' He breaks off.

'Was there anyone who might have felt anger towards her? Who might have had a motive for hurting her?'

A silence. Background noises filter into the gap: plates being stacked, cutlery gathered, laughter from another table.

Roberts says, 'You've found a body.'

'No.'

'But you think—'

'We're just taking a look at the case from other angles.' Another silence. Ellis tries again: 'Maybe a patient died, the family found it hard to accept, they felt she was to blame—'

The ugly death I still haven't managed to find.

Roberts says, 'There's nothing.'

'You quite sure about that?'

'Absolutely sure.'

Ellis says, 'Well, if you think of anything ...' He must be handing over his contact details. 'Thanks for seeing me.'

There's the faintest of buzzes. Ellis's phone? Must be. A brief pause; maybe an apologetic grimace to Roberts? Then Ellis says to the person on the phone, '*So what is it this time?*' and immediately the recording cuts out, but not before I've realised the track in the background is Miles Davis, 'So What' from *Kind of Blue*.

He was talking to me.

Sunday lunchtime, I called him to ask if he would question Catherine Gallagher's colleagues. But he'd already started.

'How many, Ellis? How many of her colleagues have you spoken to since Sunday morning?'

He barely hesitates before he says, 'The lot,' and it's like a challenge.

'The lot.' Of course. It doesn't take much with Ellis. One sniff of Catherine Gallagher's case – one hint of my interest – was enough for someone as hungry, as ambitious, as he is. He believes Catherine Gallagher was murdered and he wants the collar, and he wants to make sure he's one step ahead of me so I can't stop him getting it. 'And you were going to tell me when?' I ask.

'I'm telling you now, aren't I?'

'I want those recordings. All of them.'

'You'll get them,' he says. 'I'm done with them. Waste your time, God knows I had to.' There's an edge of bitterness in his voice: almost accusatory. 'Interviewed fucking everyone in that unit, and you know what? I got nothing. She wasn't a pain, she wasn't a bitch, but not one of them set foot in her flat, not once. Oh, there was the odd drink in a pub, the odd movie, but that's all. Parties, she'd turn up, make polite conversation but she'd be the first to leave and she was always sober. No one got close.'

'But what about—'

'The job? She was married to it. And she was good at it. There's nothing against her.'

'You're sure?'

'You told me to look for medical negligence, right? Suspicious deaths, grieving family, someone with a grudge? So I did. You know what I got? No complaints, no rumours, no gossip, not even one anonymous letter. And no hushed-up scandal either, not a whisper. Yeah, people died on her watch – she was a doctor in an ICU, course they died: at the same rate they die in any other ICU in the country. I did check the figures, Karla, I'm not stupid. So who'd wanna harm her? Some random nutter? Or a serial killer maybe—' his voice takes on the twisted brightness of sarcasm '—I could do with a serial killer, it'd look good on the CV.' Then the sarcasm drops out: his tone's got that accusing edge to it again. ''Cept you're telling me someone had motive. Which means this isn't random, it's premeditated. So there's a whole truckload of shit I haven't even got a sniff at yet. And I'm not getting any clues from you, am I? Why'd you put me on this, Karla? There's no body, there's no suspects—'

'There's something wrong with her disappearance.'

'Oh, and that's it, is it? What, like a hunch?'

'Yes,' I say tightly, 'like a hunch. What about the psychiatrist, Graves? Or have you already had a chat with him, too?'

'No,' Ellis says with heavy false patience, 'I haven't. He's next.'

If Mark Devlin could see what Catherine was capable of, then surely Graves could too.

But Ellis won't know what questions to ask. And I can't risk telling him what I know. I can't have Ellis running on ahead of me – I can't risk him finding out what's behind all this before I do, and especially I can't risk him lighting on a trail that leads back to Johanssen.

'Fine,' I say. 'I'm coming with you.'

Ellis says, 'You're *what*?'

After I've got him off the line I go back into the main room, to the big windows overlooking the dock and the office blocks.

Up here I'm safe – separate, isolated, looking down on everyone else. But now I'm going, in the company of a copper, in broad daylight, to interview an expert witness. *You must be mad.*

Isn't that why I brought Craigie in, thirteen months ago? To keep myself away from all this? To keep myself safe?

One mistake and it could all unravel. Still, I'm going.

I feel as if I'm one of Dr Gallagher's cases and I've just been woken from a drug-induced coma. I'm not going back to sleep just yet.

Day 15: Wednesday – Day 16: Thursday

Johanssen

Wednesday night: another night spent cleaning and strapping and splinting, pumping chests, breaking up fights. Riley runs triage. Drill pads around the room, eyes wide and empty, barely speaking, never engaging with anyone. Vinnie fetches and mops up; he's still talking about getting out.

Two dead tonight: a heart attack and a suicide – the last, a young woman whose skin was riddled with old track marks. She'd opened her wrists. She died just inside the clinic door, a snapshot of a brown-eyed toddler in her slack fingers. Cate's eyes have a flat hard light in them, and Riley's watching her too much.

Riley, standing outside the clinic as the morning ambulances pull away – smoking steadily, remorselessly, eyes dead ahead – says, 'She was a mess when I found her. Complete mess.

'It's what happens with the girls especially. They come in here, they don't always know what's what, where's safe. It was night, gates closed, patrols all tucked up indoors, and there she was just wandering around, out of it …' He shakes his head. 'First I thought someone had messed with her, but it wasn't that. It was something else … like, psychological. I dunno.'

Riley turns to his cigarette again, takes a drag.

'Anyway, couldn't leave her, not like that. I was in with Quillan so I brought her here. Stuck her in a room, looked after her, kept the nutters off her … She didn't snap out of it. Weeks it went on for. Wasn't talking, wasn't hardly eating. Sitting there with this look on her face. Christ knows what had happened to her.

'I asked around. Went up to the Women's Area, even got a couple of the girls to come down and take a look at her … Nothing. No one knew her. It's like she'd just popped up out of nowhere.'

'Quillan ask the screws?'

It's the first thing he's said, and Riley gives him a sharp sidelong glance, as if the question isn't his to ask. 'If he did, he's never said.'

'Then one night they brought a bloke in, one of Quillan's. Someone'd swung at him with a metal post, crushed his throat, the guy's blue. Needed a tracheotomy, you know, hole in the windpipe, put a tube in, anything'll do, biro, anything. Years since I done one of them but it's night, gates are closed, so I've got a blade and I've got my bit of biro and my hands are fucking shaking. And she's there, and I'm about to make the cut and she goes, "No." And she takes the blade and she just does it, right there – makes the incision, puts the tube in like it's nothing, like she does it every day. Doesn't talk about it, doesn't say how she knows what to do, but two hours later she eats her first proper meal.

'Next night they bring in someone else, somebody's mate. Word's got round, see? And she starts to talk about this guy, about how to treat him. Next day she asks for some paper. She makes a list: all the stuff we needed for this place. And she wants Quillan to get it all for her. Which he did, course, cos then he's got his own private clinic.'

'Hearts and minds,' Johanssen says.

'Hearts and minds. But what the fuck, clinic kept her going. You seen the marks on the wall? She counts the ones she saves.' Then with another swift sideways glance: 'You know why I just told you that? So you understand what she's been through. You understand why your life's worth precisely nothing, compared to hers. You got that?'

Johanssen nods.

For a moment Riley keeps on looking at him, as if there's some test he has to pass … At last he turns away.

He says, 'Cate thinks it's like a penance. Why you're working here. I don't buy it. You're a bit too steady for that. No, it's like a purpose. Like a resolve. I can see that in you.'

'I told you, I'm—'

'Yeah, you're making yourself useful, I got that. And you think it's safer being under Quillan's nose than somewhere out of sight, though you got that wrong.'

For a few moments after that neither of them speaks. Riley finishes one cigarette, lights another from the butt, treads the old one out.

Johanssen says, 'She said she killed someone.'

'She tell you that?'

He nods.

'She tell you why?'

Johanssen shakes his head. 'She tell you?'

Riley says, 'She got called to some house, and there was this guy there, and she was supposed to be looking after him but she killed him. That's all I know.'

They both stare across the compound, towards the fence and the council block. Beyond the wire, a snatch crawls down the street.

Riley says softly, 'You know what it's like. You do something and it fucks you up for a bit and then you deal with it somehow, cos you have to. Like you did – because you did, didn't you? Not her. With her it's never stopped. She killed that guy once and she's been killing him ever since.'

Later, when he comes down with his boots ready to go out, Cate's in the clinic at her usual counter, cleaning surgical tools with a brutal, mechanical precision, her mouth tight and pinched.

He says, 'I'm going out,' because it's the only thing he can think of.

She doesn't say a word.

Outside, Brice's crew are waiting in the compound yard.

They've spotted him: Yellow Teeth sniggers and murmurs something that he doesn't catch, and someone else laughs, but they don't move to follow him. Maybe they're waiting for Brice, gearing up for another day spent doing the rounds with Johanssen's ID card: throwing their weight around, smacking heads, demanding a name.

He steps outside the gate. Twenty yards on, the tail slots into place.

When the time comes – when he leaves with Cate beside him – they'll try to follow. So today he looks for blind spots, for places where he can hide, lose them, double back.

After an hour he returns to the compound.

He's pulling his boots off in the clinic when there's a telltale prickling in his neck and on instinct he looks towards the door to the waiting room. No one comes in, but the feeling doesn't go. He has to open the door to the mortuary (damp stains, cardboard boxes, a few body bags), then the one to the side room. The metal cots are empty. He almost misses her.

She's curled up fully dressed on a blanket in a corner, knees drawn up to her chest, arms embracing her shoulders, cuddling herself against the cold. She's asleep.

In those few seconds he sees all the details. Every strand of her dirty-blonde hair, the down on her cheek, the little pink half-moon at the base of her thumbnail. The dark shadows beneath her eyes, like bruises. Every individual eyelash.

He withdraws silently, without waking her.

Up in the bunkroom he undresses, lies down.

You do something and it fucks you up for a bit and then you deal with it—

Eight years fold to nothing.

There were three of them in the car that picked him up that day, all Charlie Ross's men. He knew they were going to visit someone called Cunliffe, though on the way there they mostly referred to him as 'the cunt' or – Sully thought he was being especially clever – 'the Cunt of Monte Cristo'. 'Cunt Dracula,' said another, and they were off: winding each other up, like footie fans off to a local derby, ready for a bit of action.

He was an ordinary man, Cunliffe: forties and overweight, sweating into a cheap shirt on a sultry summer day, in an office with the name of a cab firm on the door. He was alone.

They put him in the car, wedged between Johanssen and another man. Cunliffe tried talking, then pleading, but no one answered, and he stopped.

The farmhouse was in the middle of nowhere. No cars in the yard, no livestock. The only machinery, a hay rake paralysed by rust. They drove the car into one of the barns and pulled Cunliffe out – by now his shirt was sodden – and took him into the house.

They showed him the room with its plastic-sheeted floor, and he shat himself.

Sully and the other two took Cunliffe into the room and locked the door, leaving Johanssen in the corridor, on watch, and that's where he stood for too long, listening as the pleading turned to screams, then something else, and telling himself, *This is what your life is now, this is what you've got to be able to deal with, or they were right all along, weren't they?*

And knowing already that he was about to fail.

When finally he broke through the door, the thing on the sheeted floor, the mess of meat that used to be Terry Cunliffe, was still moving, in reflex jerks, a sound gurgling in its throat. Sully and the other two were dressed in disposable paper suits, white spattered with red. It took him seconds to realise that the thing that Sully was holding was Cunliffe's skin.

Sully looked up in surprise – he must have assumed there was trouble, that Johanssen had come to raise the alarm. He didn't think to use the knife in his hand until it was too late.

Johanssen stopped when the three were bloody pulp.

And then Cunliffe—

Do something. Do something, you've been trained. But not for this.

The police found Cunliffe's body three days later, dumped in a field: a message to Quillan, who retaliated. Sully and the other two were caught, tortured, killed.

From a payphone Johanssen rang the Scouser who'd given his name to Sully in the first place. Out of guilt perhaps, the man gave him a phone number – 'They're supposed to help people disappear but it'll cost all you've got, now don't call me again, ever' – and that number brought Johanssen to a bare room and a bright light and a woman's calm voice: 'You have to tell us everything. Complete disclosure is vital.' Karla, but he didn't know her then. All he knew was that he had a price on his head, that the man who wrote *unreliable* in his file had been right, and that what remained of his life as Simon Johanssen wasn't worth keeping.

It was months before he worked out what went wrong; what the trigger was. And it was Cunliffe. Cunliffe, standing in the hallway of the farmhouse, when they opened the door to the room and he saw the plastic sheeting, and shat himself – the spreading stain in the man's trousers, and the smell. That was it: the tiny detail that you don't want to see, or it will get its hooks into you. The tiny detail that makes them human.

Eight years since then. How many jobs? More memories tumble out, though these are bright, compressed, fleeting, like a handful of snapshots thrown across a room. An arc of tracer in a desert sky. The corpse of a man in an African street with a snake trail of blood winding through the dust behind him. The moment when a skull explodes. Somewhere behind them there's a figure, a total that he can get to if he wants …

Eight years, and every job proof that he can look at all those tiny details – up close, across a room or in a street, close enough to hear the target breathing, or half a mile away, ten-up in the sights – look at them, and now they don't affect him at all.

But somewhere in his head, behind that farmhouse door, Terry Cunliffe's screaming.

After half an hour Cate's footsteps come dragging up the stairs, and go on, to the room above. But he's still lying awake two hours later, so he hears it: a word repeated over and over again, rhythmically. Something beating against a wall. And that same small thin cry, like a child having a nightmare.

Day 16: Thursday

Karla

Ellis calls at 9.35 on Thursday morning. 'Be outside Graves's office at twelve,' is all he says. He's smug, as if he's just got one over on someone, and he ends the call without saying goodbye.

Ian Graves shares a practice with three other psychiatrists in a converted five-storey town house on a Chelsea side street. The practice draws its clientele from the ranks of bankers and brokers, lawyers and minor political figures: the unhappy rich. I wonder what drew Dr Catherine Gallagher to him; she doesn't seem the type.

I'm loitering in sight of the glossy black door at twelve on the dot but there's no sign of Ellis, so I wander down the street. It's in a sought-after area between the upmarket stores and bars of the King's Road and the railed green of the Chelsea Pensioners' grounds. Most of the properties are residential. Next door to the practice a ghost house is swathed in plastic sheeting, though there are no sounds of drilling and hammering today: someone's expensive renovation project has stalled. Among the parked cars I pass four Mercs, a top-of-the-range Lexus, a four-wheel-drive Porsche and an Aston before I reach the end of the street and retrace my footsteps.

Ellis pulls up in an unmarked car at fourteen minutes past twelve. I've changed my appearance enough to throw a casual observer – sensible shoes, a dry-looking brown wig, dark-framed glasses – and he double-takes when he sees me, then grins.

'We're late,' I tell him, needlessly.

'Early,' he says. There's the same unmistakable smugness clinging to him. He's up to something.

'What?'

'Come on.' He climbs the steps to the front door and leans on the intercom button.

After a couple of seconds a well-bred female voice crackles back at him. 'Hello?'

'Mr Ellis for Dr Graves, he's expecting me,' he barks.

The lock releases with a buzz. Ellis puts his hand on the door. Over his shoulder he mutters, 'Keep your eyes and ears open and your mouth shut, I'm asking the questions,' then he pushes his way in.

Inside what must once have been the front parlour a pretty, conservatively dressed woman with shiny hair looks up from a glass desk and smiles. Not the sort of smile you'd give a detective inspector on a murder enquiry; she must think one of us is a prospective patient. Probably me.

'We have a meeting with Dr Graves,' Ellis says.

She looks enquiringly at me, but before I can say anything Ellis jumps in with, 'We're early, if it's inconvenient we can wait,' in a tone that says, *It'd better not be for long.*

For a second she hesitates – it's as if we've presented her with a social difficulty – but then she brightens: would we like a cup of coffee? Ellis says, 'No,' and 'Thank you' as an afterthought.

'Well then,' she says, 'do come this way,' and another smile ushers us into a waiting room (modern sofas, plants, a tank of darting tropical fish). She hovers for a second in the doorway – 'If there's anything you need?' – smiles again, and goes.

She's like the idealised wife of a cabinet minister: contented with her lot, unshakeably polite, one of life's little optimists, vanilla through and through.

When the door has closed behind her Ellis says, 'Our Dr Graves is a man who prefers to be in control and doesn't like surprises.'

'So that's why we're late?'

'Early.'

'So you said.'

'He said he couldn't see us today, I said I'd be here at eleven, he says he's got an appointment at eleven, I say twelve o'clock then, he says it's a two-hour appointment, so I say, one it is, and put the phone down.'

'So we don't even have an appointment.'

'So why'd she let us in? He'll see us. Nosy bastards, psychiatrists.' There it is again, that pleased little smile.

'He'll keep us waiting.'

'Do I look like a copper?' Ellis asks. 'Answer: yes.' And he does, in his leather jacket and his designer shoes: a smart young copper on the way up; or a crook. There's that clever knowingness to him, always one step ahead of the game.

187

'People who come to this place don't want it known. So they stagger their appointments, so no one's sitting in the waiting room with anyone else. So when's the next appointment? Half past? Twenty to? They'll be turning up any minute and Little Miss Perfect isn't going to want them in here with—'

On cue the door is opened by a thin-faced man in his fifties with a neat grey beard. Immediately Ellis is on his feet, warrant card in his hand. 'Dr Graves? DI Ellis. We're early.' He grins. 'Good traffic.'

Graves looks at Ellis as if he's caught him practising some sort of low subterfuge, then he turns to me. 'And you are …?'

Ellis answers for me. 'Elizabeth Crow.'

I've come prepared: an ID in that name in my pocket, and a string of references to published papers inserted overnight into the Internet, a little pattern of tracks in the electronic snow. Now I smile and offer my hand. 'Dr Graves.'

He's a slight man, trim and carefully dressed in the sort of colours you'd struggle to remember. He shakes my hand, his gaze fixed on my face. 'Not a police officer, then?'

'A consultant,' Ellis says.

Graves is still gazing at me. 'And your expertise …?'

'Women who vanish,' I say quickly before Ellis can open his mouth.

'Well,' he says, 'do come through.'

None of us mentions the absent eleven o'clock patient.

He shows us into a panelled study overlooking a tiny back courtyard. A gauzy blind pulled halfway down the window cuts out the view of the buildings that back on to this one. Across the room a double-fronted bookcase houses professional journals and reference works behind a latticework of polished wood and diamond panes. In one corner there's a couple of armchairs and a small table with a box of tissues, a potted African violet and a pair of coasters for coffee – that must be where he sees his patients – but he manoeuvres himself behind a big Victorian desk, waving us into the upright visitors' chairs opposite. He wants a barrier between himself and us. A green cardboard file lies on the blotter in front of him. The name on the cover is Catherine Gallagher's.

As he seats himself, he takes up a pad which he balances on his knee, below the level of the desk and out of our view, and he picks up a pen.

He looks straight at Ellis. His voice is soft and calm and musical. 'Are you in charge of this investigation?'

'Yes.'

'And you report to?'

Ellis gives the name of his DCI without flinching. I think Graves writes that down, but like me he's learned to write without looking directly at the paper, and the desk hides the pad from view.

'And a contact number for her?'

My heart rate rises a notch. Graves will call to check, he's the type. Will he do it right now, while we're sitting here? If he does, will Ellis's boss back him? What about me? But he doesn't reach for the phone or rise to leave the room.

As I pull out my own notebook Graves sits back with his head tilted to one side. 'Can I ask why you've reopened the case?' He looks at each of us in turn.

'It was never closed,' Ellis says.

'But after a year, surely ...'

'It's just routine.'

Graves waits to see if he'll add anything more, but Ellis says nothing.

'I first saw her over two years ago.' Graves glances down at the green file on the desk in front on him, but he doesn't open it. His gaze levels back up at us. 'September, it would have been September.'

'Who put her in touch with you?' Ellis asks. 'Her GP?'

'She was a private patient, a self-referral.' He pauses. 'She was very guarded, initially.'

'In what way?'

'Well, for instance: she booked the appointment under a false name.'

'Is that unusual?'

'It happens sometimes.'

'And why might she do that?'

Very patiently Graves says, 'She didn't want anyone to know that she was seeking help. She was afraid it might come out. For the same reason she refused me permission to contact her GP.'

'But later she gave you her real name?'

'And, as it turned out, her real address. Not everyone does.'

'So you met her. Here?'

'Yes.'

She must have sat in this same room: the suit, the guarded smile ... Did he get past that smile? If he did, will he tell us?

'Describe that first meeting,' Ellis says.

'The format's the same with every patient. An initial consultation takes two hours. In that time I try to establish a patient's life story. We talk about their problems and how those problems affect them.'

'And what were Catherine's problems?'

Graves pauses again, as if he's thinking through his answer, though maybe he's making another note to himself. He says, 'You are aware of the issues of patient confidentiality?'

'Yeah,' Ellis says. 'Tell me, does it apply to the dead?'

Graves purses his lips.

'Or maybe you think she might still be alive,' Ellis adds.

Graves's eyes say she's dead.

Ellis presses on. 'So she told you …?'

'That she was finding it difficult to function: she felt burned-out, she had no energy. And she was very anxious. Anxious about making mistakes.'

'What sort of mistakes?'

'Mistakes in her work.' Again, as if he's stating the obvious.

'Had she made mistakes in the past?'

'I asked her that. She could only talk about a few tiny errors which she corrected almost immediately, before any damage was done. Nothing of any significance. It was the *potential* for catastrophe that troubled her. The "what ifs".' Another thoughtful pause. I'm getting used to these pauses; they're part of his style. A professional device? Leaving space for the patient to interject? Or is he making another note?

Graves says, 'Of course, at the time I thought she worked in advertising. She didn't tell me she was a doctor.'

'Would it have made any difference if she had?' Ellis asks.

'Naturally, and as a doctor she would have known it. She was in an important position, caring for vulnerable patients. I would have had to inform her employer.'

'Was there a risk to her patients?'

'With hindsight? No.'

I jump in – 'You're sure about that?' Beside me Ellis twitches slightly.

Graves turns his gaze on me. 'Depression can impact on concentration – as I say, she was anxious about making mistakes … but I felt she posed a greater risk to herself.'

Ellis asks, 'Did she tell you that?'

'No. I asked if she had any thoughts of harming herself – it's a standard question – and she said no.'

'But you didn't believe her.'

'I felt she was filtering her responses,' Graves says reasonably. 'If she'd said yes, that would have required admission – inpatient treatment – again, something she would have known. Also, I think she found it hard to acknowledge her condition. To admit that she wasn't coping.'

'She came to you for help. Wasn't that an acknowledgement?'

'Rationally, she knew she had to do something. But emotionally, instinctively ... You know about her parents?'

'Mum's in a care home. Dad's dead.'

'I meant her childhood.' Another pause. Another note on his pad? 'She felt her father judged her only by her achievements; in her accounts he emerges as a demanding man. Her mother seems to have been somewhat disengaged, colourless; present, but emotionally absent. She may have been a depressive herself – it often runs in families. Both were what we might term emotionally unavailable. In modern slang, they weren't "there for her". No one was. That early emotional experience formed her expectations of others: she transferred it to everyone else she met. No one would be there to help her: she would always be required to cope on her own. That extended to me. She knew she needed help, but emotionally – instinctively – she didn't believe I could give it. She didn't believe anyone could. My task was to change that view.'

'And would you say you failed?'

Ellis is trying to provoke him, but Graves just tilts his head sympathetically. 'My duty was to try.' His voice is sorrowful but also soothing. This must be how he presents himself to patients: a benign presence but also shadowy, indistinct ... His gaze flicks from Ellis to me and back again, observing us. The hand holding the pen glides over the pad, out of sight. *He* might be interviewing *us*. We can't get anywhere near him.

'So you tried to help her,' Ellis says flatly. 'How?'

'Initially she just wanted medication. Something to help her function.'

'Which you prescribed?'

'No. She could have been on other medication. And drug interactions can be problematic. Normally a patient's GP would advise ...'

'But she wouldn't give you their name.'

'So in her case I'd have been prescribing blind. It wasn't worth the risk.'

'It worried you, that she was holding so much back?'

'Of course; but it was in character. That habit of secrecy again: not wanting people to know.' Another pause. 'I was keen to refer her to a psychotherapist for a talking treatment. Someone who could help her get to the root of her problems, modify her behaviour and her assumptions. She refused. She wasn't ready for that level of exposure.'

'But you continued to see her yourself.'

'Yes. I normally see a patient again three weeks after the first appointment, to monitor the effects of any medication—'

'Which she wasn't taking.'

Graves ignores him. 'Then every six weeks after that. She was what we call a "good" patient. Punctual. Co-operative – at least as far as she'd allow herself. She said it helped. And I felt that at some point there might be a breakthrough. In the meantime I could offer her a safety valve: a chance to talk.'

I spot an opening again. 'What was she like?'

This time there's a small pause, as if he's assessing me, before he answers. 'In her way, a classic depressive. She had a very poor view of herself, despite her achievements. Her sleep was quite disturbed. Early-morning wakefulness, a common symptom. Diurnal mood variations – her mood was bleak in the mornings, better later in the day, but bad at night, again because of the sleep problems. She suffered depressive psychodementia – a loss of concentration and with it the anxiety that her memory was failing. Hence the fear of making mistakes.'

Ellis jumps back in. 'What about other fears? Did she ever talk about enemies? People who hated her, or might have wanted to harm her?'

Graves frowns. 'Are you asking whether she suffered from a paranoid personality disorder?'

'I'm asking if she felt threatened.'

'Catherine wasn't paranoid. She thought that people didn't like her, but that was part of the depression. As I say, she displayed many of the classic symptoms: isolation, loss of appetite, loss of self-esteem. Feelings of worthlessness, anxiety, guilt. Not paranoia.'

'Why would she feel guilty?' Ellis asks.

'She believed she was fundamentally unlovable. Her father had taught her to value herself only through her achievements. Her mother offered nothing to counterbalance that view. Without constant achievement she felt she was worthless. Place that in the context of her work. Every week she saw good people, people with spouses and children, people who were loved and valued, dying in her care, because she was unable to save them. Do you still wonder why she might feel guilty?'

I'm in again. 'But not because of anything she'd done?'

Graves says carefully, 'She didn't need to have *done* anything. The guilt depressives experience isn't rational.'

'What about what she might have done, what she was capable of?'

Graves blinks at me. 'I don't know what you mean.'

Ellis says, 'And when she didn't turn up for that last appointment – how did you feel?'

It's an obvious jab, too obvious: Graves isn't going to talk to us about his feelings. He gives Ellis that look again, that pursed reprimand that says, *I know all the little tricks.*

'I believed something was wrong,' Graves says coolly. 'She'd never missed an appointment before. And consider her personality type: she would have written a note, left a message for me. Missing an appointment would have been a significant failing in her eyes.'

'She had to be perfect,' Ellis says.

'Quite. As I say, I had her home address, and her home phone number. I tried to contact her. When that failed I went straight to the police.'

'You thought she'd tried to kill herself?' Ellis asks.

'I thought it was highly possible. And when I learned she was a doctor—'

'That made a difference?'

'In an ICU she would have had access to some extremely powerful drugs. Diamorphine, for instance: a very strong pain reliever. Barbiturates: phenobarbital – it's an anticonvulsant, often used with head-injury patients. They're controlled drugs, kept under lock and key – she would have needed authorisation to draw them – but with sleight of hand, over a period of time she could have built up a significant stock for her own use, with minimal risk of detection.'

'Do you think you could have done more to stop her?' Ellis asks.

'I think I did everything I could.' Then his voice loses that sorrowful tone, becomes quizzical: 'Though I'm curious. You've asked exactly the same questions as your colleague did a year ago.'

'And that surprises you?'

'I thought as you'd taken the trouble to call on me again …'

'We'd be asking different questions? Not always.'

Graves doesn't move, his face doesn't change, but it's like a vibration in the air, his reaction. Graves knows there's something wrong about this. Something Ellis said has given us away. Graves will phone Ellis's boss. And ask about Elizabeth Crow? That could be interesting.

'Well,' he says, 'if that's everything.'

He rises, and as he does so his hand flattens protectively across the file in front of him.

'One other thing,' Ellis says. 'She paid for her treatment with you. How did she pay?'

'Cash,' Graves says, and gives us one small, dismissive smile.

And I know: *That was all wrong.*

The glossy black door closes quietly behind us as we walk down the front steps.

'Nice bloke,' Ellis says. 'Yeah, if I was suicidal, a chat with him'd make all the difference.'

'We need to talk,' I say.

Ellis has gone back to his car. He flicks his key fob and the hazards blink. 'Too right. Get in.'

'Not here.'

'*Get in,*' he says.

I get in on the passenger side and close the door. The car reeks of air freshener. Immediately he holds out a data stick to me – the recordings of the other interviews? – but when I reach for it he doesn't let go, and his face is sour.

'You owe me an explanation,' he says. 'Don't say, "What explan-ation?", you know fucking well. Five days I've been on Catherine Gallagher's case, every spare moment of every fucking day, burning the midnight oil, turning over all the stones, and what have I got? No threats. No sign of foul play. No motive – no cock-ups, no unexplained deaths under her care, no unhappy families, no one holding a grudge against her. Colleagues hardly knew her. No one much liked her but no one hated her either. Graves is an obstructive bastard but his account's solid—'

'Graves is wrong.'

'Oh is he? What about?'

Mark Devlin's Catherine flashes before me: the woman capable of all the bad things, without the boundaries to hold her back. Fielding's too: the woman responsible for a shocking, ugly death – for whom the Program's not punishment enough—

And a professional like Graves should have seen all that, should have been on to her in seconds.

'Well, Karla? How's he wrong? What am I missing, eh? Because I've looked, and there's nothing in the hospital. And apart from one half-hearted fling with some headhunter, nothing outside it either. She was a lonely control freak and she was depressed. Karla, I've looked at everything, and you know what? Every fucking thing so far says she's a suicide. Open and shut. Except you. The only person talking about murder is you. What makes you so sure? Don't tell me it's a hunch, don't give me any of that intuition crap. You know something and you're not saying. What is it?'

But I can't tell him.

'Nothing that counts,' I say. I can hear the frustration in my voice.

Ellis hears it too. 'Right,' he says. 'And I'm supposed to believe that? What is it? A witness? Someone who knows where the body's buried? But *someone*. Otherwise how come you're so certain she was murdered? That's point number one—'

'I'm not—'

'And then we've got point number two. Why it matters to you. Cos it does matter. When did you last sit in on an interview with me? Fucking never. So: until you can give me something more, you're on your own here. Got that?'

'Ellis—'

'I'm hungry, Karla. I'm not fucking starving.' He lets go of the data stick at last. 'Call me when you're ready to talk. Now get out of my car.'

I shed my disguise in a toilet in the Victoria and Albert Museum. I want to hear those recordings – there's still the chance that Ellis missed something, that the Catherine whom Devlin knew is still lurking in her colleagues' testimony – but I have to make the usual circuitous journey home, and it's almost four before I sit down at my desk, open the directory and click on the first icon.

By the time I've finished five hours have passed, the offices beyond my window have emptied, and it's night.

Ellis is right. There's nothing.

I put my coat on and walk out, to the river.

I like the Thames at night. Its broad sweep becomes monumental after dark. I lean against the curved metal railing, hugging my coat around me. On the far bank the lights of the Hilton Pier and Columbia Wharf seem a long way away. Just then, to my right, where the river curves out of sight beyond the converted warehouses of Limehouse Reach, a light on the water catches my eye: it's a police launch, buzzing downstream towards me. It approaches – the swell cracks against the underside of the hull as it skims past – and then it's gone, but I stay there against the rail, waiting for the next boat and the next ... A commuter boat approaches from downstream and manoeuvres against the pier below me. The queue of passengers shuffles aboard and it casts off again and heads out into midstream, while at the far curve of the river a party cruiser comes into view, its lights jewelling the water with tiny reflections. Faintly I can hear music.

What am I doing, standing here in the dark? Hunting Catherine? But I've already found her. Except every time she's different, and the more I see of her, the less I know.

Who is she? Not Ellis's missing person; he thinks she's dead. Who, then? Aylwyn Roberts' ambitious, intensely private doctor, who couldn't bear to admit she wasn't coping? Ian Graves's depressive? Mark Devlin's clever woman without barriers, capable of evil? All of these, or none?

The first time I saw her I thought: *Monster*. And she is, but not the kind I thought back then; she's like a virus, replicating itself while still evolving, every version slightly different to the last, and just when I think I've got her contained, defined, she re-evolves again.

And I'm no nearer to knowing what she's done, or why, or who wants her dead, and time is running out.

So what happens now?

I stare at the river. I wait. No answer comes.

I shiver suddenly. It's a cold night, and a breeze has sprung up. Time to go home.

I'm turning away from the rail when it comes back to me, in a snapshot: Graves on his feet, the file in front of him on the desk, and his hand flattened protectively on its cover.

A little skip in my blood: *Protective of what?*

He's told us all about Catherine's depression.

What if there's another story in the file?

Phone Craigie? No, phone Robbie. Not just because Craigie will lecture me about risk, but also because the people I need to talk to don't trust anyone easily, but they do trust Robbie.

'I want to lift a file,' I tell him. 'Secure premises.'

'Specialist contractor?'

'And it's urgent.'

There's a moment's silence, then Robbie says, 'You mean Louis, don't you?'

And he's right, I do. But I wish I didn't.

Day 16: Thursday

Powell

Thursday night. He's working late again.

Spread out across the desk: the records retrieved from the Ealing flat. Pages ripped from exercise books, covered in Laidlaw's patient black-ink script. Time on his hands meant narrative accounts in full sentences, but not all are like that; some are in note form, just the hurried essentials. But every one complete.

The things we knew about. The things we didn't.

The Ealing flat was on the surveillance log – Laidlaw couldn't make himself invisible – but they'd checked it out, or thought they had. The electoral register and the bills gave the resident's name, one Arthur Burton: a recluse, in poor health, shunning his neighbours – but they saw lights going on, heard the radio and the TV. And heard Laidlaw visiting from time to time, with bags of shopping – calling out, 'It's all right, it's me, I've got my key,' or, 'Get the kettle on.'

When Powell did the walk-through of the flat – the first one in, covers on his shoes, touching nothing – he found the timer switches on the lamps and radio and TV, and the cupboards full of food.

Arthur Burton was a complete fiction, his name stolen from a child who'd died in the 1930s; a largely hollow ID with no obvious connection to Laidlaw's Russian past. His landlord was a different matter: Gordon Fox, a cover name assigned to Peter Laidlaw back in '76, after his own name had popped up on a Soviet watch list.

Someone should have spotted that.

They found the records triple-wrapped in plastic, in six different locations around the flat – in the cistern and taped to the underside of the bed frame, under the floorboards and in the freezer compartment, in the oven and in the lining of a coat – each cache spanning a different period of Laidlaw's relationship with Knox.

The things we knew about. The things we didn't.

Transactions logged in minute, careful detail: each tip-off, dead drop, brush pass, hidden message. And then, after every cool account: Laidlaw's bewilderment, excitement, bafflement, frustration. The growing knowledge MI5 was watching him. The growing sense, too, of an alliance with Knox. *He's given me a good one this time* and *They'll have to work harder if they're going to catch us out.*

Beyond that, yet another layer: the search for Knox himself.

The patient analysis of each transaction: not just the information supplied and what it might imply, but the method, and every clue that might be gleaned from that. *Dead drop in park* and *Shoes ordered by credit card – details not available* and *Brush pass in café, didn't see. Tradecraft??? Background? Is this a double-bluff?*

Got sight of the man who may have dropped off package. I attempted to follow, but failed.

The collation of the list of Russian names: question marks and strike-throughs.

Two years ago: *Maybe not Moscow after all????*

A period of stalling: Laidlaw's frustration mounting. *Though we're on the same side he will not trust me* and *This is getting nowhere.* The notes are scantier.

And then, a week before Laidlaw's own death: *Saw package man again, am almost certain.*

Details of a sighting in a street market. A ferrety-faced man – *Mediterranean origin???* – in a brown jacket, dodging between stalls. Found and lost again.

There's never any mention of Laidlaw's illness, the hospital appointments, the tests. Except in the last sentence, underlined:

I wish I had more time.

It's gone ten now. He slips out of his office, locking the door behind him out of habit, and walks down to the little kitchen at the end of the corridor. While the kettle boils he reviews today's meeting with the Section Chief. The street market's a weekly happening, every Saturday. It's got to be worth a look?

Laidlaw's description of the man taunted them both from the page. There is, of course, no photograph.

The Section Chief's nod was purse-lipped. It said, *Is this the best you've got?*

'Use local police. But keep them in the dark.' The instruction wholly unnecessary: has the man forgotten how many times he's done this? 'And no direct contact with Knox, understood?'

As if he might have forgotten.

The kettle clicks off. Beyond that sound there's another, from outside in the corridor. A door closing, the snick of a latch? A colleague working late? He goes to the kitchen doorway, peers out, but the corridor is empty, and all the doors are closed.

A shiver of something. Paranoia? Again he thinks back to the moment outside the Ealing flat: resting the crate of papers on the car roof, reaching for his keys – the flash of sunlight off a moving car—

The sense of being watched.

Day 17: Friday

Johanssen

He doesn't go far today. The weather's turned sleeting and gusty, the wind whipping needles of ice into his face. Behind him the two-man tail follows very close, hunched into their thin jackets, with no attempt at concealment. He makes it to the shops on the west side of the main guard base, and buys toothpaste and another bar of chocolate. When he comes out the two men are loitering sullenly by the door. He hands one the chocolate. 'Let's get back.' For just a second the man looks almost angry – as if Johanssen's broken a rule – but then he looks at the chocolate and relents. The three of them walk back together, not speaking, heads down against the sleet.

He's climbed the first flight of stairs above the clinic and he has one hand on the door into the kitchen when the sounds begin.

One word first, quite loud, spoken urgently. A pause, and then a phrase, rapped out. Then a small, soft whimper, barely audible.

He's carrying his boots. He puts them down and climbs up to the second floor, carefully, so the treads don't creak. The phrase comes again – four syllables.

He tries the handle; it gives and the door creaks open.

'No,' she says, and it's a plea this time.

The blackouts are in place, the room near-dark. The floor's piled with clothes and junk. On the far side of the room the bigger bundle on the mattress moves.

She's pushed herself upright against the wall. Her head flips right, then left – 'Get to a phone,' she says, and, 'No, not that.' Her eyes are half-open, but she's not awake.

'Get to a phone.' The four-syllable phrase from before: he recognises the rhythm. Then another word he can't make out, strangled up in her throat, it might be 'dragon', he's not sure, and then under her breath she starts to count: 'One-two-three-four-five-six-seven-eight—'

'Cate.'

'He'll be dead in a minute,' she says. 'In a minute.' She whimpers again.

'*Cate.*' He takes a step towards her.

The movement does it. She blinks. Then slams herself back against the wall, clutching the bedding around her, staring at him. Automatically he takes another step – she flinches, scrabbles for something in the bed, and then her hand comes up and the blade's in it, a dull glint in the gloom.

He backs, one step. 'I'll use it,' she says, and she means it, and in a second he sees what she does: Ryan Jackson, double murderer, blocking the doorway. He takes another step back.

'You were dreaming,' he says. 'It's over now.'

Still she stares at him, fist white around the knife, chest heaving, eyes wild.

He says, 'You cried out. But you're OK. I can go now. You want me to go now.'

For a handful of seconds she doesn't move. Then slowly she lowers the hand with the blade and looks down at the mattress as if she doesn't know how she came here.

He goes down to the kitchen, fills a glass with water and brings it up to her. She's pulled a ragged blue cardigan over her T-shirt, and when he comes back in she's wiping a hand across her face. The skin on the inside of her wrist's a pale film, the sinews and veins starkly visible through it.

He passes the glass to her and then backs off again. She sips, shivers, puts the glass down. Huddles into her cardigan, looks sideways at the blacked-out window. Handfuls of sleet are rattling against the glass like tiny stones.

'You called out in your sleep,' he says.

'What did I say?'

'You were counting. You wanted to get to a phone. You said something about a dragon.'

She's silent for a moment, then she says, 'I'm in a room. From the window you can see a gate. The gate has dragons on it.'

'And that's where it happened, in that room?'

She nods, then rubs her arms as if she's cold. 'I keep going back there.' She looks at him. 'What do you dream about?'

Karla. A rooftop at night. A man at a desk. The farmhouse. Cunliffe screaming. 'Just stuff.'

'The same dreams?'

'Sometimes.'

'Good or bad?'

'Both.'

Suddenly she says, with a quiet intensity, 'Tell me a good dream.'

The best dream – Karla, her hair against his shoulder – segues into his head. *Not that*. Second best, then. He says, 'It's night. I'm on a rooftop. I'm running.'

'And that's it?' As if she expected so much more.

Then for a moment neither of them moves.

She says, 'His first name was Daniel. I wasn't told his surname. He was your age. Maybe younger. Dark hair. It shouldn't have been difficult. He was already ...' choosing the word carefully: '... incapacitated. Both of his ankles broken. The left one must have been when he tried to get away, the right one ... later. And he was restrained, of course, and he'd bled quite a bit. So I thought it would be quick. But he fought. Despite everything. He fought. So it took ... time.'

She looks down. She's been twisting the hem of her cardigan in her hands. She stops now, but doesn't let go.

'Why did you do it?'

She looks up at him again, and he can almost see it, something coiled and spitting at the back of her eyes. 'Because I could.'

'Had he attacked you? Is that why?'

'*Huh*. He'd done nothing to me. He was a complete stranger.'

'Someone made you do it.'

She laughs – a hard, flat, bitter laugh, like a slap. 'No one made me do it. Any of it. That's the thing. *No one made me do it*. I could have walked away. I could have done "the right thing", whatever that was, or I could have done nothing, nothing at all. But I stayed. I stayed, for four days. And then I killed him.'

She turns her head towards the window, though there's no view. She says, 'I think you should go now.'

He goes downstairs, but not into the bunkroom. Instead he sits on the first-floor landing with his boots beside him, and listens, for half an hour, an hour, while in the room overhead she paces from one wall to the next.

After a while the door beside him opens and Vinnie comes out.

'What you doing?' he whispers, and then he looks up, and his soft harmless face creases in concern.

Together they listen to the footsteps.

At last they stop. Vinnie says, 'She's asleep,' and Johanssen says, 'Yes.'

Asleep, or just sitting there, holding the glass, thinking of the bright edge it would make if she broke it … Vinnie nods and goes back into the room, but Johanssen waits another fifteen minutes, to be sure, before he too turns in.

Lying on his bunk he goes over it in his head. The man she only knew as Daniel, who'd broken his ankle trying to get away, who'd been tied up to stop him trying again. Whose other ankle was then broken. Who had bled.

Four days she spent with him. Treating him? Or torturing him?

And then she killed him, counting the seconds while the fight went out of him.

Because she could.

He has Terry Cunliffe in his dreams. She has Daniel.

Day 17: Friday

Karla

Just gone noon on Friday. We meet in an ugly pub on the edge of a council estate in Bow: the tables sticky with spilled drinks, two spotty lads playing pool in a side room. I'm dressed in a plain dark chainstore suit, with little make-up and my hair tied back: I could be a case worker or a solicitor, or maybe someone from a charity. Robbie is beside me, sipping his pint; his smile is neutral, his habitual jollity turned in on itself. He set this up – they like him, trust him – but right now he's minding his own business.

I don't want to be here.

Louis sits opposite me, a glass of lemonade in front of him: he doesn't touch alcohol. His expression is quiet, unassuming. He looks tired, and out of condition: there's a slow roll of fat at his gut, and the circles under his eyes show purplish-black against his dark skin. Louis is rusty. They lose their touch, don't they? Just two jobs in the four years since we first met. *And whose fault is that?*

Beside him, Morag's a startling contrast: bone-white skin that must once have had an ethereal translucence, crinkling red hair scraped behind her ears. There's not a spare ounce of fat on her. She looks brittle, but it's an illusion. If Morag were the type that broke easily, she'd have done so long ago.

Louis is a specialist contractor, and his speciality is doors. Doors, and locks, and motion detectors, and alarms. Morag is his partner, but also his manager, his agent, playing the same role in his professional life that Fielding plays in Johanssen's, except where Fielding loves the business, the contacts and the negotiations and the deals, she gives every sign of hating it. She nurses her vodka-tonic with a silent malevolence, and when she turns her gaze to me, her eyes say, *Bitch*.

She too looks tired today. A bad night? More than one? A week of them, or a fortnight? Perhaps this isn't a good time to approach them, but then these two never have good times: they lurch from one crisis to the next, an unpredictable sequence of scrabbled-together clothes and late-night taxis and dawn watches in hospital rooms.

They don't want to be here either.

'How's Kyle?' I ask.

Louis doesn't look up from his drink but he smiles a slow, inward smile.

Morag's gaze spikes the air between us. 'Kyle's fine,' she spits.

'Your mum sitting in with him?'

Her look says, *What's it to you?*

Kyle is the reason they're here, the reason they do this, but Kyle's also the reason they're very, very careful.

They first came into my orbit four years ago, when Kyle was two. His particular cocktail of disabilities – it includes cerebral palsy and epilepsy – means he will never speak, or walk, or feed himself, or control his own bowel movements. They were caring for him between them, with what little support was available from the state, living on benefits and also, from time to time, the occasional job for Louis – once, maybe twice a year, eking out the money for as long as possible afterwards, knowing that if Louis were caught, Morag wouldn't cope alone, even with her mother's help.

Kyle is now six. In four years I've only ever seen him from a distance, when no one knew I was watching – thirty yards away, hunkered down behind the wheel of a battered Vauxhall, while Louis or Morag or Morag's mum wheels him out in his specially adapted pushchair. That's as close as I get.

'You got everything?' I ask, still looking from one to the other. By 'everything' I mean: the floor plan of Graves's building, the model number and spec of the alarm and the motion sensors linked to it, the number and type of the window and door locks, the floor plans of the houses on either side of Graves's building, photographs of all three buildings, front and rear, and a plan of the area with the CCTV cameras marked in. Finn and I were up all night pulling it together. The information was handed in an unmarked envelope to a pallid teenage girl – Morag's niece – on a street corner in Whitechapel this morning, as arranged: Morag won't allow such things in the house. Being careful, again.

Now she gives a neat businesslike nod. 'We got it.'

'And?'

'He needs a week.' From the side room the pool balls click and one of the lads swears.

'That's not possible. We know it's tight. That's reflected in the fee.'

Morag's mouth tightens and she gives a tiny, fractional shake of the head.

I pretend I haven't seen it. 'I can't afford to wait on this.'

But Morag has a poker player's face. 'We need a week,' she says. 'Minimum.'

I shake my head. 'Tomorrow night. If I thought it was reasonable I'd be asking for tonight. Tomorrow is as good as it gets.'

'Then sorry.'

What do I say now? That I'll have to go elsewhere?

There are alternatives. But they involve either people I don't trust, or Joe Ellis and a warrant. Right now Ellis isn't playing. But even if he were, a warrant would make it official, and I don't want the Met anywhere near this. In truth, there is no *elsewhere*. There is only Louis, and this cold red-and-white woman sitting in front of me.

I'm pretty sure she knows it too.

I lean forward, fix on her. 'Morag, it's straight in and out. Access only. Nothing leaves the building. All we want is a copy of a file.'

'A week. Or nothing.' She shrugs. 'Up to you.'

'Look. You have to put yourself out. We appreciate that. We pay more for it. In fact we pay double. You won't get another offer like this.'

Something stirs behind that poker player's gaze.

'Five days,' Morag says.

I should go to three here, but I can't. There isn't time. 'Tomorrow, and the fee still stands. Final offer.'

Morag sits back in her chair. She's thinking about it. Her fleshless white fingers tap at the glass in front of her, shifting it left a little, and then right, until it sits exactly between the two of us, as if she's a sniper lining me up in her sights.

Then she shakes her head. 'Don't like it. He's taking all the risk.'

'I'll have one man on lookout in the street, another holding the point of entry, someone else watching CCTV feeds.'

'He's still the one handling the merchandise.'

'Then we put someone else in to make the copy. Louis just opens the doors.'

'He doesn't work with strangers.'

'Then how about me?'

Robbie's sitting next to me, and so his shock comes at me sidelong.

'Tomorrow night, Morag.'

Abruptly she gets to her feet. Louis looks up as if he's just woken from a doze, and then he too rises, blinking sleepily. Is that it? Are they leaving? But all she says is, 'I need a fag.'

Together they wander towards the door. The barman – who's kept out of sight and earshot ever since we started talking – instantly reappears, and nods to them. He begins to wipe down the bar, pointlessly, glancing over at us as he does so. I feel as if I've been placed under guard.

Robbie sits back, sips his pint, says nothing. If he's ever wondered why Morag hates me so much, he's never asked.

Two jobs in four years, for ludicrously inflated fees, because they won't take charity. So Louis won't have to work for other people who aren't as careful as I am. So he and Morag can cope. And every time, the negotiation's as bitter as this: because Morag has no illusions about the fees, she knows I'm paying over the odds, and she's proud. She'd love to turn me down.

Will she? I've no idea. All I can do now is wait.

They come back five minutes later, with smoke on their breath and flecks of sleet in their hair, and slip back into their seats.

Morag says, 'We'll get back to you.'

It's not the answer I want.

'Fine,' I say. 'Do that.'

She nods once, then she says, 'And if we agree and this goes tits up, we'll shop you.'

I reach for my bag, and rise. 'I know you will.'

The barman appears again and eyes us warily as we leave. At the door I glance back. They're still in their seats, not talking: a weary black man and a brittle white woman, each staring at their glass as if looking into an abyss.

In the car Robbie blows out his cheeks. He must think I'm mad.

But I have to see that file. I have to know.

Robbie drops me near a suburban overground line. While he threads towards Graves's office to make a recce, I head back to Docklands the long way, alone.

By the time I get back, it's 3.55 and Craigie's already waiting for me in the lobby of my building, for yet another routine Friday meeting.

The usual litany of clients, sources, opportunities, threats. A minor gang boss with a history of violence is seeking help in tracing his daughter. A German client wants the floor plans of a major London hotel. Someone's asking questions about William Hamilton's whereabouts, though the rumour doesn't say who, and Hamilton, tucked up in a safe house, still won't come clean on exactly what he's done. And then Lucas Powell again: whatever he took from Ealing in that crate, it hasn't led him to my door. (Craigie adds, 'Yet.')

At the end of our session Craigie – rising, reaching for his coat – asks casually, 'And the Johanssen business?' So I tell him about Ellis's fruitless interviews with Catherine Gallagher's colleagues.

I don't tell him about my evening with Mark Devlin, or the meeting with Graves, or the proposal I've put to Morag and Louis. I don't need another lecture about risk.

Six o'clock comes and goes. Seven. I reread Catherine Gallagher's Missing Persons file, replay Ellis's recorded interviews and wait for the phone to ring. It doesn't.

Morag could string this out for days.

These lulls are part of every job. Why should this one be different? But it is. It is, and already it's started to eat at me.

By 8 p.m. I can't sit here any longer, waiting for something to happen.

I put on my coat and walk out, through the home-going crowds. The sleet's abated but the wind's like a knife. What am I doing out here? Where am I going? To look at the river again? Buy milk? I don't even know.

By the side entrance to a corporate HQ a skinny teenage girl in a cleaner's blue polyester tabard is shivering her way through a quick fag, her back to me. As I pass her she stubs it out and turns, and something drops from her bag onto the ground.

It's a cheap bracelet. I stoop to pick it up. 'Excuse me.' She half-turns back, looks at me without any trace of recognition. 'I think you dropped this.'

'Oh – oh, ta,' Morag's niece says, and then, her thin pale lips barely moving around the word: 'Tomorrow.'

Day 17: Friday – Day 18: Saturday

Johanssen

That night is more of the same: chest pains, a broken wrist, some poor bastard who's drunk bleach. A frail old guy strapped to a trolley, trying to nick something from the nearest equipment cart – Johanssen leans over, unlocks the wheels of the cart and shifts it out of the man's reach ('Sorry, pal') and the old man glares at him. Drill in his chair, motionless and unblinking, as if someone's pulled the plug on him, Vinnie eating a banana and talking about what he's going to do when he gets out, and Cate working through it all, the expression on her face closed and intent, as if she and the patient she's treating are the only people in the world. Working even through the lulls, when there are no patients: pulling things out of cupboards and counting them and scribbling lists, padding out the empty minutes with admin, locked in a cycle of perpetual motion. He's seen it before in others; once, for a time, in himself. You work and you work and you work until you're too tired to remember, until the trivia of the present has taken up every spare inch of space in your head, leaving no room for the past.

On Saturday morning she goes straight up to her room. He waits on his bunk for the sound of her footsteps on the stairs but they don't come. At last he gets up, dresses and goes out. The two-man tail is waiting by the gate, smoking and stamping their feet in the cold; he nods to them and one of them nods back. They let him get twenty yards ahead before they throw down their cigarettes and follow.

He makes the usual random circuit.

He's wheeling back towards the compound and has stopped at a junction to let a patrol pass, when across the street a scene catches his eye.

A man is slumped against a wall, asleep or drunk. Another – a little guy with flattened-down dark hair – is bending over him. It's Jimmy from the yard that first afternoon. *Jimmy's first task is to help us with a little demonstration* ... Just now he's trying to extract something from the slumped man's pocket, though it's made harder by the fact that he's having to work one-handed: his left arm's in a dirty sling.

Jimmy straightens with something in his hand. A photograph. He looks pleased. He's pocketing the photo when his gaze crosses the street to Johanssen, and for a second or two he smiles – a sudden, hopeful smile, a child's smile. But then he seems to remember, and his free hand comes up protectively by his shoulder, and the smile drops away.

They let him in at the compound gate without a word. He crosses the yard, pushes his way through the clinic doors into the waiting room. And there it is, the familiar prickle of tension.

He stops, measuring the silence. Cate will be waiting for him in the clinic.

In that moment tiredness hits him, deep-in-the-bone tiredness, and he wants it to be over.

He steps through the clinic door and lets it swing behind him. A chair is in the centre of the room, empty.

The blow comes out of nowhere.

Pain in his skull. Blood in his mouth. A ripping sound – loud – right next to him: duct tape pulled from a roll. Brice says, 'Block the doors,' and someone laughs, a breathy laugh: the thin dark one. The one with the knife.

He opens his eyes. Tape binds his forearms and his ankles to the frame of the chair, tight. He can't move.

He must have made a sound. Brice crouches before him. He presses a finger to his lips. 'Hussshh ...' One of the others, out of sight, says, 'Gag him?' but Brice smiles. He says to Johanssen, 'That's not going to be necessary, is it? Is it?'

Co-operation. Brice demands co-operation. Johanssen shakes his head. Bloody drool spills from his mouth where his teeth have cut into the lining of his cheek. Brice tuts. 'Messy.'

Johanssen swallows, hard. *This isn't it, he'll want an audience. Quillan. Cate.* But fear's expanding in his guts like a fist uncurling. There are too many blades in this room.

Brice is still crouched before him, looking up into his face. His eyes are bright and clear. 'You're looking tired, Ryan – that is your name, isn't it? And you're making mistakes – but you know that.' He pauses. 'Can I tell you what I think? Can I, Ryan?'

Johanssen nods. Brice smiles encouragingly. *Good boy.*

'You didn't take this place fully into account. You didn't, did you? You've been around, seen some stuff. This place? It was going to be easy, coming here, wasn't it? Walk in, get on the right side of Quillan, make yourself at home ...' Brice brings his face a few inches closer. 'You haven't given this place enough *consideration*,' he says.

He moves suddenly. Johanssen jerks back from the blow but it doesn't come. Brice's on his feet now, an easy casual stroll that takes him the length of the clinic. He runs his hand along the counters, opens cupboards and peers in and closes them again, lifts pieces of equipment and puts them down. Johanssen cranes round to follow him but he's strapped to the chair, and the muscles in his neck burn.

After a minute Brice says, 'I watch you taking out the body bags and you know what I think?' He picks up a bottle of fluid, reads the label, returns it to its place. 'It's a waste. A waste, to go out like that. Not that you will. You'll leave this place alive. Just ... changed.' He nods to himself as if he's been giving it some thought. 'Yeah, this place will change you. Change you for life.

'People are frightened of change, don't you find that?' He rests a hand against the sterilisation unit, taps it once, moves on. 'I mean—' he glances up at Johanssen, a look that mimics genuine curiosity '—what scares you most? The idea of death? You believe in hell? I don't.'

He's found a box of gloves. He pulls one out, idly, and then eases it over his right hand, wiggling his fingers as if testing the fit.

'Death's just like sleeping. But living on, and being changed—' he's wandering back across the room, behind Johanssen, out of sight '—say, living without something you take for granted, living without your eyes or your tongue or your hands – *your hands.*' He's right behind the chair now. One gloved fingertip brushes Johanssen's cheek, lightly, coldly, and he flinches.

Brice murmurs, 'Just think: all that life stretching out in front of you and you can't even wank. Eh? Eh, Ryan?'

Johanssen nods. What comes next?

Brice leans forward: Johanssen can feel his breath. He says, 'This place is changing you. It's got you *marked.*'

Brice's left hand rams into the back of Johanssen's neck, forcing him forward – the right grabs at his jacket and shirt and pulls them up over his head, and rips away the dressing on his back.

One gloved finger probes the wound. The pain jabs into him. His breath catches.

'You see,' Brice whispers, 'once you've made the first cut, the rest – is – easy—'

The finger probes deeper, working its way under his skin. The pain's burning now. He locks his jaw against it, squeezes his eyes closed. Lights dance against his eyelids.

'I could open you up,' Brice whispers. 'I could open you *right up.*' His laugh's soft, close, intimate. 'All we need is time.'

Suddenly Brice hauls him upright. The wound slams against the back of the chair. Brice's hand closes round his throat, squeezing. He can't breathe. He chokes.

'This is just the start,' Brice says and he raises his fist.

The blade. He sees the blade first, sees it slicing through the tape, flinches against the cut but it doesn't come. Cate is beside him, her head bowed as she works on the bindings. His left arm comes free, then his left leg. She looks up and her face is white.

'Don't move,' she says as she shifts round to the other side.

The pain in his back is raw and ragged. His head throbs. He can taste blood again.

You walked into it. You thought without proof he'd do nothing? You should have seen it coming.

His right arm comes free, his right leg. He draws a breath, tries to stand. The blood pulses in his head—

'I said don't move.' Her mouth's a thin tight line. 'What did he do?'

'My back,' he says.

She eases him out of his jacket and pulls up his shirt. For a few seconds she's silent, then she says, 'What about your head?' She hasn't touched the wound.

'My head's fine.'

'Crap. He punched you,' she says. 'You blacked out.'

She checks his eyes and his skull, then says, 'Take your shirt off and lie down.'

When he stands, the room shifts fractionally: he has to hold on to the chair for a second.

He lies face down on a treatment bed with his head turned away from her, feeling the light cool pressure of her fingertips on the edges of the wound. 'You should have had this stitched the first time,' she says. She doesn't say, *This will hurt.*

For a few minutes she's silent as she works. He closes his eyes, waits out the pain. At last she says, 'How important is it? For you to be here. How important?'

He doesn't reply.

She says, 'First it was outside the compound, and it was quick. Now it's in the clinic and he didn't hurry, did he? What's next?'

I could open you right up.

She says, 'Brice will come back, and next time it will be worse.'

When she's finished she moves away and he sits up on the bed. The wound's settled into a low raw burn. His head's still pounding.

She pulls off the gloves, bins them. She doesn't look at him. 'I don't want you in the clinic tonight,' she says.

'I'm fine.'

'No you're not.'

She raises her head. Her eyes are bleak. 'Don't make me deal with what he does to you next. Go back to America. Go back to Victorville. Get out before he comes back.'

He lies on his side on the bunk. The wound in his back throbs. When he closes his eyes he can still feel Brice's fingers digging into his flesh.

Eventually he dozes, but he dreams: the farmhouse again, but this time the scream isn't Terry Cunliffe's. It's his own.

He wakes sweating. Stumbles into the washroom, runs the cold tap into a glass, gulps it down too fast. Stands panting by the sink. The shaving mirror reflects his face back at him, strained and ghostly.

You should run.

He hasn't run from a job since Terry Cunliffe. Eight years. They said he was unreliable but they were wrong, he's proved them wrong. He won't prove them right now.

The certainty's almost physical, sitting cold and hard behind the wall of his chest, like a stone heart.

Time to finish it.

Day 18: Saturday – Day 20: Monday

Karla

An amateur would have waited until the middle of the night. Two in the morning, or three: when the side streets, even in this part of Chelsea, are quiet. But why would a woman be letting herself into an office building at three in the morning?

So it's 11.15 on Saturday night when I walk past the parked cars, heading for Ian Graves's practice. There's a taxi pulled up against the kerb thirty metres from the front door, and as I pass I can make out Robbie's heavy profile behind the wheel, but he doesn't glance at me and I'm too busy reaching into my bag for a key; except it isn't the key to this place and it won't open the door. But it's appearances that matter. The street's largely residential. If a neighbour glances out of their window at the wrong moment, I want to ensure that nothing they see looks remotely criminal.

So here I am, a respectable woman, letting myself into a building with my own key, with no attempt at concealment. See how I appear to fit the key into the lock, and see how the glossy black door swings open for me, and I step inside and close the door quietly behind me. I must work here. I must have left something behind on Friday, and I've come back after a night out to pick it up. There's nothing to worry about.

It's Louis who opens the door for me as I present my key to the lock. He slipped into the ghost house next door hours ago, and has been carefully, methodically working his way to this point ever since – bypassing the alarm and the motion sensors, easing his way past the window locks and then pulling the blinds before turning his attention to the front door. When I switch the hall light on – switching a light on is what innocent people do, after all – he flinches and blinks doubtfully at me but he says nothing. I'm halfway down the corridor when he turns the light off again, plunging me into darkness, but by then I have a torch in my hand.

The file must be here somewhere. All I have to do is find it.

At the end of the passage Graves's door stands ajar. For a few seconds I wait in the doorway, listening – a siren wails along the King's Road – then I click the light on.

Panelled walls, armchairs, coffee table, desk. I try the desk drawers first, but more in hope than expectation. They hold pens and pads, a digital recorder for dictation, a spare power cable, a computer mouse. No files.

Across the room the glazed bookcase houses only journals and books.

I go back to the hallway, where Louis is waiting for me, and nod towards the staircase.

On the first-floor landing there are three doors. One opens into another consulting room, a second hides a lavatory, a third, an office with a window overlooking the back – Louis immediately closes the blind – two desks with computers and phones, a couple of spare chairs, a photocopier, a scanner, and three filing cabinets, all locked. Louis looks at the cabinets and then at me: the look says, *Open?* It'll only take him a minute. But I shake my head. Four psychiatrists are registered at this practice. Three filing cabinets aren't room enough to store the records of one of them, let alone four.

'There's a file store somewhere else.' Two doors open off the office, but one reveals a coat cupboard and the other a kitchenette.

We move through the upper rooms. We find two more consulting rooms, a bathroom and a storeroom for spare furniture and stationery. We don't find any records.

But there was a cardboard file on Graves's desk, with Catherine Gallagher's name on it, and he made notes, handwritten notes—

I go back down to the ground floor and Graves's office.

I look at the furniture again. Then I look at the floor.

It's good-quality carpet, but it's been down for a few years and the wear patterns are starting to show: the pile's flattened just inside the door and in front of the armchairs, and behind the heavy desk where Graves manoeuvres his chair. But there's another faint patch of wear directly in front of a section of panelling.

I cross to it. Step on to it, and turn. There is no picture, no mirror, no view: nothing that would draw anyone to this point in the room.

I go back to the doorway and switch the overhead light off, then return to the panelled wall. This time I angle the torch beam at forty-five degrees to the panelling.

Above the wear patch a straight one-millimetre gap runs down between two panels from floor to ceiling.

I kneel down and run the beam along the base of the panelling at floor level. There's a gap of two millimetres between the lower edge of the panelling and the carpet. Then a few feet to the left, another tiny vertical gap in the panelling, floor to ceiling again. A concealed door.

I rise and I press my gloved hands against the panels, one after another. Nothing gives.

I step back. Louis is standing in the doorway, watching. As I move away, he steps forward. I don't need to ask him to open it.

But it's another fifteen minutes before Louis clambers off his knees, and the panelling cracks, and opens.

My torch beam plays over hundreds of files suspended on hangers from floor to ceiling in the recess.

There must be an organising principle here: alphabetical probably, but with some distinction between current patients and those he no longer sees ... G for Gallagher, where is she?

Louis' mobile buzzes softly and he walks out of the room.

I pull one file out, *Madison*, and then another, *Kirby*—

A whisper from the hallway, a single-syllable obscenity. I only catch the tone. Then the insistent beeping of the alarm system.

In one corner of Graves's office the motion sensor light blinks – on-off, on-off – as it starts to reset.

What?

Louis' dark outline appears in the doorway. I flash the torch towards him. His eyes are wide and desperate.

'Turn it off,' he whispers. 'Don't move.'

I click the torch off. The alarm stops beeping. The red light in the corner goes constant.

I am standing in the dark, in Graves's office, with a torch in my hand and the file store housing Graves's records open behind me, and no good reason to be here, and I cannot move a fraction of an inch, because if I do, the motion sensor will set off the alarm.

My eyes strain towards the dark doorway where Louis stands. I want to ask him what's happened, why he's reset the alarm system, but I can't even see his face.

Then another noise reaches me: a key turning in the front door.

*

As soon as the door opens the alarm begins its warning beep again. The light goes on in the hallway; there are footsteps and then someone giggles and a female voice hisses, 'The alarm, the alarm.'

More footsteps. Someone must have keyed in the code: the alarm stops beeping. In the corner of Graves's office, the red light of the motion sensor blinks off.

I take one big gasping breath, mouth wide to cut the noise. My heart's racing. Louis' breathing is hoarse. The dim light filtering down from the hallway catches the sweat beading his dark skin.

I search the room for a hiding place. There's nowhere.

The woman laughs, high-pitched, a little out of control. She's been drinking. She says, 'Fuck me now.'

I know the voice. It's the butter-wouldn't-melt receptionist, the cabinet minister's wife with her shiny hair and her dull clothes and her air of quiet contentment. Robbie, out front, must have seen them coming – recognised the woman from the recce he did yesterday, realised she could only be coming here, and flashed a warning to Louis. And Louis knew the first thing she'd do would be to deactivate the alarm, so he switched it back on again.

'Fuck ... me,' she says again.

'Right here?' A male voice, one I don't recognise, and nowhere near as drunk: he's the one in control here.

She giggles. 'On the desk.'

Faint sounds that I can't quite place. Then the scrape of a chair on a wooden floor, and a little surprised gasp from her, and a laugh from the man – warm, encouraging – and she moans.

Louis and I stand frozen. The sounds begin to build.

Suddenly Louis nods at me, then slips noiselessly out of the doorway into the corridor.

Follow him? No. Find the file. Be ready to move.

I click the torch on again. The file in my hand is *Eames*. I slide it back into its hanger as quietly as I can, then run the torch to the right. *Faris. Georghiou.*

In the front reception the sounds are building to a climax.

Gallagher, C. There it is. I pull it out, flick it open. The top sheet's just a form: her name, address, home phone number. I flick on: pages and pages of notes, in longhand. I have what I came for.

In the front reception, the woman cries out, once, twice, three times, and the man gives a shuddering gasp, and then the noises stop.

Where's Louis now?

If this goes tits up, we'll shop you.

Has he made his escape? Is he outside now, moving back towards the ghost house, leaving me to it?

I can't blame him. He's got Kyle to think of.

A few more seconds of silence, then, from the front reception, the clearing of throats, the adjustment of clothing.

There's no reason why they should come in here. I kill the torch beam anyway. Footsteps in the hall: her heels, his leather-soled brogues. No talking now. Maybe they're sated, comfortable. Or maybe they just have nothing more to say to each other.

The latch rattles. The front door creaks open – *Thank God*—

Then, 'Wait,' she says, 'I need to do the alarm.'

Eight seconds later, in the top corner of Graves's study the red light of the motion sensor winks into life, and the alarm starts to beep.

There isn't time to get out of here. All I can do is sit down in Graves's chair, place Catherine Gallagher's file on the desk and fold my hands over it.

Then the building goes dark, the front door closes, and the red light goes constant again.

I've lost all sense of time. I'm wearing a watch, but my sleeve covers it and I can't move. My mobile's in my pocket: it buzzes, once, against my hip – is it Robbie, or Sean? – but I can't answer; all I can do is stare at the motion sensor and try to control my breathing.

Minutes pass. Streets away, another police siren wails and flees.

How long can I stay in this position? How long before muscle fatigue and cramp begin to tell? Or will I sit here all night, and all tomorrow too? Will the receptionist let herself back in on Monday morning – her clothes fresh, shiny hair perfect, make-up unsmudged – and find me still sitting in this chair?

Robbie won't let that happen. But Robbie can't get me out of here either; for that he needs Louis. If Louis has vanished, he'll have to improvise. Call up support. Call up Craigie.

How long will it take? How long can I hold out?

How many minutes have passed now? Fifteen? Twenty? Some people have the knack of judging time. I don't. I wish I knew how long it's been.

My hands are folded over the file in a protective gesture. It reminds me of Ian Graves.

If I had light, and the file open in front of me, at least then I might know what it was he was trying to hide. At least I'd have something to read.

I'm still paralysed in my chair, hands folded across the file, muscles screaming in my neck, when there's a faint noise from the hallway and the motion sensor light winks out.

Louis.

For a moment I just sit there, frozen. Then I lean forward until my forehead rests on my hands, and I close my eyes.

Louis' voice comes from the doorway, a soft, uncertain 'Hello?' I raise my head.

He has a torch in his hand, and he plays it across my face, then lets it drop.

I don't say, *You bastard, I thought you'd left me.* I don't have to. He's seen my face.

It's gone 3 a.m. on Sunday when I get back to my apartment. Before I left Graves's office I used a small hi-res camera to copy the file's contents, obsessively checking every shot against the original page to make sure I'd missed nothing. Then I returned the file to its hanger. I left first, and alone. Robbie and Sean will stay in position until Louis himself is clear, the doors and windows closed and locked, the alarm reset. We have been careful. Nothing is disarranged. No one will ever know we were there.

I can't sleep until I've read those pages.

I plug the camera into my laptop, transfer the file, press 'Print', then set coffee on to brew.

I never drink it. Within three minutes the pages have claimed me.

Graves and I have something in common. He too is a collector of data.

The form first. Name, address, phone number. Occupation: junior account manager (advertising). The space for a work contact number is blank, so is the section for her GP's details. Then the notes themselves: every meeting over a fifteen-month period logged and detailed. There's something remorseless about the marching characters.

It's all there, exactly as Graves described it. The distant, demanding father, the emotionally absent mother, a childhood of conditional love – conditional on achievement, good school reports, exams passed with flying colours … I picture Catherine as a serious child at the dinner table, still in her school uniform, her blonde hair in plaits, fresh from her textbooks or her piano practice, yearning to impress.

Another meeting, and another, and another. The sleepless nights. The sense of worthlessness. The fear of that catastrophic mistake, of being unmasked as simply not good enough … I battle my way through the jargon to the last visit she made before she disappeared, looking for a hint of a confession, the first clue to the fact that she confided in Graves. And then I go back to the beginning and start all over again, this time looking for a gap, an edit, because Graves may have been afraid of a warrant, may have removed all mention of what Catherine did in case Ellis came back.

There's no clue. There's no gap. Just a woman's despair reduced to a set of syndromes; clever names for pain.

For all their careful itemisation of personality, Graves's notes tell me nothing.

I'm dead-ended, aren't I? *Go to bed. You're tired, you need to come to it fresh.* The old half-lie, it'll look better in the morning.

But my brain won't let me sleep: I lie there while the thoughts tick in my head, metronomic, insistent, like the drip of a tap. Still I keep coming back to the last moments of our interview with Graves—

You've asked exactly the same questions as your colleague did a year ago.
And that surprises you?
I thought as you'd taken the trouble to call on me again …
We'd be asking different questions? Not always.

—and that odd vibration in the air between us, jarring, off key … I thought he was suspicious of us, but he hasn't pursued it. What, then? What triggered that reaction in Graves? I play and replay our conversation in my head. There's nothing. Nothing but Graves with his hand flattened protectively across the cover of the file. Keeping me out.

It's there, the clue, it has to be.

There's only one person left to ask. Stephen.

And that's a good idea?

Stephen knows nothing of Karla. But keeping Karla from him has been a source of friction between us before now. Because although I'm a good liar, of all the people I've ever known, Stephen is the one who can always tell.

He lives alone in Strand on the Green, a ribbon of pretty eighteenth-century houses overlooking the river by Kew Bridge. There are three pubs and a café along its stretch of towpath. On sunny weekends their outside benches are crowded with drinkers, but today's damp and cold, and only the hardened smokers are on duty.

He opens the door, beaming. He's a big man and he almost fills the frame.

'Come in, come in. Let me take your coat. I've just made coffee, do go through.'

The kitchen is at the back, overlooking a neat lawn and a bare apple tree. Pergolesi's *Stabat Mater* filters out of his speaker system, sombre and heartbreaking.

'Heavens,' he says, 'let's turn that off. Something more cheerful—'

'No,' I say, 'leave it.'

'Of course,' he says smoothly. But he fusses over the coffee, over whether I want milk or cream, whether we should drink it in the kitchen or in the sitting room, whether we need biscuits and if so, which I'd prefer. He takes out one set of cups and then immediately puts them away again and picks out others. He knows something's up. When did I last call him out of the blue and ask to come round immediately? Show up on his doorstep when I haven't slept a wink the night before?

Finally he's loaded a tray. He lifts it and beams again. 'Shall we?' So I lead the way into the sitting room and take a seat, and let him go through the ritual of serving me while we chat about things we both know are irrelevant.

I was five when he was born: the older sister, the sensible, careful one, already aware of the gulf between our parents, a gulf which even Stephen's arrival – the spitting image of his father – couldn't bridge. Like me he was born into a war zone, and like me he became caught up in its hostilities, pressed into service by both sides. Though he had it easier; he had me to explain the rules of combat to him, as soon as he was old enough to understand: when to nod, when to lie, when to make yourself scarce. Ours was a childhood of subterfuge. No wonder we turned out the way we have.

Other people's secrets have become our business, but while I buy and sell them, my brother Stephen, like Ian Graves, is a psychiatrist. Except that his clientele's made up not of the unhappy rich – desperate lawyers, suicidal bankers – but of the criminally deranged, men

222

and women too sick for prison, let alone the 'enhanced individual liberty' of the Program. He spends much of his time in secure institutions, behind bars, quietly persuading his damaged charges to reveal their warped assumptions, their sick fantasies. And they look at this big, clever man with his air of unjudgemental concern, and for some reason they tell him.

Sometimes I wonder what he'd make of the truth about me.

He knew about Thomas Drew, of course – the relationship, and the fact I went to work for him. Knew the business was something to do with IT and security. Knew that Drew disappeared, leaving problems that I had to sort out. Knew that I walked away with a windfall, carefully invested, and never had a regular job after that … But he was a medical student then, wrapped up in his own life, and I was still the older sister, aware of the rules before he was even born, telling him only what he needed to know.

By the time he got round to asking the important questions, I already knew I was never going to answer them honestly.

Today we talk about things that don't matter: concerts we've been to, mutual acquaintances from years back, his last holiday. He doesn't say whether he travelled alone. He's gay, but his private life, like the exact source of my money, is something we skirt around. But I can't put it off for ever. At last I say, 'I need to ask you a favour.'

He smiles as if it's the simplest thing in the world, but behind that smile his mind is working.

I reach into my bag and bring out Catherine Gallagher's notes.

'I need your opinion.'

'My opinion?' He says it lightly. I'm not fooled.

'Your professional opinion. These notes—' I hold the file in my lap but I don't offer it to him yet '—were made by a psychiatrist. They concern a young woman. I'd like your view.'

The word 'psychiatrist' has made him uneasy. This is someone else's case. He looks at the file and then up at my face.

'I'm asking this as a favour. No one knows I'm speaking to you, and unless you tell anyone, no one will ever know. You won't be quoted—'

His hand wipes the air between us, as if that's the last thing on his mind.

I say, 'I simply want to know … I would like you to read these notes and tell me what you think. Today – now, if you can. Or I can bring them back some other time. I'd rather not leave them here. This is the only copy I have, and it wasn't easy to get hold of.'

I stop then. I could say more, but that won't change his decision.

His gaze travels from me to the file and back to me again. At last he says, 'It's important, isn't it? You seemed – distracted – on the phone …'

I shrug. 'A bad night's sleep.'

'Because of this?'

I had a lie lined up, but for once it fails me.

He looks at me for a long time. Then he reaches out a hand, takes the file and opens it. He glances up at me. The top sheet's missing.

'I've taken out her name. I felt it would be better—'

'Yes,' he says, 'of course.' He hesitates again, but doesn't state the obvious: that these pages have been photographed.

'Could you do it today? You may have plans for lunch.'

He smiles ruefully. 'I was planning to have lunch with you.'

'Were we going out?'

'I thought I might cook.'

I rise. 'I can fix something.'

He raises his eyebrows. He knows just how bad my cooking is.

He takes the file up to his study, a small book-lined room on the first floor. I go up once to ask him if he needs more coffee, and again to take him a sandwich, which is all the lunch he wants. The first time he looks up from the file as if he's surfacing from a great depth, and his responses are monosyllabic. The second time he's leafing rapidly back and forth through the pages, cross-referencing something, and he doesn't even glance at me. I eat alone in the kitchen, looking out at the garden. When the recording ends I don't put another one on, and the silence is like an electronic hum in my ears. The riverside path runs directly outside the front windows and from time to time people walk past, their voices suddenly loud, delivering snatches of conversation I'm not supposed to hear. But they see only the houses, not the people inside; they have no idea anyone's listening.

At last he comes halfway down the stairs. 'Charlotte?'

I go up with more coffee. He's returned to his chair. The notes are back in their file, on a table beside him. As I take a seat opposite, suddenly I'm anxious.

He sits with his elbows on the arms of the chair, his hands laced together in front of him.

'Who is she?' he asks.

'Just a young woman I … Her mother's a friend of a friend.'

Liar. But he lets it go. 'Do you know her personally?'

Safer ground now. 'No.'

'But you know people who know her.'

'I've talked to people who knew her.' Another lie, though this one's small and white. Ellis has done most of the talking; I've just listened. It's close enough.

He instantly picks up on the tense. 'Knew?'

'Knew.'

He doesn't ask if that means she's dead. Maybe he doesn't need to. He sits back in his seat. 'Tell me who you spoke to.'

'Colleagues. Her boss.'

'Friends?'

'An ex-lover; but that was just a fling.'

'Were there friends you could have spoken to?'

'I haven't been able to trace anyone who was close to her. Nor could the police.'

His look says, *So the police are involved, are they?*

He murmurs, 'And no family, of course, if you don't count the mother, and sadly we can't.' Then, 'What about the psychiatrist who wrote these notes?'

'I've spoken to him, yes. And I've been to her home.'

'Did she live with other people?'

'She lived alone.'

He sits back in his chair and frowns to himself.

'Tell me how her colleagues described her.'

'Very good at her job. Very competent. Ambitious. Driven.'

'So her depression manifested itself – how? What did her colleagues say?'

'They had no idea she was depressed. She hid it from them.'

'No idea at all?'

'None. She didn't confide in anyone. She wasn't the type.'

'And she didn't work closely with others?'

'She worked in a small team, sometimes under pressure. She had a lot of contact with a few close colleagues.'

He frowns again. He says, 'The notes say she was worried about making mistakes at work. She didn't mention that to her colleagues? She must have been anxious about losing her job.'

'She didn't confide in anyone,' I say again.

'And no one noticed anything? No anxiety? What about anger?'

'Anger?'

He touches the file lightly. 'This is an angry woman. Throughout her whole life no one loved her for what she was, only what she did. Her psychiatrist views her as a suicide risk. Suicide's a furious act. No one picked up on that?' I shake my head. 'A refusal to engage, maybe?'

'She was certainly a very private person. She kept herself to herself.'

'It would have been more than that. An absence, almost: her colleagues might have felt rejected, or unsupported.'

'Nothing like that. They didn't even realise there was a problem until ...' I stop there.

He registers the hesitation. How does his mind finish that sentence? *Until she killed herself? Until they found her?*

'But while they were working together?' he asks. 'Did they feel she was going to let them down?'

'No. She prided herself on never making mistakes.'

Stephen nods once, to himself, but when he speaks again he's changed the subject.

'Her psychiatrist didn't prescribe antidepressants.'

'She wouldn't give the name of her GP.'

A slower nod. He doesn't comment. 'Was she drinking heavily?'

'Maybe at home, though there's no evidence. Never in public. Not even at parties. One drink, two at most.'

'Physical symptoms,' he says. 'Complaining about aches and pains?'

'She was never ill. Nothing stronger than paracetamol in her bathroom cabinet.'

'What about her attendance record? Days when she phoned in sick at short notice?'

'No.'

'No time off sick?'

'Virtually none.'

'What about self-harm? Any evidence of that?'

'You mean cutting herself?'

'Possibly. But tell me about her background. White collar?'

'Highly educated middle class.'

'Then she may have self-harmed through social transgression. Proxy self-harm: screaming at her boss, sleeping with a colleague's husband. Bad behaviour, with potentially catastrophic consequences.'

I shake my head. 'No.'

'And she didn't cut herself either, I suppose.'

Something in his tone catches at my attention, but I can't put a name to it.

'She may have cut herself where it wouldn't show.'

'An autopsy would have found it,' he says. He purses his lips, frowns. It's as if he's seen something and now he's focusing on it, homing in on it.

'Tell me about where she lived,' he says.

The question catches me out. It seems irrelevant. 'Clean, tidy. Dull.'

'Not shabby? Not neglected? Any sign that she'd ceased to notice her surroundings, or ceased to care about them?'

'Very tidy. Tins lined up in the cupboards.'

'That could link to obsessionality. If she was naturally very tidy that could have been magnified by her depression. But there should have been another area that she neglected. An overgrown garden? Filthy car?'

'She didn't have a garden. I didn't see her car.'

'What about her appearance? Her clothes?'

'Conservative. Nothing frivolous but nothing shabby either. I think she took care of her appearance. She bought good clothes and she looked after them. She wore make-up. She exercised.'

'And towards the end? I assume there was some crisis—'

'No change.'

He passes a hand over his mouth. He's thinking.

He says, 'The notes say she was anxious about making mistakes at work – catastrophic mistakes. She worked in advertising?'

'She was a doctor.'

'But the notes say—' He stops. Then nods to himself, reassessing her. *Of course. She lied.* 'What sort of doctor?'

'Intensive care.'

He raises his eyebrows. 'And they really never spotted anything, her colleagues?' Then he says, 'She didn't go to her GP either, did she? That's why she wouldn't give their name.'

'She self-referred.'

'Straight to the psychiatrist?'

'Private patient, paying cash. He says she was terrified of anyone finding out she wasn't coping.'

'Because she was a doctor, yes. And doctors notoriously hide their own problems.' He sits back again. 'You spoke to the psychiatrist. How was he?'

'Protective. Maybe defensive. The notes seemed to be an issue for him, but when I read them ...'

'She took an overdose?' he asks.

'No one knows.'

'I'm sorry?'

'She was never found. The last sighting was CCTV footage from the entrance lobby of the block where she lived. She walked out of the door and vanished.'

'Who reported her missing?'

'The psychiatrist.'

He looks at me intently. 'The *psychiatrist* reported her missing? Not her colleagues?'

'She was on leave when she disappeared. She failed to turn up for an appointment. He couldn't reach her by phone, he had no work number for her, so he went to her flat—'

'He actually went to her flat? He didn't just write a letter?'

'He was worried.'

'And no one answered the door, so he went to the police.'

'Yes.'

'Saying, "I demand you look for this woman, she's a potential suicide."'

'Yes.'

'And now you're trying to find her?'

'I want to know what happened to her.'

'Do you think she's dead?' he asks.

'I'd rather not say what I think.'

'But you want me to say what *I* think?'

'Yes.'

He turns his head away and then he rises and walks the length of the room. It's not a large room, and he's a tall man: three paces take him to the window. For a few seconds he stares out towards the river – to the left a grey-white and red District Line train crosses Kew Railway Bridge, to the right the tower blocks of Brentford lumber up against the sky – then he turns to me.

'Why did you come to me?'

'Because I have to know what happened.'

'But the notes tell you what happened. Why don't you believe them?'

Because she killed someone and it was bad. Because Devlin saw the darkness in her and Graves should have too. Because I think he did but I can't prove it. I don't have a lie for that. 'I can't tell you.'

'Because you don't know why you don't believe them?'

Or that. 'I can't tell you.'

Another look: baffled concern this time. A good man in an evil universe, trying to make sense of it all. Better than I am, so much better. Better by a thousand miles. He deserves more from me than this.

I say, 'I need to know what happened to that woman. I thought the notes would give me an answer. But they don't. I've read them half a dozen times. The notes don't give me anything.'

'They give you a textbook example of a depressive.'

'Maybe I believed there was more to it than that.'

'Not in these notes.' He says it with complete finality.

It's like a weight's been dropped on me, pressing me into my seat. My head, my chest, my guts, my limbs are heavy. Because I was so sure? Or because like Ellis I've turned over all the stones? This was the last one, and I'd counted on there being an answer beneath it? An answer that would explain it all, deliver me the client, make Johanssen safe? But there isn't.

But he mustn't see any of that. I begin to gather myself. 'Then I'm sorry I deprived you of a good lunch—'

I glance up into his face.

'Everything you'd expect to see in a potential suicide,' he says. 'And that's the problem. The whole thing's too clean, too … focused. Real people are messier than this. Especially real people who're planning to kill themselves.'

'You don't think she was suicidal?'

'I don't think she was ever in the room,' he says.

I gape at him.

'Did you notice the handwriting? Too regular throughout. The ink changes between entries but there's no variation in the style between the end of one entry and the beginning of another. And there should be differences. Your handwriting changes fractionally every time you pick up a pen – sometimes you write fast, sometimes slowly, and the surface you're resting on varies, it's early morning, it's two in the afternoon, you're in a hurry, you're not, you've just had two cups of coffee, you haven't stopped for lunch … Variation. His writing should change and it doesn't. Except towards the end. Did you notice? The character size starts to fluctuate. And there are recurring phrases – he's repeating himself. He's coming out with clichés, almost. It's as if he's got tired. As if he's been sitting at that desk for hours, he's on a deadline, and he's beginning to give out.' He stops.

I can hardly breathe. 'Go on.'

'He says she's a potential suicide. He says she talked of killing herself. But did anyone who actually knew her think she was suicidal?'

'She was hiding it.'

'What if there was nothing to hide? There's no anger, there's no self-neglect, there are no lapses in concentration. She kept her home tidy, she exercised, she looked after her appearance, she was punctual, she was reliable. Where's the depressive? In the file.'

'You're saying the notes are fake.'

'We've got, what? Fifteen months of appointments here? I'd say he wrote it in one sitting. All of it. He had a list of symptoms in his head and he worked through it, checking each one off. As I said: everything you'd expect to see in a potential suicide. He's focused on delivering one message: that this woman is going to kill herself.'

He spreads his hands – 'Charlotte. I cannot be certain' – then drops them. 'But on the evidence you've given me? She was no more suicidal than you or I.'

Everything drops into place.

You look at what you've been given and none of it makes sense.

Because you bought the story. Like everyone else did: the police, her colleagues, her neighbours, the press, everyone except Mark Devlin. You bought the story.

Beyond the window the daylight throbs like a pulse.

But what if the story is a lie?

What do we have? A missing woman, and an expert witness. A set of appointments, and the notes, fifteen months' testimony to Catherine Gallagher's suicidal state. But no proof.

Her neighbours hardly knew her. Her colleagues thought she was fine. Everything rests on Graves's testimony. Take that testimony away – take the notes away – and what are you left with? A set-up.

Don't fall into the trap of certainty. Don't believe it just because you want to.

But it feels like the truth all right.

There's no family clamouring for answers. There is no body, and there will be no inquest. Easy just to accept that she's lying dead somewhere. What did Roberts say? *It's like her: not wanting to be found. It's like her.* But the notes are the weak link and Graves knows it. That gesture of his – his hand splaying across the cover of the file – and that vibration in the air between us, the one I took for suspicion … It wasn't that. It was fear.

He thinks the police are on to him. Otherwise why would they ask the same questions they asked a year ago? Because they want to catch him out.

So what did he give us? The safe answers, the things he knows we can't fault. An account of an unhappy childhood which we can't possibly verify, and a list of symptoms: diurnal mood variations and depressive psychodementia, loss of appetite, low self-esteem. *Textbook.*

That's why he hasn't phoned Ellis's DCI, checked us out. He doesn't want to raise his profile. He's hoping that if he keeps his head down all this will go away.

I've been staring into space. Stephen is watching me. His face has a look of compassion. 'Charlotte,' he says.

I push my hands down into my lap. 'I'm all right.' And I am.

'You said her mother—'

This time the lie comes out smoothly: 'She's in a nursing home. And no one else is interested. I said I'd try to help.'

Still, he knows I'm lying. He always knows. I can see the flash of frustration before he checks it. He wants to ask again. He also knows it won't make any difference.

He says, 'You need to go to the police with this. There could be perfectly good reasons why this has happened. Sometimes people want to disappear …' An echo of Devlin's words. But it isn't what he's thinking, I know it isn't; he's thinking that another psychiatrist has somehow colluded in the disappearance of a young woman, has engineered that disappearance to look like suicide so no questions will be asked. Maybe it's worse when it's one of your own.

He's still talking. 'Charlotte? Tell me you'll go to the police. They don't have to know you've seen the notes.' He's guessed I shouldn't have them then, guessed they were obtained by illicit means. 'Just tell them what her colleagues said. Tell them you have an expert who's willing to review her file and give a second opinion. Will you do that?'

I nod. Does he believe me?

He smiles encouragingly, as if I'm a patient. 'And phone me. Tell me what they say.'

I nod again, but when I look at him I can still see the same baffled frustration on his face. He knows he hasn't convinced me. And he's right.

I'm not going to the police. I'm going after Graves.

Common sense kicks in before I've even got the car to Hammersmith. Stephen's word isn't good enough. I need evidence.

Oh, there'll be more grounds for suspicion. Catherine Gallagher's 'cash payments' for treatment mysteriously missing from the practice accounts, or added late as an afterthought. Appointments always falling outside office hours – none of Graves's colleagues, even the receptionist, will ever have set eyes on her. The appointments themselves will appear only in Graves's personal diary ... But I've seen Graves in action. He'll have an answer for everything. An accounting mistake; and of course her shift patterns ruled out meetings during conventional hours, or maybe she insisted on coming at strange times because she was fearful of being recognised. The diary? I can almost hear his smooth voice: *An administrative error. Why, is it important?*

If I'm going face to face with Graves I need something that he can't dodge. I need proof. To place Catherine Gallagher somewhere else during some of those appointments. At the hospital or in the gym or on the Tube or accessing her emails or withdrawing cash from a machine – it doesn't matter where, but somewhere she left a trail. But how long will that take to find? How long can I afford to wait? Twelve separate dates to check, and one discrepancy won't be enough, we need two or three ... What if they've thought of that? What if they looked for the blanks in her life and fitted the appointments into them?

Call Ellis? See what he can find? But if Stephen's right, Graves fixed Catherine's 'suicide'. Maybe she paid him to do it. Or maybe someone else did, and Graves can lead me to them. I don't want Ellis anywhere near me when I find them.

Graves has a house in Hampstead. I send Sean there while Robbie goes to the practice in Chelsea: Graves deals with busy people, maybe he sees patients on a Sunday. Sean has the better traffic, but there's no one home in the house by the Heath. I tell him to sit tight. Graves may return at any moment.

Robbie phones fifteen minutes later. The practice is in darkness, and no one's answering the door.

I have a mobile number for Graves. Call him? I'm still staring at the handset when it rings: Sean again. He's spoken to a neighbour. Graves is clearing his late mother's house in Buckinghamshire.

It takes me less than five minutes to trace the address.

4.55 on Sunday evening. Sunset outside the window. 'Dr Graves ... Elizabeth Crow.'

A hesitation on the line. 'I'm sorry, I don't think ...?'

My turn to think, *Liar*. 'I was with DI Ellis. I'm sure you remember.'

'How did you get this number?' he says sharply.

'Some new information's come to light. I'm afraid we need another meeting. Today.'

Another hesitation. What do the words 'new information' suggest to him? I wish I knew. 'Well I'm sorry, it's just going to have to wait. I'm not in London—'

'We do know where you are.'

'Well then,' he says, as if I've proved his point.

'You don't want to know what we found?' *Nosy bastards, psychiatrists.*

'To be honest, Ms Crow, I think you've wasted enough of my time.'

'Or you've wasted ours.'

'I don't know what you're—'

Play the card. 'You lied, Dr Graves, and we can prove it.'

'Who says so?'

There's only bluffing left. 'Care to guess?'

Some silences are empty, they're voids. This one blooms on the line between us, opens up like a flower or a drop of ink in water.

I don't know what answer his mind's supplied. All I know is that I have him.

'Please stay where you are.'

Another silence. What's he going to do? Put the phone down? Run?

'A car is on its way.'

'Will there be uniforms?' Suddenly his voice is tight, tremulous. I hear him swallow.

'You'd prefer not?' He's thinking of the neighbours, the public humiliation ... 'I'll see what I can do.'

'I'll need protection,' he says. He's afraid. Good. Let him be afraid.

'That can be arranged. Just be there, Dr Graves.'

Five minutes past five. Should I send Robbie to babysit Graves? Robbie's closer than I am, so's Sean. If the traffic's good, either of them could be there within an hour. But Graves won't run, not if he thinks we have proof: Graves is either going to roll, or stand and fight. And I've met enough violent men to know when I'm at risk. He might try argument or even threats, but not physical violence. He's not the type. I don't want either Robbie or Sean exposed. If this goes the way it might, the fewer of us he sees, the better.

Instead I phone Robbie and tell him to get hold of an unmarked van, switch plates, and await further instructions. We may need to move Graves out of there, to a safe house.

And all the time: *You think you can bluff your way through this? What happens when Graves realises you don't have enough?*

Twenty past five. I leave on foot with an overnight bag: Charlotte Alton going to visit friends. A taxi, and then a five-minute walk to the lock-up where we keep a couple of the back-up vehicles: the black four-wheel drive is parked there. In the back of the garage I change into Elizabeth Crow's dowdy skirt and coat, her flat shoes and her dark wig. One last subterfuge … The charade of my 'professional' status has almost reached the end of its usefulness – before the evening's out Graves will have realised I'm not what I said I was – but by then it will be too late.

It's 7.17 and dark when I drive through a small village in the Chilterns. Houses straggle down one side of a twisting rural road. A couple of them are chocolate-box quaint, but much of the village is newer – 30s, 50s, newbuild – and unspecial. Even so there's money around: a Jag facing out of one drive, a Porsche Cayenne with tinted windows pulled up on a verge. On the other side of the road the four-wheel drive's headlights pick out a blighted winter field and a dead tree. There's no pavement and no street lamps.

I drive through the village. The houses thin out. The turning I'm looking for is no more than a gap in an overgrown hedge. I slow the car. Through the gap, beyond an area of weedy gravel, a low white 30s house squats against a background of dark trees. There's a pair of dormers in the eaves, like eyes: one of them shows a light behind it, as if the house is winking. There's a light on downstairs too, but the curtains are closed. A car is parked in the drive; the plate matches a vehicle registered in Ian Graves's name.

Graves's mother passed away two months ago at the age of eighty-eight, after a short spell in hospital; utility bills suggest the house has been empty since then.

I park in a lay-by thirty metres beyond the entrance to the drive. As I walk back up the dark road towards the house the only sign of life is a woman in a Barbour who passes me walking a fat black Labrador.

I turn into the drive and crunch across the gravel. It's a windy night: beyond the building, the trees toss and hiss at me.

I press the doorbell. An electronic chime sounds inside. And movement, was that movement? I wait for approaching footsteps, the outline of Graves's trim figure in the ribbed glass of the front door. Nothing happens. After twenty seconds I press the bell again. It's a small house: he must have heard me. Maybe he's in the bathroom.

Another minute passes. Still nothing.

I step back and look up at the lit dormer window: all I can see is an angled patch of ceiling with a pool of light cast upwards from a table lamp. No movement. The downstairs curtains don't twitch.

I pull out my torch, switch it on. A path runs along the side of the house. I make my way down it. In a side window the curtains are only half-drawn. Inside, light spilling in from a hall through an open doorway shows a bed with ornaments strewn across it – little blue and white Wedgwood trinket boxes and bud vases and pin trays, tiny china flower arrangements – and a cardboard box on its side as if it's been emptied hastily. I edge round, peer sideways to take in more of the room. A chest of drawers stands in a shadowy corner, the lower drawer open with clothing spilling out over the sides, the upper drawer pulled right out and upended, as if someone's been through the contents in a hurry, looking for something.

Another sound, close by. A door, closing softly?

I grip the torch, walk round to the back of the house. No one in sight. The trees rattle in the wind. I stare towards them. Nothing. Then turn again to the house.

Patio doors with the curtains closed, the room beyond in darkness. A lighted window with a blind pulled down, and beside it a back door with more ribbed glass in the upper panel. I wad my hand with a handkerchief and try the door. It's unlocked.

It opens into a kitchen: shabby Formica units, vinyl flooring.

I step inside, close the door behind me. No sound. 'Hello? Dr Graves?'

Across the kitchen, to the hallway. There's the door into the bedroom, standing ajar, and this must be the bathroom—

He's wedged between the toilet pan and the wall. His eyes are open and his face has an expression of mild protest. Whoever killed him used a knife. His clothes – no longer colourless – are the sticky dark red-black of blood.

Time hangs suspended; I don't know how long for. And then—

Oh Jesus.

Suddenly I want to run. Run and hide. Drive fast and drive a long way, put as many miles as possible between myself and this, bury myself where it can't find me—

Stop.

Back it comes. The sense of movement within the house just after I pressed the bell. A moment later, a door closing—

Are you alone? Listen.

There's no controlled breathing from the next room, no creak of floorboards. *Yes.*

But they knew you were coming.

Did they bug Graves's phone? Were they listening when I rang him?

I told him I was sending a car. When they knocked, he'd have thought it was the police. How many standing on the doorstep when he opened the door? One? Two? And he'd have felt a little stab of relief: *Plainclothes, they sent plainclothes after all.*

Poor bastard. Poor stupid bastard.

Or did he panic? Did he call someone to warn them it was all about to unravel?

I should have sent Robbie. No – I should never have phoned. I should have just come here, confronted him on his doorstep, proof or no proof. I should never have given them the chance—

A sound cuts through the house, insistent, staccato: a mobile ringtone.

It jars me into action. Down the short hallway and right, into a darkened living room. The phone's screen shines blue from the floor. I scoop it up. The screen shows a mobile number.

A beat, then I press the answer key, hold the phone to my ear. Four seconds of silence, and the line goes dead.

I pull the phone away from my ear, stare at the little screen.

Focus. You don't have much time.

I access 'Call log'. Go into 'Received calls'. Top of the list is that last call, timed at 19.34, from a mobile number, six seconds duration. Second on the list: 'Unknown number'. My own landline call to Graves, secure and untraceable, logged at 16.55.

I go into 'Dialled calls', and there it is. At 17.08 – moments after I hung up – Graves called that first mobile number, a call that lasted less than two minutes.

Was he panicking? Warning someone? Begging for help? And now whoever's on that number has phoned back. Checking he's OK? Checking he isn't? Checking that the job's been done? Checking for me?

They could have called from miles away. Or from the end of the garden, by the trees—

A lurch of panic. *Stop it.*

Memorise the number. Repeat it back. Got it? Good. Now switch the phone off. Don't drop it. Put it in your pocket. You're ahead of the police right now. See if you can keep it that way.

Now move. Move.

I walk back up the hallway. Part of me doesn't want to look, wants to pretend the thing in the bathroom isn't there. Part of me has to see him again. To be sure?

Everything's unchanged. It's only in your nightmares that the dead move. Still I can't take my eyes off him: I have to back away across the kitchen, stopping only when I bump into the sink.

Get out of here.

And if they're outside, waiting?

I open the back door using the handkerchief. Pause on the threshold, straining into the dark. Nothing. No dark shape, no sudden onrush.

Step out. Close the door. *That's good, don't hurry it.* Mechanical, careful, even though the blood's beating in my throat so hard it could choke me. But it's the little details that matter. There will be no prints.

I turn. On the far side of the damp lawn the evergreens rock.

Someone there?

Go. Just go.

I drive, on minor rural roads, for six miles. Six miles with the image of Graves in my head, as if it's on a loop that I'm being forced to watch again and again. My hands are clammy on the wheel. *You shouldn't have phoned. You shouldn't have given them a chance.*

At last I come to a possible spot: a gateway, a copse. The winter trees are bare, skeletal, but there's an evergreen holly, some scrubby brambles, a thickening of undergrowth. The ground is soft: the tyre marks will be there tomorrow. Nothing I can do about that.

I get out, retrieve the spare set of plates from their hidden compartment and set about changing them. My hands are cold and stiff, and filthy by the time I've finished, but Graves's village is the sort where retired civil servants pass the time jotting down the vehicle registration numbers of strangers. For all I know the woman walking the fat Labrador has a photographic memory. Every major road into London has number-plate-recognition cameras. I won't lay a trail for them.

Then I pull off Elizabeth Crow's brown wig and stuff it into a bag, along with her shoes and coat. I'm Karla again, in lipstick and heels, though I have to fight the shakes in my hand as I apply the lipstick.

I check the map, then I make one call to Robbie – precise, practical instructions with no explanation – and finally I look around, in door pockets and under seats, for anything I wouldn't want to leave behind.

I get back into the car, start the engine again, and move off.

On the way back into London the shock uncoils on me. Sometimes I'm fine. Sometimes I'm shaking. I'm cold, but when I turn the heater up it makes no difference.

I want to curl into a ball. I want to shut it all out. Then I want to talk to someone – anyone – tell them everything. It's shock, I know, this need to make a story of it, as if that will make sense of it, make it safe. I'm in shock. Ridiculous. Then I want to laugh, and that's shock too. I set my jaw: the effort makes my muscles ache.

Get a grip. Bloody well get a grip.

I can't tell anyone. Robbie, Sean … The less they know, the better. Because once you start to explain, it becomes a habit, or an obligation. And once they know, they'll be part of it, presented with decisions they shouldn't be asked to make. They don't want that. They're just doing their jobs.

Instead I stare through the windscreen at the lights of the other vehicles on the road, flashing past at coded intervals. There's a message out there that I can't decipher.

I want to forget Graves's face, and I can't.

I hit the outskirts of west London: the sodium lighting flattens the buildings into a two-dimensional frieze like a cardboard stage set.

At last I take a left and pull over, leave the engine running and get out. Robbie's waiting on the kerb, hands in pockets. As we pass on the pavement, I say, 'Get it off the road. Make it disappear.' The calm in my voice belongs to someone else.

'Plates?'

'Already done.'

Robbie just nods and slides into the driver's seat, and the car accelerates away. But I've read his big quiet features. He's trying not to look too hard at any of this, trying to take it one step at a time, but he knows something dark's lurking just out of sight: something bad has happened and we're covering our tracks. How much does he guess?

He'll know for certain tomorrow. The TV news will see to that.

I hurry back to the main road. The traffic's a steady stream belching fumes, three lanes in and three out, separated by a barrier. I have to descend to a subway to cross. The lighting's yellowish grey and the air down here is cold and damp, and smells of urine. The steps at the far end are half-blocked by a group of kids, aged thirteen or fourteen at most, smoking and talking and pulling at each other. Tinny tunes jangle out of their mobile phones. They watch me as I edge round them, assessing my vulnerability. Their confidence is frightening. One of them says something to my back as I scuttle away, but I don't make out the words and right now I don't care.

As I surface it starts to rain.

The next car is waiting for me in a side road, hazards blinking, Sean behind the wheel. It pulls away before I've got my door closed.

It hits me: Sean doesn't know the mess he's in.

We weave across the city, taking the least direct route. Corner shops and off-licences and pubs are open. People are picking up groceries, meeting friends, heading out for a Sunday night drink ... The mid-evening normality of it all jolts me. I've been robbed of my bearings, knocked out of place. The last two hours seem like a sickbed dream, stained with fever. I'm not sure what time it is, and when I look at my watch, the numbers and the hands are meaningless.

Halfway back to Docklands I say suddenly, 'Graves is dead.'

Sean looks sideways at me, briefly, then back to the road. His hands tighten on the steering wheel. He breathes out, once. His face is still.

'He was murdered at his mother's house this evening. You spoke to his neighbours; they told you where to find him. You'll be a suspect. Dump the car, then go home. Craigie will contact you with a cover story and an alibi. As soon as the news breaks, go to the police. They'll question you, but your cover will hold, I promise. I'm sorry. I didn't know this was going to happen.'

He's silent, driving mechanically, absorbing all this. Finally he asks, 'Does Dad know?' and he sounds so young.

Up in my apartment I want Scotch but instead I make myself tea with two sugars: the cliché for shock. It's almost undrinkable but I force it down like medicine.

Then I log on and send Finn details of the two calls, one to the unknown mobile, the other from it. <trace mobile. user? loc? call hist? URGENT> How long before I get a reply? The police won't need a warrant to access Graves's phone records; an inspector's signature on an S22 notice is all they'll require. I have to trace whoever's on that number before they do.

When the phone rings I jump so hard the tea slops into my lap.

It's Charlotte's phone, but I don't pick up and the caller hangs up. The message light winks at me. One message. I hit 'Play', and Mark Devlin starts talking, but he isn't talking to me, he's talking to another woman, and tonight she has ceased to exist.

I phone Robbie on a safe line. It's not a good call. I hear it in his silences, and in the way his voice goes up and down when he speaks: he's fighting his fears. Sean in a police interview room, Sean's face in some copper's memory ... 'He knew the risks,' he says. 'Had to happen sooner or later, I s'pose. Sometimes you're just unlucky.' But his stoicism's tissue-thin; a word could puncture it.

'How was Sean?' he asks, and I say, 'Sean was great. He's a good lad. We'll look after him.' And I mean it. Whatever it costs, whoever I have to bribe or smear, I'll see Sean isn't harmed by this. Somehow it's still not enough.

Then finally: Craigie.

That first meeting with Graves, lifting the file, the confrontation over the phone, Graves dead ... So many things withheld from him till now. I can feel his resentment growing on the other end of the line, but when I get to Sean's alibi he says, 'I'll get on to it.' Business first; recriminations later.

When I finally put the phone down I feel drained.

Graves faked Catherine's suicide. Graves phoned someone. Graves is dead.

I need to make sense of this. I need to pull it all together and I need to do so now. But the image of the man cuts through every chain of thought: glassy-eyed, bloody, wedged between the toilet pan and the tiles, always with that expression of mild protest on his face.

I have to put some distance between myself and that memory. Sleep. I must sleep.

I pull off my clothes and crawl under the duvet. I'm cold again.

Tomorrow everything will be different. Tomorrow I'll understand all this. Tomorrow I'll know what to do.

Sleep feels like plunging into darkness. Somewhere in that darkness Graves sits watching, making notes I cannot see.

I wake dry-mouthed to a ringing phone. The safe-line handset's on the pillow beside me. I can't even remember putting it there. The bedside clock tells me it's just gone 4 a.m.

'Yes?'

A voice says, 'What the fuck's going on?'

Ellis.

'My arse is on fire here. Remember Ian Graves? The psychiatrist who reported Catherine Gallagher missing? The one we talked to? Well he's dead, and a woman visited him just before he died. Tell me it wasn't you.'

I pull myself upright, reach for my robe. I'm shaky, as if I'm convalescing after a long and draining illness.

'Where are you calling from? Home?'

'*Jesus.*' As if I've accused him of rank stupidity: his domestic line is off limits. 'No, the phone you gave me, the scrambled one, OK?'

No point in trying to placate him. 'I had to talk to Graves again.'

'So it was you. *Christ.*'

'He was dead when I got there.'

'You sure about that?'

'Are you saying I killed him? Ellis?'

'Oh, if you'd found him dying you'd have called it in, would you? Your voice on a police tape?'

'I wouldn't have just left him if he was alive.'

Silence from Ellis. He doesn't know if it's true.

'You were spotted,' he says at last.

'Not me. Elizabeth Crow. And it was pitch dark. She didn't get that good a look.'

'You sure about that? What if they put together an e-fit?'

'Then there's a risk that Graves's receptionist will ID me as the woman who came with you to interview Graves. Where does that leave you?'

That hits him. 'Shit,' he says. '*Shit.*' He's sweating now, I can tell.

'She didn't get that good a look,' I say again, stonily.

For a moment he's silent. When he next speaks he's got it under control, though the anger's still there, just beneath the surface. 'So why'd you go back, Karla?'

Tell the truth? I can't do that. He's a copper, with a copper's instincts, and he's hungry for a collar, always hungry, and once he's got hold of this there may be no stopping him—

Don't be stupid. It's already too late. The situation's racing beyond my control. The most I can do is try to stay with it, and for that I need Ellis.

'I discovered he'd lied about Catherine Gallagher.'

'What d'you mean?'

'I got hold of a copy of her notes.'

'She told him something. And he kept it to himself—'

'Ellis, the notes are fake. And that's an expert opinion. He made it all up. She was never a patient of his. Where's the evidence to tie her to him? She self-referred, she paid cash. He never even wrote a prescription for her. All we've got are the notes, and I've had them checked. Signs are he wrote them in one sitting. Fifteen months' worth of appointments, all at his office, and I'll bet none within office hours. His receptionist won't be able to pick Catherine Gallagher out of a photo line-up.'

'And you confronted him with this?'

'I phoned him yesterday. Told him I knew he was lying. Demanded a meeting. He was going to roll. I spoke to him at five. He was dead by 7.30.'

'You phoned him? Can they trace the call?'

'I used a safe landline. They won't be able to track it back.' I'm not going to tell him about Graves's mobile. Let Thames Valley Police work out it's missing. I'm not going to tell him about the other call either.

'What about prints? You leave anything for the SOCOs to find?'

'I was careful. And they won't find the car either. Have they spoken to you yet?'

'No, but how long's it going to take? I accessed Catherine Gallagher's file, I talked to her colleagues, I interviewed Graves. They're going to be all over me in hours, asking what I know. But I'm going to get my story in first. So: what do I tell 'em, Karla?' The sarcasm in his voice is corrosive.

'It was made to look like a burglary,' I say. 'He surprised someone turning over the house, he started shouting, they panicked, they stabbed him, they fled. For now, let Thames Valley run with that. Tell them nothing.'

'Nothing? With my name in Graves's diary? My log-in against Catherine Gallagher's file? Nothing?'

'You heard a rumour that Catherine Gallagher's disappearance was worth another look. That's all. There's nothing else.'

'So as far as Thames Valley's concerned, Graves's death is a coincidence.' He says it as if he can't believe I'm asking; it'll never work. 'You want me to kill the Catherine Gallagher link.'

'For now. Yes.'

'Why?'

'Because we don't know where it leads.'

'Or because if anyone starts looking they'll find you all over this case?'

'They won't find me. And if they do, we're both in trouble, aren't we?'

A silence. Then he says, 'Yeah, but who's got most to lose?' and the line goes dead.

Day 20: Monday

Johanssen

On Saturday night he didn't work: when he came down to the clinic at 5.30 p.m. for the shift, Cate sent him back upstairs. At three in the morning shouts from below roused him again, but by the time he got downstairs it was all over, the patient strapped down, Vinnie cleaning up the mess ... Vinnie glanced fearfully at him as if he'd come to make trouble. Drill just stared at him. Wondering about the wound, probably: what Brice had done and how much it hurt.

Cate said, 'We don't need you. Go back to bed.'

An hour later Riley came up and smoked half a cigarette, sitting on Drill's bunk.

Johanssen said, 'She told you then?'

Riley drew on his cigarette, flicked ash onto the floor. 'Brice. He's going round shouting about it.'

'What's he saying?'

'First he marked you, then he got into you.' Riley shook his head. *Marked. You've been marked.*

And then at the end of the shift: feet on the stairs, and the big man with the damaged face of a boxer lumbering in. 'Mr Quillan wants a word.'

Quillan in his sitting room, in his usual armchair, hands folded in his lap. He'd heard. Of course he'd heard. 'You've had ... *trouble* with Mr Brice. Do you wish to make a complaint?'

Johanssen said, 'No.'

'He thinks the Ryan Jackson who killed those two people was a different man. He's going round the Program with your card. You know that, don't you? Course, no one knows your face; or your name. You don't have a past, not in this world. But did you think that would satisfy Brice? Was he really going to shrug and walk away? You humiliated him. And then you let him live. I'm doing my

244

best, Mr Jackson, but even I can hold him in check for only so long.'
Quillan leaned forward in his seat. 'So what will you do?'

Johanssen said nothing.

'You think simply ignoring him will work?'

Silence between them. The clock ticking in the china cabinet.

A look from Quillan: long, slow, cold. 'You have a problem, Mr Jackson. Want to know what it is? I'll tell you.' A tilt of the head. 'It's emotion – you weren't expecting that, were you?

'Because you could be forgiven for hating Brice – think what he tried to do to you; think what he'll still do – but you don't. You're Mister Rational, you're always in control. And you think that's a strength. You think that's how you'll stay alive in this place.

'Well: contemplate the idea that you might be wrong. Contemplate the idea that your rational approach isn't a strength at all, but a weakness.

'Because you don't hate him. But he hates *you*. And he dreams of making you suffer, he longs for it, and he'll work harder and go further and endure more to achieve it. Does that make him weaker than you? Do you really think so?'

Finish it.

On Sunday, for the first time since he re-entered the Program, he didn't go out; he stayed in bed, listening while the others slept, ignoring the pain in his head and the prickling of the wound in his back, gathering his strength, thinking about what's to come. Playing it and replaying it in his mind. And all Sunday night in the clinic, while he fetched and carried and strapped and held and watched, he ran through it again and again: the process, with all its little variations, all its potential hitches.

Now nothing else remains but to do it.

He doesn't need to go back to the workshop. Once you've made a recce you don't go back. Returning sets a pattern, and you want to avoid that, especially if you're being watched. But today's dawn brought fog, reducing everyone on the streets to featureless outlines, like people made of clay. Ideal conditions for losing a tail. The two men are running around out there, panicking, cursing him. Can't be helped.

So here he is.

He stands in the main room and looks up at the broken window. *One more time. Pace it out. Make it real.*

Do it while the clinic's closed.

Come here first. Sabotage the camera. (Overhead it's watching. He doesn't look up.) *Then back to the compound. She's in the clinic with her blades, or upstairs in her room, pacing, or counting the saved.*

She must come because she wants to.

A message will do it: someone needing her help, something bad, something no one else can handle. And a woman. An injured woman who's hiding here, among the broken prefabs, too frightened to leave … Already she'll be reaching for her medical kit and asking for details: where's the wound? Is it bleeding heavily? Is anyone with her? Do they know how to stop the bleeding? She'll be focused, businesslike. She trusts him. It will never occur to her that he might be lying.

She'll leave, walking quickly at his side. Unless there are things she needs to know, she won't talk: her mind will be running ahead of her, to the patient and the things she'll have to do next.

There'll be a tail. He'll have to lose it. He'll have to make her understand that losing the tail is necessary.

He can do that.

He'll keep close to her, but that won't worry her. He's just covering her back. As they approach this place she'll be a little ahead of him.

Just inside the doorway he'll pull up – 'Wait' – and put a hand on her shoulder.

There will be no premonition, no sense of betrayal, no terror, no pain. It will be quick. She'll feel nothing.

And then he'll put her out of sight, where no one will find her.

Hours later the maintenance crew will come with their tools to refix the cap on the tank, but he'll be long gone.

Again and again it loops through his head. And with it a twinge of anxiety, an ache of misgiving – the flash of something in the corner of his eye, like a tail, gone when he turns. The sense of something just beyond his range.

What is it? What's wrong? The camera? The timing? The client? The risk that it's a trap?

Nothing from Karla, nothing on the client. But Fielding said they came with references. A revenge hit, pure and simple.

And if you come here and there's someone waiting?

Then he'll be ready.

So do it. Just do it quickly and cleanly, and leave.

Outside the fog's thickened – visibility's dropped to less than four metres now – and it plays tricks with his eyes: when he peers into it, it becomes grainy, and shapes seem to move within it. His headache intensifies, squeezing itself into a knot at the back of his skull. The wound in his back feels hot and prickly against the dressing. He's tired again, and he's getting slack. Brice was right: he's losing it, making mistakes. But Brice won't strike today, even if he could find him in this fog; Brice wants him sweating and looking over his shoulder for a while longer. Sometimes he can still feel Brice's slick finger probing, probing … As he reaches the road, two figures materialise out of the fog in front of him. Something about the light makes them seem bigger and more threatening, and for a second or two he tenses, but a few feet away they resolve into ordinary, evasive men who play by the rules, avoid eye contact. Johanssen plays by the rules too, and looks away, and they pass.

He finds a payphone on an empty street. When the line connects there's a pause, then a sleepy, muffled 'Huh?' He pictures Fielding groping for his Rolex, a tousled blonde untidily asleep beside him.

'Did I wake you?' Johanssen asks, and Fielding mutters something he doesn't catch.

Background noises: Fielding hauling himself out of bed. The acoustic changes as he moves from one room to another, becomes echoey. Hallway? Bathroom?

'Well, son,' Fielding says expectantly.

'Everything's all right.'

'You sure?'

'Yes.'

Silence. Fielding testing for the lie. Johanssen waits.

Fielding says, 'All right then,' and the pressure releases in Johanssen's chest. The line goes dead.

Karla next. Give her the word. Another payphone though, a different line. The phones are monitored. He won't put her at risk.

He steps out of the kiosk. The damp's soaked through the layers of his clothes and into his skin. He's cold.

To his left a patrol vehicle rumbles out of the fog with all lights blazing and an extra man on top cover. The man looks wired.

To his right a tall figure shuffles towards him, head down, plastic

247

bag in hand. Johanssen senses the moment when the man – he's sure it is a man – registers him.

Any second they will both look away.

The man stops. But he doesn't look away.

He always was a big man, six six or six seven, and he towers over Johanssen still, but the Program has shrunk the flesh on his frame and his big raw hands stick out from his ragged cuffs. Three days' growth of grey bristle on his chin, and a cut above his eye. But it's him.

Eight years become nothing: it's night, a damp summer night, and Johanssen's back at that big house overlooking the river at Marlow—

What can you do?

Whatever I have to.

Charlie Ross. Charlie Ross, who died three months after he entered the Program – who came out of here in bits, whose partial remains were returned to his widow for cremation—

Except Charlie Ross has just walked past him.

The fog's getting thicker, invading the side streets, clogging the spaces between the buildings. He moves carefully, checking for Ross's loping stride ahead of him; checking behind himself, too, for the first sign of the tail.

People loiter in doorways or stumble down the streets. They squint at him but he's nothing to do with them, and no one interferes with him.

He turns a corner just as Charlie Ross crosses a junction ahead of him, and vanishes out of sight.

Another snatch patrols slowly down the street towards him. Another knot of wary-eyed men stare at him as he passes too close. He ignores them. He strains for the retreating shape of Charlie Ross.

Ross turns a corner. Johanssen marks it, turns it. As soon as he enters the street, a figure turns right at the other end.

Johanssen breaks into a soft-footed run.

At the corner where the figure turned he pauses, one hand against the wall, and looks right. He's not been here before.

The buildings are blurred with fog. There are sounds of shouting and banging, then someone starts to wail. A man is hanging out of a window, bellowing at the empty street. There's a bad smell of drains.

Charlie Ross is gone.

The one man who knows who he is, the one man who can link him to that night in the farmhouse and the death of Terry Cunliffe, and he's alive, in the Program. An administrative error? Or one of those freak coincidences, a perfect-match DNA sample, another man with Ross's profile cremated in his place? It doesn't matter now. Charlie Ross is alive. Charlie Ross can ID him. And he can't count on any mercy from Ross. Two minutes in the same room eight years ago doesn't buy you any favours. Not after what happened with Terry Cunliffe.

Ross was Quillan's enemy. If he survives now it's only with Quillan's permission, Quillan's favour, a tolerance that could be withdrawn at any second. But now Ross can give Quillan the one thing Karla deprived him of eight years ago: the life of the fourth man in that farmhouse on the night Terry Cunliffe died.

Part IV

Day 20: Monday

Karla

Eight o'clock on Monday evening. I'm on the roof terrace of my apartment, forty-one storeys up. The fog that's wrapped my building in wadding all day has lifted at last. The air's raw and cold. Across the dark chasm of the dock the offices of Canary Wharf still roar with light: financial institutions, stockbrokers, law firms; business conglomerates controlling factories in a Third World sweatshop the best part of a day's flight away. This could be Hong Kong, New York, anywhere.

Between the evergreen foliage and the hardwood benches, concealed speakers spin out a thin skein of melody: an early-music ensemble plays Bach. There's a shawl over my jacket and a glass of red wine in my hand. I've only managed one mouthful. Tonight it tastes like poison.

The news broke this morning: a man found stabbed to death in a quiet Buckinghamshire village, the police appealing for witnesses.

Craigie arrived at my apartment shortly after. He looked tired, but then he'd been up all night fixing Sean's cover and alibi.

'Sean's exposed now,' he said. It sounded accusing.

'I know.'

I couldn't dodge the blame. Couldn't shake his suspicion either: if he'd been running it, it wouldn't have ended like this.

'It's all reactive, isn't it?' he said bitterly. 'We don't control it.'

'We never did.'

'If they place Elizabeth Crow at the scene—'

'They won't. I can put her out of the country. Have her travelling in eastern Europe somewhere. And the online images for her will look nothing like me. If they come up with an e-fit it won't match.'

'And Ellis?'

'Ellis will co-operate.'

'Sure about that? What if he doesn't?'

'Then he's just sacrificed his career,' I said stonily.

A moment's silence between us. Then Craigie said, 'So what happens now?'

'Straight after I phoned Graves he called someone on a mobile. I think he told them the police were on the way. Maybe just a friend. But less than three hours later he's dead. So maybe not a friend.'

'You think they may have had him killed to shut him up?'

'It's the only call he made. Then while I was in the house, they phoned back.'

He shook his head. 'If they just killed Graves, they know he's not going to answer.'

'What if they sent someone else to kill Graves? Maybe they're checking the job's been done. Or maybe they did the job themselves, they're in the garden and they've just seen someone walk into that house. They're wondering who I am. Maybe they're not phoning him; they're phoning me.'

'You picked up?' he asked sharply.

'I didn't speak. Craigie, whoever they are, Graves talked to them and then he died, and I think they know why. The mobile they used will have left a trail. Finn's on it now.'

'What if it's unregistered?'

'We get the list of who else they called and where they called from. We start to narrow this down. Meantime I'll arrange a meet with Fielding. See if he knows anything about the hit on Graves. Maybe he supplied the manpower. We need to know, one way or the other.'

'So you're going to see Fielding now?' A stinging tone.

'All right, you talk to him.'

A silence. Craigie just looked at me. I thought – though I couldn't be sure – he gave a tiny, disbelieving shake of the head.

On the Program surveillance feeds Johanssen entered the workshop alone, then left. A final check before he does the job? I tried to track him back towards the compound but the fog was down there too, the outside surveillance feeds all clogged with white. You couldn't see a thing. But ever since, I've been expecting a call from him, a coded message, the trigger to get the bolts loosened on the tank. It hasn't come.

*

The lunchtime news bulletin named Graves as the murder victim. An eminent psychiatrist, they called him. His colleagues in the practice issued a statement expressing shock and highlighting his valuable work with 'distressed and vulnerable patients'. The neighbours spoke of the devoted son who'd visited his elderly mother regularly at the house, but who hadn't been seen much since her death.

Within an hour one Sean Wilson, a carpenter who'd gone round to Graves's London house with a price for a job, turned himself in for questioning.

Then at three o'clock: a police news conference. Thames Valley's show, no sign of Ellis and no mention of a link to an ongoing Metropolitan Police enquiry, but that means nothing: they may be keeping that particular powder keg dry. The detective handling the case appealed for a woman who was seen near Graves's mother's house around the time of his death to come forward. He stressed she was not a suspect; they just wanted to eliminate her from their enquiries. Were the police looking at any former patients in connection with Ian Graves's death? The detective hedged: there were signs that property may have been disturbed. 'We're keeping an open mind,' he said.

Shortly after that the phone rang, and this time it was Ellis.

'Let's start from the beginning.' *And where's that?* 'She was never depressed. She never went to Graves for treatment. All those colleagues beating themselves up because they should have guessed? They were wrong. But something was happening all right. You know what tells me that? The fact she lied about her sick mother. She knew they were coming for her, didn't she? She knew they were coming, but she thought she'd beaten them. When she walked out of her place on the eighth December? She was running. Just not fast enough. Isn't that right?'

'I don't know.'

'What do you know, Karla?'

'I have evidence that someone wanted Catherine Gallagher dead.'

'What evidence?'

I said nothing.

'Look. I didn't put myself in this position. You told me to get the file. You sent me after her colleagues. You asked me to take you to Graves. I'm just playing the hand I'm dealt. Now I want this collar, and you want to get to the person behind this.' Then he said,

'And you need an in on the Thames Valley enquiry because they're looking for you.'

'I'm either a neurotic patient or a married lover. Maybe both. I want to keep my name out of the press. No one expects me to turn up.'

'What if they realise it was Elizabeth Crow?'

'The woman seen at Graves's address looks nothing like Elizabeth Crow. Check online if you don't believe me. And Elizabeth Crow's abroad. Eastern Europe, I think.'

'You think you're so fucking clever. You were seen. No one else. Just you.'

'Someone else was there. I'm sure of it. And they knew I was coming. They knew he was going to crack.'

For a second he relented. 'His mobile's missing. Maybe they bugged it. Took it from the scene after they killed him.'

'Phone records?'

'Nothing useful.'

A lie? Or maybe just Thames Valley keeping some details to themselves.

'What about forensics?'

'Processing now. Oh, I don't expect they'll get a sniff of you, you're too careful. But they'll keep looking. And while they're looking, you've got to keep your head down. You need me,' he said. 'And sooner or later you'll realise that the only way you're going to crack this is with my help. So talk to me.'

'And if I don't?'

'Then I don't share whatever I turn up. You get to see what happens next on the TV news, along with all the other good citizens.'

'You won't turn up anything. Whoever killed Graves did it to stop him talking but it's worked against them. It's drawn attention and they don't like attention. They'll go to ground. If there's no forensics and no sightings, then you've lost them.'

'You and me both,' he said.

'Except I don't need to turn in a result.'

'Oh yes you do,' he said. 'I haven't a fucking clue why, but you do. You want to know what's behind all this and it's eating you up, Karla. Fucking eating you up. I come up with nothing – so what? Graves isn't even my case. Catherine Gallagher's a suicide. But you – you don't come up with a result and what happens then?'

*

And after that, just as the light was fading: Finn, with news of the number that Graves called.

<all records wiped Number never existed>

Someone's deleted the account.

Every detail about the phone that made that call – the complete call record and all the technical data that would tell us where those calls were made from, the cell sites, the aerial sectors – have vanished from the service provider's records.

They knew we'd look. They've covered their tracks. That's why Thames Valley Police aren't searching for the person Graves phoned. As far as everyone else is concerned they don't exist.

But records don't just vanish. Someone pressed the button.

<find who did it Someone must know>

I'm starting to sound desperate.

And finally, a call from Stephen. I sat by the phone and listened while the machine took the message. He hoped I was well. He was wondering how I got on. He didn't mention the police. He sounded concerned but not desperately worried, so he hasn't put two and two together: he hasn't linked the notes I showed him to the dead man. Maybe he's not seen the news yet. Or maybe his normal working day gives him his fill of the world's horrors. He doesn't need to seek them out; they'll come to him anyway.

The walkways below my building are almost deserted, the bars quiet. I sip my wine – it's tarry and corrosive – breathe in the cold night air and try to focus on the views, but tonight they're flat, without depth, as if they've been pasted onto glass.

Last night all I could see was Graves. Tonight I've shut him out, but someone else has taken his place: Catherine Gallagher. But not the blurred fugitive from the CCTV, nor the woman from the surveillance feed – thin, dead-faced, hugging herself against the cold. No: the woman in that very first photo, with the guarded smile, the unmistakable self-control.

What did I tell myself, right from the start? *I have seen this woman before and she was never a victim.* And yet I bought the story, just like everyone else: that Catherine Gallagher couldn't cope.

I told myself: she killed someone, and although she never gave a sign it weighed on her, plunged her into depression, and so she went to Graves. She may not have meant to tell him, but she did. That's what I thought. But none of it was true.

So who hired Graves? The people who put Catherine in the Program, to ensure there'd be a nice pat answer to her disappearance?

Or did she fix it all herself?

You want to fake a suicide: your own. But nobody believes the clothes-on-a-beach set-up any more. They want proof. Or failing that, a witness, an expert witness. That was what you gave them.

Did you have something on him, or did you simply pay him? There's no record of payment but you're smart enough to hide it. You knew that sooner or later someone might come looking. You covered your tracks.

You bought his co-operation; he faked his notes on you. He gave you the background you needed. He labelled you a potential suicide.

At work you didn't make the amateur's mistake of overacting. You didn't fake depression or anxiety to colleagues who might see through it. Restraint – emotional reserve – is part of your nature; you stuck with that.

On the eighth of December, at 8.15 p.m., you walked out of your flat and you never came back.

You thought you'd beaten them all.

And then ... what?

Catherine Gallagher half-smiles back at me. She's saying nothing.

I abandon the view. Walk back into my apartment. Switch the TV on: it goes straight to a news channel. An item on Graves's death stitches together the day's events. A daylight shot of the straggling village, another of the police tape across the gravel drive leading to the low white house: there's a blue crime tent erected over the front porch, SOCOs in protective suits emerging with bagged evidence. A photo of Graves flashes up on the screen. A cut to the news conference: the same talking heads, the same appeal for the woman who visited him to come forward. No e-fit yet. Then a reporter stands in the road in the dark with her back to the house and does her piece to camera. 'Tonight, this is a village in shock,' she says.

My phone rings: the concierge, with news my financial adviser's come to see me, for the second time today.

The moment he walks in I know it's bad.

'We've had an invitation to do business,' he says, and his face is tight with stress. 'It's Lucas Powell.'

'We treated it like a game,' Craigie says hollowly. I've made him a cup of tea but it sits on the table in front of him, untouched, cooling.

Anxiety has sharpened that narrow clever face of his, given an extra edge to all of his gestures; even his East Kilbride accent is stronger.

I say, 'Laidlaw loved the game. And it made them think Moscow.'

And we sanitised everything. But not enough. We screwed up somewhere, didn't we? We screwed up.

'What's happened?' I ask.

'You used Isidore.' When he says it I can't tell whether it's a question or not.

Isidore's a minor criminal, a mongrel of North African, French and Spanish extraction, operating out of a market stall in north London with a nice little sideline in National Insurance numbers: a canny ferret of a man whom we've used from time to time as a courier. A crook, but then I don't have much use for entirely honest people. He knows the streets, he knows how the system works, and he's more trustworthy than he looks, if only because he's been made to understand: open a package, or fail to deliver, and his life won't be worth living. He doesn't know me. There's no reason why he should. He reports to a bookie called Paulie, who himself reports to the brassy manageress of a tanning salon in Kilburn. Once, twice, maybe three out of the twenty-two times I passed information to Laidlaw, Isidore handled the package, or directed him to the drop. But Laidlaw wouldn't have got a sniff of him. Isidore's always been careful. *I* have always been careful.

'On Sunday Isidore was picked up off the street.'

'Sunday?'

'I only found out an hour ago. Police scooped him up. Straight into a van, then straight into an interview room. They weren't saying much but they were being nice to him, so then he assumed either they were softening him up or they just wanted a chat, a bit of information. Then a man comes into the room. Not a police officer, he says. Tall. Black. Nice suit.'

Powell. Jesus Christ.

'He interviews Isidore alone, if you can call it an interview. No witnesses, no tapes.'

'That he's aware of.'

'Quite. Most of the time he's just sitting around. Cups of tea. No threats, no attempt to turn the screws. Then right at the end, the business with Laidlaw. "You work for Knox. I need to get a message to him."'

'And Isidore said ...?'

'Isidore denied everything. Looked blank.' Of course he did. Isidore's never heard of Knox. 'Powell didn't push it. Gave him his card, let him walk out of there. Isidore kept his head down. He knew they'd be watching. He didn't dare contact anyone. This morning he saw Paulie, by chance. Paulie spoke to Deborah, Deborah got a message to me.' He reads the expression on my face. 'Believe me, everyone's being very, very careful.'

I nod. I trust him on this.

Craigie says, 'My guess is that Laidlaw faithfully recorded and tried to trace every message you sent him. But he didn't want to frighten you. What he was getting from Knox was good, potentially very good. He scares you and he loses Knox. But he can't stop looking. I think once – just once – Isidore was careless.'

And that was all it took: Laidlaw – old-school Laidlaw, apprentice of the Cold War – quietly hunted him down.

'So Laidlaw identified Isidore,' I say.

'But he did nothing with the information. Didn't act on it. Certainly didn't pass it on. He logged it and he stored it, and that's where it stayed.'

'The Ealing flat.' In my head, Powell lugs his cardboard crate towards the waiting car.

'Maybe the Ealing flat,' Craigie says, 'maybe somewhere else. Knowing won't help us.' He looks bleak.

'We break the chain,' I say. 'Leave Isidore where he is. Get Paulie out of there. If Powell leans on Isidore again and Isidore cracks, the only person he can give up is Paulie. Put Paulie out of harm's way for a while. Deborah too. Get them out tonight.'

We hold our nerve and we'll be all right.

'And Powell?'

'We don't go near him. He's only got Isidore, and Isidore knows nothing. We're safe.'

Craigie glances down at the cup of tea as if noticing it for the first time. His face is strained. He says, 'Powell's made this a quest. He'll keep trying. He wants Knox for himself.'

He looks tired. Up all last night sorting out Sean's cover, and this tonight … I probably look worse.

Then he says, 'I got hold of Fielding. Face to face. He blanked me when I mentioned Ian Graves. Whoever did that job, it wasn't him. But there's something else. Your alter ego Elizabeth Crow? Last night I put an online watch on those references you posted. Three hours later someone took a look. I should have spotted it sooner but Sean's alibi …' He breaks off.

Overnight … I hadn't laid the false trail to eastern Europe then. Or uploaded the images that don't look like me.

'It's not police,' I say. 'Ellis would have told me.'

Someone moving within that house after I rang the bell. The snick of a latch on a closing door. A sense of someone watching from the trees …

Craigie gets it too. 'It was whoever killed Graves. But who's that? Fielding's client? Or the people who put Catherine Gallagher in the Program? Assuming they're not one and the same.'

'I don't know.'

'Anything from Finn?'

'The phone records have been deleted.'

Craigie gazes at me. 'Karla,' he says softly, 'we don't know anything, do we?' He turns his head, pinches his lips together.

'We'll get there.'

'Hasn't this gone far enough? Since when did you put yourself at a crime scene? Since when did you put a lad of twenty-one who knows you in a police interview room?'

'Sean will be fine.'

'It's not about Sean. You brought me in a year ago to keep you safe. But now you're taking risk after risk after—'

'Craigie—'

'As if there was never going to be any comeback, as if no one was ever going to notice. Now Lucas Powell is looking for you. You should be keeping your head down. And you shouldn't be handling Simon Johanssen, you shouldn't be anywhere near him, he's too—'

'Too what?'

For a handful of seconds, nothing: Craigie's sallow face is still, but somewhere in his eyes there's a look I never wanted to see from him, and it's compassion.

Quietly he says, 'He's too important to you.'

I retaliate. 'Are you saying my judgement's clouded?'

'Are you saying it's *not*?' He stares at me but still his voice is gentle. 'Hand him over to me. You're not seeing this clearly. I will do everything in my power to make sure he's safe—'

But you won't. You won't.

It's stalemate, and he knows it. At last he rises stiffly, reaches for his coat. He says, 'Then I'm sorry, Karla, but I think we need to isolate you a little.'

'Isolate me? How?' I'm going nowhere, not while Johanssen's still out there.

He pauses. Blinks. 'What I mean is, I think you and I should routinise our contact more.'

Routinise? For a moment I don't get it, and then I do.

Craigie has begun to distance himself from me.

As soon as he's gone I walk into the kitchen and tip my wine down the sink. I ache with tiredness, but I know I won't sleep, and I can't stop, and I don't want to sit by the phone any longer.

The lift takes me down to the dank, overlit basement car park. I thrust my hands deep into my pockets and walk past the ranks of my neighbours' cars – luxury models, every one – to my parking bay, my heels ringing on the poured concrete. A camera swivels on its stalk to follow me: the concierge must be watching.

The Merc gleams in its slot, the bodywork like black glass. I touch the wing mirror lightly – it's been fixed – then slide into the driver's seat, shut the door – it closes with a satisfyingly heavy clunk – and rest my hands on the wheel. The interior still has that smell of newness, chemical, faintly toxic.

When I touch the ignition the engine purrs into life. I slide the car out of its space and turn it towards the ramp, flashing my keycard at the sensor. The security shutter slides up, and I'm away.

I drive aimlessly through the evening traffic, edging between lanes, dodging the buses, picking lefts and rights at random. First the glass canyons of Canary Wharf. Then Commercial Road: run-down side streets, shuttered shops, late-night grocers doing Monday evening trade. Then cutting north-west, through the high-water mark of hopeful new money. Beyond it, in the fashionable East End: restaurants and bars, the premises of media start-ups and graphic designers, the gallery with its display cases of rotting meat, the blue neon of a boutique hotel. A building site, cranes slumbering behind hoardings. Then south: the City, emptied out for the night, the pubs quiet, the shops and coffee bars blank and closed, litter racing the cars down the streets. The Merc slides through the grid of traffic cameras. If they want to track my every move, they can. I've always counted on slipping beneath their radar. I wonder if I'm on it now?

Graves knew what this was all about. Now Graves is dead. The person who phoned him knows too. That record is deleted. At every turn I'm blocked, and they're good. Good enough to wipe a whole phone record at source. Like me, but stronger, more powerful.

Now they know Elizabeth Crow's on to them. Of course. That ID's thin; it won't take long to break. They'll know soon enough she's just a fiction.

One consolation: they don't know she's me.

And if they saw you in Graves's garden?

It was dark. The disguise will hold.

And Simon Johanssen? Do they know about him?

I don't even know who they are.

There's a hidden architecture to this job, an architecture of false doors and secret passages, dead-end corridors, high windows into rooms I can't locate. Catherine Gallagher stands behind one of the windows, polished, aloof, but she's not alone. Other people move through that building. They leave traces – shadows, footsteps, a door closing on the far side of a room, a bolt slid home – but however hard I try I can't get sight of them.

For the first time it hits me: that maybe I never will.

Johanssen hasn't called yet, but he will. He'll go to that workshop with Catherine Gallagher. Never mind that we don't have any in-surance, never mind the risk. He's committed himself. He's going to do it anyway. He's been going to do it from the moment Fielding first told him about the job.

Not safe, a voice in my head still whispers. *It's not safe*. But that's the irony of it: he's known all along, and he's made his choice. And I can't stop him. Because he doesn't care about *safe*. He only cares about *impossible*.

So walk away. Just walk away. Phone Craigie. Hand over the job. Go back to being Charlotte Alton. Charlotte Alton has a good life, doesn't she?

And just at that moment – as I'm pulled up at a red light on the Embankment – I look across the road, and there's Mark Devlin.

He lives in an elegant painted house with a Notting Hill address that only seven figures can buy. Three buttons on the entryphone, and his name on the middle one. The flat's main room's an expensive space, stylishly furnished but with bachelorish touches: the over-sized screen of a home cinema system, skis propped against a wall, an e-reader wedged against the arm of an Italian sofa. Through a doorway, in the kitchen, he busies himself with a bottle of red and a corkscrew, pours me half a glass – no more, I'm driving – and hands it to me.

'Nice place.'

He smiles. This one's rueful. 'An inheritance. I'm doing well but not that well.' Then, 'Take a look around, I know you want to.'

I wander over to a bookcase by the window. Ignore the battered crime novels and the travel guides. Go straight for the photos.

Mark Devlin, impossibly young, in an academic gown, surrounded by other students, laughing at the camera against a backdrop of granite-grey architecture; a lifesize skeleton completes the line-up. Then older, with a group of male friends, in morning dress: a wedding. A ski trip, a mixed group goofing around outside a chalet – he's flushed and grinning beside an elfin dark-haired girl.

I glance up. The real Mark Devlin's leaning against the door frame, jacket off, tie loosened, cuffs pushed back. Nursing his wine glass, smiling slightly. He looks clean, and fit.

I turn back to the photos. Devlin, in his twenties, with a girl, his arm hooked around her waist. Not Catherine Gallagher. But then why would it be? Gaunt tired Catherine, hugging herself for warmth or comfort with the life drained out of her face ... but she would have been different when they met, she would have been the polished woman in Johanssen's photo, with the smile you couldn't get past—

Don't think about her. Don't.

I look again at the photo. Devlin and the girl are outdoors: dark trees in the background, monumental stonework and wrought iron. And the girl ...

'She was outside the restaurant.' I grope for the name. Hannah. *Anna*. Same delicate loveliness. The look she gave me now makes perfect sense. 'You look very young.'

An adjustment in his smile. 'Anna and I go way back.' The same line as before. Same sense too of prickling awkwardness.

Should I change the subject? The idyllic childhood, the house in Wales ... 'This your country pile?'

I'm half-joking but he says, 'Don't be fooled, the house is very ordinary.'

'Still in the family?'

'I should sell. I don't go much these days. Time.'

I look again at their faces. They were together once, and happy. And then what? It ended. Probably he strayed. But he kept the photo—

'She wants to be with you.'

It comes out too soon, too fast. Straight away I'm ready to apologise, but he smiles, a different smile – 'And not the other way around?' – a smile with a thin rind of sadness. He looks at the photo. 'She dumped me four months after that was taken.' Then he twists that smile into something rueful. 'It broke my heart.'

'But you're still in touch – you're still close.' Just thinking of her conjures it up, the look she gave me, that brief dissecting glance – the look a woman gives a rival. 'You're sure she doesn't want …? The way she looked at me, as if she thought …'

He shakes his head. 'You're wrong. We're just friends. We're close – she needs me, she has problems, she wouldn't cope alone – but we're just friends. Don't ask me to explain, I can't.' Then he says, 'And you, what about you? I'm not supposed to say you look tired, am I?'

'You're not.'

He glances down at his wine glass for a moment and then he says, softly, 'At *Götterdämmerung* you wore green. You're excellent company and you're patient with bores. You're wealthy but you're not complacent: there was a time when you didn't have much money. You're extremely smart. You don't like people who ask personal questions. So I'll try not to. But you look like you haven't slept for days … It's all right,' he says suddenly, 'I know you're – *careful* about how close people get to you. I don't want to pry. But … do you want to be with him?'

Is it the wine? The tiredness? I don't know. I don't say, *Who?* I say, 'It's not like that.'

'Sure?'

I'm not sure of anything right now. Still I say, 'It's something else.' Back in the apartment with Craigie, the moment he asked me to step aside – 'I can't let him down. He needs me.'

'You're afraid if you walk away from him it'll all come crashing down?'

I nod. Suddenly I can't speak.

He says, 'We're more alike than we know.'

I bite my lip, stare out of the window. He pretends to be interested in his wine.

'So what do we do?' I ask.

He says, 'What we have to.'

265

All the way back to Docklands those words are chiming in my head.

I park the car in its slot, take the lift up to my floor, let myself in, close the front door and stand there, in the dark, listening to the sound of empty rooms, the faint electronic hum of the building ... I reach for the light switch, and my mobile chimes.

A text from Finn. One word. <RESULT>

Two days have passed since Graves phoned someone on that unknown number, shortly before he died; and they phoned back. Two days since every detail of the account attached to that number – every trace of its existence – was deleted from the service provider's system.

But I'm looking at the record of a pay-as-you-go phone, no owner ID available, no call history until two days ago. A dedicated phone, kept charged up, sterile and blank: they knew it might happen one day, that Graves's story might come into question, and they gave Graves a number to ring if it did.

And on Saturday night he called.

There's the record of that call: the one that told them I was on my way, I knew the notes were fake, the game was up. And after that, the call they made to Graves's mobile number at 19.34. To check up on him? Or on me.

Two calls. Two sets of technical data. But only one location.

They could have fled minutes after the last call was made. The trail could take me to a deserted building, an empty road. But if it does, why go to the trouble of deleting the record? Why bother, if there's nothing there to find?

One location, and I'm going.

Don't ask me to explain.

Day 20: Monday

Powell

Monday night, late, in the office again. More surveillance logs: new ones this time, on the movements of the man called Isidore.

They found him on Saturday, surprisingly easily, and just as Laidlaw had described him – slight, ferrety-faced, olive complexion, dark hair, even the brown jacket was the same – loitering by a market stall, an outfit selling mobile phone accessories, alongside a girl with bleached hair and poor skin. They tracked him all that day and into Sunday, then had him picked up off the street. An unofficial chat, that's all it was: Powell playing it relaxed, unthreatening. (True janitor style, that: keep them off their guard. Wasted on this one, though.) Isidore Maksoud chewed gum, drank tea, nodded at his suit – 'Nice, that, where'd you get it?' – and blanked the name Knox. Then they let him go, but not before Mitch had confirmed the man's flat was now bugged.

Since then they've watched him around the clock. The Section Chief's idea, and all the reports are going to him too. But it's a waste of time and energy: Isidore's suddenly restless, moving between locations constantly, and greeting almost everyone he sees – a word here, a handclasp there, a muttered aside ... *He knows we're watching. He's saturating us.* Too many contacts to trace and identify, let alone follow, and any one of them could link to Knox.

We won't find Knox like this.

So what then? Wait? How long? He doesn't even know if Isidore passed the message on. Does Isidore have the first idea who Knox is? From what he knows of Knox, he doubts it. But what else has he got to go on?

And all the time, the same question as before lurks in the background: *What if you don't find Knox?*

There are cases that open and never get closed. The mole you never find, the traitor you never name, the leak you can't locate, that drips and drips from decade into decade. He's seen cases like that, though he's never had one, and he knows: they inhabit you, those cases, they suck your life like parasites, they take away your sleep, your marriage, your children's childhood, and they leave you old and stinking of regret ... He's never had one, and he won't start now. He won't.

But what if you don't find Knox?

His tea is cold. He gets up, goes out, locks his door, walks towards the kitchen. It's late, but as he passes down the corridor, behind him another door opens. He glances back. It's Leeson, mug in hand, heading for the kitchen too. She smiles at him briefly, the smile you'd give a polite stranger who's held a door for you.

Leeson tonight, but it could be any of them; they're all loitering around him. Carter, bluff and hearty as ever – 'We still haven't had that drink.' Kingman from Special Branch, respectful, keen, playing the same angle as before – 'I've heard so much about you'; hints that he'd like to benefit from Powell's experience. Morris watches him over her glasses, witchily; she gets closest to asking what he's working on. Leeson holds back more, but she's watching too, and working all the hours. Heavy caseload? A big push?

Or because the Section Chief's lie about his activities stuck?

He's come to clean out the shit. What do they make of that? He's going through their files? He can't reassure them: janitors don't share their cases, and everything on Knox is embargoed. Still, it would be nice to talk to someone. He thinks of Mitch's pasted-on friendliness, Bethany's cool recording-angel stare, noting his failures for some day of reckoning ... Another flash of staggering loneliness. He smothers it.

He got too used to normality, didn't he? Straight desk work, standard office hours. In Washington he advises on security, writes memos, reviews procedures, mentors people more junior than him. Works within a team. Goes home to Tori and Thea – *Thea* ... The years passed and he forgot what this job involved: the long hours and the isolation, and what that does to you. When he first moved over from MI5 they told him: *Janitors are the loneliest people in intelligence. No sounding boards, no one to get it off your chest to. Get used to it.*

He steps into the kitchen. Fills the kettle from the tap. Behind him Leeson slips through the doorway, nursing her mug. The room's tiny, a glorified cupboard. He clicks the kettle on, turns to her. 'You're on the late shift too?' Half-question, half-statement.

She smiles a platitude – 'That's the way it goes' – and slides her mug beside his. There's a tea bag in it already. The kettle begins to mumble. He folds his arms, leans against the counter. They wait.

What if you don't find Knox?

Should he bring Isidore in again? Lean on him? How much does he know? Not much, not Knox's ID, but something. Someone hired him to deliver that package, someone with a name, a face … He'll say he can't remember, but people do, if you just bring the right pressure to bear, but what's the right pressure?

He can't afford to fail.

He's tired … He rubs his face. Beside him Leeson stands, chin down, sunk in her thoughts, not looking at him. The kettle rumbles on its plinth, begins to steam.

He says, 'I've got a subject who won't talk,' and senses Leeson's twitch of surprise. Her head comes up fractionally.

'He knows something. Not sure how much.' He shakes his head.

He hasn't spoken to her like this before. To anyone in the building, even the Section Chief. It's OK: he's giving nothing away.

'We've had a chat. He's smart. They're always the worst, the smart ones, aren't they?'

She doesn't answer, but then it's not really a question. She doesn't look at him either, and he's grateful for that, for her allowing him the space to talk.

He says, 'And there's pressure for a result. Of course. Increasing the temptation to get the thumbscrews out.' Leeson shifts on her feet – uncomfortable? – but they've barely exchanged a word, she might not get his humour. 'Only joking.'

The kettle clicks off. He turns and pours the water into their mugs. Leeson's tea bag stains the water green, and smells of peppermint.

But if we go in hard, and Knox finds out …

He takes a teaspoon, prods his own tea bag, then squeezes it against the side of the mug, scoops it out, drops it into the wastebin. Opens the fridge and fishes out the milk.

You need Knox to know he can trust you. Don't run at this too hard. You'll only lose it.

He says, 'You can become too obsessed with the risk of failure, can't you? And failure's such a dirty word.'

He glances across at her. She's perfectly still, watching him. Then she gives a careful smile and reaches for her mug. She says, 'It is' – it hits him, how controlled she is – and suddenly he remembers that other case: the MI5 ops list put out on the open market, the tip-off from Knox, the tech ops guy whose name she got too late, when he'd already fled … There's a wound still open somewhere. He wants to say, *We all have failures.* Then he remembers he's not supposed to know.

Back in his office, he sips his tea.

Threatening Isidore won't work. So: wait and hope? For now, at any rate; until he comes up with a better plan. There'll be another meeting with the Section Chief tomorrow. More pressure for a result. And another warning: that he's to have no direct contact with Knox. *Irrelevant, when we don't know who he is.* But the Section Chief's antsy about that, as if Knox carries some contagious disease and he could be infected, as Laidlaw was: begin a secret life, keep hidden records, and ally with his source against his masters.

He looks at his watch. In Washington it's half an hour to bedtime. Thea's in pyjamas, with her milk, ready for Daddy's call and then a story … He picks up the phone to dial, but another thought cuts in – of Leeson, in her office, contemplating failure – and he feels a pang of guilt.

Day 21: Tuesday

Johanssen

Run. You should have run.

A straight choice, no middle ground: either stay in and do the job, or pull out immediately. *And he saw you, didn't he? He knows who you are. So go. Go now. Phone Whitman. Ask to be lifted. Walk to the nearest patrol and hand yourself over—*

And then what? Phone Fielding? Tell him you've pulled out?

How many jobs in six years? And all clean, all fine, each one burying Terry Cunliffe a little deeper. But walk away from this one and then what?

And then what?

The job simply moves on to someone else. Because there'll always be someone else. Never mind what he said to Fielding, someone will find a way. Someone who won't be careful, or quick. A man with a knife. A man without rules. For a second he sees her – abused, bloody, thrashing in pain – *Don't. It's not your problem.*

Still he hasn't run.

Yesterday he came back to the compound and lay awake on his bunk – *Did he recognise you? Can you be sure?* – listening for the sound of footsteps on the stairs, Quillan's men coming for him at last, Charlie Ross at their backs, pointing the finger: *Yes, that's him.* Until the gates closed for the night and that was it, he was trapped there, in the clinic, watching the door, while the argument went back and forth in his head, though the answer was the same: *You should have run.*

Midnight, then 1 a.m., 2 a.m., 3.00. Riley smoking under the overhang. Vinnie mopping the floor and talking about the first meal he's going to have when he gets out; and about his dog, of course, he loves his dog, he's going to see his dog again – but his eyes keep going anxiously to Cate ... Cate, still and closed off from everything, mouth thin and tight, eyes stained with sleeplessness. And Drill in a

271

chair, his gaze flickering between their faces, his head tilted back as if he's tasted Johanssen's fear in the air and now he's trying to trace it back to its source.

You can abort the job for your own safety.

Or you swallow the risk, phone Karla, go ahead anyway.

It's 4 a.m. before the third option comes to him.

Find Charlie Ross, and kill him.

He pulls on his boots at the foot of the stairs. Cate's up in her room still. The yard is empty. He crosses to the gate. It's opened, and out he goes.

Johanssen walks, and the tail walks with him. He stops, and the tail stops. He makes no effort to lose it – that would only make them suspicious – but he's aware of it all the time, like a physical pressure.

He has given himself one day. One day in which to comb the Program for Charlie Ross, though the men behind him mustn't guess: he has to make it look random and aimless, and he can't ask questions either because those questions, like everything else, will be reported back to Quillan. So: locate Ross, lose the tail, deal with him. Then make the call to Karla, confirming the job, and return to the compound as if nothing's happened.

Or fail, and make the call to Whitman instead, and leave before the gates close.

He walks for an hour. Down the road from the Skills Development Centre a refuse collection gang under armed guard tosses waste bags into the back of a crusher. A snatch takes up the rear. On the pavement by the white admin building Quillan's men barter cigarettes. Overhead rainclouds gather.

Charlie Ross is nowhere. Not hanging around outside the boarded-up chapel. Not watching the lads kicking a football on the waste ground. Not buying tobacco in a little shop, not shovelling food in the canteen, not loitering in the handout queues. Charlie Ross has ceased to exist. So who was the man in the fog? A ghost? But there's no such thing as ghosts: if they existed they'd have haunted him long ago.

No, the Program has swallowed Charlie Ross whole.

Swallowed him up, but any second it may spit him out again.

*

It is now 11 a.m. If he's to get out before the gates close he must phone Whitman at four, latest.

Five hours in which to find Ross. Already he can feel it: the slow slide towards defeat.

Terry Cunliffe, disinterred, grins at him.

Don't look at this as a failure, he says.

Day 21: Tuesday

Karla

Docklands was already waking when I left the apartment at four this morning, lights moving on the roads, taxis dropping traders off at their glass fortresses, the early shift timed to pick up a Far East afternoon's trade on the Nikkei and the Hang Seng. I took a cab towards central London, then doubled back to the lock-up, anti-surveillance drills all the way. I chose the small blue hatchback, the car bought to replace the black four-wheel-drive we had to scrap after Graves's death, only because it had a full tank.

It took me two hours to drive here, another hour to get in position. Two more hours have passed since then. All I've done is watch.

I'm standing in a fringe of damp laurels. Twenty metres away, across a wintry lawn, a red-brick Edwardian house slumbers. It sits in an upmarket residential swathe on the Berkshire–Surrey border near Wentworth. Close by, corpulent stockbroker mansions squat behind high walls, but this house is smaller, less guarded. It's tucked away down a leafy private drive with three other properties, all old houses on big plots. The other houses are out of sight, and silent, the inhabitants at work or on the golf course or the massage table. Occasionally the leathery leaves around me stir, or a blackbird alarm-calls in a neighbouring garden, but there are no voices and no footsteps.

From my vantage point I can only see the rear of the house: at ground-floor level, a back door that must give on to a kitchen or utility room with a window beside it, a pair of French doors, and another window. A patio with sheeted garden furniture runs the whole width of the house; at the far end of it, beyond the kitchen door, there are a couple of outbuildings in dark wood stained green with age.

No lights are on inside, and in two hours there's been no movement. Maybe I'm already too late? Maybe they've gone, cleared out, and they won't be coming back. But security cameras jut out from under the eaves: I daren't cross the lawn to peer in through the windows. I'm hoping that, with the records of the calls deleted, whoever's here thinks they're still invisible. I can't afford to let them know they're not.

Years since I last did live surveillance. I'm out of practice, cold and hungry. This morning's cup of coffee is a distant memory, and the bottle of water I brought was empty by nine. The blood stopped circulating in my feet an hour ago; my lower limbs have locked. Still I wait. This address is all I have. The property's held in the name of a shell company which also pays the bills; the directors are nobodies, stooges paid to put their names to a piece of paper. There's no landline listed for the address and no one on the electoral register. The trail begins and ends with the one simple physical fact that those calls were made and received in this house. There's nowhere else to look.

I shift my position in an attempt to keep warm, and stare at the windows.

Just after ten a lamp goes on inside, but it might just be a security light on a timer. No shadows cross behind the glass.

Around 10.30 it starts to rain.

I hear it before I feel it, pattering down on the laurels around me. Then it begins to seep its way through the leaves, dripping into my hair and down my neck. The temperature drops one degree, and then another.

You're a fool. You're here, alone, without support, watching a house that's probably empty. And even if they come back – even if you get a shot of a face – even if you can ID them – what then?

Graves phoned them before he died, and they called him back. Now they're covering their tracks. But that doesn't make them Johanssen's client. And unless you can trace that client, you are nowhere.

The rain peters out. I'm promising myself anything, anything at all, just to get through another hour, when a light goes on in the kitchen, and a man's face appears briefly at the window.

My camera's tucked inside my jacket. I fumble pulling it out. My fingers no longer work. I hold my breath.

Come back, come back, by everything that's holy come back.

Another minute. Two. Nothing.

Risk approaching the house? Too dangerous.

A third minute, a fourth …

The kitchen door opens. A man walks out. I freeze.

I know him.

Dark at the back of a warehouse. A bright light. A man in his sixties with the handsome face of a patriarch, sweating through his golfer's tan – and Craigie's voice, steady, measured, the facts at his fingertips.

William Hamilton. William Hamilton, the ex-Big Pharma boss, the man who could have been one of Charlotte's cronies with his expensive casual clothes, his cultured air. Less than three weeks ago I stood in that warehouse, not listening while he told us about his fraud.

He's different in daylight, greyer somehow, older, more diminished. But it's him.

He pauses on the terrace for a second, head back, breathing in the air. Music escapes behind him through the open door: a recording of a piano piece, something familiar and sad.

What's he doing here?

And in the same instant I know. This is a safe house, and we put him in it.

I haven't moved or made a sound. But he turns and looks across the garden towards me, and for a frozen moment he seems to stare right at me. His face is pinched and strained but there's a resolve about him too, as if he's ready to take on all-comers. Any second he'll come across the lawn—

But then it begins to rain again, pattering down on the leaves around me, falling on Hamilton's bare head. He looks up into the sky, then turns back to the house.

I step out of the cover of the laurels, into the open. 'Mr Hamilton. *Do not turn around.*'

Shock. An instant bracing against a coming blow, as if I might attack. A fraction of a second in which I'm sure he'll turn. Then his shoulders drop.

He says, 'Oh, you've come.' As if he knows me. As if this was inevitable: that he expected me all along.

But he can't. He can't know about Karla.

Does he misread the silence as a different denial? He says, 'You think I don't know who you are?' Fear and sadness and a sort of bitter irony.

'Who do you think I am?'

276

Trick question. He doesn't answer that.

He says, 'What have you got? A gun? A knife?' A little wobble on that last word 'knife'.

'I haven't got anything.'

'You're lying.' Then, 'You found me: how?'

'Graves phoned you here. I traced the call.'

'And when I phoned him back it was you who answered, wasn't it?' And then, rapidly, on a rising wave of anger and despair, 'Why did you do it? Why did you kill him? He was just a friend doing me a favour. He knew nothing.'

'I didn't kill him.'

A whiplash savagery: '*Got someone else to do your dirty work?*' He draws himself upright, lifts his head, fills his lungs. I cut him off.

'I didn't kill him; I found him. He was already dead. Whoever did it didn't hesitate. I'm guessing they're also after you, that's why you're hiding here. Mr Hamilton, if I'd come to kill you, what am I waiting for? No one's watching.'

He says, 'You won't do anything to me until you've found out where she is.'

'But *I already know*. She's in the Program.'

I cannot see his face, but I can see his body, the way the convulsion hits him. And I can hear the sound he makes – a groan, a sob? – out of frustration and grief and something that opens up at my feet, so deep that I can't begin to measure it.

He masters it. But something about him is now stooped, as if in two sentences I've aged him a decade – more – and suddenly he's a very old man.

I press on, hardening my voice this time. He has to understand that he must talk.

'I didn't kill your friend, Mr Hamilton. I don't know what half of this is about. But I know Catherine Gallagher's in there because she killed a man and it was bad—'

'She's in there because *I put her there*.' He pulls himself up a fraction. 'Don't you know who I am?'

Out it comes, from memory, as if by magic; or as if Craigie's voice is in my head. William Arthur Hamilton, ex-Director of Collaborative Ventures at Hopeland, the medical giant – he was a middleman, an intermediary, lining up big corporate and government jobs—

And Hopeland have the healthcare contract for the Program.

Not Hopeland by name; a wholly owned subsidiary. But they

staff the Emergency Medical Centre outside the wall; they run the armoured ambulances. And Hamilton was the contracts man: he pulled the strings, knew everyone. He could spin some line just like I did to get Johanssen in there, quote national security and pull rank, skip procedures, cut through red tape, and not leave a trace. That's the how.

The why is something else.

'Yes,' I say. 'I know who you are.'

'And you know what she did,' he says. 'What are you? Police? A *journalist?*'

I could lie. It's what I do. Try to persuade him I'm on his side, on Catherine's side … But the lie fails me; or maybe there just isn't time. 'It doesn't matter what I am. But I've been on the trail of the people behind this for weeks, ever since I learned there was a contract out on her life. I know what she did, but that's only the half of it. I thought Graves could tell me the rest, but I was too late. So now I've come to you. Mr Hamilton, who's behind this?'

He says, 'You mean you don't *know?*' Then, 'What do you think will happen if I tell you?'

'I can get this stopped.'

I say it with every ounce of confidence I've got but he laughs, sick and bitter. 'You can't stop them. Why do you think I put her in the Program? You think I did that lightly? You think I don't know what it's like in there?'

Another silence. When he speaks again his voice is flatter, but also gentler. 'She turned up on my doorstep in the middle of the night – December the thirteenth, a year ago – and she told me everything. *Everything.* So I know exactly what she did. I have no illusions there. But her father was a friend of mine – I've known her since she was a child – I couldn't let them—' He stops, gathers himself, goes on. 'It was the only place she'd be safe from them, the only place they wouldn't look.' He pauses; turns his head slightly as if he might see me out of the very corner of his eye. 'If I tell you what this is all about, they'll do to you what they did to Ian Graves.' Then he says, 'And if they find out where she is, they'll kill her too.'

I don't reply. I don't know how to tell him. I only realise he's measured my silence when it's too late – when he says, faintly through the patter of the rain, 'But they already know, don't they?'

'They do.'

For a second I think he's going to ask me if I'm sure. But he's heard my voice, and he doesn't.

'Then it's over.' He bows his head.

The rain is falling on him, soaking his shirt, plastering his thin grey hair to his skull, exposing his scalp, raw and pink and frail.

'Tell me what this is about. Tell me who they are.' I'm leaning towards him as if that might make a difference, persuade him to talk—

'Why? *You – can't – stop – them.*'

'Do you think not knowing will make me safe? It didn't work for Graves.'

Cruel, that. He hesitates, but not for long. 'I'm going in now.'

'Mr Hamilton—'

'Be grateful that I haven't seen your face. So if they ask I can't tell them who you are, no matter what they do.' He pauses on a thought. 'Unless they're watching now?'

A silence. Simultaneously our heads go up, both of us straining through the rain for something beyond it, as if we might be able to hear them, whoever they are – as if by listening we would know they're there.

Of course there's nothing.

Then he takes one, deep, steadying breath and walks back into the kitchen, closing the door behind him. The kitchen blind goes down.

I'm standing by the laurels, soaking wet.

I should go to that door. I should hammer on it until he lets me in. But he won't, will he? He won't.

That's when I realise: someone deleted that phone record. It wasn't Hamilton – he hasn't the resources – and it wasn't us. That only leaves the client.

They have exactly the same information as I did.

They can trace him here.

And again I'm listening to the rain. What if I'm not the only one who's watching?

I slip back into the shrubbery, and away.

It takes me twenty-five minutes to work my way back to the car, looking over my shoulder all the way. Then I drive to Staines – anti-surveillance drills again – park on a street and phone Craigie.

'Hamilton,' I say. 'We have a problem.'

A silence. Then Craigie says tightly, 'You're on a mobile. You know we can't talk—'

I make it cut and dried: 'Hamilton put Catherine in the Program. She's not being punished in there, she's hiding. And whoever wants her dead is on his trail. Craigie, he's blown. They can track him down the same way I did. Get him out of there.'

A silence from Craigie. But then he says, quietly, 'All right. Where are you?'

'I'm on my way back – Craigie? Be careful.'

I'm light-headed with tiredness and hunger now. In a café I buy a takeaway coffee and a bacon roll, and a bar of chocolate. I'm soaked to the skin. The girl who takes my money gazes at me pityingly. 'You should try to get warm,' she says as if she's wondering whether I've got a home to go to. I try to smile at her but my face feels frozen. She gives me more change than I'm owed. I'm climbing back into the car when I find a twig in my hair.

I dump two packets of sugar into the coffee and gulp it down. It burns the inside of my mouth. I swallow half the bacon roll too fast and then can't face the rest of it. I eat the chocolate instead. It gets me halfway back to Docklands before my energy levels crash again. I eat the rest of the bacon roll as I drive, one-handed. I feel nauseous.

More anti-surveillance drills. Am I being followed?

I hit roadworks, then a major accident. The police hold the traffic in a queue while they clear the road. In all it takes me three hours to get to the lock-up. The image of Hamilton, and everything he said, loops in my head all the way.

December the thirteenth: it had all just happened then, and she was running ...

Five days had passed since that final sighting, captured on CCTV: Catherine Gallagher walking out of her life. I looked at that image and I thought, *This woman's killed, and it's caught up with her; this is the getaway.* But I was wrong. Maybe the woman in the hallway in her coat is still untainted; maybe there's no blood on her hands just yet. But she's walking into a future where all the bad things will happen. I wonder if she knows.

At the lock-up I don't have a change of clothes, only a spare coat which I slip over my wet clothing. The damp has wicked right through to my skin now: I'm freezing. I try to tidy my appearance in the hatchback's rear-view mirror. My hair's dried badly, and when I put on lipstick my skin looks as white as paper.

I pick up a taxi two streets away from the lock-up, and get it to drop me at London Bridge. I take the Jubilee Line back to Canary Wharf.

I walk the last half-mile head down, praying I'll meet no one I know.

In the bathroom I strip off my wet clothes and step into the shower. The hot water pummels my chilled skin. I stand there for ten minutes, then scrub myself half-dry and pull on my robe.

Craigie can't just walk into that safe house; not if someone's watching. How long will it take him to pull a team together, get them into position, get the area swept for other interested parties ...?

But things are happening. Hamilton knows what Catherine did, and Hamilton will talk – Craigie's ruthlessness will see to that. A matter of hours and we'll know everything.

The phone is ringing: the concierge. I have a visitor.

Craigie arrives buttoned into his overcoat, clutching his briefcase as if it might afford some protection. He looks harassed. This isn't the *routinised* contact he was looking for.

But still, he couldn't resist. He's sent his team off after Hamilton, and now he's come here to find out what this is all about. That's what this business drills into you: the insatiable hunger for information, the endless need to know.

'William Hamilton,' he says. 'How did you track him down?'

'You put him in a house near Wentworth. The call Graves made before he died? Finn got hold of the deleted record: it was made from that house.'

'You've been there?'

'Spoke to him – he didn't see my face. He's the one who put Catherine Gallagher in the Program. Got Graves to provide the suicide story as cover. Craigie, she's not in there to be punished. She's hiding.'

He says, 'That phone record: we didn't delete it.'

'I know. And Hamilton doesn't have the resources. Has to be the client, making sure they got to him before we did. They go for Catherine, they go for Ian Graves, they go for anyone who's helped her—'

'So why didn't they go for him straight away? You said that they could trace him to that house. Why wait?'

'I don't know. Just tell me he's out of there now.'

'Oh, he's out of there,' he says, but grimly, and something in me lurches.

'I sent someone in to ring the bell – a delivery driver with a package, no big deal. He was just going to make sure Hamilton was OK, look out for surveillance. The door was on the latch. The lights were off. Our man went in—'

And Hamilton was gone.

No sign of disturbance or a violent struggle. No sign of Hamilton's wallet or passport either. Hamilton just grabbed a few things and left, alone. The CCTV recordings showed him leaving.

And it was me who triggered it – appearing in that garden, telling him I'd traced the call. Making him think the safe house wasn't safe at all. That's why he's fled.

Perhaps he doesn't realise he's put himself in the open—

No. I think again of the way his head bowed, when he said, *It's over*. He simply doesn't care.

Craigie leaves to supervise the ongoing search for Hamilton. I check my messages. Still Johanssen hasn't phoned.

Monday, late morning, Johanssen went back to the workshop. A final check, I thought. It's Tuesday afternoon now, gone four o'clock, the day dipping into evening. He should have called by now. Why hasn't he?

Suddenly an old clip flickers across my vision: Johanssen in the street, the blond smiling man – a message, a threat, a kiss ...

My spine prickles. No one's watching the surveillance feeds today. *So phone him.*

I pull up the contact number, the one he gave me for the clinic. Already I'm trying to get the words straight in my head. The Program lines are monitored; someone could be listening. But it's not as though I have anything to tell him. I just want to hear his voice.

I dial.

It rings – once, twice, three times.

It's still daylight. The clinic will be shut, but Johanssen's close, only half-asleep nearby—

Someone picks up.
Three seconds of sound, maybe four. That's all I get.
Male voices baying in a nearby room.
A man screams.
The connection cuts.

Day 21: Tuesday

Johanssen

Three o'clock. He's crossed and recrossed the Program so many times and still he keeps coming back to the place where he last saw the man.

The housing here is the worst in the Program: the windows broken, the gutters collapsing, the air sour with raw sewage. Quillan's men on the corners are fewer and more indifferent and the patrols pass blank-eyed. Today there's a neat pile of human shit in the middle of the street and someone's screaming from a window. He leans against a wall. Behind him the two men who've been following him note his action and pause at the neck of an alleyway. After a minute two more wander over to join them. Once in a while they glance in his direction, as if he's an exhibit, an animal in a zoo; as if they too are wondering what happens to him next.

He closes his eyes. His head throbs.

Twenty-four hours since their paths crossed in the fog. If Ross were planning to cash in his sudden knowledge with Quillan he'd have done it already, wouldn't he?

But maybe that's what he's doing right now – maybe he's standing at the compound gate this second, demanding to see Quillan. And Brice. Brice will be there too, thrusting the ID card into Ross's face, watching as Ross nods—

So go now. Don't wait. You're never going to find him. Phone Whitman, get out. Then go and see Fielding. Tell him what happened.

Already he can feel the shame pooling in his mouth like saliva. He gulps it down.

Deal with it. It's over.

Someone has come to stand beside him, just a foot or two away. He glances across. It's Jimmy.

Suddenly he's more tired than he's ever been before, and nothing matters.

'Hello, Jimmy,' he says.

Jimmy smiles shyly at the pavement.

'You all right then?'

Jimmy nods.

'That's good. You look after yourself—'

Jimmy reaches into his jacket one-handed – the dirty sling makes it awkward – pulls out a wad of photos and thrusts them at Johanssen.

'Photos,' Jimmy says earnestly. 'Photos.'

He takes them. Why not? The first one's a snap of a caravan park. The second – a different size – has a small boy in a Man U strip running across a living room towards the camera. The third's a wedding line-up.

'Where'd you get these then, Jimmy?' he asks, though he already knows.

Jimmy says proudly, 'Mine.'

Johanssen shows him the boy in the Man U strip. 'He your lad?'

Jimmy nods happily. He points to another that's fanned its way out of the stack in Johanssen's hand. 'My house.'

The same house. The house at Marlow.

It's new but built to look old, three broad gables and a turret behind, an expensive wood-framed conservatory to one side, box hedges and steps going down to a lawn. He's sure of it, even though he saw it only once, eight years ago and in the dark – even though the shot doesn't show the river sliding by at the end of the lawn. In the photo a couple are standing on the steps. The woman wears a pale blue dress. She has a sweet face, though the last time he saw her, she didn't even look at him; she only looked at Sully.

The man beside her in the photo is Charlie Ross.

'You know this man, Jimmy? He a friend of yours?' Jimmy just stares at the photo. 'You know where he lives now?' Jimmy's eyes wander and he opens his mouth. 'You mustn't tell anyone where he lives. Not me, not anyone. All right?'

Jimmy looks at him uncertainly.

'Here – here.' He thrusts the photos back at Jimmy. 'You take care of your photos, now.'

Jimmy nods happily. 'My photos.' He takes them, then awkwardly pushes them back into his jacket pocket.

'Bye bye,' he says and he walks away.

Johanssen watches him go.

Jimmy's almost out of sight when he stops and for all of ten seconds looks sideways at a building opposite, and his mouth moves, forming words. *Mustn't tell.* Then he nods to himself, satisfied he's got it right, and goes.

Johanssen waits six slow minutes before pushing himself away from the wall. As he does so, the party of onlookers breaks up, the tail peeling off to follow him.

He walks in the opposite direction to Jimmy, then cuts back in a ten-minute loop that will take him to the building where Jimmy stopped.

When he turns into the street, the tail is ten seconds behind him.

A little snapshot of misery. A woman sobbing, a scuffle in the mouth of an alley, a man who glares at him as he passes – Johanssen switches his eyes away, ducking the confrontation. The ever-present smell of drains and shit.

Any second the tail will turn into the street. He reaches the point where Jimmy stopped, and looks left.

It's the worst block in the worst area. Weeds have sprouted in the concrete apron in front, and cracks run through the stained precast panels that make up the building's outer skin, gaps opening up around the windows. The stench of drains is strongest here. A man with pasty white skin is slumped on the step by the main door, hollow-eyed, empty.

Behind him, in the doorway, is a face.

One second, two at most. Johanssen doesn't break stride.

Behind him the tail turns into the street and Charlie Ross steps back into the shadow of the doorway, but Johanssen can sense him watching, all the way down the street.

Do it now. Don't wait. Do it now.

He cuts down a side street and then through an empty building, doubling back while the men following him are still running around trying to pin him down. Giving them the slip will attract suspicion, but it can't be helped. No one must know about this.

He goes to ground until he's sure the coast is clear, then slips across to the block where he saw Charlie Ross.

He is unarmed. It takes more speed and more focus, and you have to be closer, that's all. Ross is a big man but he's aged and the Program's taken its toll: as long as he's alone, there won't be a problem.

The broken man is still slumped in the doorway. When Johanssen steps over him he doesn't flinch but he whimpers.

Inside, weak light filters through dirty windows. The stench intensifies.

Charlie Ross, the big man, in a place like this ...

There were lilies in the hallway of the house in Marlow, an armful of them in a big vase, standing guard on a pillar. They glimmered over the woman's shoulder as she opened the door, and crossing the polished floor he caught their sickly reek. He doesn't know why, of all things, he remembers the lilies now.

Two men with dark closed faces stand in the gloom at the foot of the staircase, talking softly. One of them's smoking, the glowing tip of his cigarette like a beacon. Their self-possession marks them out: they don't live here. Are they Quillan's? He doesn't recognise them. They hand the cigarette between them, oblivious to him as he passes.

Quickly he climbs the two flights of stairs.

At the top the corridor stretches away left and right. The left-hand fire door is wedged open, the foot of it gouging itself into the floor: the frame has buckled. Beyond it, the corridor's almost blocked by a barricade of wood and debris. He turns right simply because there is no barricade.

He goes door to door without knocking. Behind the first a thin old man wearing only a dirty shirt is lying motionless on a makeshift bed. The second door's jammed shut from the other side. When he shoulders it open, six women – the youngest maybe twenty, the oldest in her fifties, all with used faces – are huddled around the walls, holding their breath.

Behind the third door cockroaches scuttle across rotting food on plastic plates. No one else is home.

The fourth door is locked. He's turned sideways ready to put his shoulder to it when shuffling footsteps approach, and the lock rattles. The door opens a crack.

In the half-inch gap is the eye of Charlie Ross.

'It's you,' he says after a moment. 'I thought you'd come.'

And you waited? You knew I'd come, you know why I'm here. Why didn't you run?

The roof must have started to fail. The ceiling tiles are stained and peeling away, and damp is spreading down the walls. An old sofa sags in one corner of the room, piled with bedding. A radio emits a tinny scratch of sound in a corner. Ross turns it off.

'How long has it been?' he says.

'Eight years.'

'Eight years.' He pauses a couple of seconds as if those years are passing in front of him, then he says, 'I'd offer you a seat, but ...' and he gestures around the room. Apart from the sofa, a small table and a cardboard box, there's no furniture.

Back in the house in Marlow he didn't offer Johanssen a seat; but everything was different then. Now he's dressed in clothes a size too small for him. Grey bristles sprout from his chin. Most of his front teeth are missing. He must be sixty but he looks eighty.

For a moment they stand there in silence. Then Charlie Ross says, 'They looked for you. You disappeared. I thought they might have found you.'

'No.'

'They found the other three.'

'So I heard.'

'But not you. You were always going to be different. I'm glad, you know? That they didn't get you. If anyone had any right to kill you, it was me.' And Ross smiles as if this is a shared memory, something they can joke about now. Then he says, 'Where did you go?'

'Just away.'

'But you came back to the business, didn't you? Or you wouldn't be here now.'

For a second both of them look around the room. The windows don't fit and the cold blows in around the frames. Ross says, 'It's a long way down, isn't it?'

'You could do better than this,' Johanssen says, and in the same moment he knows he's wrong.

Ross says, 'Any better than this and you have to fight to keep it. You get tired of that after a while.' And he looks tired, tired to the bones. 'I didn't expect I'd ever see you here.' But then he seems to rouse himself, stands a little straighter. 'I never talked, you know. Whoever shopped you, it wasn't me.'

'I know.'

'How long have you been here?'

'Couple of weeks.'

'Takes a bit of adjusting to. But you're in with Quillan.' He nods to himself.

Johanssen says, too sharply, 'Why d'you say that?'

Ross gives him a look. He says, 'The way you came in here. Like you're untouchable. You're in the compound then?'

'Clinic,' Johanssen says.

Ross looks briefly interested. 'You got some medical training. After what happened?'

'Before that.'

'So you're saving lives.' Ross says it as if it makes sense to him; he nods to himself.

Johanssen says nothing.

'He's a fair man, is Quillan. He leaves me alone now.' Ross's gaze is steady and he's got that head-up posture again, as if being left alone is something to be proud of: a mark of character. Though they both know different.

He leaves you alone because you're broken now. He leaves you alone so people can point at you and say, Wasn't he Charlie Ross?

Then Ross says, 'He doesn't know, does he? He doesn't know it was you.'

Johanssen shakes his head.

'Best keep it that way, eh?'

Get on with it.

The distance between them is no more than four feet. Johanssen takes a slow breath, filling his lungs, gathering himself. Ross just stands there, waiting: a tired scarecrow of a man with half his teeth punched out and nothing to fight for.

Ross says, 'It was the beginning of the end, that night, you know? When you did what you did. Oh, we cleaned up afterwards, but that's what it was. The beginning of the end.'

Johanssen takes the second breath. On three he will move.

'But not for you.'

The third breath comes and goes. Suddenly he's tired too, tired of all of this.

'If anyone asks, you don't know me,' Johanssen says.

It takes a second before Ross understands. Then he nods and drops his head a little. 'I don't know you,' he says.

'You looked at me in the street because you thought I was someone else.'

'Of course,' Ross says. 'And that someone else …?'

'Is dead,' Johanssen says.

289

Ross pauses, then nods to himself.

Johanssen turns towards the door.

Ross says, 'That's not why you came here though, is it?' Then he adds, 'You needn't worry. I was never going to sell you out to Quillan. If he thought I knew something ... Well, you've met Brice, I'm sure. He'd want to be *thorough*. I don't fancy that.'

'No.'

'So don't come back.'

After the door has shut behind him, Johanssen stands in the corridor for a moment, listening as Charlie Ross's soft footsteps shuffle away.

Ross won't hurt him. No one can even connect them.

Charlie Ross is not a risk. He doesn't need to die.

As he walks down the stairs it loops in his head. *Charlie Ross is not a risk—*

Outside the late-afternoon light is dull and cold, like tarnished metal. The dark is drawing in.

The man who opens the compound gate looks at him and then away as if there's something he knows but mustn't tell. There are others standing around in the yard, groups of twos and threes: they too turn and look at him but no one speaks to him.

Anxiety tightens in his gut, clears his vision, sharpens his breathing. He breaks into a run.

Through the main door, through the waiting room – a man, one of Quillan's, sits in a chair with a baseball bat across his knees. When he sees Johanssen he doesn't get up.

Johanssen pushes on into the clinic.

Riley's standing there, his eyes wide: his mouth moves, but no sound comes out.

A chair lies on its side in the middle of the room, duct tape on the arms and back. There's a long smear of blood across the clinic floor. In a corner of the room a male human form, middle-aged, soft-featured, is propped half-naked against a cupboard like a broken doll, the limbs twisted at all the wrong angles. Drill's bending over it. For the first time he looks perplexed.

Vinnie.

Riley's fists are working. He finds his voice. 'Fuck it, they locked us out, all we could do was fucking listen—' The last word strangles itself. Riley is crying.

The door to the side room is open a crack. *Please no no no—*

Johanssen crosses the room to the door. It swings away from him.

She's forced herself into a corner, behind one of the broken cots. Her breathing's raw-edged, as if with each breath something inside her is tearing. Her face is porcelain-white, eyes staring, sightless, and she is rocking, rocking.

He crouches on the floor beside her.

Everything changes.

There were five of them with Brice this time, and they blocked the doors so no one could intervene. But for once she wasn't alone in the clinic; Vinnie was with her. That was the only reason they picked Vinnie, because he was there.

And she must have known what was going to happen because Riley, hammering at the doors, heard her begging Brice to take her instead, not Vinnie – heard her say, 'I deserve it, I deserve it,' and Brice's reply, 'No, you deserve to watch.'

They gagged her and taped her to the chair.

'Watch his eyes,' Brice said. 'Watch his eyes.'

Later, in the little room upstairs, after they've sedated her, he'll sit by the door and stare at the marks on the wall – she counts the ones she saves – and he'll fight with it. He'll force himself once more to pace it out, make it possible, make it real: *Through the streets, across the waste ground, pausing just inside the doorway, her silhouette ahead of him, his hand reaching for her—* Over and over, rehearsing the event, testing himself with the moment of impact and the aftermath, because there isn't room for anything else, he has a job to do, or it'll be Terry Cunliffe all over again—

He will fight with it, but by then it will be too late.

Day 22: Wednesday

Karla

I phoned Whitman. 'For Christ's sake, get him out.'

Gone four, and the gates close at six. Too late already, though Whitman must have heard something in my voice, because he said, 'I'll try.' He failed.

All last night I camped on the Program surveillance feeds, looking for Johanssen, that four-second snatch of sound – a man, screaming – repeating in my head. I was sure he was dead. Dead, or broken beyond repair.

At 6 a.m. the phone rang: my safe line.

I swear, when he first spoke I didn't know his voice.

Now I'm in Tower Hamlets Cemetery, among the dead of the Victorian East End: iron founders and corn merchants, small trades-men and their wives, vicars and physicians and schoolteachers. Their monuments crowd between the bare trees and through the frost-blighted undergrowth: slab-like chest tombs, obelisks and Gothic pinnacles, open bibles and angels, and rank upon rank of headstones, the DEARLY BELOVEDS, the IN LOVING MEMORYS. They don't bury people here any more; it's a place of contemplation, a public park, an outdoor classroom even – local primary-school kids come with jars to dip the ponds and look for butterflies in summer. But no one's here today, at eleven on a Wednesday in early February; no one but me and a man slumped on a bench, his head bowed.

I don't like to meet in the open. There are surveillance issues to consider. So I've dressed myself like a charity worker or a church volunteer: a practical do-gooder with a satchel of sandwiches and the address of a local shelter.

I stop a few metres away from the man on the bench. He might be drunk, or stoned, or asleep. 'Hello?'

He doesn't move, but his eyes open.

I come a pace closer. 'Are you all right?'

But he isn't. I know that already.

'I'm not doing it.'

He's pulling out? That doesn't happen, ever. But suddenly I'm back in those four seconds of sound: the baying male voices – the man screaming—

'Are you hurt?'

I've come to sit on the other end of the bench. He turns his head and looks at me as if I'm speaking another language. 'No.'

'I tried to reach you yesterday, I phoned the number, someone picked up – I heard—'

'It wasn't me.'

For a moment neither of us says anything.

'Vinnie,' he says. 'His name was Vinnie.'

And you knew him. 'He's dead?'

'Yes.'

'Because of you?'

'Yes.' Then he says, 'They made her watch.'

Oh sweet Jesus.

The smiling man with the angelic features, whose speciality is torture … It's Terry Cunliffe all over again. And all because of Johanssen. He knows he has to pull out, that's why he's here: he's a mess now, and the risks are just too great. But he's staggering under the weight of that decision. He sees a job and he commits to it. Turning away from this one makes it a failure, doesn't it? Guilt and shame and inadequacy rolled into one.

'Does Fielding know?'

He turns his head away, stares down at the path in front of us. 'Not yet.'

I take a breath: let the cold air fill my lungs, and then release it, slowly.

Already I know what I must do. Return Johanssen to the south London flat. Talk to Fielding – he'll be pissed off but it can't be helped; he'll just have to find someone else to do it. The man with the knife … I turn that thought away. Tomorrow, begin to ease Johanssen out of Ryan Jackson's ID and by careful stages back into his own life and then away—

'All right,' I say. 'We'll get you out of this.'

'No,' he says, 'I've got to go back in there.' Then, quite simply, 'I've got to get her out.'

Oh Jesus, she's turned you. You got too close and she's turned you.

A middle-aged couple come along the path towards us. They glance at us, curiously: the vagrant on the bench and the woman with the satchel. Maybe they can read the tension between us. They pass, but five paces further down the path the woman glances back over her shoulder. I nod to her: it's OK, it's fine.

It's not.

The surveillance feeds again: Johanssen and Catherine Gallagher, in that workshop, talking. I saw them and I was pleased, wasn't I? Thinking, *This is good, she's confiding in him, this is how we'll get to the truth*. Not realising he was getting sucked into her world.

It doesn't matter how close he stands to his target, as long as he maintains that other distance, that cold psychological space that lets him do the job and not wake screaming. He's lost that distance now. She's turned him.

'She knows they sent you for her?'

'No.'

'She ask you to get her out?'

'No.'

'But you told her you're doing this.'

'No.'

But she's clever and she's ambitious and she'll do anything to get what she wants. She was never a victim and she doesn't intend to start now.

'We don't even know what happened.'

There's a silence. He sits, eyes dead ahead, so still. And I know: *She told you.*

He says, 'His name was Daniel. She never knew his surname. My age or maybe younger. Dark hair. He was injured: broken ankle, other wounds. She was called in to treat him. He was kept in a room; from the window she could see a gate with dragons on it. She stayed with him for four days; I think in that time he was tortured.'

'By her?'

'I don't know.'

'And then she killed him?'

He looks down. *Yes.* 'He struggled. It took time, got messy. Blood.'

'She tell you why she did it?'

'Because she could.'

I'm staring at him. He turns his head away.

'She said her patients could have been another species.'

Six years now, so many jobs, and every time his targets never suffer, regardless of how sick and twisted they are, regardless of what they've done. He makes sure of that. But this woman ... I don't understand.

'Why?' I ask. 'Why get her out?'

He doesn't reply. He's struggling with this one. At last he says, 'She has nightmares.'

I don't know what to say. I don't think he does either. He shakes his head as if it's all beyond him – as if he doesn't understand himself. And something crawls into my head: *You care for her.*

'I have to do it,' he says. He turns and looks at me. 'You can do anything, Karla. Help me get her out.'

They're together, aren't they? He loves her. And he'll risk it all for her, his life, reputation, that perfect six-year record, all to get her out. To let her live.

He loves her. Like a blow: *he loves her.*

I want to walk away. I want to go through the cemetery gates and out into the street where the Mondeo's waiting, head back to the lock-up ... I can't leave him here. What will he do? Go back in there? Try to protect her? And all the while Brice—

I can't let that happen.

'All right,' I say. 'I'll pull something together.' The part of my brain that does this stuff is working, pacing out a process, ignoring how I *feel*. It's as if I've been in an RTA, a smash, and I've just walked away from it: I know something inside me's broken and it's bad, but I'm still anaesthetised by shock, on my feet and moving. Sometimes it doesn't pay to think too much. If I can just keep going I'll be fine.

'Can you do it, Karla?'

The truth is, I don't know.

A day ago we could have leaned on Hamilton. He put her in the Program, he has contacts; maybe he can get her out. And he's still out there somewhere. We're looking. People on the run sometimes return to childhood homes, places where they once felt safe; or they seek the anonymity of big cities. He was a director of Hopeland; he could still have a spare key to a corporate flat. Finn's getting details of all possible locations. Craigie's got search teams out at targeted addresses. I even called Ellis with the name – 'And who the fuck

295

is he? Or is that something else you won't explain? Jesus fucking Christ.' So far there's nothing.

But what if we don't find him?

Catherine Gallagher's an anomaly. An inmate with no record on the system. A tip-off to the authorities would do it – that would get her out. It's keeping her safe beyond that; that's the issue. We don't know who the client is, but they have reach, and resources: within an hour they'll know she's out of the Program, and they'll be taking steps.

'Go back in there. Try to keep her safe. Don't leave the clinic; listen for a call. I'll be in touch as soon as there's a plan. Through Whitman, probably. He'll need a meeting. There are visiting facilities; he can use them. We'll get her out as soon as we can. Afterwards …' That hurts. *Ignore it.* 'You'll both have to disappear, for good.' It comes out harder than I expected. 'We can fix it, it's what we do.' A new life far away from this, together. *Just deal with it.* 'You'll want to be with her as soon as possible but it takes time—'

He says, 'It's not like that.'

You don't have to pretend. The oldest failing, that: falling for a target. It's pride that makes him deny it. I wish he wouldn't. I want to say, *Please don't lie to me. I'll get her out but please don't lie.* I cannot. My throat has closed.

I swallow. *Deal with it.* 'It doesn't matter.'

'No,' he says, 'it does.'

Very gently his hand closes over mine. He's head down, not looking at me. Then he whispers, 'It's all right. I know you don't want me.'

His fingers uncurl. Release. He draws his hand away. Still he's not looking at me. 'I'm sorry,' he says.

At first, nothing. Nothing at all. Something has exploded in my head, so loud it's stunned me. I'm reeling from the shock of the concussion. For seconds, minutes – I don't know how long – I sit there, and still I don't know what to say.

He says, 'You saw what I was like, after Terry Cunliffe. I knew you'd never …'

I want to say *I knew Terry Cunliffe* and *You tried to save his life* and *That is why—*

And in a minute perhaps I will, but right now I can't. So I just take his hand in both of mine, and hold it, and wait, and wait.

*

Fifteen minutes later I leave Johanssen on his bench, a film-wrapped sandwich from my satchel beside him. I look back once, before the trees close him off from view. He hasn't moved.

Will he be safe in there? He says he will. The lie is in plain sight, but I can't call him on it. He has to go back and protect her, save her, the way he failed to save Terry Cunliffe eight years ago. Because he believes it's the only thing to do. That's how he makes it right.

A breeze picks up, sweeps across the cemetery. The undergrowth shivers around me. And in my head a woman in a dark coat crosses the hallway of her building. It's impossible to make out her expression.

I cannot trust her, but somehow I must save her.

Whitman's standing on one of the paths. His men are somewhere close too, out of sight, guarding the nearest exits. As I approach, he puts his mobile to his ear. 'OK,' he says into it. 'Move in and pick him up.' He kills the connection. 'Well?' His face is pale and tense.

'Take him back.'

He says, 'Program Administration's getting jumpy. This paperwork won't hold much longer.'

'One more time.'

'Call Washington, Laura. I mean it,' he says. 'Or we're screwed.'

I've left the Mondeo just outside the main gate. As soon as I've got the door closed I phone Craigie, but there's no news. I tell him to keep looking, end the call before he can ask me what happened with Johanssen, then start the engine and pull away. Already I'm on anti-surveillance drills. Two miles from here I'll dump the car and walk. A bus, the Tube, a change of clothes, another car ...

Johanssen's already on his way back to the Program. The torturer Brice smiles from his mugshot. And then there's Catherine. Once again: it all loops back to her.

The man called Daniel: what did he go through? But somehow Catherine walked away from it. Persuaded first Hamilton and now Johanssen to risk their lives to try to make her safe. What's she capable of?

You kill once and it changes you. Forget the nightmares, forget how troubled she may be. She knows now that the barriers can be breached. And she can do it again.

My phone rings. The display tells me it's Ellis. He says, 'We need to meet.'

Ten minutes later I find out why from Craigie. Hamilton is dead.

It takes me hours to get to Harringay. Dumping one car, picking up another, then a taxi, a bus, the Tube, each journey doubling back on the last. Still, it's only three when I arrive: trading hours, but the tyre fitters are gone, the big main doors shut. A handwritten sign says CLOSED – ELECTRICAL FAULT. A lie, and one that's cost me. The owner's at his desk surrounded by paperwork. I go through to the back room, switch on the heater and the TV, select a tatty armchair and surf the channels – a bad movie, a quiz show, an old drama on repeat. I stand up, stretch my legs, try a different chair, move the electric heater and move it again. I go to the front office and fetch myself a tan-coloured cup of evil-tasting coffee, which I drink under the plastic gaze of glamour models. I'm tired almost to the point of despair, but I can't settle, and I can't leave.

It's almost 3.30 before the door opens and Ellis walks in.

'How?' I ask him, and he says, 'Don't you know? I thought you knew fucking everything, Karla. I thought your boyfriend would have been on this hours ago.'

'Police aren't releasing details yet.'

'Oh really?' He looks pleased. So he's pulled some strings, had it hushed up so he could have the news all to himself? *You bastard, Ellis.*

'So, William Hamilton,' he says. 'Where does he fit in? Don't tell me: you don't know. Or is it a secret?'

I don't need this. 'Just give me what you've got.'

He raps it out: 'William Arthur Hamilton. Former Director of Collaborative Ventures, whatever the fuck that means, at Hopeland. Retired. Lived in a village in East Sussex. Been away for a few weeks, don't know where yet. Lights on in his house last night. He was found this morning in a wood near his home. Dead, no obvious signs of violence. Post-mortem's tonight.'

Did he just give up, go home and wait for them to come? Or walk out into the dark with a pocket full of pills, beating them to the punch? I'd like to tell myself he didn't suffer, but I saw him at the house in Wentworth, just yesterday: suddenly old, and convulsed by grief. He cared for Catherine, didn't he? He tried to protect her, and I stepped out of those laurels and told him that he'd failed.

Ellis is watching me.

I get to my feet, reach for my bag. We're done. 'So why the meeting? You could have told me this over the phone.'

Ellis stands between me and the doorway. He's going nowhere. 'I figured we could use a little chat.'

'About?'

'All the things you're still not telling me.'

I don't have time for this.

'Eighth December, Catherine Gallagher walks out of her flat and vanishes. Looks like she killed herself. A year passes. Then suddenly, four in the morning, you're on the phone. You want to see the Missing Persons file, you want me to talk to her colleagues, you corner the shrink who claimed he treated her, you get her notes lifted ... You go to meet Graves alone; Graves turns up dead, and you tell me the suicide story was a fake. You want to talk to this guy Hamilton. Now he's dead too. And all this for a girl you said you never even knew. Why? Why, Karla?' He's fixing on me. 'There's a big hole right through the middle of this. Fill it, Karla. Tell me the truth. Put me on your side.'

'I can't.'

'Why not?'

I say nothing. His stare holds mine. I don't move. He reads me, swears, and walks away.

After he's gone I force myself to wait five minutes before I leave the workshop. In the front office the owner is still bent over his paperwork, stabbing at the keys of his calculator with a sort of fury. He doesn't look up as I pass, and I don't say goodnight.

The client floats at the edge of my vision. *Like you, but stronger, more powerful.* Catherine must pay, but not just Catherine – Graves and Hamilton too. They died because they tried to help her, but I've got Hamilton on my conscience now: I drove him into the open, to despair, and to his death. No point in whining, *I didn't know that it would come to this.* It's hardly an excuse.

And I get to make up for it by saving Catherine Gallagher. Who murdered a man called Daniel and then fled. The irony of it all twists in my face – and twists again: I'm doing it for Simon Johanssen's sake – how many has he killed?

My mind is jumping.

Daniel, no surname, thirties, dark hair. Injured before Catherine ever appeared on the scene. Tortured afterwards. For information? Who is he? Get Ellis to trawl Missing Persons, dig up the possibles? *Too late now.*

And Johanssen's heading back into the Program, driven by forces he doesn't understand, to save her. *She has nightmares . . .*

I need to move her and I'm out of options. I'm down to the one person who can get her out.

I'm down to Lucas Powell.

A deal on information, in return for Catherine's safety—

He wants a prize. He'll try to take you down.

The network for himself. Me as his stooge. Or replaced completely. And then what?

The price I pay. For Graves, Hamilton. For Johanssen. All of this.

I look up. Twenty yards away a woman in a raincoat turns her head. I can't see her face, but something in the movement reminds me of that girl: Anna, the one outside the restaurant, the one in Mark Devlin's photograph—

It comes at me from left field, like a blow.

Devlin in the foreground, his arm around Anna's shoulders, both so young. Monumental stonework in the background, and a complication of twisted wrought ironwork, fantastical Gothic shapes. Behind that, dark trees: somewhere rural. *The house is very ordinary.* The house he doesn't visit any more.

On top of each gatepost is a dragon.

'Ellis?'

A hesitation before the aggression kicks in: he's wondering if I've changed my mind. 'Well?'

'Mark Devlin's alibi for the night of eighth December.'

Ellis says, 'You are fucking joking—'

'Please don't hang up. You saw him outside his office, you asked him for an alibi, he couldn't remember. You told him it wasn't urgent. He called you back.'

A silence on the line: Ellis weighing this one up. 'What is this? You screwing with me, Karla? You trying to jerk my chain?'

'I need it, Ellis. His alibi.'

A silence. *Please, please tell me—*

He says stonily, 'He was at his place with some girl called Anna. I got her details too, and checked it out. His alibi holds. And he's all wrong for it.'

6 p.m. before I'm back at the apartment. Three messages on Charlotte Alton's phone: someone calling about a fundraiser, an invitation to a

dinner party, and Mark Devlin: what am I doing tonight?

Straight to the office. Log on. Fingers on keyboard – a house in Wales, a family property … I drill my way down through all the data. *Devlin Devlin Devlin*—

There it is. An address up in the Brecon Beacons. I pull out the postcode, fire it into a map, and up it comes, a small pink square surrounded by trees, close to a reservoir. A satellite photo gives another view: two buildings in a clearing, the main house and another, smaller, set at right angles to it – a garage, workshop, stable block? You can't make out the gates.

The nearest house is half a mile away.

In the month they were together, did Devlin take Catherine there? And when the time came, did she remember? A house in a forest, remote, usually empty—

Not hard to find out Devlin was safe in London on the eighth December.

And after Daniel was dead and she'd moved on—

Devlin's voice: *I never saw it coming.*

But he saw something when he went to that house.

Bloodstains? Sweet Jesus, the body? *She was capable of things other people aren't.*

Yet Mark Devlin didn't go to the police. He cleaned up after her. Another one on her list, along with Hamilton, and Johanssen: another man stepping in to save her. I hope I get to meet her one day: I'd like to know her secret. Though Devlin's different. He doesn't care for her like they do. Her hold over him is something else entirely.

I set the map to print, and go to change. I'm halfway out the door when I realise: if the client knows Mark Devlin covered up for Catherine, they'll come for him, too.

Day 22: Wednesday

Johanssen

Inside the Induction block, behind the same armoured-glass screen, in the same room without natural light, the same clerk who processed his first entry just over two weeks ago fiddles with an application form, and snatches glances at him.

Can the man see it in him, the change? He thought he'd dealt with that.

All the way back in the car with Whitman and the other two he felt it: as if a bank of switches in his head had flipped, the lights had changed, the colours were all different. All he could think of was Karla.

But he can't be going back in there like that, and so he's put it in a box – something solid, lead-lined – closed the lid and sealed it, and then buried it deep, and now he must forget it: the cemetery, her hands tightening around his, her breathing ...

Later. When it's over. Not before.

The usual routine. The strip-search. Dressing. Back out into the corridor again. Whitman waiting, the dough-faced clerk still beside him, clutching his paperwork, shifting uneasily, on the edge of saying something – what? But when the escort steps forward nothing happens.

Outside. The tarmac, the view of the wall. The sentry booth. The gate sliding open. He steps through it. It clangs shut behind him.

Somewhere deep inside, that box is buried. Still a faint Geiger-counter tick of emotion tells him that it's there.

He gets back to the compound just before 6 p.m. There's a man on the clinic door, another in the waiting room, both Quillan's. Protection; just too late.

And where's Brice now?

He goes past them without a word.

In the bunkroom kitchen Drill's eating alone. When Johanssen pauses in the doorway he looks up. His expression is blank, impassive. He's waiting for the next development, for things to get interesting again. Johanssen goes on up.

Riley's at the top of the second flight of stairs with his back to the closed door of Cate's room, smoking a cigarette. His face is raw with sleeplessness.

'Where've you been?' he asks, but quietly, as if the door isn't closed, as if noise might disturb her.

'Out.'

Riley grunts. 'Out,' he repeats softly, bitterly, to himself. 'Oh yeah, doing a deal with your Americans.'

'She asleep?' Johanssen asks.

'Still sedated.'

'I need to talk to her.'

'That's going to help her, is it? That's going to put Vinnie back together?' Riley looks at Johanssen, hard. 'You know what I think? You should have done what Brice told you to the first time, given that thief a kicking. Or if you couldn't even do that, you should have had the guts to take your punishment. So you'd have lost a finger or two. Better than this, eh? Her strapped to a chair while Brice breaks every bone in that poor little bastard's body.' He takes another drag. The cigarette's shaking in his fingers. 'He came for you – you know that, don't you? He was going to wait for you to get back. Only she was down there and Vinnie—'

Riley stops, breathing hard. Emotion's working over his face.

For a minute they wait on the stairs in silence.

Johanssen asks, 'You been here all day?'

'Yep.'

'Anything from Quillan?'

'Just his muscle downstairs. Too fucking late,' Riley says. 'He should have known. He lets you stay, lets you wind Brice up, and then he sticks a tail on you so Brice can't get to you— What did he think, that Brice was just going to forget about it?'

'Quillan's not touched him?'

'That's right. Well done. And he'll come back for you. Not today, not tomorrow cos Brice is smart like that – he knows when to stop, when to back off, leave you sweating, wondering what's around the next corner. He'll wait till he's good and ready. But he'll come back. So.' He looks up at Johanssen. 'You know what happens now.'

'What happens?'

'You get the fuck out of here.'

'I can't leave her.'

'Can't you see it? You're next. You stay and he'll come back for you, and she'll step in because she can't help herself. And it'll be worse than Vinnie. Worse for you, but I don't give a fuck about you, you make your own choice. But worse for her. I won't let that happen. You're leaving. Tomorrow, when the gates open. If I can only do one thing for her then I'm doing that. You're out of here.'

Johanssen says, 'If I leave her here, she'll die.'

'Brice won't kill her. Fuck, he won't even kill you; he wants you alive, he wants you suffering. Even Vinnie wasn't supposed to die, Vinnie was a *mistake*.'

'I didn't mean Brice.'

'Who else is there? Unless you mean all the mad bastards out there.' Riley jerks his head towards the outside world. 'I think you'll find she'll take her chance.'

Johanssen says, 'Get something to eat. Get some sleep. I'll sit with her for a bit.'

'You look as wrecked as I do,' Riley says.

Johanssen shrugs.

As Johanssen passes him on the stairs Riley grips his shoulder. 'He was actually fucking getting out, was Vinnie. Done his tariff, one more month to go. I mean it, mate,' he says. 'You're out of here.'

Johanssen opens the door a crack, and then an inch, two inches. She's lying on the mattress. The sedative's still working: her face is slack, her limbs still. He steps inside the room, closes the door, crosses to her, crouches. Her drugged breathing's slow.

He'll get her out. He will. Karla will find a way—

But Brice is out there still. Why hasn't Quillan made a move against him? What's he waiting for?

Day 22: Wednesday – Day 23: Thursday

Karla

It took me time to gather what I needed. The car – a souped-up ten-year-old BMW – from one lock-up, supplies from another. Craigie phoned while I was packing rucksacks. He must have tried the safe landline first; he knew I wasn't at home. 'Where are you?'

'Something I need to check out,' I said.

He couldn't ask what, not on a mobile, not Craigie. All he could say was, 'Karla . . .'

'I'll be careful.'

And I called Devlin, on his landline, just to be certain. When he picked up, there was music in the background, and he said, 'You got my message? We must get together,' in a way that told me he had company. Less than two hours since he rang me; some other woman – Anna? – must have answered her phone. That's good: if he's not alone, he's safe. I laughed, told him I'd call back some time, hung up, and switched Charlotte Alton's mobile off.

I was on the road just before 9 p.m.

The M4 and the Second Severn Crossing are quicker by half an hour, but there are front-facing cameras on the bridge, snapping drivers' faces. So I've come across the other way, the M40 through the Chilterns, then the A40. Just past Oxford I stopped in a lay-by for a slug of coffee and switched Charlotte's phone back on. It chirruped into life: another message from Devlin, timed just after ten. 'You're not free tomorrow, are you?' I switched it off again, and drove on.

West past Ross, Monmouth, Abergavenny, Ebbw Vale – towns fast asleep, just scattered lights in upstairs windows, the blue glow of a late-night TV movie, the pavements empty and the roads deserted. At Merthyr, by a roundabout, two coppers in a patrol car eyed the Beamer, saw I was a woman and turned away.

Then north, into the Beacons: the bulk of the hills black against the night sky. The roads shrank. On bends the headlamps picked out snatches of landscape, conifer forest and moorland, tussocky grassland, the red eyes of sheep and cattle grazing in the dark.

At last, on my right, the paler glimmer of the reservoir; left, the trees rising beside the road. I slowed down, looking for the turning. There it was: a tight hairpin. I took it slowly, killing the headlights on the turn. Drove up and into the trees, and there were the gateposts, a Gothic dragon squat and sullen on top of each. The wrought-iron gates were propped open, and overgrown. Beyond them was the clearing, and the house, in darkness.

I parked the car and got out. And here I am.

The air is cold, and damp, and soft, and smells of leaf mould. There's a stream running nearby, a constant rush of water; beyond it the hiss and rattle of the trees – for a second I'm back in Graves's garden, but this time no one's watching. I turn 360, scanning, allowing my eyes to get used to the dark. The woodland screens me on all sides: no view of the reservoir, or the road. No lights anywhere.

I turn towards the house.

Devlin's right: it's big, but nothing special. I cross to it, peer in through the windows, then turn away towards the drive, but the trees curve around the clearing: you can't see the gates from here.

The other building's two-storey, like the house. Garage doors and what might be a workshop on the ground floor. A glazed door on the end; through it, stairs going up. A handmade sign by the door reads, THE ANNEXE. It looks like it was painted by a kid.

I pull on latex gloves.

The lock's a simple one, but I'm out of practice. It takes me minutes to pick it. Inside it's pitch dark. I pull shoe covers out of my pocket and put them on as I step over the threshold, then shield my torch with my hand to kill most of the light, switch it on, and go up.

First two doors: a kitchen cubbyhole and a little toilet/shower room, clustered around the top of the stairs. Then a corridor. First bedroom on the right, second one straight ahead, both completely empty: no furniture, no carpets, just bare boards and painted plaster walls. The place has been stripped and is very clean.

I go to the window of the furthest bedroom. On the edge of the dark clearing, the stone gateposts glimmer.

I go back down, taking the shoe covers off at the threshold, to fetch what I need from the car.

It was Thomas Drew who taught me crime-scene processing. He

argued it was an essential skill. You need to know what traces you are leaving, and you need to be able to detect others' traces, either in order to make sure you've erased them, or because the proof may be useful for blackmail purposes. So I learned it all: how to secure a sterile corridor, pick up fibres, lift latent prints, process semen stains on dirty bedding. And look for blood, of course.

I need two journeys to bring everything from the car. Before I close it up for the last time I take another swig of coffee from my flask, and listen, but there's no sound from the road.

This time before I go up the stairs I put on a SOCO's paper suit.

In the kitchen I pull down the blinds, then get out a little battery-operated nightlight, put it on the work surface, switch it on. Then I go through the flat. There are blinds at all the windows and I pull them down too. The nightlight emits only a faint glow, but I don't want it leaking out into the dark empty night.

Back in the kitchen I prepare the Bluestar fluid, popping the tablets out of their foil packages and mixing the solutions. Two containers: the pump spray for the floors, the paint-gun-type aerosol with the more concentrated mixture for the walls. I may not need both but it pays to have them ready. I swill them round to let the solutions mix, then take them through to the furthest bedroom. Then I go back, and move the nightlight part-way down the corridor, so its glow just reaches the bedroom door. I leave the camera on its tripod propped up in the kitchen. A SOCO would take photographs; but a SOCO wouldn't be doing this alone, and I don't want to waste time setting up the camera if there's nothing here to find.

I return and stand just inside the bedroom door. The faint pale glow of the nightlight is the only illumination, but my eyes have adjusted, and you have to do this in near-dark.

A little room. Big enough for a small double bed, a chest of drawers, a chair, not much else. *Assume there was a bed in here a year ago: in the middle of the floor, with space around its sides ...*

I start in the far corner of the floor, working my way down under the window, spraying as I've been taught, in steady even strokes, from half a metre away. I'm waiting for the telltale glow of a luminol reaction, the thirty-second steady blue fluorescence that tells you it's blood; but nothing comes.

I take one pace back and spray again.

And there it is: the first bright bloom of spatter, an arc of glowing droplets, left to right.

307

One more pace back. Spray again. Another glowing arc pulses into life. This one runs up onto the skirting board. I swap the pump for the aerosol and continue spraying, chasing the arc up across the painted plaster. It runs out three feet above the ground. It's smeared where someone's wiped it.

It happened here.

A voice inside – it might be Drew's – is telling me: *Be systematic. You need evidence. Get the camera now. Set it up. Respray. Get shots.* But I can't break away; I can't stop spraying. The bright trails surge and glow before my eyes, surge and glow, hypnotically – the violence of one death recorded in spatters and spurts of blue light. One loops right up the wall to the ceiling. Another goes along towards the door – breaks off – a clear gap – then a fat bright splodge – a smear—

And then, as clear as day, a handprint. The size of mine, maybe a little smaller. A woman's hand. Catherine.

I stare at it as it slowly fades to nothing.

Respray. Get shots.

Because this is all the evidence I may get. All that's left of the man called Daniel.

And in that moment I know. I'm going to get that woman out of the Program, but I'm not going to ignore what she's done. Not until I know everything.

I turn towards the door. In the corridor beyond, the nightlight falters.

A footstep, and a man's outline blocks the door. He's holding a shotgun.

He says, 'Charlotte, what are you doing?'

I swear I never heard a car. He must have parked it somewhere along the road, and run from there. Not with the gun: the gun comes from the house. He let himself in, got the gun, loaded it, and came up here, all so quietly – a late gift from all those childhood holidays, the games of hide and seek, knowing exactly which stair will creak—

I say, 'This is where she killed him, isn't it? I'm spraying with luminol – it discloses bloodstains.' And then, ridiculously, 'Do you want to see?'

Of course he doesn't. He's seen it all already.

I say, 'I know you didn't do this,' and he says, 'If I'd had any idea that she …' and we both stop, and together we look back along the wall, but the smears and arcs and spatters have all faded. We're standing in the near-dark of an empty room again.

He says, 'It was such a mess. He was—' He stops, swallows. He saw Daniel.

'And she left you to clean up.' The walls, the body, everything … I wonder where Daniel is now. In a shallow pit among the trees?

'I didn't have a choice. She'd gone. I couldn't go to the police—' He breaks off again. *What did she have on you?* But later, I can leave that one for later. There are other more important things to deal with now.

What did I do to bring him here tonight? Somewhere along the line I showed my hand. Too obvious an interest in Catherine? In the photo? Or was it the phone call? Did I let something slip?

But he followed me; and someone may have followed him. And he's standing there with a gun, and he doesn't know who I am any more or whether he can trust me.

He turns and looks at me. He says, 'You're collecting evidence. Why, Charlotte?'

'Because I had to be sure.' I sound calm, though my heart is hammering. 'And because I needed you to talk to me about what happened. Unless I had evidence you'd just deny it.'

'Why should I talk to you?' His back is to the door, the corridor, the nightlight; I can't see his face. All I've got to go on is his voice. And in it something's shifted.

'Everyone involved in this is in danger – everyone who's helped her get away. Two are dead already.' I don't want to say, *You could be next.* 'What brought you here tonight?'

He says, 'You were seen,' and I hear it again, the change in his voice, but this time it's like a shutter going down, a part of Mark Devlin closing itself off, and for the first time I'm afraid.

Seen? At Graves's house? Was it Mark Devlin watching? But in that case—

Devlin is the one who murdered Graves.

I've got this backwards. Mark Devlin isn't Catherine's protector. Mark Devlin is the client.

You need to be in control of this right now.

'All right,' I say, making it firm, businesslike. 'Do you know who I am?'

'Probably not Charlotte Alton,' he says. There's a bitter little twist there. I ignore it.

'I'm not police, and I don't make moral judgements. Catherine killed a man. It was horrific. You got here too late; you couldn't have stopped it. All you could do was clean up afterwards. But then you went after her. To put right what she'd done. And eventually you found her. You've hired someone to do the job, haven't you? Because you can't get at her where she is.'

A silence from Devlin. Then he says, 'I liked you. I really, really liked you.'

Another kick of panic. I smother it. 'We can still sort this out.'

He says, 'I was warned you'd say that.' He lifts the shotgun, just fractionally. 'I have to make a call.'

My heart lurches.

'We're going to the house now,' he says and he points the gun at me.

If he killed Graves, he'll use it.

How many chances on the way out of here? The staircase and the corridor are narrow. We'll walk in single file: me in front, him behind. Top of the stairs: I'll turn before he does, with the kitchen on my left, the camera tripod propped within reach, but I won't have space to swing it cleanly, and before I'm down the stairs and out the door he will have fired.

'All right,' I say, and move to step past him. For a second he has to step back, lowering the gun. I'm still holding the Bluestar aerosol.

I spray it in his eyes.

He howls. Behind me something clatters, but I'm in the corridor now. I kick the nightlight – the plastic casing shatters against the wall, and it goes out. Turn at the end of the corridor and throw myself down the stairs. How long before he realises he's not blinded? I'm out the door now, running for the car. *Keys, keys.* They're in my pocket, under the SOCO suit. I have to rip it off. For a second it fouls my ankles. Then I'm out of it, keys in hand, hurling myself into the car.

Car key in ignition. The engine fires. One glance towards the building – the door bursts open and there's Devlin running, with the shotgun. I crunch into reverse, pull back and spin the wheel – where is he? – aim the car towards the gates and floor it, feel the pull of the acceleration as the Beamer's rear wheel drive digs in—

Bang. The windscreen crazes over in front of me, dozens of tiny cracks and splits. I can't see ahead but my foot's still to the floor. *Bang* again, another starburst – then an impact. The car shudders violently, bounces, throws me to one side – then I'm clear and still accelerating – and then—

I see them in the undamaged edges of the windscreen, the second before I hit them. Trees.

I don't know how long I've been sitting here. The engine's stalled, but the headlamps are still on. Their light reflects up into the crazed patterns of the windscreen. It's oddly beautiful.

I can't move: everything has locked. Then something scratches at my side window and I turn my head, but it's just a twig. I turn my head back. Shift my shoulders experimentally. Prise my hands off the steering wheel. My fingers are like hooks.

The driver's airbag hasn't deployed. Interesting, that.

Devlin Devlin Devlin

—had a gun—

In the rear-view mirror the wreckage of undergrowth and saplings is lit red by my tail lights.

Beyond them there's the clearing, and a low dark shape.

I sit there for another minute, not taking my eyes off the mirror, watching. The shape doesn't move.

Get out. Get out. You have to.

Undergrowth is packed against the door; I have to force it open, then push myself along the bodywork. Twigs claw at me until I'm past the car. Its track has scarred the woodland: broken saplings gleam palely. The air smells green, and damaged.

I reach the edge of the trees.

He's like a rag doll wrapped up in torn clothing, limbs with joints where they shouldn't be. His head and chest are crushed, deformed, his scalp half torn away, his features mangled and out of shape.

I know he's dead, but still I have to touch him.

I torch the Beamer. There's old newspapers in the house, fire-lighters, even a disposable barbecue. I add the SOCO suit. The car's cigarette lighter makes a spark. I crack the driver's window, wait until it's caught, then back away.

The shotgun lies twelve feet from Mark Devlin, both barrels discharged. I leave it there. Leave everything in the annexe too: the Bluestar sprays, the camera, the broken nightlight, everything.

As I walk down the drive, past the sullen dragons, the Beamer's already billowing acrid smoke.

I reach the road, turn right, keep walking. A few hundred yards, and there's a small car park overlooking the reservoir. Mark Devlin's silver Audi's parked under the trees. I turn away from it, get out my mobile. One bar of signal. I call Craigie. Give him a code I thought I'd never use. Then switch off the phone, and stand among the trees, and wait.

Mark Devlin leans against the doorway in his flat, wine glass in hand, clean and fit and alive, and smiling. *Breathe in too deeply and you feel dizzy.*

Day 23: Thursday

Johanssen

At 1 a.m. the pattern of her breathing changes. By two she's starting to stir, and then her eyes open. Ten seconds of blankness. Her forehead creases as if she's trying to remember something. Then her mouth distorts and she sucks in air and her body convulses under the blanket. 'No—'

He's already across the room. 'Cate—'

As he reaches her she flails. He grabs for her wrists, catches one, misses the other. Her arm whips round, her hand clawing at his cheek. He jerks his head back, clutches at her loose arm, grasps it. Her body arches away from him. He's talking to her, hushing her, but she's fighting him, fighting Brice, fighting all of them. The noise she makes is barely human: the only word he can make out is *No*.

'Cate, it's me, it's—'

She hurls herself against him, driving her head into his chest. He releases her wrists and wraps his arms around her, pulling her close and tight, hushing into her hair while she struggles against him. She's tiny, like a small bird in a net or a starved cat in a bag. He never realised how tiny: nothing but skin and bone and sinew.

Suddenly she stops fighting. She huddles against him, shaking with adrenaline, gasping for air.

On the floor below a door bangs. Feet pound up the stairs – one man, moving fast. The door opens: Riley, eyes wide and frantic.

Against Johanssen's chest, Cate's head moves. He pulls away from her a little. Saliva drools from the corner of her mouth. He wipes it away with a thumb.

'Where were you?' she whimpers. 'Where the fuck were you? You could have ...'

Her face crumples and she begins to cry. He draws her against him.

Riley turns and steps outside, pulling the door until it's open just a couple of inches. He slumps down onto the stairs with his back towards them. After a moment he puts his head in his hands.

For a while she cries. Then for a while after that she could be sleeping, he's not sure. Then he looks down and her eyes are open, a faint slick reflection glancing off the whites.

'Vinnie,' she says. Her voice is a whisper.

'I know.'

'Didn't deserve that,' she says. 'Didn't deserve that.'

Her gaze is elsewhere. Another memory has slid in beside the first, the gate with dragons on it, Daniel, all that blood. In her head, on an endless loop, they're playing. And they'll go on playing, for weeks, months ... Even years from now, when she's far away from here, living a different life, those memories will still have the power to ambush her. He knows that. In his own head, beyond a locked door in a remote farmhouse, a man still screams.

Around four in the morning she stretches and moves away from him, and tells him she needs to piss. He stands outside the door while she urinates into a bucket. He's alone: Riley has left his post at the stairs.

There's a window at the top of the staircase looking out over the yard. Outside a light rain is falling, no more than a mist. Over by the gate half a dozen men loiter under the floodlights. Their voices, blurred by distance and glass, drift across the yard to him. If he opens the window he'll be able to smell their cigarettes, but he doesn't move.

Quillan hasn't touched Brice. What does that mean?

From behind the door he can hear Cate moving around, shifting things. He goes back in. She's fully dressed now, but still holding a bundle of clothes. She puts them down and rubs her face with one hand, distractedly.

'I have to get back to the clinic,' she says. 'I have to work.'

'Clinic's closed.' Then he says, 'I'm going to get you out of here.'

She just looks at him dully.

'You have to leave the Program,' he says. 'They know you're here, they're coming for you. I'm going to get you out. There are people waiting on the outside who'll make you safe.'

Her head comes up a fraction. 'Coming for me? To kill me?' she says. She doesn't sound afraid. But she's on some sort of time lag, the words reaching her belatedly, stripped of their impact. They haven't hit her yet.

'Yes,' he says, 'to kill you.'

She frowns. 'How do you know this?'

'I'm the one they sent.'

A long moment's silence, then she says, *Do your job.*'

'No,' he says – she can't have understood. 'You have to trust me. We can get you out. I've talked to someone – they've got resources, they can do it: a day, two days. We just have to keep you safe, then they'll get you lifted. New life, new ID.' It sounds so simple, so cut and dried. *We do this, and this, and this* … Like a child's story, with magic and a happy ending.

'No,' she says. Her voice is flat now. 'I'm not going anywhere. Just do your job.'

'I can't,' he says.

'Why not? Your girlfriend—' She stops, and her face changes, the realisation clicking into place. 'You're not Ryan Jackson, are you?' She gives a tiny, sickened smile. 'So Brice was right.'

'I can't do it. Not this time.'

Her eyes snap open. 'Why not? You know what I've done. Don't I deserve it?'

As if her death is something she's earned by killing the man Daniel. As if there's some simple balance sheet somewhere that says her debt's due … He thinks of Terry Cunliffe suddenly, of another balance sheet, another debt, this time with his name against it. He can't tell her.

He says, 'You have nightmares about it. Sometimes you're afraid to sleep. You count the ones you save, but there'll never be enough—'

'And that makes it OK?' She's folded her arms – that stiff protective gesture, shutting him out. Her expression's tight and cold. He doesn't know what to say.

She says, 'If you don't do it, what then?'

'They'll send someone else.'

'Then let them.' She turns away. 'Now go.'

He wants to say something more. He doesn't know what it is.

But when he reaches the door, she says, 'If you're not Ryan Jackson, who are you?' and she's looking back at him. 'Do I get to know your name?'

He shakes his head. She thinks about it and then she nods.

'You've done this sort of thing before,' she says. 'The killing part.

315

It doesn't usually bother you.' He looks away. His gaze snags on the scratches on the wall. Slowly he starts to count.

She says, 'I'd like it to be you, if there's a choice. At least it would be quick.'

She turns away again.

He goes down to the bunkroom, pulls off his boots, lies down. Quillan's men stir and mumble in the waiting room below. If the phone rings, he'll hear it.

No sound from upstairs: no scratching at the wall.

Over on the bunk opposite, Drill lies stretched out on his back, still as a marble figure on a tomb. But he too is awake, and the whites of his eyes glisten in the dark.

Day 23: Thursday

Karla

Just after 4 a.m. an estate car pulls into the car park by the reservoir. Its number plate matches the text that I received an hour ago, the last time I turned the phone on. It parks beside Devlin's silver Audi, and a man gets out. He goes to the back of the car, lifts the tailgate, pulls back a blanket, takes out a Thermos, drinks coffee looking out across the water. Then he screws the lid back on the flask, replaces it, walks a little distance away, and with his back to me unzips his fly and begins to piss.

The tailgate of the car is still up. I climb in and pull the blanket right over me.

Footsteps as the man comes back. The tailgate slams down right next to my head. The driver's door opens, the car shifts on its springs, the door shuts. The engine restarts, and we're away.

Two hours of driving. I tune it out. Try not to think at all.

At last the car stops. The man gets out and walks away. Ten minutes later someone else opens the tailgate and pulls back the blanket: a woman with bleached-blonde hair, a hard mouth, too much jewellery. We're in a big garage, almost empty. Without a word she leads me to a van, helps me into the back. There's nothing inside except another blanket. When she shuts the door I'm completely in the dark.

Someone gets in the front and starts the engine. The woman? Someone else? Craigie's using people I don't know. To them I'm just another client: some poor bitch who's got out of her depth and has had to buy a rescue. It's not far from the truth.

It's gone 9 a.m. before I'm back in Docklands, in clothes that aren't my own. Through the door, straight in the shower, scrub myself hard, robe, into the main room. TV on: news channel, mute the

317

sound. I've gone beyond hunger, tiredness, even shock. I've switched to automatic.

Devlin's dead, but that doesn't mean it's over. He was going to call someone else, someone who's still out there, still in play – someone who warned him about me, someone who knows—

So call Craigie, get him over here. Then call Powell. Get Catherine lifted. Do it.

For a second the glowing smears and smudges from the wall, that small bright handprint, flare out at me. With Catherine in Powell's hands I'll never know who Daniel was, or why he died. But right now there's nothing else I can do.

I'm reaching for the phone when someone hammers on my front door, and I freeze. I don't get surprise visitors.

Ellis's face bulges in the spyhole. But he shouldn't be here, he knows this place is off limits, he's not allowed anywhere near Charlotte Alton—

His hand comes up. His warrant card is in it. This time it's official.

I open the door. 'Ms Alton?' he says. 'DI Ellis, mind if I come in?' And then he looks beyond me into the main room and grins, a savage grin that doesn't come anywhere near his eyes. 'Oh good,' he says, 'are we on?'

I turn. Through the open doorway, the TV shows a helicopter shot: forest, a winding ribbon of road, a flat expanse of water. Police cars parked at angles on the road. And then the clearing: more police cars, and a red fire tender pulled up beside a crime-scene tent. The Beamer's hidden by the trees. The house is untouched. The annexe is a blackened, smoking ruin.

I have to make a call, Mark Devlin said. When it didn't come, did they come looking? And it was a mess when they arrived: the burned-out Beamer buried in the trees, and Devlin—

They could have cleaned it up; but that would have taken time and manpower, and I could be coming back. They did the next best thing: destroyed the evidence of Daniel's murder, and left.

When I turn back Ellis is watching me. 'A few questions, if you don't mind, Ms Alton.' He gives the standard phrase a vicious spin: 'It's just routine.'

He stalks into the main room behind me. I gesture to a seat. He doesn't take it. Immediately he's checking out the room, his gaze going from wall to wall to window, like a dealer pricing the furnishings. 'Nice place you got here, Ms Alton – or can I call you

Charlotte?' Then, quick as a knife, 'Thanks for the heads-up on Mark Devlin, Karla. That call of yours, it really got me thinking. Decided I'd better double-check his alibi. I called round his flat first thing this morning. Was on my way to his office when the news broke. You do know he's dead, don't you? You don't seem that surprised. Or that upset.'

He turns and begins to wander down the room, away from me: another casual survey. He says, 'He was mown down by a vehicle attempting to leave the scene. They found a shotgun, both barrels discharged, car crashed in the trees. Whoever was in that car, he tried to stop them.' He turns, glances back at me. 'Is any of this news?'

I say nothing.

For a long moment he watches me. Then he says, 'You've always tried to keep me from the truth. First time you called me? You knew she was dead. You didn't know who did it, you didn't have a motive, but you knew.' He shakes his head. 'What've you got? A body? But then why not tell me? Or a witness. That's it, isn't it? Right from the start you've been protecting someone. Who is it, Karla?'

I just blank him back.

He stares at me. He's read me. His look's close to contempt. 'I should have you in an interview room,' he says. 'I should be sweating this out of you.'

'Then why aren't you?'

A pause, and then his voice takes on a sneering, official tone. 'I understand you knew Mr Devlin socially. Can you tell me when you saw him last?'

So that's the way we're playing it. 'I spoke to Mark last night. He'd left a message, suggesting we meet up. I called him back, but by then he had company. Do check the phone records.'

'Oh, I will. And where were you?'

'Here, at first. Later I went out.'

'Anywhere in particular?'

'Visiting friends. In London. Nowhere much.' *Don't push it, Ellis.*

For a moment we square up to each other. Then he says, 'This isn't over, Karla,' and he leaves.

I walk into the office. All the unanswered questions ... I slam a lid on them. *Powell. Nothing else for it. Contact Powell, do a deal, get her out of there, make Johanssen safe. Get this all closed down.*

There's a message light flashing on one of the machines. I hit 'Play', and Whitman says, 'Laura, I really didn't think you'd do it.' He sounds pleased.

The message ends immediately.

I call him back. 'Do what, Mike?'

He says, 'Square it with Washington. I got a call from a guy I know in the Department of Justice. *He'd* had a call from someone in your department. We had one of those conversations – nothing stated, but he's in the loop. He sounded impressed; you pulled some weight on this one. So, we're fine.'

Someone in your department. But he thinks Laura's something in intelligence …

Oh no no no.

I end the call. Redial. This time it's Fielding. He answers as usual, with a grunt.

'Johanssen's client—'

He says, 'You do my fucking head in, you know? How'd you work it out?' Then, as if he knows I won't reply, 'Yeah, I saw the news.'

'Mark Devlin. You said he came with references.'

'That's right,' he says. 'D'you think I'm stupid? D'you think I'd send Johanssen in there without—?'

'Who supplied the references, Fielding?' Nothing. Try again. 'You said you didn't know the guy. He could have been anyone. But you knew he was fine, he could be trusted, because he came to you through someone you've worked with before.'

Still nothing. Then, as if it hurts to say it: 'The guy had a code.'

'And this code told you what?' *Please no—*

'That he was safe. I told you— Fuck it, Karla. Sometimes I get approached to sort stuff for people who can't be seen to be involved.'

'Intelligence.'

For a moment Fielding says nothing. Then, more quietly: 'Johanssen's done the odd job for them. He doesn't know.'

'They don't use people like him. They've got their own.' The Spec Ops unit that rejected him, for starters.

'Oh yes they do,' Fielding says. 'They do when they don't want to use their own.'

'And when's that?'

'What do you think? When no one wants to admit how badly they've screwed up. When they want it all just flushed away so nothing touches the sides. I told you: it's fine, he's safe. So when's this wrapping up?'

'Devlin's dead,' I say. 'You don't have a client.'

He says, 'Oh yes I do.'

Safe. That's the irony. I wanted to protect him all along. But from the outset they were watching: watching him appear in Program Reception with his fake ID, watching him go in and out through those gates, ready to step in the moment he was challenged. Watching over him, to make sure he did the job.

Like you, but stronger.

Smarter too, and better at keeping themselves hidden. But still like me: deleting Catherine Gallagher the way I'd delete an inconvenient file, wiping it from the record because it's their job. Intelligence.

Intelligence, interrogating a man called Daniel. Who was he? A terrorist? A traitor? But someone who had to be made to talk, and fast. But torture's something they can't do, so they set up the blackest of black ops, fronted by civilians, all deniable. Catherine Gallagher supplying medical cover: brought in to keep the man alive, keep patching him up so they could start on him again the next day and the next, so he didn't die until they'd got everything they wanted – because that's what clever, ambitious Catherine was good at, keeping people alive. They'd have known exactly what buttons to press with her. *Use your skills, help your country, fight terrorism. You'll see how grateful we can be ...* Easy to agree when you already believe your patients are another species.

Catherine Gallagher persuading Devlin to let them use the house. And when it was over, Catherine Gallagher killing Daniel and walking away, leaving Devlin to clean it up. That's why he couldn't go to the police. I have experience with these people: I know how they work. *Co-operate and this will go away. Talk and you're in the frame.*

And when they tracked Catherine down to the Program, Devlin fronting negotiations with Fielding, with just a nod to say he's one of theirs ...

And if I phone Powell now? I've read his file. He's a company man, and a janitor. Good at cleaning up inconvenient messes, flushing away the shit, just like Johanssen. He's not the one behind all this. He wants a deal with Knox and he'll say anything to get it. But however many promises Powell makes, the moment Catherine enters his protection, a clock starts ticking.

He'll tell me that she's fine – abroad, with cover, a new life. I'll never be able to prove him wrong. But I know: if I place her in Powell's hands, she's as good as dead.

And that matters, does it?

Isn't this what's coming to her? She sold out on an intelligence deal, supervised a man's torture and death. Isn't this payback?

Contact Powell. Just do it.

I don't move.

I promised Johanssen, didn't I? That I would keep her safe. Because saving her somehow makes up for Terry Cunliffe. Somewhere a voice inside me says, *He'll never know*, but I know I can't trust it. I'm not going to lie to Johanssen now.

But there's something else.

I'm back in that dark room with the bloodstains glowing blue on the walls around me. A man I still know only as Daniel died in that room for a reason. I'm going to find out why.

Day 23: Thursday

Johanssen

He sleeps, and then he wakes, eats, sleeps some more. Cate's up in
her room; Riley takes her food, can't get her to eat it. Johanssen
doesn't go up. He listens for her movements – footsteps, scratching
– but there's no sound.

Quillan's men still loiter downstairs. Where's Brice?

Riley comes in and says, 'I thought you were leaving.'

He says, 'I'm waiting for a call.'

He sleeps again. At some stage he dreams.

He's in the clinic, and they've just brought Terry Cunliffe in. The
man's a mess of raw flesh but he isn't screaming. Instead he looks
at Johanssen expectantly, as if this is his problem, his responsibility,
something he's expected to fix, and Johanssen feels panic rising
because it's too late and there's nothing to be done.

Then he's back there, in the office, in front of the man at the desk.

'This is no reflection on your abilities—'

He wakes on an intake of breath. It's four in the afternoon.
Outside, distantly, someone's shouting.

Then he hears it, from the room below: a phone, ringing.

There is a playground – you can see it through the glass of the Family
Room, in the dusk: a patch of blighted grass, a few swings and a
climbing frame, a flimsy shelter and the stained concrete bowl of a
paddling pool, drained for the winter. A shallow puddle of rainwater
has collected in it. Around it all, a six-foot-high metal fence: another
prison within a prison.

The building he's in is tacked on to the wall, beyond the strip of
waste ground. It's where the visitors come, and there's a handful this
afternoon. Strained women trying to make conversation with their
men, sullen kids who don't know why they're here, an elderly couple
who sit close, bright-eyed, tearful, holding it together for a heavy

323

tattooed guy who must be their son and who's wishing they hadn't come … Opposite Johanssen, Whitman looks jumpy and unwell, and eyes the guards uneasily. He delivers the message without quite looking at Johanssen. 'She says there isn't any other way.'

Johanssen nods, and goes.

Quillan's men are waiting outside in a pool of floodlight on the edge of the rubble. Four of them today: a bodyguard. But they haven't had sight of Brice's crew. He wonders where they are, and what they're waiting for.

All the way back across the Program he watches for them, but they don't appear.

He reaches the compound gate at last. Lights in the windows of the council block, and in Quillan's building too. He looks around: one more quick survey, fixing it. The next time he leaves it must be with her.

Will she agree? But why should she? *She counts the ones she saves.* That's her defence against the guilt and the nightmares, and it's kept her going for a year: the hope that somewhere all those lives add up, that one day she'll look at that wall, count the marks and think, *Enough.* Now he's trying to take even that away from her. And leave her with what? The memory of those two deaths, Daniel's and Vinnie's, and no way to make them right?

Still it comes back, like a reflex: *She's wrong. She's wrong. You have to get her out.*

He's crossing the yard when someone falls into step with him. The man says to Johanssen pleasantly, 'Sorry I missed you. Next time, eh?' It's Brice. The light from the gate catches his smile and then he's gone, strolling across the tarmac, hands in pockets, humming to himself.

He opens her door quietly. She's asleep, over on the mattress by the window; he can tell from the easy rhythm of her breathing. He closes the door again and settles down against it. Replays what Whitman said to him, begins to pace it out. It's cold on the stairs. He doesn't mind. The cold will keep him awake.

Day 23: Thursday – Day 24: Friday

Karla

It's late now. I walk from room to room. The blinds are up: beyond the glass the city glitters indifferently.

I've had my meetings, made my calls. Craigie first, late this morning – Craigie looking edgy and reluctant, but only hours before he'd exfil'ed me from a crime scene where a man Charlotte Alton knew was killed. By rights I should have been keeping my head down, and he shouldn't have been here. But we needed a team in place as soon as possible; there wasn't time to waste.

I kept it cool, and hard, and practical: boiled it down to pure risk management. Made all my points as if no one could doubt them. That tomorrow isn't far too soon for this. That we can minimise the risk and everyone's exposure. That given the right set of circumstances we can pull it off – as if this isn't way beyond our comfort zone, our capabilities. When I'd finished he went quiet, and his face took on an odd immobility. At last he said, 'This is for him.'

'He is our client, yes.'

'And he's just gone native.' I knew what he was thinking: *unreliable*. At least he didn't say it. He sat back, then he said, 'You've already decided,' and he shook his head. I've lost the bigger picture, haven't I? My judgement's clouded. We don't stand a chance.

'You don't have to be a part of this—'

He looked me in the eye. 'You need me.'

He could have walked out when Drew did. He's not leaving now.

Then Whitman, over the phone, with the message he had to deliver. And there it was in his silence on the other end of the line: the penny slowly dropping, the realisation of what this had to mean. He believes I'm Laura Pressinger, who works in intelligence, pulls some weight, gets Washington on board. Even so, he knows what this sounds like, and it sounds bad.

325

And finally Ellis. I hesitated before phoning him. But tomorrow he'll be all over this anyway, and I need him on my side.

Ellis didn't answer. I left a coded message.

Until he calls back there's nothing more I can do, but I can't settle. I've tried music, television, a book. I've tried routine paperwork. I can't concentrate. It's as if the cogs of my mind have all been filed smooth: nothing catches.

I'm so tired. The past keeps coming back to me in snatches, like disconnected fragments of a dream. I'm in Graves's consulting room with Ellis, and Graves is making notes I cannot see. I'm back outside the gallery under the too-bright street lights with Mark Devlin saying, so seriously, 'I can't just leave you like this.' I'm stepping out of the laurels, confronting William Hamilton – 'Oh, you've come,' as if he's been waiting for me all this time, and can't believe it's taken me so long.

I'm in a corridor at the Royal Opera House, and for a fraction of a second, less, Johanssen's hand's in mine. A signal, in a code I thought I understood but didn't, at all, until yesterday.

Do not think of him. You can't afford to think of him. You have a job to do.

But still I can feel it: the shape of his hand in mine.

The plan will work. It has to.

But you're up against intelligence. How long do you think you can keep her out of their hands? A month? A week? A day? And in that time will she tell you the truth?

And what will you do when she does?

At last I stop pacing and go to bed. I need to sleep tonight. Tomorrow, and the day after, and maybe the day after that, I could be working double shifts, and sleep will be something I snatch in odd hours, so I'm lying in the bedroom with the lights out and the blinds down. But tonight sleep won't come. The part of my brain that deals with these things is still turning, numbering off all the elements we need to have in place for this to work.

And it's too many, isn't it? I'm out of my depth already, before I've even begun.

So I'm still awake in the early hours of Friday when the handset beside me rings.

'It's Ellis.'

In those two words I try to gauge his mood. 'You got my message.'

He just grunts.

'This is a heads-up, Ellis. Get a good night's sleep. Tomorrow you find Catherine Gallagher.'

A five-second silence, then he says, 'I *fucking* knew it.'

'Knew what, Ellis?'

'You knew all along where they put her. Why now? Why not a week ago? Two weeks? All this time I've been—'

'Things have moved on.'

'Then why wait until tomorrow? Give me the location now. We can start digging as soon as it's light. What earthly fucking difference is it going to make now?'

'We're not ready.'

'Karla—'

'Get your head clear and get some rest. I'll give you all the information I can, as soon as I can. You can't help her now. But tomorrow she'll need you.'

'Spare me the *CSI* crap about bringing her murderer to justice, Karla,' Ellis snarls, 'I know my job.'

'But you're not looking for her murderer,' I tell him. 'Your job, Ellis, will be to keep her alive.'

I've told him I'll deliver her to him at an address he'll be given tomorrow. I've told him I'm relying on him for her protection. Perhaps I should have told him more. But no: the less he knows about what I've planned, the better.

So here I am: piece by piece, bolting together the machine that will save Catherine Gallagher. But the second it starts up, this whole mechanism could spin out of my control, and if it does, there's nothing I can do to stop it.

Part V

Day 24: Friday

Johanssen

They opened the clinic at eight, two hours late. It's been a quiet night since then, the cases trickling through. Cate works in silence. But just after one, as he helps her with a heart case – laboured breathing, chest pains – she murmurs, 'How much longer?' As if she knows he's watching the time tick away. As if she's watching too. But when he tries to catch her eye, she turns away.

He gets Vinnie's mop and cleans the floor. Someone's got to do it.

At three he goes to stand outside the main door, beyond the awning, and tilts his face up to the sky.

And if she won't go?

The men talk and smoke on the gate: their voices and the smell of their cigarettes drift across the tarmac. Figures shift behind the windows of the council blocks beyond the wire. Everything is a million miles away from him.

The door swings open behind him. He turns, expecting Riley, but it's Cate.

He looks at her once, then away. *Find the words. You've got to find the words.*

She says, 'Brice spoke to you.'

'Who told you?'

'Riley saw it.'

'Riley say where Brice is now?'

She nods towards the wire, the gates, the council blocks, the night. 'Out there somewhere.' Then, 'He's coming back for you. You have to leave.'

'Not unless you do.'

'And if I don't?' He doesn't answer. 'If you stay Brice will—'

'Yes.'

She wraps her arms around herself, that protective gesture, or she's cold again. After a minute her head drops; she's standing in the litter of Riley's fag ends and she stares down at them as if they demand all her concentration. He thinks of Vinnie suddenly, always cleaning – Vinnie should have swept them up—

She says, 'Why are you doing this? Why is it so important to you?'

The past unfurls in pictures. An office with a uniformed man behind a desk. The lilies in the house in Marlow, and Charlie Ross, gold watch and business shirt – *What can you do? Whatever I have to.* A hallway in a remote farmhouse—

He doesn't answer.

She says, 'You think you can save me.' Her eyes are huge, unfathomable in her wasted face. 'What if you can't? What if it's impossible?'

Karla on the park bench in the cemetery. Karla holding his hand.

'It's always possible,' he says. *You've got to believe it's possible.*

After that they fall silent. He glances down once: she's looking out across the yard, but her eyes are blank.

It's 7.55 a.m. when he touches her arm. The flow of patients has stopped. The very sick and the walking wounded are waiting for the first of the morning ambulances. She's sitting on a chair over by the sink, head down, but at his touch mechanically she starts to rise as if he's brought her another case.

'I'm going now,' he says.

Riley's over by the sink, scrubbing up. At the words he turns and looks at Johanssen.

Cate says, 'For good?' He nods. 'Then I'll walk out with you.'

When she goes upstairs to get her coat Riley comes across. 'This is it then?'

'This is it.'

Riley says, 'You haven't got your stuff,' and Johanssen says, 'They'll only take it off me. You have it,' and Riley nods.

The door to the stairs opens. She's wearing that bulky padded coat, the one that's too big for her.

He holds the outer door for her, but when she reaches it, she turns. 'I'll be all right,' she says to Riley. She could be saying sorry.

Day 24: Friday

Karla

Friday's dawned, chill and grey. My coffee tastes of nothing. But that's what it's like when you're in the middle of a big operation: everyday life ceases to register. Food, sex, sleep become irrelevant. You live in a constant state of preoccupation. There's only the job.

It's happening today, even though it's too soon: we're not ready, we don't have enough people in place, there's still too much to do. But I don't say it and neither does Craigie, on the other end of a secure phone line, and that's why I chose him in the first place – for his diligence, his doggedness, his ability to work to the task. He's been dealt a hand and he'll play it.

'Surveillance feeds?' I ask.

'I'm in,' he says. 'Compound gate.'

It's on my screen too, the men on sentry duty stamping and smoking in the cold early light.

'Everyone ready?' I ask.

'Standing by.'

The clock on my screen clicks over to 08:00.

At the command posts the shutters are rattling up, the snatches nosing out into the streets. The main gates are opening too, the armoured ambulances rolling forward in clouds of exhaust, the guards' faces pinched and white with cold.

Please God, it's all about to happen.

The Program's surveillance cameras pick them up as they reach the compound gate: Johanssen, and beside him Catherine Gallagher bundled into her oversized coat. She walks as if she's in a trance.

I say to Craigie, 'We've got some movement.'

'I'm on it,' he says.

The men on duty exchange uneasy glances. There's a shuffling

333

of feet and then the gate unlatches. Out they go. Immediately they turn left.

Their departure's caught someone out. They've reached the next corner before two figures detach from the group on the gate and begin to follow.

Johanssen and Catherine Gallagher turn the corner. I switch to the next surveillance camera. It takes me just a few seconds to get there, but when I do the street it shows is empty.

Day 24: Friday

Johanssen

After three minutes he's sure they've lost the tail. He doubles back, leading her through side streets. Down an alley, and through an unlocked door into an abandoned small-business unit. The lights are out. He doesn't switch them on. Enough grey daylight seeps through the window to show a room full of waist-high tables. Scattered across them in heaps, and in sacks against the walls, are plastic toys and crayons to be packed into pouches and given away with children's fast-food meals. No one's been here in months. A soft fuzz of dust has settled over everything.

One block away sits the main command post with its fortified garage.

She's followed him without a word. When he turns she's right behind him, her breath faint and pale in the cold air.

He says, 'You've got it?' She doesn't move. 'Give it to me.'

She reaches into her padded coat. Brings out the syringe, the needle in its protective case, the little vial of fluid. He takes them from her. Her hands are cold.

He places a chair – 'Sit down' – then he plugs the needle into the syringe and fills it, checking the dose. She just sits and watches, passive. She's stopped arguing, stopped making decisions. Become somebody else. He doesn't know if he should be afraid.

He says, 'Take off your coat. Roll up your sleeve.' She doesn't move.

He says, 'They'll only rush you out if you're unconscious. Don't be frightened.'

'It's not that,' she says.

She shrugs her coat off, rolls her sleeve right up. He takes her arm in his free hand to steady it, prepares the needle. Muscle, sinew, bone; no spare flesh. Her skin's blue-white. When the needle goes in, she sighs.

He steps back. 'You'll be all right.'

She says, 'You should cut me. The blood will panic them.'

'No. Unconscious is enough.'

Footsteps outside. Running footsteps, coming close. A voice. 'Down here?' Just feet away. He turns his head towards it. Holds his breath. Beside him Cate stirs – moves restlessly – for a moment he's almost afraid she might call out. How long before the drug takes effect?

He moves towards the door. The lock's already broken; all they need to do is push. He closes his fist, plants himself, waits for the handle to turn.

A different voice, further away. He can't make out the words.

'All right,' the voice outside says. Behind him Cate shifts again. 'All right.'

The footsteps retreat.

Another movement at his back. He turns. She's still in the chair, the fabric of her top pulled up with one hand, her midriff bare—

The blade in her other hand draws a careful line across it, in red.

He's across the room, grabbing at the blade. Blood surges.

She looks at him. 'I should feel something,' she says. She's shaking. Her eyes are wide, imploring. 'I ought to feel *something*.'

He yanks her upright, on to her feet. Drags her to the door, jerks it open one-handed, wedges it with his foot, scoops her into his arms. Her head lolls back.

In the alleyway two men turn and straight away back off, wide-eyed. He runs past them into the street. Blood's started to surge through the fabric of her top. *It didn't go that deep, it's superficial* – but she's bleeding far too much.

He reaches the main road.

There's a snatch coming towards him. He runs straight at it, shouting.

Day 24: Friday

Karla

I'm jumping from camera to camera, street to street, at random now. If I see two figures together I pause but it's never them. I pause too for anyone who might be Johanssen, even though he shouldn't be on the streets alone, she should be with him. We need to time this to the minute. Where is he now?

Craigie says, 'What's happening, Karla?'

He's watching too, and he's as much in the dark as I am.

'Do you have a fix on them?' he asks.

'Not yet.' I make it sound calm. As if he's fussing, unnecessarily. It doesn't feel like that.

I'm cursing myself: I'm an idiot, this needed three pairs of eyes, or four, I should have had Sean on it, I should have had Finn.

Now Johanssen has slipped through the net of surveillance cameras, and vanished.

As he always planned to, of course. He won't do it anywhere the cameras can watch.

Command posts, then. He'll take her to a command post, won't he? I split the screen – six tiles, then nine – and begin to fill them with images of armoured doors and razor wire and aerials—

Suddenly Craigie says, 'I've got them.'

'Reference?'

I'm still stabbing at keys, trying to get on the right camera when Craigie says, 'She's bleeding. Karla, why is she bleeding?'

All the things we talked about. How long it will take them to ID her. Where she'll be taken, and by what route, and whether there'll be a police escort. But not this.

She shouldn't be bleeding.

She's in the armoured ambulance now. Craigie's eavesdropping

337

on their comms, but when I ask, 'How bad? Life-threatening?' he just says, 'Don't know yet.'

If this is bad we may have to abort. Let them take her to a hospital – *Shit shit shit, not that, we can't deal with that.* They'll ID her in hours. The news will break – for all Ellis's efforts it will break. Fielding will discover where she is. He'll send someone else to do the job, someone we can't identify. Can I tip Ellis off about the hit? Surely he can get protection for her, saturate the place with uniforms—

In the background, that insidious whisper: *They're intelligence. They brought Johanssen in because she was in the Program, but any minute now she'll be out. They killed Graves, and Hamilton, without any help from Fielding. If she's in hospital, she's already dead.*

'We lift her anyway.'

'What?'

'We lift her anyway. Warn the team she's hurt. And get that doctor standing by. Have they ID'd her yet?'

A silence from Craigie; in the background a chatter of other voices, distorted by scramblers, broken up and fired through the phone system and reassembled in his other ear: the ambulance service, Program security, police, everyone—

'They've worked out she's not an inmate. That's all.'

'What else?'

More chatter.

'The armoured ambulance has reached the Emergency Medical Centre … OK.' A pause. 'They're going to transfer her. Civilian ambulance.'

'Projected route?'

'Coming up.'

'Police escort?' Please no.

'Yes.' *Shit shit shit* again. 'Karla …' A warning note in his voice. He knows: we cannot risk a battle with the police.

'How many cars? Monitor it. And pin down that route.'

Another pause from Craigie, then: 'Volunteer. They think she's got to be a volunteer and the system's screwed up.'

But they're not taking chances, are they? 'Route?'

'On it now.'

Seconds later it fires up onto my screen: a pulsing red line, bright and arterial, tracking through a map. All guesswork, mind.

'They're moving out now. Just one police car. Blue light.'

'She's a volunteer, she doesn't need an escort.' I'm saying it as if they can hear me, as if I can will them to believe it. Then: 'We need that car called off. Give them something more important to do. A report of gunfire off the projected route.'

'Gunfire?' Craigie sounds alarmed.

'Yes, gunfire, suspected casualties – Fuck, Craigie, just *make something up.*'

I don't get to watch it happen. The CCTV cameras have gone down; we saw to that ourselves. I only get to listen, and imagine.

The same manoeuvre rehearsed last night with dummy vehicles, over and over again, in an old aircraft hangar in Oxfordshire. The ambulance, stripped now of its escort, slows for a tight corner and meets an unmarked van head-on, on the wrong side of the road. The ambulance brakes sharply, tries to drive round – another van draws up tight beside it, a third vehicle behind. It's boxed. The ambulance driver reaches for her radio. No one stops her. Help won't arrive in time.

Two masked men have already opened the ambulance's side door. They go in. One plants a meaty hand on the paramedic's chest and says, 'We're not going to hurt her, mate.' The voice is Robbie's. The other cuts the stretcher straps, pulls off the oxygen mask—

And then they're out, the woman limp between them, the dressing on her belly stained with blood. They put her in the back of one van, jump in with her, and all three vehicles pull away in different directions.

In my ear Craigie makes a tight exhalation. Shock, relief, elation? I don't know. He says, 'All right, everyone's clear,' and he says it in a voice I've never heard from him before, the voice of a younger, braver man. I wonder if he's shaking.

'It worked, Karla,' he says. 'It worked.'

It did. We got her out. Already the vehicles are vanishing off the streets into workshops and lock-ups, the crews dispersing; Catherine's in the back of a big Mercedes with tinted windows, heading for a discreet house in a north London suburb while a small quiet man tends to her wounds.

She's hurt but she will live. And we will talk.

I sit back in my chair, then reach for my computer mouse and close down the map: its insistent red trace vanishes. And there, behind it, is the Program surveillance feed. The street is empty. Johanssen's gone.

I start to click through options. Street after street, view after view. He'll have called Whitman, arranged to be lifted. Maybe he's already heading for a gate.

Still no sign.

But everything is fine, isn't it? The job's done, she's safe, he's coming out—

I don't know where the fear comes from, but suddenly I'm scared.

I click from camera to camera, looking for his face, his walk – *Not him, not him, not him.* Where is he? Perhaps there's trouble and he's gone to ground. I pick up the phone, dial Whitman.

'Has he called you?'

Whitman says, 'No.'

A heartbeat frisson – *Kill it.* 'OK, don't wait, just get him lifted.'

A pause, then, 'We got a problem, Laura?'

I don't know.

I end the call. Go back to the surveillance feeds. A man walking purposefully with a bag of tools. Two men and a woman passing along a street – the woman's laughing. A snatch patrolling. A blond man pausing in the neck of an alley, and looking down it, smiling—

A momentary spinning sense of vertigo, as if the ground's suddenly dropped away from beneath my feet and I'm falling already. The man is Brice.

He nods as if satisfied, and moves down the alleyway, out of view.

I pull up the Program map. Click through its levels until I reach the street plan with its scattering of icons. Yellow squares are cameras. There's the alley: no yellow square, no camera.

I'm blind.

Back to the phone call, all of three days ago. The man screaming. They made her watch. *Brice. Please no.*

And then I see Johanssen.

He's moving at a fast walk, his head going left-right-left, as if he knows he's being pursued and they're all around him. Any minute they'll come into view—

He's heading for the alley.

I need to think clearly. I need a plan. But all I can think is, *No. No.*

Day 24: Friday

Johanssen

First he only hears them. Running feet, somewhere close by and moving parallel to him. How many? Three men? More?

Then up ahead too, their path converging with his. He ducks down a side street but now they're on the other side of him as well, closing in on him, closing off his options.

He needs to go to ground, let them wash past him.

Behind him, someone shouts.

An alley opens up to his left. He turns into it. And there's Brice just fifteen feet away – head thrown back, feet planted, his hair a pale halo. 'I told you you were making mistakes,' he says, and he's smiling.

Johanssen pulls up and as he does so they step into place behind him. If he turns he'll see them closing in: a man to his left, two more to his right, someone else—

The first blow is to his head, the second to his guts. He doubles. He'd fall but the men hold him up. Another blow and his mouth fills: warm salt-and-iron. A fourth, and this time the men on either side let go.

He hits the ground, rolls, tries to curl into himself but they're on him, pulling him open, pinning him there, and Brice is looking down on him.

He says pleasantly, 'You know what they say? What doesn't kill you makes you stronger? Do you believe that?' and suddenly Johanssen notices his hands: the pale synthetic film of the surgical gloves is slippery with blood.

Later – how much later? He's not sure—

They have strung him upright, from the hooks in the ceiling of this room: strung him up high, on tiptoe, then put ropes on his ankles, and tied the ropes to rings in the walls, pulling them tight, spreadeagling him so he can't even stand: his whole weight rips through his arms and shoulders, burning the muscle, twisting the joints, the ropes cutting into his wrists. But when Brice speaks it's as if they're alone, just chatting. Not here, under the lights with people watching. He sees men he recognises from the gate, the clinic ... Drill's there too, at the edge of the group, detached curiosity on his face.

And Charlie Ross. What's left of him. He's dead, but it didn't come quick enough. One eye socket's empty; one hand has stumps for fingers. The mouth's fallen open and the lips are drawn back, the gums raw and bloody: the last of the teeth have been ripped out. Pain's distorted the features into caricature. Still Johanssen knows him.

'What I don't get,' Brice says, 'is why you let him live. Why you didn't just kill him when you had a chance. *Compassion*, Simon? I can call you Simon now, can't I? And that crap story about him thinking you were someone else, some dead guy who used to work for him ... Did you think that would fool us? Soon as he gave us the name, I knew. Though it took a bit longer to get him to confirm it. Two fingers before he really started to talk. But he told me everything, you know. Eventually.

'Well, Simon Johanssen, the fourth man from the farmhouse ... Here you are, after all this time, right under Mr Quillan's nose. You even got him to protect you. Bet that felt good, didn't it? It's not going to feel so good soon. Never mind, eh?' Brice looks into Johanssen's face and he smiles, a sick parody of sympathy. 'You're scared, aren't you? It's in your eyes. Well, not much longer to wait now,' he says.

He moves: a slow circuit, out of sight, then back, to stop in front of Johanssen again. His thumb strokes the blade in his hand.

He says, 'I've had a while to think about how this might go. Anticipation's a pleasure in itself, isn't it.' He tilts his head to one side. 'No?'

He says, 'I've made all sorts of plans for you. But you know what? You've given me cause to rethink. Oh, it's all going to happen: your fingers, castration, your eyes ... Always save the eyes till last, if you can. But given who you are, given what you did, we'll make it like Terry Cunliffe all those years ago.' He smiles again. 'We'll start with your skin.'

He steps behind Johanssen, close. 'Feel this?' he whispers. A cold point of pain at the back of his neck. 'This is the knife I'll use to take your skin off.'

Brice jerks the blade – it slices through the collar of Johanssen's jacket – and then he draws it down in a long clean rip. The second cut slices through his shirt. The dressing's still on his back. Brice tears it off. He makes a little soft '*Hah*' when he sees the wound. 'She stitched it,' he says. 'Sweet.' The tip of the blade touches the wound, bites – hot, white. Johanssen jerks and pain rips through the tendons in his shoulders. 'Shhhhhh,' Brice whispers. 'Shhhh now.'

Four feet away Drill is watching. His face seems to float in the gloom, intent and curious.

'So tell us. Tell us what you did to Terry Cunliffe, eight years ago. Was it like this?'

The blade's singing against the wound. Johanssen bites down on the pain.

'Did Terry Cunliffe scream?' Brice says softly. Johanssen can feel the man's breath on his back. 'I bet he did. I bet he screamed like an animal. Do you remember that? That sound, that's going to be the sound you make.'

The blade probes again. Johanssen chokes.

Brice says, 'It's like peeling an orange: the trick is to remove as much skin as possible in one piece. I shall start ... *here*—'

The pain goes deeper. Goes white again. And there's Brice against him, pressing close: his shallow breathing, his sweat, his excitement. He says, 'Open your eyes, Simon. Open your eyes. Go on. Look who's come to watch.'

He opens his eyes.

There's Quillan, leaning on his cane, his stare hard and cold. The man with the boxer's face stands just beyond his shoulder. On the other side is Riley.

Quillan says, 'Simon Johanssen, why did you come here? You knew this would happen.' Then to someone else: 'Cut him down – Oh, come now, Mr Brice, don't pull that face. It's hardly a fair fight.'

Drill steps forward with a knife. The ankle ropes first – as his weight shifts the pain burns up into his shoulders as if someone's poured petrol on him and lit it. The other ropes are tied off on a cleat in the wall. Drill loosens them – Johanssen whimpers as the joints realign – then just lets go, and he falls, and lies there. The pain keeps catching in his throat: he has to swallow it down in gulps.

Quillan shuffles towards him – tiny, careful steps. He says, 'Oh,

I've heard all about you, Mr Johanssen. No, not from him—' a glance at Ross's corpse '—I'm afraid I wasn't there for that. But Sully and the other two – remember them?' Then he says, 'You tried to save Terry Cunliffe. You see, I made them talk, those three, and they went to great lengths to blame each other, but the one thing they agreed on was that you tried to save him. But you failed. You made a fuss; you didn't make a *difference*. Terry died. So: is that why you're here, under some fake ID? To atone for that?' Quillan pauses. 'You're not saying much.'

He's on his knees now. He sucks in air. 'Cate …'

'Evacuated with stab wounds. She did it in front of you, did she? Don't flatter yourself: you weren't the cause. From the moment she arrived here, she wanted to die.' Quillan tilts his head. 'Enough talking. It's time to get this done. Stand up. I said *stand up.*'

He rises in slow painful stages. Finally stands, swaying on his feet. Quillan beats one hand against his thigh, *slap slap slap*, a mockery of applause. 'Oh, well *done*. You know where we are now, don't you, Mr Johanssen?' He smiles that stretched smile of his, gone in an instant. 'Right back where we started – you remember? In the yard, all that *showing off*. Well, time to do it again.' Then aside, 'Someone give him a blade.'

It's Riley who presses the knife into his hand. He pats Johanssen's arm but his eyes are sliding away already. Brice is standing on the other side of the room, turning his own blade over in his hand. Blood already on it. Then he smiles.

Quillan says, 'Go on then. *Impress me.*'

Across the room, Brice begins to circle.

Johanssen grips the blade, but the grip's weak, his fingers numb and stiff.

He cannot do this now – he cannot do it. He has to, but he can't. He's got nothing left.

There is no choice.

First breath. It catches in his ribs. Second. He tries to work his shoulders, balance the knife, get his feet moving. *Go on the third.*

For a tiny moment he thinks of Karla – of her hand in his, of all the things he hasn't said to her – but it's still good, to think of her now, because he knows what comes will drive everything else out of his head, even her. Then Brice lunges.

Johanssen sidesteps, tries to fall back – too slow. The blade nicks his forearm, hot, stinging. He stumbles. Brice spins. Takes another step, sideways, the knife weaving in his hand, that smile. *He's not even trying yet.*

Beyond him, Quillan: hawkish, watchful, just like before—

Johanssen tightens his grip on the knife but the blood's surging from the cut in his arm: his fingers are slippery with it.

Brice lunges again.

Johanssen parries, high – for a fraction of a second connects, before Brice throws himself backwards out of reach, but the contact is enough. The blade pops out of Johanssen's grip, goes skittering across the room. His fist closes on air.

Brice is breathing hard. Knife in his right hand, his left pressed against the side of his neck. When he pulls his fingers away there's blood on them.

He says, 'I'm going to strip your skin,' but this time it sounds different, and he's no longer smiling.

Brice lunges a third time.

Johanssen goes down.

Brice is on him. Brice has got him by the hair. He says, 'First I'm going to break your jaw and then cut out your tongue' – and his fist comes up, without the knife this time—

And then Brice's eyes fix, and he folds.

Johanssen's on the floor, just breathing, letting the pain come and go. Brice is on the floor too, on his belly, head turned towards Johanssen: his eyes are open, and he too is breathing, but badly. The knife – Johanssen's blade, it must be – quivers in place between his vertebrae. His bowels have voided. The room smells of shit.

Riley kneels beside him, very pale, quite still. He's ex-army, killed at least once; forgot what it was like? He says, 'Bastard had it coming.'

Johanssen staggers to his feet. To reach the door he has to walk past Quillan. The old man is still leaning on his cane. He's watching Riley. He murmurs, 'I always wondered what it would take to make him snap.' And then he glances sharply at Johanssen: 'You thought it was you I had in mind? Oh, I knew you couldn't do it; you didn't care enough.' He nods at Riley. 'Not like he did.'

Brice is still on the ground. Eyes still open. Still breathing, in gasps. He hasn't moved. No one has touched him.

Quillan says, 'I suppose he'll need a doctor,' but he says it without interest.

Across the room Drill's watching Brice too. He must have picked up Brice's fallen knife. He holds it close, caressing the blade, and there's a look of hunger in his eyes.

Johanssen walks out through the door, into the bright day.

He's wandering, still shirtless in the cold and bleeding, when the patrol picks him up.

Much later, in the back of Whitman's car, stitched and strapped up and muffled with painkillers, he hears it on the car radio: an injured patient snatched from an ambulance, on a street in east London, in broad daylight.

They don't give a name.

Day 24: Friday

Powell

Five more days. No leads. Where does he go from here?

Yesterday he had Knox's delivery boy Isidore Maksoud brought in again. The Section chief's idea – 'And go in hard this time.' He didn't. He's got nothing to go in hard with. The package Isidore handled for Knox contained a tip-off about laundered money and friendly young men with oddly blank smiles and terrorist connections. *What can we charge him with? Supplying information that benefitted national security?* And it's the wrong play with Knox, in any case. Knox won't respond to threats.

And so, more tea, more chat. Did Isidore pass the message on? 'Who to? Told you, I don't know no Knox' – Isidore grinning at his own alliteration, delighted with himself. Powell came back to the office with a sense of emptiness, to find Kingman in a foul mood, Leeson looking like she hadn't slept, and Bethany pointedly running out of tasks. He shut himself in his office and sat there, staring down the barrel of his own failure.

The case has died on him.

He knows what happens next. He writes his report, which summarises all the evidence, outlines the steps he's taken to investigate, and reveals precisely nothing. He is then sent back to Washington – to Tori and Thea, and his colleagues – no one any the wiser that he's failed.

It sits in his mouth like dust.

He thinks of Knox. *You talked to Laidlaw. Won't you talk to me?*

But Knox likes to choose his confidants. He'll choose somebody else.

And that's it, isn't it? That's what Knox offers: the sense of being chosen. It's the subtext of all Laidlaw's careful notes: Knox chose him, made him special. And although he tried to track Knox down, Laidlaw was never going to hand him over to MI5, or let MI5 take

347

Knox away from him. Because Knox *chose him*. He understands that now.

But Laidlaw's dead. Who'll be chosen next?

The Section Chief wants it to be him. How many times has the man ordered him not to talk to Knox? The moment contact's made he must back off, hand Knox up the chain of command, let the Section Chief make all the running – let the Section Chief be the one that Knox selects.

But if Knox calls, if Knox chooses *him*, he knows: he'll disobey that order in a heartbeat.

He was leaving the office last night when he saw Leeson again, this time without her seeing him. She looked fragile. Suddenly he was struck by a surge of fellow feeling: *We're the failures on the team, aren't we?* He's growing used to her quiet reserve; it disconcerts him less now. And talking to her that time in the kitchen did help. He'd like to return the favour, find something positive to say to her, before he leaves. He knows it's not entirely altruistic – it's as much for his benefit as hers. He needs to feel he's done some good somewhere, that something positive came out of all this.

He must be careful what he says, that's all. There is so much he's not supposed to know.

He'd better read the file.

The tip-off first, though this file doesn't say where it came from, just that an MI5 surveillance list turned up on the open market, and was attracting bidders; that steps were taken – successfully – to secure the item and neutralise the threat. Leeson was tasked with hunting down the seller. She found him soon enough: a tech ops officer called Fenty – smart but chippy, lacking social skills, passed over for promotion, soured with resentment. He'd left no clear electronic trail but twitched right through the interview. That night he went home, packed a bag and vanished. Leeson put out an alert, went after him. She came back a week later, empty-handed. He can read her exhaustion in her own report.

Officially she signed off months ago, but he's prepared to bet she's been on it every waking hour since then: calling in favours, scouring for leads, sure that Fenty's out there somewhere, and one day she will find him ...

His tea is cold. He picks up his mug, leaving the file on his desk, steps out into the corridor—

There she is, coming down the corridor towards him with her coat on, walking fast. When she sees him, for a second he'd swear she flinches. Odd.

'Leeson,' he says. Already it sounds too formal. He wishes he could remember her first name. 'I was hoping I'd catch you.'

She's pulled up. She says, 'I really am in a hurry,' but her eyes don't leave his face. He has the odd sensation she's measuring him, measuring the level of threat that he might pose.

He steps back into his office doorway to let her pass. She doesn't move.

He says, 'I thought perhaps we could have a chat,' and immediately wishes he hadn't; it sounds so staged. He tries again. 'We spoke on Monday night – you probably won't remember – about a case I'm working …'

She says suddenly and quite clearly, 'Have you reported yet?'

'Not yet. Some loose ends I still have to tie up.'

'The Section Chief is in the loop, of course.' That's brittle, with a little sting to it.

He thinks of his own planned disloyalty. 'Not entirely.'

Something shifts behind her gaze. A tiny reassessment. She says again, 'I really have to go,' but this time it's thoughtful.

He nods. 'Then I won't stop you.'

She walks past him and down the corridor. But at the end she turns, and looks back.

He grabs his coat, locks the office. She's taken the lift; he hits the stairs. When he comes through the fire door at the bottom he's panting. Her footsteps echo across the basement garage, baffling him. He walks along the row of cars, and there she is, between the concrete pillars, the key to her little red Citroën in her hand. She looks up and sees him, and stops; then glances round as if they might not be alone. Her eye goes to the CCTV camera. This will be on the record. He can't tell if she's reassured or not.

He doesn't want to say, *I'm worried about you; I know something's wrong.* Makes do with, 'I need to talk to you.'

She says, 'Of course you do.'

She unlocks the car – the indicators flash – and gets in, closes the door but doesn't start the engine.

He walks to the passenger door. Hesitates, opens it. Hesitates again. Gets in.

She's staring straight ahead.

'You know what the problem with us is?' she says. 'We always have to know everything.'

She starts the car.

Day 24: Friday

Karla

Ellis says, 'What the fuck?' I can't tell if he's impressed or shocked or angry. I doubt he knows himself.

One in the afternoon. He's at the house in north London: high walls, electric gates, good security. The neighbours are all offshore business types with complex financial arrangements, expensive life-styles, dubious friends. They won't ask questions. Catherine's in a back room, out of sight.

On all the screens in my apartment the news channel's looping the same footage, with the sound on mute. I wonder if Ellis is watching it too.

'Snatched out of an ambulance? In daylight?' He adds scathingly, 'Nothing like keeping this low profile.'

'It was the only way, Ellis. Nobody got hurt.'

'And now I'm supposed to babysit her?'

'Ellis, the moment her picture crossed your desk, you'd have ID'd her. You'd have turned up at my apartment waving your warrant card and demanding to know what I'd done with her. This saves us both a lot of time. Or are you saying you don't want to be in on this now?'

For a moment he's silent. All along he's wanted the inside track. He's got it now, but it's not what he was expecting. He thought that with Catherine in his hands he'd be able to control what happens next. It hasn't quite worked out. And it's dawning on him that just by being there he's in up to his neck.

At last he says, grudgingly, 'I'm saying it's put the entire fucking Met all over the case. Any minute now someone's going to put a name to her. And when they do, who's the first person they're going to call? They'll want my arse in the office yesterday.'

'Then phone me. I'll have someone standing by to take over at the house. I want you on that investigation, Ellis.'

'So I can fuck it up for you?'

'Give them the benefit of your theories. She's been hiding in the Program. You don't know why, but she must have been scared. Hamilton put her in there; Graves covered it up. They were killed because they'd tried to protect her. But no one could get to her in there. Then she got injured, got evacuated, and someone pounced.'

'So they'll think she's dead? And what about Mark Devlin? Where does he fit into this little picture?'

'They don't need to know.'

'And I don't either, eh? I talked to the guy, Karla, remember? He shagged her half a dozen times, he hardly knew her. How come he ends up dead? Don't tell me: you don't know. And someone's still coming after her, and you don't know who they are either.'

I can't tell him about the intelligence link. He'd only freak. 'We're on it, Ellis. As soon as I've got something—'

Bitterly: 'Yeah, right.' Then he says, 'Or I could decide to bring her in myself. Could say I had a tip-off, turned up at this address, there she was—'

'Then she'll be dead within an hour, and you'll never find out who killed her.'

'Within an hour? I'll have her in protective custody—'

'*It won't be enough.*'

A silence follows, but he doesn't argue.

'So how's she doing?' I ask.

'How the fuck should I know? Doctor's stitched her up. She's conscious, yeah? But weird.'

'It's just the anaesthetic wearing off. He'll give her painkillers too.'

'He tried. She wouldn't take them. Something about needing to feel it.'

What's that about? Guilt? Masochism? I wonder if she's likely to confess. I need to get over there; I need to talk to her. Tonight? Tomorrow? A brief spasm of anxiety. I don't know what it means. Johanssen's safe, she's safe, we've got this under control ...

'All right. Call me if anything changes.'

I'm about to ring off when he says, 'Oh, Thames Valley's got an e-fit coming. The woman who was seen near Graves's house? Though you were right: it doesn't look a bit like you.'

I put the phone down. Suddenly I'm so tired. I want to walk into my bedroom, crawl under the duvet, sleep – no: I want to see Johanssen, right now.

The memory slices across my vision again: he's bleeding on a Program street, stumbling, dazed. What did he go through in there? Whitman says he'll be fine. How would he know?

How long till I can see him, talk to him, touch him? How long until it's safe? A month? Two?

And there it is again, that same unease. A glimmer of something at the edge of my vision. A sense of something bad I can't quite place, something I knew once but have forgotten. But I keep getting this. Fragments of memory and a deep sense of misgiving. It's sleeplessness and stress that does it. I'll be all right soon.

My phone rings. Charlotte's phone. I stare at it a moment, then pick up.

A woman's voice, uneven with emotion, says, 'Charlotte? Charlotte Alton? It's Anna – you won't remember me – I was a friend of Mark Devlin's …'

Anna. The woman outside the restaurant that night. The girl in that earlier photo, so young and so in love. The woman watching him with other women, the one who wouldn't cope without him … He said she didn't want him in her life – *not like that* – but he was wrong, she was just waiting for an opening, waiting for her turn to come again.

It hits me fresh: it's never coming now.

A sudden rush of feeling I can't kill. 'Anna, I'm sorry—'

'It's all right, it's all right,' she says hurriedly; her voice wavers. For a moment I think she's going to cry. Then she says, 'I'm trying to talk to everyone who knew him. Someone must know what happened to him that night …'

Gently I say, 'I don't think I can help you.'

'But is it OK if I just come and talk? It helps, you see, to talk about him—'

I shouldn't say yes. Not now. 'Well … all right.'

'This afternoon? You'll be at home? *Thank you.*'

She puts the phone down. What have I just done? *You still feel guilty, don't you?*

Coffee. I need more coffee. Then Craigie's coming for our usual Friday meeting, convinced we have to stick to our routine. I was too tired to argue.

I walk to the kitchen. Put the coffee on. Stand there blankly while it brews. I must phone Anna back, confirm a time. Don't want her arriving while Craigie's here. I wonder how she got my address.

On the kitchen screen the news is still playing, talking heads this time. And then a caption: IAN GRAVES MURDER E-FIT.

And there it is. The face of the woman seen outside Graves's house, the night he died.

Ellis was right. It doesn't look like me. It looks like Anna.

How much time? How much time?

I click into the building's CCTV, go to the lobby camera and then to the one that scans the walkway directly outside the building's front doors. No one's loitering. Click to the service bays at the back. A couple are clutched in an embrace, hungry for each other, and oblivious. There's no one else.

How long before she gets here? Five minutes? Ten?

Devlin's ex, the girl who couldn't have him, the one who simply followed him around – best cover of all, the disappointed female, the nice woman no one's particularly interested in. My own stupidity hits me like a slap. Charlotte Alton's played that card for years.

Anna is intelligence. She's been behind this from the beginning, and now she's coming here. She knows that Charlotte Alton's on the trail of Catherine Gallagher. She knows I was at Graves's house – and Devlin's on the night he died. She thinks I know where Catherine's hiding. She wants that information. And then she wants me dead.

She doesn't know the other cards I'm holding: Karla, Knox. Those are my trumps. I'll play them only when I'm ready. She'll search the place, but she'll find nothing. Already I'm loading up the software, the program that will fry everything on my system, burn out the data and all connections to the network, wipe out all the trails – to Johanssen, Craigie, Whitman, Robbie, Ellis, Finn—

The fear knifes through me: how long has she known? How long has she been watching me? If she knew before two days ago, she could know about them all.

There isn't time to warn them.

I hit 'Execute'. The warning flashes up, in red: '! This will delete all data.' I hit 'Yes'. Already I'm shaping up my deal: working out the price Karla will demand for co-operation. No one goes down but me.

I grab the scrambled phone. Text Craigie first: 'Abort'. Then Finn: a close-down code to wipe the phone's account. My fingers fumble over the keys – press 'Send' – then flip the phone's back off, pull out the SIM. With scissors, slice it into tiny, brittle chips.

Run to the roof garden, to the rail, toss the chips out into the wind, forty-one storeys up.

Back to the office. On the screen a timer reaches zero: the screen goes blank. I'm cut off from the network.

Now get out of here.

Coat. Bag. Keys to the Merc – but she'll know it. Go on foot? One last glance out of that big main window. Has she got people out there already, behind the blank watchful office windows opposite? Can they see me now?

Go. Just go.

There's no one in the hallway when I run to the lift, no one there when the lift doors open on the lobby. The concierge turns his head to me and smiles and I smile back, automatically, as I walk past him and out into a Friday afternoon.

Get out of here. Get as far away as possible. Then contact Powell and set up the deal. Intelligence gets Knox and access to the network. My team goes untouched—

And Catherine?

I scan the area. Is someone waiting at the end of the lime-green bridge, or among the tourists on the walkways, or across the dock where the smokers gather, outside the bars? Impossible to know, at this distance.

I turn, and there he is, just feet away. A tall black man in a good suit. Lucas Powell.

But you're too late. Forty-one storeys above us those electronic brains have emptied, leaving just the vacant corpse of technology, the low-level current ticking through it like a pulse, like brain-dead patients on life-support—

He holds out an ID card with curious formality. He says, 'You need to come with me now. Please don't try to run.' The sweat is beading on his brow. He turns his head a fraction, glances back. Eight feet behind him Anna's standing, hands in the pockets of her mac, watching, serene and lovely.

Powell says quietly, 'She has a gun.'

It's only then I realise he's terrified.

She walks behind us all the way: under the concrete legs of the DLR tracks, away from the Docklands monoliths and out towards the ordinary streets of Poplar. Before we reach the tracks, Powell says,

355

'There are cameras everywhere here, you know?' and he's saying it to her, but she just says, 'I'll get the footage wiped.'

Like me, but stronger.

Just then we pass a pale-faced man in a dark overcoat, briefcase in one hand, staring at his phone. He glances up once, sees me, sees Powell, and instantly switches his gaze back to his phone, as if we'd never met.

Day 24: Friday

Powell

He tried to talk. Walking into Poplar, and at the garage while he secured the woman's wrists behind her back with cable ties – Leeson holding the gun and hissing, '*Tighter*' – right up to the moment when Leeson duct-taped his mouth, he tried to talk. And even lying in the back of the van he's rehearsing, telling himself it's not out of his control yet. He's been on courses – hostage negotiation, high-pressure situations – he knows the things that you're supposed to say. *Stay calm, be persuasive, show that you can help her.* She has to see there's been a misunderstanding, but they can get it sorted. Go somewhere, sit down and clear this up—

It sounds so trite and thin.

All the time he's wondered how this could have happened, how it could have come upon him quite so fast – as if he should have seen it in a rear-view mirror, bearing down on him before it hit. There should have been some premonition of this.

The woman from Docklands is quite small, mid-thirties maybe, elegantly dressed. The moment he saw her he thought how tired she looked. She hardly spoke on the walk to the garage in Poplar; the shock had made her passive. But now, sitting in the chair in this new location – an empty building in a light-industrial park, he's guessing – her eyes are wide and desperate above the tape gag. She must be so afraid.

The cable ties are cutting into his wrists and ankles. He tries to relax. Control. Somehow he has to keep control.

Leeson steps towards him. Rips off the gag. 'Where is she?'

He doesn't even understand the question.

He makes his voice calm, measured. 'Leeson, you know why I was brought in? To investigate a source called Knox. He's been supplying MI5 with intel through a retired Moscow handler, Peter

Laidlaw. Knox trusted no one else. Laidlaw died suddenly three weeks ago, MI5 lost contact with Knox, my job has been—'

Leeson takes a pace across the room and strikes the woman, hard: one smart clean blow with the flat of her hand. The woman's head whips round, but the gag's in place: she hardly makes a sound.

Leeson draws breath, steps back as if nothing's happened.

She says, 'The first week I wasn't sure what you were doing. I was watching Bethany and Mitch. I hadn't worked out they were just the smokescreen. Then one week in, a Met DI called Joe Ellis pulled the MisPer file on Catherine Gallagher. Was it supposed to look like coincidence? Some nosy copper, digging in the files?'

'I don't know anyone called Joe Ellis.'

A pace, hand raised – the woman flinches from the blow but she can't move away and it catches her across the face again, and this time she makes a small, sharp, desperate sound through the gag.

Leeson says, 'Joe Ellis is your handy way of asking questions. Pretending he was investigating a murder too, as if she really might be dead.'

In the chair opposite, the woman blinks away tears. Her cheek's raw from the blow. Leeson looks at her, but calmly, dispassionately.

She says, 'I didn't know about this one until Wednesday night. She's very good; you must be proud of her. She was all over Mark ten days ago, but women always were. He never could resist the damsel in distress. And I didn't put it together, even when I saw Elizabeth Crow – Crow looks older, plainer, heavier. But I was trailing Ellis on Wednesday afternoon. There's a tyre workshop – you know it, of course. On Wednesday it was closed. I saw Ellis go in, I saw him leave. Five minutes later she comes out. And of course I've got the number she gave Devlin, so I got on her mobile account straight away. She checked her messages halfway through to Brecon – we guessed where she was heading. She'll have told you all about the evidence she found. Shame she didn't get pictures.' She pauses. 'Well, Lucas? Or should I call you Powell? You only ever call me Leeson.'

He wants to say, *I don't know what you're talking about. I don't know any of these names. Mark, Elizabeth Crow, Ellis, Catherine Gallagher ...* He looks at the nameless woman opposite. She knows what's coming. His powerlessness washes through him.

Leeson says, 'You knew of course that Catherine was alive; you knew just where she was. You knew, presumably because Hamilton told you, once you'd got him tucked up in that house. Did he know you were also using him as bait? You realised I could trace his calls. You were just waiting for me to come after him, weren't you? Only I know what a safe house looks like. Shame you couldn't keep him there. And the moment you lost him, you should have called time on it. But you wanted to have all the little pieces before you trotted off to the Chief with your report. That's why you still didn't make a move against me. You hadn't got her yet. Until this morning.

'So what did you want to talk to me about? After you pulled the file on Fenty, but before you made your report to the Chief. What were those last few loose ends you had to tie up?'

He doesn't answer. He doesn't know what to say.

After a moment Leeson says quietly, 'You're going to tell me where you've put her.' She waits, and then when he doesn't reply she says, 'I presume you know what I did to Fenty.' She glances at the woman on her chair. 'Don't think that I won't do the same to her.'

Fenty? This is all about Fenty? The tech ops guy who tried to sell that file—

The missing week in Leeson's life, after Fenty disappeared. The things he said to her in the kitchen at work, *the pressure for a result, time to get out the thumbscrews*, how she twitched—

The pieces drop into place with a tiny click. She didn't lose Fenty, did she? She found him.

He doesn't understand the rest of it – the names, or where the woman opposite fits in. But he knows with utter certainty that Fenty's dead.

He says, 'You killed Daniel Fenty?'

'Of course not. All I wanted him to do was *talk*. Where is she, Powell?'

'I don't know. I swear it, I don't know.' *I've never heard of Catherine Gallagher. I don't know what any of this is about—*

Leeson blinks. She's thinking. He can see it. *Believe me, please, believe me.*

She says, 'There is a possibility you're telling the truth. It could be only Ellis knows. He's not reported in. That's why you were waiting.' Then she adds, 'You understand, I have to check.'

She goes to stand behind the woman's chair. She says, 'I'm going to break her fingers now.'

The woman's eyes widen. She's trying to suck in air against the gag, and then her head goes down. She's bracing herself against the pain. He says rapidly, 'I've never seen this woman in my life. I don't know who she is.'

'Really? Do you think I wasn't watching? I must say, you're very good. Looking at you, when she came through that door, I'd almost believe you. But I was looking at her too. And she knows you.'

Day 24: Friday

Karla

She bends one finger back and back and back. Nothing can hurt this much, nothing. I'll sell Catherine Gallagher out, I'll do it now, please just take off the gag—

I feel it snap.

The room turns red, then white. My ears are full of hissing. It hurts so much I'm going to vomit.

Something crashes nearby. Powell is yelling. But he's become irrelevant, lost in the whiteout.

At last the room comes back, in a strange, sick, bleached-out form. My mouth is full of bile. I gulp it down. The pain in my hand is now a background roar. I focus on my breathing.

Powell's on the floor, the chair pulled over on its side. He's saying, '*Please, please, please,*' as if he doesn't know that it's too late, it won't make any difference.

He says, 'I don't know where she is, I don't know ...' His face is twisted, unrecognisable. 'Why are you doing this, Leeson? Why?'

Anna's standing over him. She says, 'You know what was on that list. The name of every last man and woman under surveillance in the UK, and precisely how they were being watched – every bug planted, every phone tapped, every car tracked. Some of these people are nobodies. But some of them want to hurt us, and hurt us badly, except they think they're under our radar – they think we don't know what they're planning. And what does Fenty do? He puts all that up for sale to the highest bidder. But he gets the protection of the law. He gets a solicitor, he gets *rights*. We work to keep this fucking country safe—' She knows she's losing it. She stops. Her head comes up. She straightens. 'These people have forfeited the right to our protection. I only did what had to be done. I had to make him talk. I won't be punished for it.'

She walks out of the room. When she comes back, she's holding the roll of duct tape. She squats down – he says, 'Please don't, we need to talk—' She says, 'Shut up or I'll break another of her fingers.' She tapes a new gag over Powell's mouth, and then she rises and gets out her phone, and walks away, thumbing keys. Just before she passes out of earshot, I hear her saying, in a different voice, 'DI Ellis?'

Two minutes later she comes back. She looks down at Powell again. She says, 'You'd better hope that Ellis talks.' She goes, without a glance at me.

I would have sold Ellis like a shot; Ellis, and Catherine Gallagher. I would. I'm not that good with pain. The moment she takes off the gag I'll give her everything. The network, Knox, the lot. I wonder if it will make any difference. She works with Powell, she's a janitor, but they've kept Laidlaw's source a careful secret: she's never heard of me.

And Karla's already fading into nothing. Her tracks have gone from Charlotte Alton's flat. Her mobile's dead. Her right-hand man has watched her leaving, under arrest, and will be shoring up his own position; I can't blame him for that. Johanssen's sleeping in the safe flat in London, oblivious, under Whitman's care ... I want to be beside him in that bed, listening to the rhythms of his breathing, wrapped up in the warmth of him—

Do not lose it now.

After a while Powell makes a noise. I've closed my eyes – I'm still trying to think this out, spot the gap in the fence through which I can wriggle, the manoeuvre that will turn this all around – it means that I don't think about my finger, and that's a good thing – but now I open them. From behind the gag comes a quiet, rhythmic moaning, and with every moan he's beating his head against the floor, again and again.

He has a wife in Washington, and a child. I wonder if it's coming home to him: he won't see them again.

He doesn't know it, but he's just like Daniel Fenty: back up against the wall, being asked for answers that he cannot give, with no one to believe his ignorance, and no exits in sight.

Craigie and I found out who took that list, although she took some tracking down. She worked in an administrative role within MI5, acting as liaison between departments; until we contacted her she thought that she was safe. We made it clear our role wasn't to punish traitors – we wouldn't be passing her name on to her superiors – but that we wouldn't stand by while she sold secrets to terrorists. If in future she had information to trade, she should come direct to us. She's contacted us twice since then, but only with little snippets of data, useful rather than spectacular. I don't like her – she's very focused on the money – but then few criminals are in it out of love; it doesn't bother me.

She mentioned that they'd pinned the blame on Fenty; that was what made her safe. The fact he'd run did suggest that he was guilty, but if he was, then I don't know of what. Perhaps simply of crossing Anna's sights. Perhaps that was enough.

But Anna caught him.

I wonder what she told Mark Devlin. That Daniel Fenty was a colleague injured in a black op, on the run? Someone who needed a safe place and a doctor who wouldn't talk? *Help me, Mark …*

And so Mark Devlin helped: with the house, and with Catherine. He must have sat in his London office, or in his beautiful Notting Hill flat, believing that what he'd done was good – while Anna went to work on Daniel Fenty, with Catherine Gallagher in support: clever, ambitious, cold-hearted but skilled, and vouched for by Mark Devlin.

If Fenty had been guilty, he'd have cracked. He was in technical operations – a boffin, a geek. He'd never have withstood hard-core interrogation. Anna would have turned in a prisoner, a confession, a result. Fenty's injuries would have aroused suspicion, then been explained away. Catherine would have been bribed into silence: a prestigious new posting, a research budget, all in recognition of her valuable assistance. If she'd had misgivings, she'd have buried them.

Fenty would have lived. If he'd been guilty.

But Fenty wasn't guilty, and he couldn't crack.

Anna must have shown Devlin the body. *She did this to him, and now she's set you up to take the blame.* Or maybe she just appealed to his sense of rightness, the same blind sense that had him stepping out in front of a speeding vehicle, believing he could make it stop.

Catherine killed this man. Bringing the police in won't help. It's up to us to put it right.

They cleaned the house, disposed of the remains. Then Anna spent a year looking for Catherine. At last she found her in the Program.

But she'd been looking over her shoulder too, and when Powell arrived to run some hushed-up investigation, she thought he'd come for her.

Across the room Powell has stopped moving. I doubt he understands what's going on. I like him much more than I thought I would. I have a sense of him already: smart, straight-down-the-line. Copes with the politics of intelligence less well than he believes. An honest man, and they're always hard to manage. No wonder they sent him off to Washington. I think back to his file: the child's a girl, her name is ... Thea. *Well remembered. Clever you.*

Oh, yes, I know everything now.

I hear her coming back before I see her. She walks in and instantly I'm trying to read her. Did she corner Ellis? Her face doesn't give anything away. I'm sweating, cringing, gulping, searching for the first sign she's coming to me – already I can feel her touching my fingers, squeezing so gently on the broken bone – the pain's already singing in my ears—

She comes over and looks down at Powell. One long quiet moment.

She says, 'Now we wait.' She goes again.

She isn't going to hurt me this time.

Ellis has talked.

Day 24: Friday

Johanssen

Johanssen's drifting.

He's back at the south London flat, and he's alone; no guard this time. He overheard Whitman releasing the two British guys with a story about reinforcements – 'And he'll be no trouble; you've seen the state he's in' – then Whitman too went out, though he'll be back. He's got a wife in Paris, even showed Johanssen a picture before he left, of a pretty dark-haired girl with wayward eyes. Whitman wants to wrap this up as soon as possible: 'Yeah, we'll do it properly, but since Laura cleared it with Washington …' He shrugged. He left behind a phone, one of Karla's specials, heat-sealed in a soft plastic envelope. Johanssen broke the seal and called Fielding on it, reporting in on Cate's evacuation – 'She was wounded, there was nothing I could do.' Fielding said, 'You heard someone snatched her?' and Johanssen said, 'Heard it on the news. The client?' and Fielding muttered something dark. He's pissed off, thinks it's the client taking matters into their own hands, and he's lost out on his fee.

Johanssen called Karla, but the line was dead.

The drugs are still muffling his senses. Through them he can just catch the ghostly outlines of pain – his head, his arms and back, his shoulders, torso, neck … He'll ease off the painkillers in a day or two, but first he needs to sleep.

The afternoon ebbs. He lets the TV drone in the corner, a low-level distraction while he dozes on the sofa: the sound mingles with the sounds of other TVs in other flats, the child coughing its smoker's cough next door, a woman talking on her mobile in the corridor outside: 'I told him, I said I hope you're fucking proud of yourself.' The sounds wash over him. He's entering a period of transition, like decompression, as if he's a diver who's surfaced too fast out of a dark depth and this scummy flat's his hyperbaric chamber, a place to wait it out until he's in a fit state to rejoin the outside world. The days will pass. He won't go out. He'll keep the TV on round the clock. The wounds will heal, the bruises yellow and fade, the stiffness ease; the pains will become aches. He'll mend. A few more days of this and he'll move out of here, shed Ryan Jackson like a discarded skin, return to his own life. And Karla. Karla.

When the phone rings, he gropes for it, thinking of her, suddenly hopeful.

Fielding says, 'Client's got us a new address for the target.'

An address. Through the fug, the world shifts; and then the floor seems to drop away as if someone's blown it out from under him. Karla isn't answering her phone.

'Where did they get it from?' he asks. He hopes his voice sounds normal.

'Some copper, hired to keep an eye on her – a freelance job, the Met's not in the picture. Apparently she's alone in the house.'

'So where's the copper?'

'Toss-up between an operating theatre and a slab, I'd say. They want it done today. Can you handle it?'

Automatically he says, 'Course.'

'You sure? You don't sound—'

'I'm fine. I can do it.'

'All right then. The place is fucking fortified, but our copper friend's provided the entry codes.' Fielding pauses. 'Just one thing: client wants proof. You know what I'm saying?'

Proof? He doesn't understand, and then he does. He says, 'You trust them?'

'Oh yeah. Ask Karla if you don't believe me. She knows who they are.'

He tries her phone again. Still dead. And then he tries the old number, the one he phoned before, when he came back, the one that was answered by the Scot. *He works for me. He's safe.*

The number isn't recognised.

Outside it's early Friday evening, heading for night. The light's a fading winter grey and it's raining. He walks with his head down, trying not to limp. A man who's been beaten stands out from the crowd. He must be careful. But the rain's on his side: people hurry past under their umbrellas. Nobody looks at him.

Still he's putting it all together, through the fog of drugs, pain, adrenaline. Karla compromised. Or missing. Or running. *She knows who they are.* Cate alone, abandoned in that house … The client wanting proof.

The car's parked in a lock-up in Dalston. He opens the door, slides into the driver's seat – the pain shoals around him, then recedes again.

Somewhere in his head a voice he's heard before is reminding him to run.

The house has high walls, electric gates. He wonders if they've got it under observation; walks round once, sees nothing. *But you don't these days, do you?*

There's an entryphone by the gates, with a camera and a keypad for the lock. He keys in the code; the side gate clicks; he steps inside, and it swings to behind him. He's in a drive. Big white house with blinds drawn on the windows. One sleek black Mercedes slumbering on the gravel. No lights on anywhere.

The front door's locked. Another keypad. He walks round the back. A swimming pool is covered for the winter, a strange synthetic turquoise. The blinds are down on this side too. He goes back to the front door, keys in the second code. Pushes the door open.

She's standing in the hall as if she's been waiting for him. Face white as paper, features drawn – sharpened by pain but dulled by something else, something he's seen before. One hand clutches her belly. Through the thin fabric of the robe she's wearing, the dressings bulge.

She says, 'It's you.'

'Get dressed,' he says.

She moves towards the staircase, but stiffly, her body automatically protecting itself against the pain. He wonders what she's taking. Anything?

At the foot of the stairs she stops. 'Why are you here? Ellis went out. Some woman called from Scotland Yard – she said they had to meet.' Then, 'He asked if I'd be all right on my own,' as if it's some sick joke.

'They know you're here,' he says. 'We've got to move you.'

She thinks about it. She says, 'It's all going to pieces, isn't it?' but as if she doesn't care.

He doesn't reply.

367

She nods and goes up, slowly.

She was like that in the makeshift workroom before he injected her. Passive, spent.

He finds a downstairs bathroom, slips his jacket off, checks a mirror. He's bleeding through the back of his shirt.

She doesn't want to live.

It's full dark when they leave. She doesn't ask where they're going. He walks her to the car, two invalids together. Thinks, *we don't have a prayer.*

She gasps a little when he helps her into the passenger seat, but that's all.

He climbs in on the driver's side, shuts the door. She's looking straight ahead.

She says, 'Ellis told me William's dead. His friend Ian. Mark Devlin too.' She turns her head to him. Her eyes are without emotion, the spark gone out of them. 'It's all because of me. Because I was flattered. She said it was for the good of the country, it was all about saving lives. She said he'd talk. Hours, that's all it should have taken.' She stops. He says nothing. She turns away. 'At the end of the first day Daniel told me what was going to happen to him. He knew already, but I didn't listen. I didn't believe it could go that far. Four days, I put him through four days of that, because I didn't want to know that I'd been wrong. I should have killed him right at the start, when he asked me to.'

She turns away. 'You haven't told me we'll be fine.'

He says, 'I'll sort something out.'

He gets out the phone, calls Fielding again. He says, 'I've got her.'

'They still want proof.'

'They can have it.'

Day 24: Friday

Karla

She shows us the gun again – nine mil, with a suppressor – before she blindfolds us and unties our feet. She takes Powell first, then comes back for me. She walks beside me, a firm grasp on my arm, the gun's muzzle brushing my jaw. She doesn't touch my damaged hand, still cable-tied behind my back, and I'm pathetically grateful. So this is what you become when confronted by the imminent reality of pain: how docile, how easily dominated.

She steers me to the back of the van. The bumper brushes against my thigh. 'In you go,' she says, quite coolly. I lift one leg to get my knee up on the sill, she gives me a push, and down I go face first, the van's floor smacking into my nose. I cry out; the gag muffles it. I breathe in and taste blood.

She lifts my feet into the van and shuts the doors. A moment later the engine starts, and we move away.

Powell lies beside me. We are touching.

Another journey comes back to me, the one from Wales. An unmarked van, a hard-faced woman with too much jewellery, Mark Devlin dead, and the misery and shock and guilt still washing over me.

And I start crying.

I don't know if it's for Devlin, or for Powell's little girl. Or if it's simply for all the bits of life I haven't had yet, and now never will.

Day 24: Friday

Johanssen

He comes to the place on foot, through the darkness. Friday night, and everyone's gone home. The street lights shine down on deserted pavements, tatty old industrial units, the odd dumped car. The roads are slick and wet, and don't look right. Everything's been tainted with a sickly sheen. The drugs have worn off now, and he's dragging the pain behind him like a weight – the pain, and the knowledge he shouldn't be here, he's not up to this.

He doesn't have a choice.

The area's still crappy, desolate: the litter in the gutters, the air of abandonment, that London's wealth has passed by on the other side of the road and left this place behind. The gates are closed, but someone's cut off the padlock and unlooped the chain. In the yard, among the broken fairground rides, an unmarked van is parked.

He circuits, checking for surveillance. Then goes in.

She's standing alone in the warehouse: a woman with brown hair, the sort some men would call pretty. She's wearing a tidy coat, and shoes she doesn't plan to run in – she looks like she's just come from the office, but she's sharp, this one: she spots him early, when he's still feet away. And she has a gun.

He stops and lets her look at him.

'Hello,' she says at last. Her voice is educated, calm, polite.

'You found it OK, then?'

She nods. Her expression's neutral. She's looking at him carefully, measuring him up. How much of the damage is detectable? How much can she see, or guess?

She says, 'You're not what I expected, for a killer.'

'No?'

'No.' Then, more businesslike: 'Any issues at the house?' He shakes his head. 'So ... proof.'

'In the car.'

370

'And where's that?'

'Half a mile away.'

He sees her register that. 'You're careful.'

'You have to be. You want to see it now?'

'Not yet.' The gun hasn't moved. She's wary. Another long look. Johanssen feels the world shift beneath him.

The woman's seen it. 'Are you all right?' she says. It's calculating.

'Just some problems getting out of there.'

'You're wounded.'

'Nothing much.' He looks again at the gun, the assurance with which she holds it, with which she speaks. The level of control. He says, 'I was told the client was civilian.'

'And I'm not.' She seems to take it as fair comment. 'Your boss dealt with someone else at first. I'm just tidying up. You know you've done this sort of thing for us before?'

'I don't know who you are.'

She seems satisfied. She says, 'I'll need to see that proof. But first there's two more in the van,' and his heart stumbles.

They go outside together. She lets him lead, keeps out of his reach, watches him all the way; he's still trying not to limp. All the time he's aware of the gun in her hand, unwavering. His heart is beating very fast.

He opens the van door.

Two, tied up, blindfolded, gagged, both alive. A black guy in a dirty suit, and—

Not this not this not this

The woman says, 'We should do this inside.'

The street lamps' glow brightens, then recedes. *Do not fucking screw this up, not now.*

Karla first. She's lying prone, her head turned to one side, hands tied behind her back, one finger twisted oddly; someone's broken it. Suddenly he wants to strike out, hard and fast, but the woman's backed off, the gun still in her hand – *Don't let it show.* He reaches in, turns Karla with his hands – she whimpers through the gag – half-lifts, half-drags her to the van doorway. When the light hits her face he sees her nose is smashed, blood crusting her nostrils and round the gag.

Around him everything shifts again.

As soon as she's out, the woman takes Karla's arm and settles the gun beneath her jaw, but Karla doesn't flinch, and then he knows that it's been done to her before.

He reaches for the man, less gently, hauls him out, and back in they go: Johanssen leading the man, the woman behind with Karla and the gun. And all the time he's trying to work it out, how to set this up. The man's the shield if need be, the man can take the bullet when it comes, the man can buy him time—

They're inside again. The woman releases Karla and backs off, keeping him in range. Karla stands there mute, head down, swaying a little on her feet.

The woman says, 'The target. You use a gun?'

The room blanches. *Don't lose it now.*

He says, 'There wasn't time to pick one up,' and Karla jerks, and the woman sees it, and something flickers in her gaze.

'Do her first,' she says.

'All right,' he says. Then, 'You mind if I take the blindfold off? I like to see their eyes.'

The black guy moans.

Johanssen reaches out. Karla trembles when he touches her. The blindfold's just a strip of cloth, knotted tight. He pulls out the knife and starts to cut through it. *If she can see, she's got a better chance.* But all the time he's focused on the gun, his mind groping towards it across the space, measuring the distance, the trajectories, the odds. Ten feet between it and him. The woman looks like she's handled one before: the recoil won't take her by surprise, and range won't be an issue. Can he take the gun? How slow will he be, crossing those ten feet of space?

The blindfold falls away. Karla blinks.

The woman says, 'Get on with it.'

Karla's head comes up and she looks at him—

Now.

He pushes Karla down.

The first shot goes wide, punching a hole in the air inches away from his ear, but he's already moving: eight feet of distance, six now but he's slow, his blood's sluggish and his feet won't respond and the gun comes round again and it kicks and there's the muzzle flash—

Something punches hard into his jaw. It hurts less than he thought it would, and then much, much more.

He's down.

He cannot breathe. His mouth is full of blood and bone and teeth. He's choking.

He looks up. The woman's standing over him. The gun points to his head.

Movement, fast – a flash, bright and hard, at the edge of his vision. Just like before.

The world breaks into fragments.

The woman turning from him with the gun.

The bright arterial spurt of blood—

And Karla beside him, on her knees. Trying to say something through the gag. He can't make it out.

He can't breathe.

Then nothing, because his sight has gone.

There is no pain.

He's on a rooftop, with the street lights and the tail lights of the traffic below so bright, and everything else so clear and sharp: the rain on his skin, the slickness of the roof tiles, the rough grain of the stone parapet under his hands.

A simple exploit – A to B – and this time they will never stop him.

He is alone on that rooftop and he is running, running towards a light, and a woman steps out from behind the light and says in a voice he knows, 'I think it's time you saw my face.'

And then he's gone.

Day 24: Friday

Karla

She comes out of the shadows, between the dusty Christmas decorations. She's pale and thin, her skin almost grey, but she has a knife.

Perhaps Anna sees it. I don't know. Perhaps some instinct just tells her that it's coming, because she half-turns, and that's my chance, because I'm on my feet again and charging – she sees that too, and the gun comes back to me—

The blade goes home.

An arc of blood spurts. She drops the gun.

She reaches for her throat but it's too late, and her eyes say that she knows. She half-turns – I think she wants to say something to Catherine – and Catherine strikes a second time. I know it happens, though I don't see it. I'm on the ground now, at Johanssen's side, head down, still gagged, my hands still tied behind my back. *Please please no—*

I'm there the moment when he stops, and fails.

These are the things I will remember later.

Johanssen's body beside me, eyes fixed, not moving, jaw smashed by the bullet. Catherine trying frantically to get the tube into his throat. Running feet and someone ripping me away from him. Powell bellowing into a phone. Me clawing at a stranger's face (gag off now, hands free), one finger broken, useless. Someone shouting, '*Get her out of here.*'

And fighting, fighting, fighting all the way.

Epilogue

Day 55: Monday

Karla

The elderly woman in the coffee shop is struggling. She cannot cope with her tray (a small latte, a muffin, a glass of water) and her stick at the same time, and there are no empty seats. But just then a pale young girl by the window rises and offers her chair – 'I'm just off anyway' – and the elderly woman accepts. She settles in place, sips her coffee and stares out, blinking vaguely at the traffic and the suited people and the buildings. The coffee shop sits on a busy street in Victoria: accountants' and lawyers' and travel agents' offices mix with government departments. The elderly woman must be meeting someone – a son or daughter who works in one of the buildings, maybe. Occasionally she seems to glance at one door in particular – an odd blank door without a nameplate – but mostly she watches it out of the corner of her eye. She only speaks once, softly, to herself: 'Good job we've got all day.'

In my earpiece Robbie says, 'Copy that.'

I will wait as long as I have to. Because sooner or later he'll emerge. And I have to see this out.

Thirty days have passed since that Saturday morning in the police station: the interview room, the cups of coffee, the questions, the pain, the lies. The way they looked at me – cautious, speculative – and the way they spoke so I couldn't overhear. But they seemed focused only on how much I'd heard at the scene, and the risk I'd repeat any of it later. Damage limitation. I was just an innocent bystander, wasn't I? The woman who, like Daniel Fenty, unwittingly became a blip on Anna Leeson's radar, and made herself a target. How could I be anything else?

So I played dumb, and shocked, and it was easy. And finally they extracted a promise that I wouldn't talk to anyone about the night's events, and they said, 'You can go now.'

Stephen was standing in the station's waiting area. He insisted I came home with him. I didn't argue. By then I could barely speak.

He didn't ask about the young woman whose psychiatric history I'd asked him to read. He didn't ask what had happened to my finger. He still hasn't, though one day he will.

I stayed at Strand on the Green just one night, refusing Stephen's offer of a sedative, lying awake through the dark hours, obsessed with one idea alone.

I phoned for a cab as soon as I decently could the next morning.

I needed Craigie, I needed Finn, I needed Robbie and Sean, but they were nowhere. I was tainted now.

An hour later another janitor arrived, a woman in her late fifties, very sharp. I was being handled. I played along.

But that one idea had got into my blood, like a virus, and there was only one cure for it.

I spent two days isolated in my apartment, turning away visitors, screening calls, listening to the official version on the news – a version that left Anna Leeson dead by her own hand, alone, in a warehouse full of Christmas decorations and broken fairground rides – and felt the past few weeks being rolled up like a carpet and put away out of sight.

At last Craigie arrived at my door, but all he wanted to talk about was my share portfolio and the performance of my securities. I kept telling him, 'I need more data,' and he said, 'This is all I've got.'

And that's the way it stayed: twenty-nine days of half-life and grief in limbo. Until last night, when they brought the man to me.

Powell

It ends as it began, in the Long Room, the soundproofed box over-looking the inner courtyard, though this time someone else is doing the talking; all he has to do is listen. It works for him: he's dead on his feet, strung out and laid low by the events of the last two days; not that he'll let it show. If there's one thing he's learned, it's that you never let it show.

'All right,' says Suit One brightly, 'so Anna Leeson works out where Catherine Gallagher is—'

'And she can't get access to the Program,' Suit Two chips in, 'so she gets someone hired to do the job, with the American Whitman providing cover. Whitman confirmed it when we tracked him down in Paris: the woman that he knew as Laura Pressinger was definitely Leeson. We can't double-check it – she did something to disrupt CCTV feeds the one time they met recently, and she wiped all records from her phones – but we've spoken to Langley, and Whitman's reliable.'

Suit One picks up: 'And in any case Whitman won't say a word. He's family – in a distant-American-cousin way – and he's very keen to work for us; these French girls must be expensive.'

Suits One and Two both suppress an oily smile. He wonders who they are; where they've been whistled up from. Special Branch? MI5? He wasn't told their names – perhaps that's information released on a need-to-know basis and someone's decided he doesn't – but even if he had been told, would he have remembered? The room's coming and going around him. Any minute he'll be flatlining.

Suit One resumes: 'We're not sure where Mark Devlin fits into this. He seems to have provided the house where Fenty was taken, whether knowingly or unknowingly we're not sure. His death could be self-defence, but if it's murder—'

'—We must assume Leeson was involved—'

379

'—Covering her tracks again. Now, obviously it's in the public domain that Devlin and Leeson were ... *friends*—' Suit One congratulates himself on the euphemism '—but that works for us too: he dies under suspicious circumstances, she's unbalanced by the loss. We still going with suicide for Leeson?' The Section Chief nods, cautiously. 'Well, there you are. As for the other parties in the know—'

Suit Two picks up: 'Hamilton and Graves are out of the picture. Graves, we've already got the burglary option. Hamilton was probably killed in case he talked, but she was clever there, it looks like suicide.'

'Oh, certainly suicide.'

'And while there are some oddities in the records—'

'—For three weeks before his death we can't pin down his movements—'

'—We can spin that as a nervous breakdown.'

Tweedle-Dum and Tweedle-Dee. Powell's losing track of which one's which. Now more than anything he wants to go to bed, and sleep. He's far too tired for this.

'DI Ellis?' the Section Chief asks beadily.

'Ah, *poor* Detective Inspector Ellis: getting it so right and yet so wrong. Because in fact he wasn't even warm. He thought he was looking at a murder. Still, nasty injuries. Leeson really went to town there – some mistaken belief he knew where Catherine Gallagher was. He's still on sick leave. He's been co-operative so far. Likes to think he's smarter than us—'

'But he's ambitious; we can work with that.'

The Chief again: 'He won't suddenly recall the details of the attack?'

'We're certain, sir.' They smile in unison.

Powell says, 'And Charlotte Alton? Do you think she'll forget?' and they look at him as if surprised to find he's actually in the room.

Suit One recovers first. 'Ah, another case of wrong place and wrong time. She knew Devlin, though not well; had dinner with him a week earlier, and Anna saw them together. And she and Ellis use the same garage.' He shrugs. 'She became hysterical at the scene, didn't she? I think that says it all. I doubt she'll come up with anything we can't discredit.'

'Though she does have influential friends,' Suit Two says, more cautiously, and Suit One seems to pull up slightly: *Oh yes.* Bankers and lawyers and that politician woman – a Home Secretary in training. Influential friends indeed.

Suit Two says, 'The main thing is, I think we've convinced her not to *complicate* the issue. She doesn't seem to recall much of the incident. Terror, shock ... Plus we've assessed her and she's open to influence. We think we can control her.'

Powell thinks, *So she's become a footnote*. He remembers her straining against the gag, her eyes the moment her finger snapped, and something turns inside him. A month gone and he'll still wake sometimes in the night, drunk on his own brand of terror. Is she the same?

The Section Chief says, 'Shall we turn our attention to the third party? The hired man who changed sides? I take it we still don't have a name for him.'

The Suits exchange glances. 'We're having a few difficulties with that.'

'You think he might have been one of ours, do you? A cleanskin? In which case someone knows but they're not saying. Well, certainly *he* won't be talking now.'

Another glance between the suits. Neither of them comments.

The Section Chief says, 'And we can get rid of Catherine Gallagher, can't we? She still wants to go back into the Program?'

He visited her himself three days ago, in the isolated house in Shropshire which her minders ensure she never leaves; they spoke only briefly. She said, 'You won't want me talking about this.' When he told her he was still awaiting a decision on whether she'd be prosecuted she said coldly, 'I won't.' He still doesn't know what to make of her: sometimes he thinks the whole thing's left her no more than a shell; but then that shell seems to have been constructed out of Kevlar or titanium, or some other substance formed under extreme conditions, and impossible to break ... Sometimes there seems to be nothing left of her, and sometimes there's simply nothing that he can get a purchase on. He doesn't know whether to be afraid for her, or of her. Mostly he's both.

Suit One says, 'She could remain officially missing, in return for her ... co-operation.' He means her silence. 'Though isn't the Program coming up for review? Won't they close it down? Still, in the short term—'

Powell says, too clearly, 'And Fenty? What's the official story there?'

The Suits look at him and shift uncomfortably in their seats. It strikes him for the first time that they don't know who he is either.

He pushes on. 'Fenty never stole that missing file. Never posted it on the open market—'

Suit One says quietly, 'We can't be sure of that.'

'Oh yes we can. And that won't go away. Whatever you do to hush this up, whatever you do to buy off or discredit any of these individuals—'

Suit One gives an almost embarrassed smile. 'With respect, we've made bigger things go away.'

Powell says coldly, 'Have you ever heard of Knox?'

When the Suits have gone, the Section Chief says, 'We couldn't have known how badly she was broken.' It's the only comment he's made about Leeson so far. Powell thinks, *Oh yes we could.* He doesn't say it. He missed it too.

'So what do we do now?' the Section Chief says bitterly. 'Wash all the dirty laundry in public? We can't have sources making terms like this – doesn't Knox realise?'

'Knox wants Daniel Fenty in the clear. His parents are in their sixties. When he disappeared they were left with no illusions: their son was a traitor. We've got to put it straight.'

'Tell them he's dead?'

'I don't know.' The argument's been looping in his head. He can't give them a body to bury: the searches of the hillsides round Mark Devlin's house have so far turned up nothing. And what's to be gained from telling them the truth about the four days Daniel Fenty spent in that house, begging Catherine Gallagher to kill him? Perhaps this time it's kinder just to lie: let them believe he might be out there, safe, thinking of them, wanting to come home ... 'But tell them that his name's been cleared.' He pauses. 'And make that public too.'

'*Sweet Jesus.*' For a moment the Section Chief looks savage. 'And if we don't?'

'Then Knox puts it out there. All of it. It will be across a thousand websites in an hour, and we'll be tainted by it. *And* we'll lose Knox. To the Americans if we're lucky. If we're not ...' He lets that hang in the air between them.

'And how does Knox know about it in the first place?' The Section Chief glowers at him. 'Don't tell me we've sprung a leak.'

'I'll look into it.' He doesn't add, *I think Knox knows things about this even we don't know.* It's only a feeling; he can't be sure.

'I thought we were good at sweeping things under the carpet?'

'It's this or Knox goes public. With all the evidence. At least this way we get to control the process. And we do get something in return.'

The Section Chief says, 'Will it be worth it, do you think?'

Powell doesn't reply. His mind has suddenly jumped back twelve hours: he's seated in an echoing room, with a hood over his head, while a voice distorted by electronic technology – a voice that from now on will always be the voice of Knox – is telling him exactly what the terms of their future business will be.

'I said will it be worth it?'

Powell shakes himself. He says, 'It's Knox.'

After a moment the Section Chief says, with some distaste, 'You sure you're quite all right? You shouldn't have gone.'

Powell wants to smile but doesn't. He says, 'It wasn't my idea.'

'And did Knox come up with anything else? Anything that we can work with? We have to find who we're dealing with—'

'Nothing, sir.' And there's that first small lie: the one he realises now he was always going to tell. *You're turning into Laidlaw.*

The Section Chief sighs heavily. 'All right,' he says. 'Do what you have to.'

He'll phone the Fentys tonight, when he's ready – when he's got his story straight, his resources sufficiently recovered to manage the situation, deal with all their questions. But not yet.

Now he'll go home and try to sleep … The flat is chaos, Thea moving through it like a storm, casting up glittery pink debris on all sides. The place is far too small, he thinks, and smiles.

His rental car is parked in the basement car park, but he's too tired to drive. Instead he leaves by a side entrance and hails a taxi in the street.

And knows he's being watched.

Karla

There's a crackle in my earpiece: Robbie. 'He's on his way.'

I'm not looking directly at the door when he comes out but I see him anyway, stepping out to the edge of the pavement, hand raised to hail a cab. He looks tired. He's been up all night, hasn't he?

So have I, but I don't feel tired at all.

Robbie says in my ear, 'Do you want him tailed?'

Powell leans in through the taxi window and his mouth forms his own address; then he straightens, he looks up, and he nods at no one.

We have a deal.

The man in the hood, who shook in his chair, his knees twitching to a rhythm he couldn't control. He wasn't ready for it, or for the thirty-six hours that had preceded it: thirty-six hours of anti-surveillance drills and manoeuvres and precautions. Twice he was strip-searched and then ordered to dress in different clothes. Four times he was blindfolded and moved – in vans and in the boots of cars and stumbling through empty buildings in the dark. At each stage he was given the option of quitting, but he never took it, despite everything he went through with Anna Leeson. Those were the terms Knox had set, and he couldn't let himself refuse.

He's a tough man, a determined man. He's going to be difficult to handle. Craigie's not happy. But a deal is a deal is a deal.

I turn away – even though at this moment I look nothing like Charlotte Alton – and the taxi moves off.

'Karla?' Robbie says.

The elderly woman in the coffee bar says dreamily, to herself, 'Let him go.'

Last night we talked about Anna Leeson, and Catherine Gallagher, and what happened to Daniel Fenty: things no one but Powell himself should know. But Knox is still an enigma, isn't he? He knew about the maternity unit bomber, the ricin plotters, the Aiya Napa shooting; why shouldn't he know about all this?

Then at last, buried in all that talking, to a man who'd been awake for thirty-six hours: 'The hit man Leeson sent to kill Catherine Gallagher, the one who changed sides and took a bullet in the jaw, the one who saved your life—' and Powell twitched '—you've told everyone he's dead. Why did you do that?'

He paused before answering, and that was all I needed.

Johanssen is alive.

Johanssen

They come with questions: two men in suits, who lie when they give their names. They sit in visitors' chairs beside the bed, in the little first-floor room overlooking the grounds, press pen and paper into his hands, fire questions at him. When he doesn't write, they say, 'You can just nod, or shake your head?' And then they try again: questions about how he was hired, who put him in the Program, how he got in and out, who he reports to ... Sometimes he pretends he is asleep, but still they question him, as if they've guessed. He listens with his eyes closed, senses them watching for a reaction, but doesn't give one.

Each time they stay for an hour. They think they're good, but every visit leaves him with a clearer picture of the limits to their knowledge. One thing's certain. They still don't know his name.

And sometimes he gets visits from the other one: tall, black, educated accent, good suit, desk-man's hands. The one tied up with Karla in that van. The one Johanssen would have used to block a bullet, though he'll never know. Each time he too sits beside the bed and talks, but only about what happened at the end, and he doesn't ask any questions.

None of them came today.

Today he's had another visitor, though he didn't see or hear them: he must have been asleep when they called. But when he opens his eyes, there it is, on the cabinet beside the hospital cot: a little red and purple Christmas bauble, almost bald of its glitter.

He doesn't touch it, just leaves it there.

Beyond the window a breeze has got up. Across the lawn a flurry of blossom drifts from the trees like pale pink snow.

His jaw's been wired while they rebuild it: surgery, and then more surgery. He can't talk or eat solids; he's lost weight. But he will heal, though he may never be what he was. He's not sure if that matters. Not sure what he will need to be when he gets out of here. It's too early to say.

There are other changes too. He still dreams, but they are quieter. The man behind the desk seems muted, cautious; his opinion matters less. Johanssen still goes back to the farmhouse, and sometimes there's the screaming, but sometimes he's just standing in that hallway all alone, and doesn't know what he's doing there. He counts it as a temporary respite – must be the drugs. You don't fix things that easily.

He hasn't dreamed about the rooftop at all. But he has dreamed of Karla.

And one day he'll be ready to leave, and find her again.

He passes the time with that sniper's habit: reducing the world to its dimensions.

Two metres to the window. Three metres from the window to the ground.

It is all about distance.

Acknowledgements

The following have generously allowed me to draw on their knowledge and experience during the writing of this book: Katie Ben, Tony and Jane Lee, Gill, Gerti, Clive, Claire Mitchell, and Sarah Ramsay. Huge thanks to all of you, and apologies for any errors of interpretation or omission, which are entirely the author's.

Very special thanks to Geoff, for location scouting, and all the rest.

Thanks to Frankie Edwards for late night emails, sounding-board facilities, and names.

To my initial readers: Jean for her wisdom and advice, Pat for encouraging me to go for it, and especially Lesley, not just for reading and commenting with more insight than I could ever muster, but also for the Friday phone calls and the BFI sessions.

To the Moniackers generally, for always keeping me in the loop. You know who you are.

To Alison Sage.

To Mark and Simon for reminding me what a thriller is supposed to do; especially Mark for structural analysis, and Simon for 'the *Quantum of Solace* moment' and for telling me to do it in a sentence.

To Judith and the team at Greene & Heaton, Grainne at Fletcher & Co, and Sally at The Cooke Agency, for all their support.

Many smart and terrific people have been involved professionally in the publishing of this book. I can't hope to name all of them, but special mentions are most definitely due to Barbara Heinzius at Goldmann Verlag for getting the ball rolling; to Shunichiro Nagashima at Bungei Shunju; to Bill Thomas and Coralie Hunter at Doubleday; and to Laura Gerrard at Orion.

And finally to Bill Massey, good bloke and great editor: for his patience, intelligence and humour, for his willingness to walk into the minefield, and for getting me to write a better book than I knew I could.

About the Author

Helen Giltrow is a former bookseller and editor whose writing has been shortlisted for the Crime Writers' Association Debut Dagger Award and the *Daily Telegraph*'s Novel in a Year competition. She lives in Oxford. *The Distance* is her first novel.